march becomes dawn

vanessa zian

Cover Design - Lori Jackson Designs
Design Concept - Willow Winters

Hambright Editing

by vanessa zian

Dog Tags & Lace Series

Midnight to December

Ruby in July

Mine after October

March becomes Dawn

Standalone

The Lifecycle of a Crush

*To my children—the best miracles. Shine, innovate, charm, and discover, just as you already do.
But don't read this until you're fifty.*

content notice

My books weave in subplots of trauma and may be triggering to some, but there's good reason for it. I'm all about the happily ever after, so you will absolutely get that. But my aim is to leave the reader with the ultimate narrative full of truths, no matter what the trauma. We all have experienced some at some point, whether it be "small t" or the "Big T" kind.

We learn by sharing stories. We heal by tweaking the narrative. And we soar when we can join forces and journey together. It's what I'm here for, and I'm so glad you are too.

one

. . .

The gift of looking backwards is this—the reflection offers glimpses of the person we once were, now clearer in the light of who we've become in time.

With love, Lace

lori

fifteen years old

WHEN JAMES BLAKE walked into my English classroom, looking very James Dean-like in a white t-shirt and with an unlit cigarette dangling from his slightly parted lips—a dagger of rebellion—my heart began pounding in my chest. I'd never spoken to him before, but his reputation preceded him. The teacher, a bitter old woman in desperate need of a new wardrobe and less obvious fake teeth, coldly directed him to take the cigarette and put it in the trash. I watched in fascination as James placed his books down on a desk, none of which were the right ones for this class, I noted, and sauntered up to the teacher while removing the cigarette from his mouth. He placed it behind the teacher's ear, saying, "There. Maybe you need it more than me." An audible gasp filled the classroom.

"Did he really just do that?" someone whispered.

"What a jackass," someone else responded. A few other giggles filled the otherwise silent vacuum.

All I did was stare in fascination.

The teacher lifted one saggy arm toward the door, index finger extended as if performing a hex, voice icy as she commanded him out of the classroom and to the principal's office. With a smug grin, James grabbed his books and obliged, but not before saluting her, stating, "Thank you, ma'am," and pressing his back to the door.

And then his eyes caught mine. I was busted for staring, yet I couldn't look away. He held my gaze momentarily. A silent exchange passed between us, it seemed, as he mouthed what I think was, "Hi."

I mouthed, "Hi," in return, then smiled. He placed a dramatic hand on his heart as if my smile had somehow stopped it, then grinned back at me, shaking his head slightly. My pulse quickened at this simple interaction, and somehow, I knew James Blake was going to be changing my life.

Our moment was interrupted when Ms. Cantankerous shouted, "Out!" and James glanced back at her, assuring her he's going, he's going. He turned and opened the door with one last look at me, keeping eye contact the entire time his body exited the room, until the closing door was the only thing to break our spell.

"HE'S BAD NEWS, YOU KNOW," my friend Steph was saying as we were walking out of class.

I rolled my eyes. "Seriously?"

"What?" she asked as if she didn't understand why I would question what she said.

"You sound like a cheap headline on a magazine at the checkout aisle of the grocery store."

"Hey…mean," she said, flicking my shoulder. "I'm serious, don't even think about it, Lori." But then she smiled, eyebrows raised playfully. "Unless this is some twisted attempt to piss off your mom?"

I pondered for a moment. "Some appeal there, sure."

"Alright, fine," Steph acquiesced.

"So, I have your approval then?" I said with a nod. We stopped in front of my locker, and I pulled up on the lock. The door swung open with a loud clang.

"I'm just saying I heard his family has got some problems, that's all."

I paused the shoving of my books in and looked at her. "Like what?"

Her blonde ponytail swooshed as she glanced around us before returning her attention to me, lowering her voice. "You know— dad's an alcoholic. And not the fun kind. Typical Vietnam veteran story. And his mom's apparently a worthless pushover. They live in some trailer park outside of town."

The hallway was crowded with backpacks on kids scrambling to their next destination, the squeak of lockers swinging open before slamming shut with a jolt to my nerves. I swapped out my books and tried to shut my own locker as softly as I could.

I always found school to be a chaotic bore. I wished I had gone to an art school or something far more intriguing than that generic public school busting through the seams with sweaty teens and subpar curriculum that I had little interest in. It was the same thing every single day, wake up and repeat.

We continued down the hall again and I nodded at Steph's gossip, absorbing the information. Little did she know, all her words did was further spark my interest. I assured her I just admired James's boldness, and she countered that I just thought he was hot. I laughed and pled guilty, which seemed to appease her.

We chatted some more—more like she continued to go on about tonight's dance and all she was planning—and I silently listened and fought my boredom.

"What are you going to wear to it?" she asked. "I've got a tube top and mini skirt that you could borrow if you want," she offered, knowing my mom was strict and wouldn't want me in anything above the knee.

I shook my head. "No, thanks. I have something else in mind."

She groaned. "Don't wear something weird, alright? You're pretty. Wear something cute to show that off."

I ignored her comment, knowing my clothes might not be considered the trendiest, but I didn't care about that. See, Steph and I were really friends more out of convenience than anything. Sometimes I would think I was her pet project, or something she was trying to figure out. Like she didn't really understand the creative soul that I was. I also knew she thought I was pretty and a threat to her, so her friendship was all in an effort to conform me and join in her little posse. Then she could gush in our crowd of "friends" and brag all about how she dressed me up, don't I look fabulous, how hopeless I'd be without her. Maybe we were frenemies?

I promised to give her all my best efforts and that I'd meet her out front of the dance later so we could walk in together, figuring at least it was something my mom would let me do. She was fine with me going to dances, knowing they were under the careful supervision of teachers, overworked and exhausted as they were and hardly paying anyone much mind. I'd like to imagine the teachers were really there at those dances having steamy love affairs, sharing joints and talking spiritedly about philosophy or far-off places they wanted to travel to over the summer, their teaching-kids gig simply a paycheck that held the singular perk of summers off. I felt less sorry for them then.

I parted ways with Steph, rounded the corner and bumped into a wall of white with a scent of cigarettes and cheap cologne.

James.

The bell rang and the rest of the backpack-clad students scurried off into their next classes, doors swooshing closed behind them, taking with them the stench of lead and teen spirit.

A quiet settled in the empty hall, and neither one of us moved. James stared down at me, so much rugged handsomeness so unlike the other teenage boys I was used to, and my stomach flipped at the look he gave me.

"Hi again," he said.

I leaned against the wall behind me, the cinderblock cool against my now clammy palms. "Hmm, not sure about that," I said. "Does a silent hi really count enough to say 'again' at this one?" I offered a half smile, emphasizing the "again" in a tone I hoped was conveying a light tease.

He grinned. It was a beautiful sight. "And then I awoke."

I scrunched my eyebrows through my nervous and confused smile. "You awoke?"

James nodded, stepped beside me in a lean against the wall that mirrored my own. He popped a foot up on it and took the stack of books that were in his hand to balance on his raised thigh. He raised his arm and grabbed the small pencil that was behind his ear. I watched with interest as he scribbled something down on the blank page of the notebook sitting on top of his pile of books. I leaned over to read what he was writing, absorbed in the rough foreword slant of his handwriting, a contrast to the thick loops and curls of my own.

"'A pretty girl's joke. And then I awoke,'" I read out loud.

He paused, looked back to me and pointed the pencil in my direction. "You're the pretty girl in question, in case you're wondering."

I nodded and raised an eyebrow before leaning my head back on the wall behind us. "I had a feeling I might be," I said, loving the flutter in my belly. "So you're a writer?"

James returned the pencil to its perch behind his ear. "Unofficially, yeah. Mostly poems. Nothing good, though."

"Maybe try and hang out in English class a little more then," I said. "Unless it's just that you don't like Ms. Cantankerous."

"Ms. Cantankerous?" Warm hazel eyes stared down at me. He had a little hair stubble on his face, a decent amount for a teenage boy, and without warning, my hand reached up to drag a finger along his jawline, mesmerized by the tingle of its short spikes. James closed his eyes as if the touch were something he wanted to absorb.

I had no idea what I was doing. I'd never even truly kissed a boy before, not beyond an awkward series of pecks, let alone reached up and touched one's face like this. Someone I'd never even actually met. There was something empowering about his presence, though. A very inexplicable draw I felt, a tide impossible to fight against, so instead I floated along. James and I had made eye contact a few times in hallways or classrooms, his gaze always stirring something in me, and I'd wonder if he at all felt the same thing, or if I was just an accidental figure caught in the unassuming wander of his eye. I liked to think it was more, but before our silent exchange earlier that day, we'd never had any real acknowledgment of one another.

"It's what I call the English teacher. Ms. Cantankerous," I explained, reluctantly dropping my hand. "It's fitting, and such a fun word to say."

He nodded, clearly amused. "That it is. And what about you... your name's Lori, right?" he asked.

"Yes. Lori."

"I'm James."

"I know. James Blake," I said, drawing out the "k" with a little pop.

"Shit," he said, dropping his head down in defeat. His eyes glanced out the side to reach mine, and a wicked smile stretched across his face. "That's not good news for me then, is it?"

I shrugged and turned my body to face his, leaning my shoulder against the wall. "I don't like to judge people based off dumb rumors. I'd rather get to know someone myself first."

"I get it. You're an idealist, you see the good in everyone, don't you?" he asked, turning to face me as well. We were inches apart. Was it my imagination, or had he stepped closer to me?

"I like to think so. There's always more to the story, don't you think?"

We stood there like that for a moment, face to face in our side lean on the wall. My skin was humming with an energy in James's presence.

"You look like a good girl," he said, eyes on my mouth then back up to stare into mine. "The type that shouldn't be late to class, and definitely not out in the lonely hallway talking to strange guys."

I wanted to reach out and touch him again, feel the stubble on his face, but he was making no attempt to touch me in any way, so I didn't. Was he interested in me? Or was I just amusing to him? He seemed older than me, though I knew we were in the same grade.

I sighed dramatically. "Oh, James. You really shouldn't jump to conclusions, you know. I'm an average student, I'm known for being late and getting my head stuck in the clouds with way too many creative ideas, and I'm what my mom likes to call a 'free spirit,' though not in a good way."

"Ahh, see you weren't listening. I said you *look* like the type that shouldn't be late to class. Not that you actually are that type."

"So what does someone look like that doesn't care about being late?"

He pulled his gaze away from me and looked up at the ceiling, and I started to worry he was bored of me already and going to walk away. "I don't know, I was just going for smooth."

"Oh," was all I responded. I hadn't expected that. Was his cool stance faltering? Because of me?

I had the urge to reassure him. I reached up to touch his chin, wanting to be sweet about it, but I felt more like a curious creature exploring a new land. His eyes shot down to my hand, then back to me.

"I got something on my face?" he asked with a smirk.

I started to pull my hand back and away, embarrassed, but he reached up and grabbed it, keeping it in place.

With his hand over mine like that, the contact went from feeling inquisitive to intimate. He held my gaze, and my heart pounded in my chest. "I like your...your stubble," I said.

A wolfish grin crept across his face, sending a cupid's arrow to my heart. "It's a start."

The world momentarily stilled around us, locking us in this odd encounter like a spell. But then far too soon, as if afraid to hold on any longer, he released my hand and resumed his position with his back on the wall. I did the same, wondering what this thing was between us. Or if it was all my imagination. Was I dreaming the whole encounter? Why did talking to him feel so different than talking to any other boy?

I didn't want our conversation to be over, so I grasped to retrieve our topic. "Technically we're all supposed to be on time, right?" I had no idea where I was going with this point, I just knew that I wanted to keep him talking to me. "Not just certain types of people."

"I guess you're right," he nodded, gaze back up to the ceiling tiles above us. "But if I were to guess, I'd say you don't mean disrespect in being late, you just recognize what your time is worth. And time is a non-renewable resource."

I nodded, genuinely agreeing with his assessment. "I like it."

Another side glance over to me along with an eyebrow raise. "You know what I like?"

"What?"

"I like that you chose to be late to class so you could stand out here with me instead."

Oh my God, I'm in love.

A thought jumped into my mind, and while I knew the ridiculousness of it—I didn't even know this guy!—I had a feeling I very soon would.

"You going to the dance tonight?" I boldly asked. I did a silent prayer that he would say yes, yes, he was in fact going and that I would get the chance to dance with him, feel his arms wrapped around my body, swaying in the dim lights of the dolled-up gym, smell his stale cigarettes and masculinity in my grasp. It was the only way I'd get a chance to know him, as there was no way my mom was ever going to let me go on an actual date with a boy. Definitely not one from "the wrong side of the tracks" as I knew she'd refer to a guy like James, once she inevitably did some digging and figured out more about him and his family.

"I wasn't planning on it," he said. My heart sank. "But if you are, I will."

It was the most beautiful sound, James saying he would go if I was going. I nodded my head. "I'm going. I—I hope you will too."

James grinned and I was flooded with relief. "Then I'll see you tonight, Lori."

"Bye, James," I said.

Neither one of us moved from the wall.

two

. . .

lori

present day

THERE'S SO MUCH potential in a good first date, if you really give it a chance. I want to believe that. How else can you find a connection? I won't say soulmate—no. I already found that once. I consider myself lucky in that way, even if it ended in a reality I wouldn't put on my worst enemy. But I had it once.

I mindlessly twirl my hair as I try to listen to the man before me, my thoughts wandering to the strange online world that has offered us the access to a stream of potentials. There's hope there, but the hard part is moving through the awkwardness of it all. Dating in the adult life is a slightly painful dance of the stumble through pleasantries wrapped in wondering if someone is for real, or if they're looking for a good fuck. I've accepted that, I really have, painful as it is.

But I'm not looking for just sex. Not now, at least.

I look with hopeful longing at the potential love conquest in front of me. He could be something, I think as I casually sip my coffee. I want him to be. The ache of loneliness has been gripping in a chokehold on my chest, and I really want this new guy to work, but all I can think is that he could use a decent haircut. Or a little scruff, maybe. The clean-shaven look combined with the long hair is wrong on him, somehow. I wonder if it's rude to suggest that.

I've had a string of bad dates, lately. It saddens me that I'm beginning to lose hope.

I take a deep breath in, the scent of cappuccino tinged with vanilla soothing me. It's a cute little cafe. There are mismatched tables and chairs, two small sofas dressed in hunter green and pumpkin orange velvet. The whole place has that comforting, cluttered feel to it. Very urban for our quaint little Main Street.

Our date location was my choice.

Now, look, I used to love dating and meeting new people to potentially join forces with—I'll be a romantic until my dying days—but lately I've been feeling downright exhausted in moving around the chess pieces of the dating game.

Actually, scratch that. Chess would be interesting. Come to think of it, I haven't even played in years, barely remember the rules.

My dating encounters have been awkward and dull texting conversations, lots of one-sided talk and pleasantries, with me attempting to yank the chains to unlock something interesting with a force fit for prize-winning bodybuilders. These texts are generally followed by meetups where I grin and bear it, determined to draw out a personality, or a pulse, from the damn corpse sitting in front of me.

Or directly beside me. That's the worst, when they do that—slide in the booth directly next to you so that you're forced to strain your neck to face them. I really should try suggesting dates that put a little space between us. Like mini-golf. Or Frisbee.

But what else am I going to do, I can't give up hope. Love is a religion I will always subscribe to. It can set your soul on fire and bring about a feeling of being alive that is so fundamentally necessary, it's like oxygen. I've felt that in my past. Felt romantic love of epic proportions down in my core and beyond. I ache to feel it again.

I try and focus on the man in front of me, longish hair and all, and get re-centered in hopes of interest in my date. Maybe he just hasn't found the right barber shop.

It's not that he's unkempt, per se. Just a little unruly. What's the difference, you ask? Let me go ahead and tell you—unruly is the type that's unconcerned with bothersome tasks like scheduled haircuts and matching clothing. Thus, the man in front of me now.

Unkempt, on the other hand, that's the real danger, because it means that they just don't care.

"Are you interested in getting a haircut anytime soon?" I blurt out to my date. His name is Harrison, so with a name like that, I'm hopeful.

Large, round brown eyes blink back at me. "A haircut?" He runs a hand through his hair, then does a shake as if in a shampoo commercial—his hair is beautiful, I admit. I instinctively glance around looking for cameras. Harrison shrugs, looking a bit sheepish. "I suppose I am due."

Oh geez, now I just feel badly for saying something. "I'm sorry, I didn't mean to insinuate that! Ignore me, I can be quick to blurt out my thoughts sometimes. You really do have great hair."

He lifts a hand to wave in assurance. "It's okay. And thank you. Your hair is beautiful as well." He smiles kindly at me, then shifts a little in his seat.

I smile and sip my coffee again. My eyes wander over to a couple two tables down, both in their twenties, I'd say. They're attractive and I can't help but wonder what they're doing, nestled together with laptops propped open in front of them. What kind of jobs might they have that they come to this hipster little coffee shop and work. Some dazzling careers, I like to think. I often dream about the dazzling career I could have had—maybe I could have been an actress or a painter, or maybe a teacher or something. An art teacher. My late husband Richard used to tell me I could be anything I wanted, then he'd slap my ass and say it's a good thing I didn't need to, because he couldn't bear sharing me. Ironic, really.

"What kind of work do you do, exactly?" I ask Harrison. White teeth shine back at me. Dental health is important, so he's got that going for him.

"I'm in the dental field."

Ha! Go figure.

I'm going to need him to clarify, though. There's an income level difference between hygienist and actual dentist. The former means not exactly wealthy, and I'm not a snob or anything, it's just that I'm not sure I'm good with an income level at this point in our lives that's going to struggle to pay bills. Not that Harrison's old, because he's the same age as me, if I recall, and I'm far from old—just over the fifty mark, I'll leave it at that. No need for specifics because I'm really young at heart, and I have the legs of a twenty-year-old, and a yoga certification that keeps me fit. Really, I've been told that I could pass for thirty-five. People have even asked my daughter and me if we're twins. I get a kick out of that, and Reggie's usually a good sport about it, even if it is a bit of an insult to her. I was only twenty when I had her and her twin brother JJ.

"Dental field is vague," I say with an eyebrow raise. "Receptionist at the office?"

He chuckles and shakes his head. "Alright, alright, I see what you're doing. I'm a dentist," he says with a conceding head nod.

Now we're talking. "Why not just say that then? You should be proud." That, and it would explain a busy work life that makes being on top of haircuts a bit more challenging.

"I appreciate that. And I am proud, it's just that it can feel like bragging sometimes. 'Hi, nice to meet you, I'm a doctor.' I try not to lead with that," he says with a humble laugh.

I nod in agreement. "Makes sense, I see what you're saying. My daughter's a physical therapist and I help her out at her clinics. Do you have any children?" I dart my eyes out the window, my attention caught on the swirls of flurries hovering about above the brick sidewalk. Snow would be lovely, I do hope we get some this winter. Our Pennsylvania climate used to get wonderful snow, but these days a proper snowfall rarely ever happens.

I glance back to Harrison as he responds. "I do, in fact. One heading off to college this fall, another in tenth grade, then our whoops baby. He's eight, my ex-wife and I had certainly not been planning another child. We had already been functioning more as roommates at that point than anything, figured we'd wait a few more years until the kids were older before divorcing. Then he came along. We tried for a while longer for his sake, but the fights got bad, and we figured it would be better if we went separate ways." Harrison reaches for his phone, scrolls through before sliding it over to me. "Those are my three, they're my world."

"Hmm, they're beautiful," I murmur with a nod and smile. "And your ex? How is co-parenting with her?"

"Great, actually. Turns out we're far better friends than we were husband and wife. I devoted a lot of time to my practice, which was a big part of our problem. I can admit that. Still do hyper-focus on work, though I'm far better than I used to be. But now she can't be mad at me for it," he says with a grin and wink.

My mind imagines the perfect co-parenting team they must be, seamlessly navigating dual holidays and birthdays. It's sweet. I'm happy for them.

We chatter on a while longer, and he tells me about how great Accident Baby's arm is, how as a leftie he's sure to be a pitching success. I smile politely, making a joke about the hair commercial he's auditioning for every time a strand falls in his face and he shakes it away. He laughs easily and says how funny I am, how I'm beautiful and he's so glad to finally have matched with someone so easy to talk to.

But I'm not feeling it, I'm just not. On paper Harrison seems like the whole package, at least as close to the whole package as I can expect at our age.

But there's absolutely zero spark. We need spark, I tell you. Maybe he's a little *too* whole package, if you know what I mean.

"Harrison," I say, stretching my arm across the table to grab his hand. "I've really enjoyed talking to you, but I'm not sure I'm…not sure I'm ready for dating," I lie. "I've been widowed twice, and I guess I've underestimated how long the grieving process would take." I try and give my most genuine smile, because I'm stretching the truth big time. Richard died eighteen years ago, it's not exactly breaking news. And my first husband died about three decades ago.

"Oh, I'm sorry to hear that, Lori." Harrison nods encouragingly. "Do all you can for yourself, grief knows no time limits."

"You're sweet, I'm sorry if I wasted your time."

"What? Not at all! I really enjoyed meeting with you." He hesitates, and I suppose he's debating if he should continue. I know that look all too well, the consternation of whether or not a person's next words will be received well.

He goes for it. "You know, counseling has been helpful for me through some of my darker moments after my divorce. I know it's certainly not the same thing as losing someone you love, but I unearthed a whole lot more than what I thought I needed during the process." He shrugs. "It works, who knew."

I nod enthusiastically as if I know just what he means. "Oh yes, absolutely." I throw in a smile and say, "Friends? And maybe in six months I'll be in a better position for dating," I say breezily, knowing full-fledged I'm immediately losing his number. I don't want to hurt his feelings, though, because he didn't do anything wrong.

"I'd like that, if you're up for it." He gives my hand a gentle squeeze. I scan his reasonably handsome face and consider one last time if I should give him a real shot. Maybe I'm being too quick to dismiss.

But, no, I've resolved to not do anymore pity dating. I get too caught up in it, and then have the hardest time cutting loose. The next thing you know, we're several months in and I'm struggling more and more with each day to feign interest. I slowly pull away, but they never seem to take the hint. Eventually I end up saying yes to a proposal, only to have to break their hearts at the last minute with some fib that gets me out of it.

That's a joke. That's only happened once, not several times.

I blabber out some pleasantries and promises of reaching out when I'm ready, and grab my coat and scarf with one final smile. I rush out the front door with a strange weepiness of frustration. I have no idea where it's coming from, but I feel slightly ridiculous in the bubbling emotion.

I burst outside into the crisp morning air, inhaling a cleansing breath. I button up my pea coat, thankful for the brisk chill to cure the suffocation of my frazzled nerves. Then take a step to my right and bump straight into the soft cashmere of a coat on the chest of someone walking by.

"Oh boy, so sorry!" I say as I stumble back, feeling like a confused puppy that's lost their way.

"Lori, is that you?" the man I've accidentally accosted asks. I look up to meet the blue eyes staring down at me, flooded with relief as I take in the familiar and handsome face beneath a smooth wave of black hair.

"Why," I beam, "if it isn't Dom Francesca."

three

. . .

lori

fifteen years old

IN THE QUIET shadows of the school hallways, James would kiss me.

The first time he kissed me, I wasn't really nervous, because I hadn't expected it. It had been at a dance, the one I had boldly asked him about the first time we exchanged words. I had been hanging out off to the side of the dancefloor, chatting with Steph and a few kids from our usual group. The low lights and spinning globe of colorful rainbows complimented the forced cheeriness of the one-hit wonders pulsing through the speakers.

But then I saw James there, lingering in the shadows and watching me with intensity. Some boy was sneaking me a beer, laughing and attempting to flirt with me, and when I caught sight of James, I instantly jolted back, as if the boy were now a leper and I needed him far away from me. My stomach dropped when I glanced back over to James, knowing he had seen the interaction.

His eyes held firmly on me and the other boy, and I thought I had ruined this thing between me and James. But then the slowest of smiles crept up his face, soon joined with a subtle shake of his head as if to tell me I knew better.

I abandoned my group, the cheap beer and all the things I suddenly had no interest in. I could hear the boy calling after me, asking me where I was going. But I glided over to James, an invisible rope between us pulling me into a world I knew was far more interesting than stupid dances and cocky kids thinking they knew everything and were better than everyone.

Before I even had the chance to stop short in front of him, James grabbed my hand and led me out through a back door. Not the main double doors of the gym where teachers were surely standing by to keep track of whereabouts, but a different one, a door in a corner that I had barely ever registered before. A door solely for deliveries, maybe, or some other mysteries belonging to the Gods of running a school, and beyond the concerns of us students.

From that point on, I would forever look at that door with a kind of enchanting longing. I would stand in the midst of every dull gym class, the rest of the world moving silently around me as if playing on a screen from a reel set in fast motion, with me standing frozen in time, and I would stare at that dark blue door of steel, and I'd allow my mind to float to the beautiful memories of that night. Of James and how it all started at that door.

How he had grabbed my hand and pulled me through, as if that door were a portal to another universe where only he and I existed.

I followed with flutters in my belly down meandering halls, quiet depths of a school building that suddenly felt more magical than I ever dreamed possible.

When we were safely alone, the thrum of the music a mere muffled drum beat of bass in the distance beyond, he gently pushed me back against the cool cinderblock wall.

"Do you like that kid?" he asked. Straight to the point. I saw anger in his expression, and I was worried he was mad at me, but his eyes told a different story. His eyes were tender. Hurt, even.

"No. God, no," I said. I reached up to his face once again, as I had when we first met, amazed at how easily I could do so with him. But it was all I could do, words felt like they weren't enough. I needed to touch him and assure him where my interests were.

"Good," he said, and the next thing I knew his mouth was on mine and my head was spinning with a dizziness of my unexpected first kiss. It was reckless and wonderful, I had no idea what I was doing or how my mouth was supposed to move, but James was showing me, and I allowed myself to melt into the foreign taste of another person's tongue exploring mine. A taste that quickly became a homecoming in the weeks to follow as we stole every possible moment we could find between the hours of the school bells.

***

"YOU'RE TOO GOOD FOR ME, you know," he would say sometimes. It killed me when he would say things like that. He'd close his eyes and I'd see the pain in the tension of his shoulders, and I'd wish I could reach up and snatch the words from his mind, eradicate the thought as a cancer that had no place here in the otherwise thriving pulse of our blooming affection for one another. The thought that he wasn't good enough for me was so far from the truth, it might as well have been values from another planet. Another universe.

I knew things were hard for him at home. Not because of rumors, but because of the small glimpses James would share with me, but only if I pressed. It was as though he wanted to protect me from his world, from his broken parents, a father who apparently liked to drink and beat up anyone nearby, and James would tell his younger brothers to go and hide, or leave their trailer and head to the spot he had instructed them to months before. The safe place he had designated for them. I'd see bruises or a busted lip now and then on James, but at least when he was in school, I knew he was okay.

It was the days when he was absent that crushed me.

But when he'd tell me I was too good for him, I'd wrap my arms around him and breathe in his scent, the cologne I managed to buy for him that I noticed he wore religiously every day. And I'd tell him he was wrong, that *he* was too good for *me*, because I felt like a naive little doll in comparison to all he was going through at any given time. I didn't know suffering like that. Not back then.

"I GOT YOU SOMETHING," I heard his voice behind me. I closed my eyes as I placed my hand on the cool metal of my locker door, wanting to shut out all other senses so that the only thing I could hear was James. "A little something for my girl," he said, and I could feel the weight of his arm wrapping around my shoulder.

When I opened my eyes again, I saw his hand in front of me, holding a slim rectangular package dressed in brown paper and wrapped with a small, red ribbon. I went to retrieve it from his grasp, but he yanked it away. I spun around to face him, grinning with excitement, eager to know what he had for me. The expression in his eyes was pensive at first, as if looking at me were something to be taken seriously. I loved when he would look at me like that.

But then he slipped into a smile and said, "Curious?"

I nodded eagerly. "Gimme, gimme," I said as I scanned around his body to see where the package hand had gone, reaching behind him to snatch it from behind his back.

He stepped back and shook his head. "After your next class. Meet me at the lake." I gave him a mock punch to his stomach, and he laughed before kissing my cheek, then retreating with three steps backwards. He turned around and walked away, and I watched his back as he lifted out my gift to the side, teasing me with it, and then he slipped it in his back pocket.

"So mean," I muttered to myself.

The rest of that afternoon I watched the clock above the door in my classroom with agony, the hands moving like the last drops of honey in a nearly empty bottle—taunting. When the final bell rang, I flew out of my seat, ignoring Steph's tease of, "Fine, fine. Go rush off to your boyfriend." She had actually been far easier to deal with since I started seeing James. Apparently, she liked knowing I was off the market, and the rest of the guys she liked to run her way through were no longer paying any attention to me. James had a way of possessing me as his, and he had an air of "Don't fuck with me" that simultaneously drove me wild and kept any others at bay.

Our routine went something like this—I'd fake some after-school club I had to attend, stay late and meet James at the predetermined spot he had designated, a state park with a cozy lakeside beach near our school. Those first few weeks I struggled to shake the worry I'd feel that today would be the day he wouldn't show up, and I'd round the corner of the narrow trail leading up to the beach, trying not to cling to hope, bracing myself for the shame and hurt upon the realization of his absence. I feared he'd get sick of me in due time, a warning no doubt ingrained in me by my mother. Dad wasn't exactly faithful, and Mom therefore attempted to impose on me the lack of faith in men I imagine she herself wished she had found sooner.

That was never the case, though, not even once. James was consistent, and he was determined to bring out the absolute best in me during our stolen moments in our secret corner of the beach, under the quiet canopy of rustling leaves. We had branded the cove as our spot. James was smart, I soon learned—far smarter than I was. Not only was he a wonderful writer, he also had a knack for math, which amazed me. He helped me with my dreaded pre-calculus, and next thing you know I was getting A's on tests. When my mom questioned my sudden shift from being a B's and C's student to now getting Honor Roll, I explained that I was doing after-school tutoring, proud that I could say that without it being a complete lie.

I helped James too. Whereas before me he had been surly and reserved in school, now my own good rapport with teachers (Ms. Cantankerous aside) had been stretched out to him. Our junior year we managed to have a few classes together, and we fell into an easy rhythm of sneaking held hands under our desks, winning over teachers with our pushback in friendly debates.

But that afternoon back in the early days of our dating, when he gave me that little gift full of promises, I knew I was done for.

I found him under our tree, his back against the trunk and his legs stretched out in front of him, one ankle crossed over the other. My gift was sitting next to him, and he darted his eyes down at it, then back at me. "Go on, open it," he said.

I grabbed the gift and perched down next to him, the spring air of March surrounding us in a blanket of new beginnings. My fingers couldn't work fast enough as I slipped off the ribbon and unwrapped my gift.

There was a folded white paper sitting on top, and a slim tin case of watercolor pencils underneath. Expensive ones—ones I had mentioned wanting because I had used them in art class and loved how beautifully they blended beneath the feathered strokes of a wet brush. My mom wasn't one to support my love of art—she had zero desire for a starving artist daughter—and I never got around to buying these for myself.

I stretched up to him and kissed him, wanting to devour him in that moment.

"An artist deserves the best tools," he said when I reluctantly broke our kiss.

"It's not fair," I said as I nestled into his chest and unfolded the paper that had been on top. "A writer doesn't need anything but paper and a pencil, what can I possibly get you?"

"You're the last gift I'll ever need."

My eyes scanned his poem, my breath catching with the line at the end. But I returned to the top of the page, eager to drink in his work, and I both laughed and cried while reading. I loved every word.

To my pretty girl—

Stolen moments in crowded hallways
And my eyes would find you always
My dream girl, flesh and bones
I craved to know and be known
But could she see me?
Then you did, and I awoke

You finally smiled, and my heart beat wild
My dream girl saw me too
I found your locker. Fine, call me a stalker
But I had to have more of you
And then you stayed, and I awoke

Your creativity—my muse
Your sensitivity to all around—
A healing potion to any scar or bruise

Fuck, now I'm screwed
I've tasted the finest wine
Divine. All mine.
With that first sip, I awoke
I'll do all I can to make you feel that too
If you'll let me

I love you
-forever yours, James

So that's how it happened, that's when James and I started saying those three incredible words to one another. We were in love. James was my soulmate, my destiny. It was clear from that day on, and I never again questioned his presence at our spot. It was as reliable as the rising sun.

four

. . .

lori

present day

DOM SMELLS GOOD, he always does. Some spicy cologne that screams masculinity. Broad shoulders fill out his coat, begging for warmer climates in order to be shared with the world. I've seen him in a t-shirt before. Believe you me, I know what's hiding under that sin of a jacket.

Seeing him like this just about erases my disappointment from moments ago, my date that deflated my initial excitement like a sad birthday balloon drooping on a humid day. I feel eagerness in making the most of our unexpected run-in. Dom Francesca has always sent little flips straight to my core. So much potential there —if I could ever get him to really notice me, that is. Sure, we talk and exchange pleasantries now and then, running in mutual circles like we do. But my crush has held steady for a few years now, an unanswered call.

I flash him my brightest smile possible. "So sorry for crashing into you like that," I say, hoping my voice doesn't sound too obvious in my complete lack of sorrow about plowing right into him. The word "sorry" could more accurately be replaced with "thrilled" at seeing the big fish out here in the wild.

Dom is that kind of stoic man that keeps his emotions close to his chest, if you know what I mean. Former military with all the husky sexiness that accompanies that kind of gig. Now you may know him as—and listen to this because you're going to love it, drum roll, please—Father to famous musician Ruby Francesca.

That's right. Our Grammy-winning gem Ruby is Dom's daughter.

He's very protective over her, too, but always within the realm of support. And Dom has the movie star good looks that *would* be related to a famous person—smoldering with smooth, tan skin that is so right given his piercing blue eyes. How do I know him, you ask? Well, he's an overall friend of a friend, I guess you could say.

Dom would never go for little old me, though. I think he sees me as "too much," though I'm determined to help him see that my too much can be lots of fun. My heart starts skipping in my chest, I'm always a little nervous around him.

"Careful where you're walking, you just rob the place or something?" he asks with an eyebrow raise, hand in his coat pocket gesturing to the cafe behind me. With his other hand, he repositions the strap on his shoulder attached to a black canvas briefcase.

I blink back at him and laugh. "Hardly! Just escaping a bad date, actually." I glance back toward the cafe, kind of hoping my abandoned date walks out so Dom can see.

The universe is on my side. Harrison steps out and I twirl my hair a little, mumbling, "Nice meeting you," as he takes in the man I'm out here with. Then the guilt kicks in because I'm not trying to make Harrison jealous—or, God forbid—think I planned this. "Just ran into an old friend!" I shout out after him, my words falling on his back as his head shakes in defeat. His hair really is too long for my liking.

Dom briefly glances over to Harrison before turning back towards me. "See? That's why I don't date."

My heart sinks at hearing this. What single person resolves not to date? Especially when I'm standing right here in front of him? We could be so beautiful together, I can just see it. I'm instantly envisioning a scene with the two of us, Dom scooping me up to carry me fireman-style, me in a white dress, him in a tux, spinning me around on a beach. Or no—maybe a vineyard in Tuscany, rolling fields of grapes and rustic pale orange stone buildings surrounding us.

I'm not giving up. "You know, has anyone ever told you that you look like John Stamos?" I ask, a little flutter of my eyelashes accompanying the question.

Dom nods at me, reaching a hand up to run along his jawline. "Yes," he says, ocean blue eyes blaring into mine. He smirks and returns his hand to his pocket. He's looking at me like we're in a game, and it's my move.

"Really?" I raise my shoulders in a shrug. "Guess it's an accurate resemblance then."

He fully smiles now as if amused, but then breaks eye contact and looks down the street. I don't want our conversation to be over, so I blurt out, "Who else has told you that?"

He looks back at me again, face serious now, and he tilts his head to the side. "You have, Lori."

"Oh. I have?" *I have?* I flush with a little embarrassment. Apparently, I need new material.

He shrugs. "Several times. And I always answer the same way." The corner of his mouth raises.

"I see. And that is?"

"That I wouldn't even know who that is if it weren't for you."

It's all coming back to me now. Yes, I have mentioned his John Stamos resemblance before. "Right. Of course. And what do I usually say to that?"

It's the thick, dark eyebrows and deep-set blue eyes that really solidify the comparison. The smolder—and it's looking at me now, making me wonder if Dom at all finds me attractive. He licks his lips before responding. "You offer a celebrity rundown. You explain that he's an actor, and then you ask me what actor I think you look like."

I laugh, pleased that he remembers the conversation. Or conversations, plural, rather. Does he ever think about me?

"Ahh," I nod. "I do recall," I say with my best side shoulder shrug, raising it to my chin with a side glance back to him that with any luck, comes off as hopelessly adorable. Fingers crossed. "And?"

He hesitates, but I see a flicker of something in his eyes. "I say I'm no good with celebrity names."

"Naturally. Though surprising given your celebrity daughter."

He grins at that. It's lovely. "It starts and ends there, what can I say?"

"I'm happy to give you some suggestions. Of my celebrity look-alike, I mean."

"No need, I already know. You answer for me—Julianne Moore, I think is what you say." His face is serious at first, but then his mouth turns up with a hint of a smile, and I feel a little hopeful in the look he's giving me. He turns his head to look down the busy street again, brows furrowed, and I allow myself to momentarily enjoy the way his short dark hair flutters around the tiniest bit in the wind.

I feel disappointed, though, even if he did manage to remember that I look like Julianne Moore. I blurt out, "Oh, well, sorry for boring you with repeated conversations, apparently. My memory isn't the greatest."

Dom turns back to me, and I see kindness in his eyes. "Sorry, that may have come out wrong. Wasn't meant to be rude. Listen, I..." he says before looking back down the street again, and I wonder what's got him so distracted. Why he isn't offering to help me recover from my bad date and have a do-over, but with him instead.

"I have to go," he finally says. "I'm meeting someone."

Please don't be a woman, I think. Better not be if he says he doesn't date. I nod and smile. "I'll let you go, then."

"It was good seeing you again," he says and steps forward for a handshake just as I reach up on my tiptoes for a hug and attempt a cheek kiss. He jabs his hand in my belly, and I pull back.

"I was going for a hug! I think we're beyond handshakes, right?" I ask hopefully. He nods and I go in again, this time feeling his rigid body in my arms as he returns my hug with stiffness. And not the good kind. I decide against the cheek kiss, now feeling too shy for it. I've known the man for several years now, but I guess I'm not exactly his cup of tea. Oh well, it's fine.

Or—maybe I'll reach out to him later today. A little text to apologize for my boring conversation. I'll keep it light, make a joke of it. Yes, I could use this little exchange as a jumping-off point to actually conversing with one another. It's worth a shot, and besides, I have nothing to lose.

five

· · ·

dom

H E HAD SEEN Lori Meyers multiple times over the years, had always found her attractive, as most anyone objectively would, but he never had the interest to ask her out. Lori is light and bubbly—sure. But also a bit scatterbrained, from what he can tell. Dom knows his own limitations of patience with that kind of thing.

And now here she is bumping right into Dom on the street, as she explains that she's escaping some date. He says the first thing that comes to his mind, telling her he doesn't date, though he's surprised by his regret in that statement. He worries that now Lori will think he's celibate or something.

Which, these days, isn't far from the truth.

"Has anyone ever told you that you look like John Stamos?" Full lips taunt him. The chestnut hair surrounding her face whirls in the breeze, and the brick and stone of the building behind her frame her slim body. His eyes scan the bit of exposed skin on her chest peeking out beneath her scarf, and he resists the urge to completely look her up and down. He peels his eyes away to look down the street.

Maybe it's been too long since he's fucked anyone, who knows, but Dom can't deny that he's turned on by her. The various passersby walking around them barely register in his mind. It catches him off guard. Lori's beautiful, it's true. Captivating, even. But something in the back of his mind blares a warning signal to stay away. He doesn't do high-maintenance.

He mutters out some semblance of a response that he realizes too late comes off as offensive, because she pouts in her return statement, and Dom's quickly filled with regret. *God, she is radiant,* he thinks as he stumbles through their unexpected exchange. A vibrant orchid in comparison to his stoic self. Better suited for someone else, without a doubt. Someone who could whisk her away and give her all the spontaneity and entertainment she would surely want. Dom doesn't have the time for that.

He wishes he could match her light spirit in some way, so that he wasn't coming off like such an ass. He called her out on her repeat topic of conversation, and he worries he hurt her feelings. He should have said something else, something sweet, at least. Maybe told her that yes, she's mentioned the resemblance before, but that he *likes* hearing it from her. That would have been much better. Maybe then he could have gotten a laugh out of her.

Lori and Dom had been acquaintances thrust into one another's lives thanks to their children. Her daughter, Reggie, is married to Xavier, an old military friend of Dom's, and his own daughter Ruby is mere weeks away from marrying Xavier's nephew. All this to say that Lori and Dom run into one another at the occasional events, holidays, etc., and as two people in a similar stage of what you might consider fully adult middle-aged life, they tend to gravitate towards one another. Conversation is usually simplistic with subtle undertones of flirtation on Lori's end, and Dom a mere observer to the Lori Meyers show. They have one another's phone numbers, procured by some excuse of logistics a year or two ago, but he's never reached out to her. Has he thought about it? Sure. But the full desire to do so never seemed to reach him. What would he even say? Ask to meet up for coffee? How generic, and Dom notes that, as he's just learned, the last guy to try that with her didn't have much luck. No—a date with Lori would surely be a waste of time and energy.

He wraps up their conversation, increasingly uncomfortable in her presence and aware that he's due to meet someone in ten minutes. Being late is not something he's a fan of, so he extends a hand to shake hers just as Lori goes in for a hug. He swears to himself for being an unaware ass in the presence of this woman who is nothing but sweet and a little chaotic.

When the brief minutes of their awkward encounter end, Dom retreats down the street, shaking his head to himself. He'd all but committed to the bachelor lifestyle since he divorced Ruby's mom about fifteen years ago. Military life had made it hard to settle down with anyone else, and after learning what kind of person his ex Pearl really was—is, rather—he finds it hard to know who to trust. Things had proved so bad with Pearl that he and Ruby had long ago cut her out of their lives.

Now he finds it easier to keep to himself.

But he's still a red-blooded man that—as he has just been reminded—can very easily feel the thrums of desire stirred up by a beautiful woman, different as Lori Meyers is to him. He wouldn't even know where to begin, however, on trying to pursue anything with her.

The closest thing Dom Francesca has had to a relationship recently was with his daughter's PR manager Jules, of all people. Turns out Jules was more interested in using Dom for sex more than anything serious, not that he minded. He only worried about complicating the professional relationship for Ruby. Thankfully, the very direct, very driven woman that Jules is, meant that she had a clear goal with a clear end point in talking to Dom. Great sex— Jules turned out to enjoy immediacy, something Dom was pleased to learn. They'd fuck in dark halls after meetings, Jules pulling him in, lifting her skirt and a leg for him to hold while he pulsed his body into her against a wall. Or she'd throw the upper half of her body down on a conference table of an abandoned room, her ass inviting, and he'd ride with all his might, praying no one would walk in, but too consumed to care.

Jules made a clean break when she decided she was done with him. Dom was more than fine with that, especially since he had the feeling bedrooms were never going to be their thing, and while immediacy has a time and place, he also enjoys the slow and drawn-out event that can be lovemaking now and then.

With thoughts of Lori Meyers in his bed now clouding his mind, he heads back down the street and around the corner to the office building he had been directed to, willing himself to clear his thoughts of Lori naked. He needs to get focused.

He walks the few final steps to his destination—a historical society that could potentially help with a task. In true Pennsylvania fashion, the building is red brick with windows trimmed in crisp white paint. The door sports what looks to be a fresh coat of white as well, though the brass knob looks as old as the building itself. As he turns the relic, all he can think is that hopefully, any archive materials are stored in safer confinement. Maybe he could volunteer here, he wonders, figure out a way to assist. Retiring from the military has a way of making him feel aimless, and while he used to keep himself busy with assistance in his daughter's career, Ruby's now reached a level of success that goes beyond Dom's area of expertise. He could use a hobby.

He steps over the threshold and takes in the musty smell typical of these historic buildings. The carpet is the industrial brown variety that a public space offers, but everything else maintains a kind of time-capsule presence. Old portraits of various war figures adorn the walls, a staircase with the signature white wooden spindles sweeps up welcomingly. He gives his name and the name of the person he's meeting to the ancient-looking man at the front desk, and watches with minor concern as the man's biscotti-sized fingers shake and thumb through a book that Dom assumes is the organization's version of a calendar. No computers here, he muses. They take away from the historic appeal, perhaps.

The man directs Dom up the stairs, and he makes his way, appreciative of the old wood flooring beneath his feet that he imagines the carpet downstairs is covering in attempt at protection. Once on the second floor, he taps lightly on the door the greeter had instructed him to, second one on the right. A whisper of "Come in" beckons him into the tiny office. A beaming woman that looks to be about a hundred and five rises from her seat behind a desk. A fluff of her cotton ball hair catches a purplish hue from a beam of sunlight coming through the window behind her.

"No, no, don't get up," Dom says to her, scared she'll keel over at the effort.

"I insist!" she says, making her way over to him with a heavy lean on the desk for support with each passing step. He instinctively reaches out to her just in case, brittle arm in his hand, and he wonders how much this fossil is really going to be able to help him.

Thankfully, a moment later a younger man steps into the room behind Dom and joins them, and Dom can't help but feel relieved that there's someone here that potentially still has their faculties. Is that ageism? He wonders if he's being too quick to judge.

"Carl," the cotton ball says to the man, "this here is Dom Francesca! Do you know who that is?" Her chapped lips grin and Dom knows what's about to happen. Ruby's fame is a blinding torch he now carries around.

"Yes, of course I do, Sis. You've made it clear who would be stopping in today, but don't make the man uncomfortable. And sit down, will you?" Carl instructs to Dom's relief before turning to him. "Word travels fast around here, be warned. Not too much excitement happens, so when Ruby Francesca's father called about some old letters, you better believe everyone was talking. I think you may have breathed a decade of life back into old Sis here," he says with a wink to the woman.

Sis sits back down and tells him to "shut it," which has Dom laughing. He takes a seat in one of the leather studded wing chairs to the side of the room, Carl shutting the door and sitting beside Dom. "Now, tell us about these letters," he prompts.

Dom pulls out a slim black case from the laptop bag he brought in. He reaches in and produces a folder before handing it to Carl. A glance back to old Sis reveals she is staring at Dom and grinning, little interest in the letters, apparently.

"We found them years ago when doing renovations in our house. Tucked away in a secret spot in the floorboards," he explains.

Carl places the folder on his lap and reaches forward to the walnut desk. He pulls on a brass handle, revealing a lump of soft, white cotton, and Dom watches in bemusement as Carl retrieves the archiving gloves before slipping his hands through. With a final tug of the fabric at his wrists, he gingerly opens the folder in his lap and pulls out the papers. Dom thinks back with some guilt to the number of times he's handled them without any protection. Is Carl being extreme or was Dom being reckless?

Carl flips through the yellowing stack, a divot forming between his brows. "They all say, 'Dear Dog Tags,' and are signed, 'With love, Lace.' Is that it?" He looks up at Dom in disappointment, and Dom shifts uncomfortably in his seat.

"So is that where Ruby got the name of her song?" Sis asks, her grin now expanding to depths Dom fears her papery skin may not be able to handle. He's surprised she even knows who Ruby is, given that Ruby's fanbase is generally under the age of forty.

He clears his throat. "One of her albums, yes. She named it 'Dog Tags & Lace' out of inspiration from these letters. We tried to research them years ago but were always told there's nothing anyone could do for us, since there weren't any envelopes with them or any real names or information other than the dates on each one."

Carl looks back down, rattling off a few. "1945...1946...this one is from Christmas." His eyes skim through the cursive German writing. "Weihnachten."

Dom reaches back in his bag. "I had them translated. Here," he says, pulling out a stack of white papers with the typed English translations.

"All in German, hmm," Carl says, nodding. This fact seems to interest him a bit more, though he quickly follows with a shrug and shuffles the letters back together, handing them over to the ungloved Sis. "Interesting, without a doubt, considering the limitations on civilian mail to other countries at the time. But without any other info, I'm not sure how much we can dig and find. Are you looking to donate them here to our archives or what?"

Sis briefly looks down at the letters before handing them back to Dom, her face revealing clear boredom. "Is Ruby here in town for a visit? Maybe joining you?" He sees the dance of hope in her pale eyes.

Dom takes the papers and tucks them back into their case. "Um, no, unfortunately. She's not in town right now, she's back in LA," he quickly explains before giving his case a quick pat. "These letters served her as inspiration only in the unique signature. The letters reveal no names or anything identifiable, just that signature at the end of each."

"So what exactly brings you in here today?" Carl asks.

Dom sighs with frustration, getting the feeling he's on a fool's errand here, and that his name sparked interest thanks to Ruby with no real hope of actual assistance.

"My daughter Ruby writes her songs, and she was hoping I might get some more information to help inspire her next album. It was a shot in the dark. I told her I'd give it another try but by the look you're giving me, I'm guessing there's no real hope."

Carl turns a little in his seat to face Dom. "I wish I could help on that front, I really do. The thing is it's an old town, there's hundreds of old letters like this that we receive. A lot of times people just want help in locating any surviving family members so they can return the letters to them, offer up family keepsakes." He shakes his head. "They're obviously referring to World War II and are a wonderful piece of history in their own right, but I'm assuming you've thoroughly read and found no other useful information? Patterns of terms that might have been a code, or town names or anything?"

Dom glances over to Sis, smile now gone and what looks to be heaviness on her lids.

"No, nothing useful like that. They seem rather purposely vague. We know that the writer was a German girl—or woman, rather—writing to an American. She mentions originally being from Cologne and escaping arrest due to her political views. The letters appear to all have been written from a farm on the countryside shortly after the war ended. She rescued an American pilot and helped him escape, that's who 'Dog Tags' appears to be. But nothing solid, no names. Since the war had just ended, you get the sense that the writer still lived in some fear and didn't want to reveal too much."

"Explains the vagueness," Carl says, nodding in agreement. "There are other places better equipped for that kind of thing than we are here, specialists in the field you could try. I could give you some names. At the very least, they'd make a great addition to a collection, but sounds like you'd rather keep them."

"For now, yes," Dom confirms.

"Well, your daughter's an artist. Tell her to read through and fill in her own blanks." Carl smiles now as if coming up with a grand idea. "Bet her next album gets her another Grammy."

Dom nods and smiles in return, rising and noting dear Sis appears to have officially dozed off. "Thank you for your time," he says, extending a hand before heading out, down the creaky stairs and out the front door. As he walks down the street in defeat, he half wonders if Ruby put him on this simply to try and keep her father busy. If she really wanted to know the writer of these letters, he's sure she'd have directed him someplace other than the small historical society in town. Her team would have the resources to know where to turn.

He sends Ruby a quick text as he strolls down the two blocks toward the parking lot, flurries swirling around him with increased speed.

> D: No luck, honey. Sorry I couldn't be more
> help.

He makes his way to his car, reeling at the pointlessness of this afternoon's excursion. Although it wasn't a total waste, he thinks, as he did get to run into Lori.

He decides to send an additional text, attempting to be quick about it before he loses his nerve.

> D: It was good seeing you today.

He hits send and unlocks his car door before climbing in. "Fuck it," he says to the empty space.

> D: You looked great as usual.

He hits send again.

lace

. . .

September 1945 ~ South Germany

Dear Dog Tags,

I can still remember with perfect clarity the way my ears perked in high alert, the sound of you rustling in the darkness of the brush reaching me first in the agonizing seconds before the sight of you came into my line of vision. I held my breath in fearful anticipation, sure this was the end, that my hiding place had been found and I would be carried away in powerless restraint.

And then you emerged, a bloodied and battered shadow hobbling amongst the tree line, nearly unrecognizable as human. I thought my heart might explode out of my chest. My thoughts that the mysterious figure before me was a risk to my freedom melted away, as it was evident you were in no condition to capture so much as an incessant fly. You were in just as much danger as I was, in your own fight for life.

I soon learned in the following days to come, it was actually me that was the answer to your freedom. I could feel it in the marrow of my very bones that I was meant to rescue you.

Do you remember those first words you said to me? You knew I was German, and as a wounded American soldier, this had to be terrifying for you, even if I was just a girl of barely eighteen. How could you know if I was safe, or if I would turn you in?

But you pointed to your own chest, and you said those first strange words.

Dog Tags. Followed by your explanation.

American. Crash.

Even through your broken German I could feel your pain and fear, and I wanted to reassure you that I meant you no harm. I uttered an English word I knew—safe. And I told you my name.

You shook your head just the tiniest bit, and I could see a kind of reverence when you looked at me. It was then that you said my favorite words.

You. Lace. Marvelous lace.

A charmer, even in what easily could have been the last moments of your life. Perhaps you were delirious, come to think of it.

But in the depths of my confusing mix of emotions, I thought you were naming me "Lace." Imagine! I had no idea you were in fact trying to describe the rare and delicate grace you felt I possessed as your savior. While I laugh to think of our language barrier those first hours and days, it still remains one of my favorite moments.

That's when our love story began. And I thank God for the gift you are to me, terrified as I remained in those early days together, lost in the shadows of so much uncertainty of what was to come.

But we found our way, didn't we, Dog Tags?

With love,

-Lace

six

. . .

edie

SHE TAKES A deep breath, determined to calm her spiraling nerves as she walks up the pristine slate pathway. The pool house that serves as a guest home mirrors the brick of the main house, a miniature version of the structure with a matching sloping charcoal roof and wide French windows. Edie can imagine the beauty of the space in the summertime, when the pool is open and the garden is bursting with a rainbow of blooms, the windows open on cooler days, inviting a breeze throughout the shadowed shelter of the patio spilling beneath the cover of the extended roof.

Today the pool area appears sleepy—canvas stretched out to cover the water like a blanket, the garden at rest and dotted not with vibrant blooms, but only with the sporadic evergreen holly bush. She feels like an intruder in this quiet space, and in many ways she is, a realization that brings some guilt. In fact, the cocktail of guilt and apprehension she feels stirring in her belly are having her second-guess the decision to come here at all.

But she had to meet this woman, the one person that might finally help her learn something about her biological father. Edie's research had revealed that her father and this woman would have been married when Edie was conceived, twenty-two years ago.

Which has led Edie to a turbulent number of questions. That's the thing about finding answers—it usually only unravels more mysteries.

The fact that her father had been married was a surprising revelation that had come most unexpectedly. Edie, of course, knew there had been some sperm donation made to her mothers; obviously the two of them hadn't conceived Edie on their own. But when Edie would ask about who this mystery man was that had assisted in her creation, her moms were vague, explaining that he was "just a donor." When Edie would confront them on having been aware of subtle chatter alluding to more to the story than an anonymous donation, her moms would freeze, wide-eyed. Then they'd babble on in rapid waves that they would tell her about it later, when she was older. When the time was right.

Apparently, later was a whole lot longer for them than it was for Edie. So, she took matters into her own hands. And here she is now.

With another deep breath, she marches up to the door. Knocks twice with force that she hopes is loud enough to be heard, but not so loud that it's obnoxious. Is the woman she's hoping to meet home? Should Edie immediately state who she is, why she's here, or would it be better to come up with some other excuse for her surprising arrival? The frazzled thoughts run through her mind in the agonizing moments between her knock, the silence, then the daunting sound of footsteps increasing in volume with each stride. Her practiced speech now seems laughable, because nothing can prepare her for the encounter she's about to have.

seven

. . .

lori

WHEN EDIE MACKENZIE shows up on my doorstep, asking for Lori Meyers and claiming to be the secret daughter of my late husband, my first thought is, *She's so much younger and prettier than me.* Really, that's all I can think! Not, "What the hell did you just say?" or, "I'm going to need some proof of that!" The girl could be Richard's female twin, it's uncanny. I immediately believe her, as Richard was known to stick his penis in places other than me. Apologies if that's crude, but it's true.

I'm a curious soul with a love of people, so no—I'm not immediately shocked or turned off. Not at first, anyway. Nope, all I can think is how pretty and young this Edie girl is. And that my day just got a whole lot more interesting.

Look, what would you do in my shoes, turn away the poor thing? She appears to be about twenty or so. She had to have been a small child when Richard died, meaning she's gone most of her life without a father. Her biological one, anyhow. I can't help but have a pinch in my chest at that. It's not her fault her father was a playboy. And I'm a sucker for a lost soul, what can I say?

Edie's hair is a vibrant sandy blonde with faded pink streaks framing her face. Strong jawline, wide-set eyes framed by chunky plastic glasses, red with speckles of black, and I wonder if they're fake. Her smile stretches ear to ear, her eyes are a piercing blue, just as her father's were. In fact, the resemblance is so striking, it's like the girlish ghost of Richard is here to haunt me. It's a bit jarring in that way, which is why after I confirm that yes, I'm Lori, my first question of, "Are there more of you?" is the thing to fly out of my mouth during this strange encounter. I'm not sure I could handle a multiplication of his ghostly presence. One feels like enough.

"Right," Edie says as if she expected this question from me. "Other than the older ones from his first marriage, no. Not that I know of or ancestry.com knows of, anyway!" She shifts her weight from her right foot to the left, the strap of her overalls slipping as she does. A tiny long-sleeved pink crop top is underneath, and I can see the smoothness of youthful skin peeking out the open sides of blue denim.

Her teeth are chattering, and my next thought is what in the world is she doing out in February weather without a coat. So there you have it. If you're wondering what you might be thinking if a flesh-and-blood secret pops onto your doorstep like that, you might be surprised at how rudimentary it feels. Because for me it was simple, and in this order—that she's young and pretty. Whether or not I should be expecting more secret love children like her. And why doesn't she have on a coat?

"It's chilly outside. Come on in," I offer as I move aside.

She flashes another wide smile and steps in past me. "I'm from Florida, still not used to Pennsylvania winter weather!"

"Florida? Long way from home," I say. "Did you travel all the way up here hoping to find Richard?" Oh gosh, my heart sinks at the thought. How will I break it to her that he's died? She'll be crushed.

I walk her into my kitchen, a buttery cream that feels like a cozy hug, and I'm thankful for the setting if I'm going to be crushing sweet Edie's hopes at meeting her father. My own heart saddens at the thought of Richard, my mountain of a man. While far from perfect—proof standing here in my kitchen of that!—the truth is he *had* pulled me out of my depths of depression in the darkest time of my life.

"No, I actually live in the area here, now," Edie says to my relief. At least she didn't make the trek over here from very far. "I just started my master's program this past fall here in Philly, so I guess Florida really isn't my home anymore."

"Oh? What are you studying?" I ask as I gesture for her to take a seat. Edie pulls out a chair from the small kitchen table. The guest cottage on my daughter, Reggie's, property doesn't offer too many options for seating, so we are relegated to the only place that allows more than one person. It's a pool house, really, with two small bedrooms, a kitchen and bathroom. No real living room space, so hosting guests is a bit of struggle this time of year when the patio and its furnishings are tucked away for the winter.

I should probably mention that this property was originally owned by our dear philandering Richard, prior to his seduction of yours truly. Reggie and her husband, Xavier, purchased the home from me a few years back, moving my mother and me into this pool house bungalow. Family is everything, and I love having my daughter and two grandchildren so close by. (Though don't you dare call me grandmother; I'm too young for that. I'm Nana Lori to them.)

I debate what to do with myself. Do I sit and join her or remain standing? Offer her some tea? I opt for standing, and I look down at her with an encouraging smile.

"I'm studying Social Work," Edie replies to my question.

A girl with a savior complex. Girl after my own heart. "Tough field, you like helping people?"

Edie grins, all that youthful spirit emanating out of her like fireworks. "I love it. Every bit of it."

"I've always been a helper too," I say, leaning against the tiny strip of kitchen counter that runs beside the table. I know I should be a bit more hesitant with what this girl is doing here now, what her intention is, but I can't help but love her already! I've been known to quickly invite people into my world and then get burned when they turn out to be far less harmless than I originally thought. But I refuse to be one of those horrible, cynical types. "Now I specialize in yoga instruction for those in their golden years of life," I explain. I place a hand beside my mouth. "Alright, old people," I say with a conspiratorial laugh, and Edie laughs too, mumbling out that yoga for old people sounds "adorable." Hopefully I'm easing her nerves, I could tell she was nervous when she first introduced herself. My eyes might have gone wide, I admit. But I admire her courage in coming here.

Which leads me to my next question, "How did you know to come to this door and not the main house?"

A look of guilt, perhaps, passes on Edie's face. "I did some research and knew your daughter Reggie lived in the big house and that I could find you here. I'm good at finding things out, it's part of my job."

"Your job? Are you a detective or something in your spare time? A PI?" I ask, hopeful my playful tone is coming across. I push forward from my lean against the counter as I decide to sit and join her at the table. When I pull out the chair directly across from her, the sound of its legs drags on the tiles and pierces the quiet. I wince at the sound, realizing I need music or something. How do I fill the air with some ambiance for this most unusual meeting of two?

She laughs and rifles through her bag, pulling out a business card. "No, here," she says, sliding it across the table to me.

I scan the card and mutter out, "Heirloom Hunter?" I hand the card back to her, my interest now piqued. "What does that mean?"

"It's just a little hobby, really. I help people connect historical documents, memorabilia and whatnot to any surviving family members."

Now *that* sparks my interest. "Really? Anything juicy?"

A giddy nod confirms what I want to hear. "Oh yeah. You'd be amazed what pent-up desire and longing churn out. Especially through war times. Mostly you get the random pocket watch or knife or something. Letters filling the recipient in on day-to-day things, trying to create a sense of normalcy. But every once in a while, you stumble across the good stuff."

"Sounds like you've had a lot of experience."

A frown fills her face. "Not so much actually, no. Mostly just my own personal research in established collections, but I have matched up a few things with people. Nothing super exciting. Actually, wait! There was a military jacket someone found at a consignment shop that had identifying info in there—and something else." Edie leans forward in her seat. "Ladies' stockings in the pocket. Were they from his lady friend? Or did he himself enjoy wearing them? Who knows?" she says with a mischievous eyebrow raise. She's such a cutie pie. Her enthusiasm is contagious.

My mind wanders back to seeing Dom the other day. I had watched him after we parted ways as he walked into the historical society building. "Interesting," I say. "Does it pay you anything?" Curiosity in this young woman is quickly blossoming beyond the startling knowledge of her being Richard's daughter. A budding Heirloom Hunter—now *that* I can get on board with. I can just imagine the wonderful bits of history she gets to see. Glimpses of lovers connecting, dreams unfolding. How romantic.

"Pay much?" she says. "Not exactly. Currently I work for an agricultural non-profit, I'm really hoping to be a grant writer or something along those lines. The heirloom hunting is more of a fun side gig, but there's a somewhat famous lady on TikTok that's making waves for this kind of thing." She shrugs. "It's cool."

I nod and lean forward to place my elbows on the table, rest my chin in my interlaced fingers. "So, social work, grant writing aspirations, and crafty research to find people. Sounds like you've got it all figured out. And so young."

She huffs back a laugh. "Hardly! No, I'm the type to want to have my hands in a little of everything. My moms are constantly telling me I'm like a cartoon rocket spinning in swirls with power too big. They say that with love and encouragement," she blurts out as if she had indirectly insulted them. "My moms love my spirit and tell me to keep on moving and fighting, exactly as I am."

Her words resonate with me. I was once like that too. Feels like a long time ago, I realize with sadness. And then I shake that ridiculous thought. What am I even saying? Of course I'm still just as spirited as ever!

"Moms? No dad, then?" I confirm. "Other than your bio dad, of course."

Edie nods emphatically. "Yeah, and just to confirm, I never even met that bio dad. I have the hunch that my mom must have been momentarily swept off her feet by Richard, never knowing he was married," she says. "At least that's my guess. My mom is definitely not someone I believe could have an affair, I just don't see it. But they've never actually told me anything." She looks down, her voice quieting. "I had to dig and find out who my dad was on my own."

I take in her sadness and push back from the table, rising from my seat because this girl deserves a hug. "Oh, sweetie. All those years of wondering, can I give you a hug? Is that okay?" I ask through a small smile. When she nods, I step closer to her and lean down to awkwardly embrace the sweet thing. "The world has a funny way of working, and I'm so glad you're here and I'm having the chance to meet you." I release her, grab her shoulders to give a warm smile before settling back into my seat. I scoot it a bit closer to her, not wanting to have the table so prominent between us. "If you're right about that, if your mom was unaware of his marriage to me, it makes sense. I was hardly naive to Richard's infidelity, but your father was definitely a man who could catch you in his web. And spin that web in exactly the way that suited him. He, um, he died of a heart attack, are you aware of that?" I ask tentatively.

She nods, thank God. "Yeah, after I found out who he was, I

found his obituary. I was disappointed, I have to say. But there was some relief learning that he died so many years ago, it's not like I missed much anyhow. It's why I came here to you, so that I could learn a bit more about him. You feel like my only hope. I've tried to reach out to my half-siblings on social media. I messaged them but got no response." She tilts her head to the side. "Though it sounds like Richard wasn't the most virtuous of people."

I stretch my arms across the bit of table space between us to grab her hands. "Edie, your dad had his flaws, sure. But he could be incredibly kind as well." I shrug. "He took me and my daughter, Reggie, in when we had nothing, and within just a few weeks of us even dating. Moved us in here to this place," I say with a gesture to the property beyond. "It was his house before Reggie bought it. He was...my hero, in many ways. I was twenty-five, had just lost my husband and son in a car accident. All four of us were in the accident, actually. Reggie and I survived, my boys didn't," I say quietly, wondering when the last time I spoke those dreadful words out loud even was. I feel numb as I say them.

"Wow," her saucer-like eyes say with a blink behind her glasses. "That's terrible, I'm so sorry."

I pull back my hands and decide to busy myself with the task of making some tea. I rise and start opening cabinets, willing my mind to not allow any of the flashbacks that love to burst through my conscious, most unwelcome. "Well!" I say brightly. "It was the way it was meant to be! I've learned to trust and have faith in that kind of thing. Life has been good to me, no worries there. And now I have you!"

I pull down two mugs and my basket of teas. Fill and plug in the kettle to boil some water. "Wait until Reggie meets you, would you be interested in that? She may not be your blood, but Richard was a father to her for many of her childhood years."

Edie pushes her glasses back from her face and rises to stand next to me. She leans a hip against the counter, folding her arms across her chest. "I mean, yeah, if you think she'd be okay with that.

I can't help but feel curious about him, I'd love to learn as much as I can. Actually, this whole thing was prompted by one of my classes."

"Oh yeah?"

Edie raises her eyebrows up. "Yeah. Guess professors don't always think about how tough that kind of thing can be, looking into your 'family constellation' as they call it."

"Maybe that's exactly the reason for the assignment," I suggest. "Because there's often unanswered questions. Gives students a chance to discover."

"You're right, they say one of the goals of the program is to move through your own subconscious obstacles. Then you can more effectively help others when working in the field. So, yeah, it's what started this whole rabbit hole of me trying to find answers."

"Do your moms know that you're here? That you figured it out?" I ask while mindlessly twirling a stray strand of my hair.

She shakes her head. "Not yet, but I'll tell them. I'm not sure why they're so secretive about it all, it's not like they would need to fear losing me to him!" Her eyebrows pinch together. "Although I wonder if they even know he passed."

My mind starts rolling in curiosity of who Edie's mom is. Was she a willing conquest, fully aware she was playing with fire by way of a married man? As much as Edie in her naivety wants to believe her mother had no idea, I have the distinct feeling she did if she was so secretive about it all these years.

But I leave that to myself. A young girl is fragile, and she wants to believe the best in people, her mother especially. I'll be damned if I'm the one to take that from her.

There's a darkness that passes over Edie's lovely face, and I reach a hand over to her arm. "I'm sure you've had a lot on your mind with all this. It's a lot to take in. Are you alright?"

Her eyes meet mine with a small smile. "Me? I mean, it is, yes. But here I was worried about you and how *you'd* feel."

The glass electric kettle starts to reveal tiny bubbles beginning to rise. I watch them in fascination. "I distinctly remember the first time Richard came home with the scent of another woman on his coat. I was mad as hell, but also madly in love with him," I say with a shrug. "I know that sounds terrible, but we had a connection, you know? We were both broken in many ways I suppose. So I forgave him. Believed him when he said it was a mistake, that it wouldn't happen again."

"My moms always say, 'Once a cheater, always a cheater.'" Edie unfolds her arms and tucks her hair behind her ear. "Sorry, maybe that's not the right thing to say."

I huff out a small laugh. "Well, they're not wrong, in my experience. It definitely did happen again in Richard's case, but by that point he was in the last months of his life, little did I know. He passed before I really even had the chance to think what to do about it. Water under the bridge, it was so many years ago. Life moves on."

Edie purses her lips. "I suppose so. Although what a terrible thing, he dies before you even get the chance to face off with him, and he just gets the last word." There's softness in her sweet little young and naive eyes.

"Please," I laugh, waving her off. "He was the least of my concerns. He was a force, that's for sure, but so am I. An expert at creating the destiny of my dreams. Want some tea?" I ask.

An amusing thought pops in my head—the fact that Richard turned some woman a lesbian. He would *hate* that. The man thought he was God's gift on earth. Too funny, really.

"Please, sure," Edie responds.

"Green tea okay?"

"My favorite, actually."

I nod and place a tea bag in each mug. "I just wish I could see the look on his face if Richard knew he repulsed a woman so much that she no longer wanted men!"

"Oh, well, I mean my mom has had boyfriends as well as girlfriends, from my understanding. Says she loves all humans, so not sure Richard could really take credit for that."

"Just let me have that, Edie. More fun that way, don't you think?" I turn and give her a wink, lean against the counter as I wait for the kettle to finish boiling.

"Whatever works for you," she says, but she smiles. "Do you have any photos of him? Videos or anything?"

I nod. "I do, lots stored up in the main house in the basement. I can set up a time for you to head up there, meet Reggie and her husband too, if you'd like." I study Edie's face and if I'm not imagining, I can see the sadness in her eyes as she considers this. "It may not be the exact long-lost family uniting you'd hoped for, but it's something. In life we just have to see the bright side of things, even if it's hard at times. Better to move on and move up."

"I suppose so."

"You suppose so?" I huff out a laugh. "You don't seem convinced, but trust me on this, love. It's the best way to go. You'll see that as you get older."

The kettle clicks, indicating it's ready and I carefully lift and pour steaming water into each mug.

"I guess I just wish I could have met him."

"It wasn't meant to be, sweetie. Best not to focus on that."

"Yeah, but...the pain of it is still there," she says softly, "and it can pop up sometimes when I don't expect it. Wish I could figure out how to tackle it better."

I lift my tea bag in a steeping motion, and flinch when a droplet of hot water splashes on my finger. I put the burned finger in my mouth to temper the pain. "No, no, sweetie. It's a choice we have, happiness. We can feel sorry for ourselves for the hardships, or we can decide that each day is a new day. Face what's ahead with fervor. No sense in dwelling on what you can't change, right?" I nod to her mug. "Your tea should be ready, just be careful."

"Thank you," she says as she gingerly lifts her own mug. A strand of pink and blonde hair falls in front of her face as she gently blows into the steaming cup. She sips with an approving nod before looking back in my direction. "I really appreciate you talking to me. I know I could have emailed you or something first, but after having no response from the messages to his other kids, and with you being so close by, it just felt like fate that I should meet you, if that makes sense."

I grin. "I know exactly what you mean. And listen, while it might hurt to think of the father you never knew, just think of the wonderful thing it is that now you can meet me. And Reggie and our little crew here. With a fresh slate! Had we known about you when you were growing up, it might have been under much more tense circumstances." I lean forward to her. "Though make no mistake, I would have welcomed you with open arms no matter what. The actions of a child's parents are in no way the child's fault."

Edie nods. "I think you might be the nicest person I've ever met, Lori."

My heart beams with this. Completely bursts with warmth! "Oh my gosh, you are so sweet. I'd hug you again, but I don't want to spill my tea on you." I fill my face with what I hope to be the most warming of smiles. This girl needs love during her time of all this discovery. And I'm going to be the one to give it to her. "Well, let's go have a seat," I say, walking back over to the table. "Tell me more about your studies, what classes are you in?"

Edie joins me and settles herself in her chair. "Well, there's the family therapy course I mentioned that has prompted all this. I've done the basic Counseling Skills class, Human Development. And, actually, right now I'm in a Grief Counseling class?" her voice lifts at the end as if in question.

"Are you asking me if you're in the class?" I say with a small laugh.

She blinks and sets down her tea. "No, I mean, obviously I know what classes I'm in. It's just...well, I have to do this interview. For a project? You mentioned losing your first husband and your son, and, um, one of my big semester papers is on interviewing someone that has experienced loss."

"A project?" I whisper the question as if trying it on.

"Not a project, that's a poor choice of words. An assignment, I mean. I have to interview someone that has experienced grief of losing a loved one, but it has to have happened over twenty years ago. You know, so that the person is healed. I'm not supposed to be going into actual grief counseling or anything, just hearing the person's story and how they moved through it, that's all." She purses her lips to the side in concentration.

Is this girl insinuating I be the person she interviews? No—she can't be, right? "So, this person would be like a case study for you." My breath is getting short, my chest rising and falling rapidly as my vision starts to go a little fuzzy. I'm not sure what's happening, but it suddenly feels very hot in here. I push my tea away from me.

"It's just to learn about how someone heals, and what's helped them. I'll find someone, I'm sure." Edie's cheeks flush, but I'm having a hard time concentrating. I blink a few times in hopes to clear my vision.

Is this panic? *A project for her class,* the nerve. A project! A person's life is not a project.

I try and shake away my trepidation. Of course that's not what she means. She's just trying to help people and learning how to do so. My thoughts feel disjointed and I'm mildly aware that my chest is heaving and I'm struggling to breathe, but I attempt to say my next words anyway, make this girl understand.

Make *myself* understand why I'm having such a reaction on something I had long ago buried away deep beneath the trenches of my mind, poured over with the heavy cement of a man like Richard Meyers, the top layer planted over with the prettiest of flowers any garden shop could find. Why that buried something is threatening to burst right on through all the mortar and dirt and blooms.

A burst of images infiltrates my mind. The hospital. Casts.

Whispering for my babies. For my James. My mother hovering over me—the last person I wanted to see.

Telling me James and JJ were gone. My spew of vomit after hearing her words.

I swallow down the vomit that threatens to erupt now. "Edie," I start. "Listen carefully to me." My words are slow and steady, despite my sudden gasping for air. "No matter if it's been thirty years or twenty years or mere hours—the loss of your child is not something you ever truly get over," I say, a shakiness evident in my voice. "You understand me?" A hesitant nod. "Instead, it's a tank, a heavy war tank that sits in your chest, in your heart, and you carry it with you in every passing moment. In every breath that you take that you feel should have been theirs. In every memory that floods your mind that can never be simple and pure joy, because you know it's a memory that precedes a hell on earth."

I look at her in expectation of a response, but it seems our Edie is frozen solid.

My eyes well with tears, but I power on, irritated by her sudden silence. What, no comforting words to offer the grieving mother and widow she burst in on? I smile, but it's a smile laced with torment. "The loss of your sweet and innocent," I say with a dark laugh, "innocent and most *undeserving* child!" My voice is shrill and louder than I really mean it to be, and I see a flinch in Edie's shoulders. I should be calmer. She didn't mean harm, I can see that.

A tear escapes despite myself. A tear, after all these years! This must be misplaced frustration. Yes, it's just the idea of Richard's secret child catching up to me, now that I've had a minute with the girl.

"Oh my gosh, I'm so sorry. Forget I said anything." I can see Edie gulp.

I always hate when someone says, "I'm so sorry." It's almost like saying, "Oh, poor you...that's a *you* problem that I'd never have."

With a heavy sigh I mumble out the words that seem to want to escape. "It's fine. I think I'm just realizing that this is all a lot to take in."

"I'm so sorry."

Please make her stop saying she's sorry.

I plaster on a smile. "Look. Let me try and explain unexpected loss like that, alright? So that when you do find your person to interview, you have a better understanding." At the very least she can learn a lesson in all this. Maybe I can save the victim she tries to bully into her *project*. "Loss like that is a curse brought upon a person's existence." I wipe abruptly at my welling eyes, the threat of tears that are really more anger-fueled than anything. I'm determined to stop them. "You don't truly heal from that," I whisper. "Ever," I say with a stare as directly as I can manage into the girl's eyes.

She nods, dropping her gaze momentarily before returning it back to me. "But I have to believe you can," she says. I open my mouth to counter that healing is not some switch you get to just turn on, but she continues. "I may not know loss like you do, but I know the feelings of wondering what could have been. There's a kind of grief in that as well."

"What do you mean?"

She gives me a little half shrug. "I feel like that about my father. I always wondered about what could have been if I knew him. My whole life I've imagined him being out there somewhere, and I'd think about the relationship we could have if I only knew who he was and could find him. And then after learning that he died, wondering how it might have been different if he hadn't, and I had found him now." I can see the emotion in her eyes as she says this.

"I suppose that's true."

She nods. "In some ways I think meeting you is my way of trying to heal and move through that."

I nod, not sure what to say to that exactly, and we sit in a silent staredown. My mind starts to wander to the thoughts of what life would be like if James and JJ were here now. It's too painful, though, and I shake my head in hopes to chase away that stream of thought.

I think I'm welcomed out; this feels like enough for one day. "You know, my mother will be home soon. She's eighty years old, might be a bit much for her to meet you. Maybe it's time you head out."

I watch as her round eyes blink, then she quickly breaks eye contact to gather her bag, her movements stumbling and awkward. She rises and rushes toward the front door. When she gets there, she pauses and turns back to me. "I really didn't mean to upset you, I swear."

"It's fine," I say, my voice in contrast to the words uttered. I glance down at the Heirloom Hunter business card still sitting on the table. "I have your card. I'll be sure to be in touch," I say. I have a feeling we both know that's unlikely to happen any time soon.

On the other hand, I don't want to shut her out. She's a piece of Richard that I could have right here and now. There's a pull I feel in that.

I just need time to process all of this, that's all.

Edie gives me one last look, pity flooding her youthful face. "I really appreciate you taking the time to meet me, Lori. I'm not sure a lot of people would have done the same." She adjusts the strap of her bag on her shoulder, and a flinch of concern pulls at me for her lack of a coat in this cold.

I rise and make my way over to her by the door. "Pick yourself up some winter gear, maybe," I say, offering up a small smile. "Be well." She nods once, thanks me again and walks out the door.

I blink back the threat of more tears, refusing to let this girl be my undoing. A surprise daughter, talking case studies for a project, teaching me about healing. Oh, the ignorance of youth.

My eyes scan around the room, itching for something to busy myself with. Squash the squall of emotion that's creeping along the edges of my mind. I take a few deep breaths and try and steady my hands. There are thoughts that want to burst in and rain on my parade, but I don't have the mental capacity to face them right now.

I need a distraction. Something, anything.

I see my phone on the counter and go to grab it, opening my texts. I read the one from Dom the other day. The one telling me I looked great, as always. I have to pull the screen back and forth to find my focus before I can even fully read the words I'm looking for. But I get the focus eventually. Yes, there it is. Dom's text telling me it was great to see me.

I type back, my fingers moving furiously across the glow of my screen.

> L: You up to meet for a drink sometime? I'll try for some fresh conversation. No more John Stamos references, Girl Scout's honor.

I add a wink emoji and two clinking glasses.
A moment later my phone vibrates.

> D: Would love to. Saturday okay? I can pick you up at seven.

> D: Where do you want to go?

I smile.

> L: Sounds great. Any place romantic.

> D: Done.

eight

. . .

lori

sixteen years old

JAMES AND I managed to hide our relationship for a solid year before my mom found out about us.

Everyone in school knew we were together, so it was inevitable that word got around to my mom. The day she approached me about James, I about died, sure that the fantasy of romance I had been living in was now over.

She had walked into my bedroom one Saturday afternoon. Saturdays had become miserable for me, because it often meant I had to wait two more days before seeing James again. Mom leaned against my door frame, arms crossed and looking stern.

She got straight to the point. "You know, I had a most interesting lunch with Stephanie's mom yesterday."

I tensed. There'd been numerous times I had lied and told Mom I was at Steph's house when, in fact, I had taken the car to pick up James, and we'd roam around town like two fugitives, thrilled with our borrowed time together, unable to keeps our hands off one another as if afraid each meeting would be our last one. For all the intensity and euphoria of those moments—me pushing the boundaries of my curfew—the moments of having to part ways were like their own kind of torture. A price to pay for a few hours of bliss.

I cleared my throat and tucked my knees under my chin, my bed beneath me squeaking. A bed I fantasized about having James in one day. "That's nice, did you two have fun?" I asked as casually as I possibly could.

"Ahh, yes. Although not as much fun as you and James Blake are apparently having." Her tone was like acid.

My heart stopped. The room spun around me wildly. I didn't know what to do with myself. I had the sudden urge to scream, or to cry, or to throw something in a fit of desperation, all in the realization that my bubble of love was now completely burst, and I'd be grounded forever.

I debated trying to deny it, but I had the feeling it was far too late for that. So I held my chin up as high as I could, and looked my mother directly in the eye. "So, you found out about James then, huh?" I said with a smile, followed by a shrug. "Guess it was just a matter of time. You want to meet him?" My hope was that the nonchalance of my response would assuage her, but my heart was pounding in my chest, and I felt downright nauseated in the thick silence as I awaited my mom's response.

We were in a staredown, a silent duel of sudden death, the continuation of my happiness at stake.

"I hear he's got some family problems."

"He's a good guy, Mom," I rushed to respond. "He takes care of his little brothers and his own mother, and he's the one that's been tutoring me and helping me with my grades, and he's actually so much more than what you'd think if all you know about is his family and where he's from." I was babbling on like an idiot, my mouth a motorboat spewing out a splash of words in reckless waves.

Mom's face was unreadable. Eventually she simply dropped her arms and spun around, leaving her back to me. She turned her head over her shoulder, staring down at the floor before saying, "You're not to see him outside of school anymore, Lori Raina. Do you hear me?"

"But you don't even know him!"

"I know men!" Her declaration startled me, but then I saw her shoulders drop in a heavy sigh. "I know men, and they pressure you, trust me." Her voice softened to a whisper. "Teenage boys especially."

I hated what she was alluding to, as if James was just some run-of-the-mill prick. I knew where her fears came from. Not just from my dad, who was known to be unfaithful. But from her own teenage misfortunes. She gave up a baby when she was sixteen, and she never let me forget it.

I tried to get through to her. "Mom, stop it. You don't get it, James is *good*. He's not like that."

I stared at her with a silent plea for her to trust me and believe me. The frustration I felt in not being able to convey this to her was nothing short of maddening. How could I make her possibly understand this?

There was one thing I knew would help make it clear, but I couldn't tell her the intimate moments that James and I had in the back seat of my car, where I had been begging him to take me, all of me, and how he'd refrained. How I could feel his erection and see the agony and frustration of his hunger for me clear on his face, but he'd breathe out, "Not yet," saying that this wasn't the place. That I deserved better than the back seat of a car for my first time. I couldn't tell her the respect he had shown me, or the way he fulfilled a need deep within me, one that nourished me.

"They're all good at first, Lori. But I know you, you're reckless when left to your own devices. You'll end up pregnant and your life will be ruined, and I'm not letting that happen. He wants to see you badly enough? You think he cares enough about you? Then he'll do it between the hours of 7 a.m. and 2 p.m. Should be perfectly fine with that." Then she walked out the door, closing it behind her, leaving me.

I looked around me, consumed with a need to find anything I could to throw. A book found its way into my hands, and I threw it at the door, the bang nothing compared to the burst of sobs escaping my mouth. She was going to make my life miserable, I knew it. She'd keep me locked up, demand I be home immediately after school, relentless in her control over me, committed to keeping me from being happy.

I flopped backwards onto my bed, crying in frustration over the cruelty of being a sixteen-year-old girl with zero agency, yet having stumbled across the very thing that had awakened my whole being.

Eventually, I fell into a deep sleep, and I dreamed of the day I could get the hell out of there. I dreamed of the day I was going to run off with James, be free, and we'd finally start our life together, just the two of us.

lace

. . .

December 1945 ~ South Germany

Dear Dog Tags,

Today is the two-year anniversary of my escape, and it brings to mind the desperation I felt in those months leading up to it. Desperation causes one to do crazy things, to take risks that seem impossible not to take.

My first crazy thing started out innocently enough. As a teenage girl I had a wonderful group of friends, and we enjoyed hiking and camping, playing guitar and living within the fantastic world of freedoms. Such innocent things, no?

How do I explain—I'll say that my friends and I soon become frustrated with the oppression surrounding us, freedoms slowly being stripped away as any activity not in direct support of those in power was quickly viewed as being just as offensive as if we were the enemy. A silly thing like choosing to hike with friends—which I should add meant not joining the youth groups breeding future soldiers to fight the war—all that became something viewed as *outright rebellion. Those in power can be very subtle and crafty in their intentions at first.*

Up until you disagree with them.

And my friends and I disagreed. My next crazy and desperate thing I did started with small pranks, flyers my friends and I would hide in hymnals in church, graffiti on buildings, all messages of warning for people to wake up. Who would know a group of teens would be viewed as outright enemies in such efforts? Still, we carried on. We felt we had to.

One winter in particular, I'll not soon forget. My home city of Cologne had been ravaged with bombings. One would hear the sirens, clamor into shelter, air thick and damp, the basements dark and never the right temperature—either freezing, or sticky and suffocating.

I still shudder to recall the feeling of sitting, feeling the rumbles and waiting for death.

That winter, in the wake of Christmas, our gift was that no death came. Others were not so lucky.

We had been looking for survivors in a pile of stone and cement, and I heard a woman crying with such anguish, I thought she was physically hurt. Upon reaching her, I learned her pain was not in a broken bone or a crushed limb, but the pain was in her heart. She had survived, but her children had not. I feared ever feeling a pain so searing as that.

My own mother died during her childbirth with me, and my father had been arrested and later killed due to his communist association. I was living with my aunt, but I remained a fighter. I refused to be a quiet prisoner to the realities of tragedy surrounding us.

To suffer in silence was to deny the suffering in the first place. I was not going to be numb and blind in the name of self-preservation, for self-preservation without honesty and virtue is no self-preservation at all.

Late one night, my aunt and I heard a knock on our door. I was terrified, as I had already heard about others in my group being arrested. Here one day, gone the next. Was this my time?

With pounding hearts, we opened the door, and imagine the relief at seeing not men there to execute my doomed future, but a friend of my aunt's, warning us of whispers that my name was on a list. My arrest was imminent.

My aunt packed a bag for me, and with heavy heart and little hope for survival, I set out to escape. Death while on the run would be a victory for me, far better than the death I could face in captivity. There is no price to be had to measure value in one's freedom.

My freedom came on a freight train. My next crazy thing was jumping on that train, a girl on the run at just sixteen years old. I was heading south, I knew, but no clear idea exactly where. I went as far as I could go, then jumped off and hiked further until I found a farm. Yes, the farm where you found me. The couple there took sympathy on me and allowed me to stay in hiding so long as I could work. By then, desperation was as grave as ever.

My darling, when you came into my world, you woke up something inside of me that had been lying dormant. My heart had grown rather cold with terror and anger, and you came and breathed it back to life. The tenderness you possessed, even while risking your own life in your fight to help end the suffering happening in my homeland, that tenderness taught me more than you could know.

Because of you, I learned that tenderness and happiness may exist along with the battles and horrors of our reality. We need not choose one or the other. We may have both.

There is something utterly beautiful about that, Dog Tags.

With love,
Lace

nine

. . .

edie

SHE TAPS HER fingernails on the tattered makeshift desk in front of her, appreciative at having successfully kicked her nail-biting habit. The sound comforts Edie in the otherwise silent and bare office space, and she pauses momentarily to admire her alternating blue and black polish. Work is slow today, most of the pop-up trailer office is out on a community project helping an elementary school in preparing to construct a garden for their outdoor classroom space. A project she herself had helped set into motion, though she refuses to be disappointed at her lack of an invitation to be in attendance there today. Edie would go where she was needed, and apparently today, Roots-N-Riches, the local agricultural non-profit organization where she currently holds a part-time position, needs her here to hold down the fort.

With a sigh she leans back in her chair, checks the clock for the umpteenth time, as she's eager to have the rest of the team return. When they do, she'll upload today's photos, sort through and edit to find the best ones to feature on social media, finalize this week's newsletter, and, in that way, she'll feel more involved.

For now, she waits. At least she's able to get some studying done, she reminds herself, though now her embarrassment over her Grief Counseling assignment is clouding her spirit and interest.

She still can't believe she actually did it—she braved meeting Lori Meyers, the person that would know her late father better than anyone. It was a whirlwind of emotions, the entire interaction. Edie was shocked with how open and friendly Lori had been, and hope had bloomed in her heart that maybe she hadn't been crazy in finding her and reaching out. Maybe Edie would get answers to questions that had ached in her heart for so many years. Maybe she'd even find a new kind of modern extended family in all this, as Edie has often felt like a lost soul, trying to find her way.

Then Edie is slammed with the recollection of how the whole thing ended. While guilt threatens to dampen her mood at the memory, Edie reminds herself that she in no way meant harm. Lori was the one to offer up the history of the losses she had experienced. It's not as though Edie had pried, right? Lori had been so gregarious and kind, it almost felt like they had known one another long before, not at all like the interaction of two people meeting for the first time and under such uncomfortable circumstances.

Edie had felt so certain that the burning question mark she carried around her whole life would finally be tamed. Lori had seemed so thrilled too, at first. Was it her imagination that they had a connection, a joined sense of love and enthusiasm for the world, or was that Edie's hope running wild?

No matter, it seemed that hope was now squashed, as Edie felt pretty sure Lori was now going to have nothing to do with the secret daughter she had at first seemed so interested in.

This sense of loss hurts Edie, because there's really no easy way to explain what it's like to move through life, always wondering who your dad was, or if you'd ever reach the day of meeting him. Wondering where he was now and why he didn't have any interest in knowing his daughter. Edie remembers the end-of-year projects when teachers would hand out paper neckties, with prompts to write a sweet poem to give to your dad on Father's Day. Edie would complain to her moms about it, and they would give the same response—"Mother's Day is for Mama, and Father's Day is for Mom." As if that was it, all so simple.

What little Edie really meant wasn't that she didn't like giving paper neckties to her mom—she loved both her parents very much and found great joy in giving them the small crafts of her creations. The problem was that she didn't like having no idea who this mysterious man was that had contributed to her birth. Even at a young age, she knew enough to understand that a man and a woman were required to create a child. She also knew there was more to it than the story her moms told her, the tale they spun that the man that had assisted in her creation simply wanted to help out a couple unable to have children on their own. Edie understood that this was a man they knew but didn't like very much. They referred to him as Richard, and every once in a while, when they thought she was out of earshot, Edie would catch a drift of something like, "But she got Richard's blue eyes," or "Richard would have a fit if he knew." They'd quickly hush when they realized Edie's small ears were hiding around the corner. All Edie could think was who is Richard, and where was he now?

And more importantly—why didn't he have any interest in meeting his daughter?

With a heavy sigh, Edie picks up her phone to call her mom.

As expected, she gets an answer after the first ring.

"Is everything alright? What's wrong? Have you been harmed, are you in a cellar somewhere?"

Also as expected, her mom reacts with faux alarm given the fact that Edie has been avoiding her calls. She hasn't been sure how to broach the subject of finding out the identity of her biological father, or how her mom would react.

"There she is. My eternally hilarious mother. Missed me, I guess?" she says in hopes to keep the mood light before she reveals her recent mission.

"Hardly. Just assumed you had finally joined in on the wrong crusade and had been kidnapped by the opposing side."

Edie rolls her eyes at her mom's sarcasm before playing along in her own response. "How wonderful to be kidnapped in the name of saving the world. Think of the media attention it could bring to whatever the cause! Would you pay my ransom?"

Her mom scoffs. "Do you even have to ask? Edna, I would go to the ends of the earth and back for you."

Edie smiles. "You didn't answer the question. Would you *pay*?"

"'Course I would. No price too high for my baby. Better yet, I'd offer myself in exchange."

"That's all I need to know." Edie rises from her seat to stare out the back window to the field beyond. Acres of land where the organization's latest trailer office sits, getting ready to be converted into yet another farm once the funding comes through. "Mama, I have something I want to tell you, but you have to promise not to get upset about it, okay?"

"What, what's wrong?" Edie can hear the instant alarm in her mom's voice.

"Nothing, I'm totally fine! Just listen and don't be mad."

"Edna, I can hardly guarantee I won't be upset over something when I have no idea what you're going to say. But now I really am concerned something's wrong, are you alright?"

"I'm fine," Edie repeats, amazed at how nervous she is to present this. That she found out who her father is—not like it's a crime. And yet, the butterflies in her stomach are in their own dance, and she's thankful to have the safety of the phone and a thousand miles between them.

With a breath, she begins. It feels like a confession. "I'm in a class where we had to map out our family constellation."

"Okay. And?"

"And I did a DNA kit and found out who my father is."

Silence on the line. Edie waits for her mom to say something, but she's met with proverbial crickets, so she powers on. "Richard Meyers—that's my biological father."

"Oh my God—"

"And I know that he died several years ago, when I was little." The words come out in a rush. "I'm sorry I didn't tell you I was doing it beforehand. I wasn't sure how you'd react, since you always dance around the subject." Done, confession made.

Edie feels the heat in her cheeks and breathes through the tightness in her chest. She waits in agony for her mom's response but hears nothing. She momentarily wonders if that was all a waste, and they somehow got disconnected. "Mama, are you there?"

"I'm here. Yes."

"Are you mad?"

A heavy sigh lands in Edie's ear. "I'm not mad."

"Okay." Edie tries to think of something else to say, but she comes up short. She's dying to know what her mom's possibly thinking.

Eventually her mom's thick silence ends. "I guess I knew this day would come eventually," she says quietly. There's minimal anger in her tone, to Edie's relief. Instead, it sounds more like irritation mixed with defeat.

"Why didn't you ever tell me who he was?" Edie asks, trying not to sound whiny.

"I think I hoped I'd be six feet under and wouldn't have to deal with it," her mom replies. Edie hears her mom flop into a chair as she speaks.

"Mama!"

Her mom chuckles. "Sorry, that was dramatic. I think I'm in shock, I was not at all expecting this, Edie."

"I know," Edie assures her, almost apologetically.

Another heavy sigh from her mom, and Edie braces herself to hear what she'll have to say. "I don't hear from you for several days, and then you call me and tell me this?" There it is—the reaction Edie was expecting. Her mom's words feel like they're scolding her, and Edie's frustrated with what she knows in her heart is basic information she had a right to know.

She tries to find her courage to get some more insights into the secrecy of it all. "Is it because he was married? Did you know that, is that why you never talk about it?"

More silence. A gust of wind blows and Edie watches as the wild field flutters with brown debris, dormant and dry through the winter.

Eventually her mom responds. "Yes, I knew he was married. Not at first, though."

"So he lied to you? Was he your boyfriend? Did you love him?"

Her mom sighs in exasperation. "Edie, I really think this is a conversation to have in person, don't you?"

"Well, yeah, but I've tried that, remember? You never wanted to talk about it, so here we are." She feels her irritation building. Her mother—a woman that's never shy with her opinions—is now being painfully locked up. Is Edie dumb to expect that taking initiative would suddenly put an end to a lifetime of secrecy?

But there's one more thing Edie needs to confess, she remembers. And if that piece doesn't get her mom talking more, she supposes nothing will. Figuring that it's now or never, Edie prepares to share the other bit of her recent findings.

"There's one more thing, Mama."

"Stop being cryptic, what do you mean, one more thing?"

Edie closes her eyes, as if blocking out her vision will make this next part easier to share. It doesn't, but she powers on anyway.

"I found my dad's wife. His second one, Lori Meyers. And I met her."

EDIE LIFTS HER GLASSES TO her head, rubbing her eyes as she reflects on the phone call she just had with her mother. Both big bombs dropped, first that she found out who her father was, and the second—perhaps harder one—that she met with Lori Meyers. Edie had braced herself as she awaited her mom's reaction to that one. It was not all that surprising—a warning to stay away.

After discovering Lori and knowing her marriage and Edie's own conception overlapped, Edie felt certain her mom had no idea of Richard's marital status. Her pure-of-heart mama had been duped, Edie was sure of it. She was able to reach a greater state of sympathy for her mother, a greater understanding in the secrecy. How awful it must have been for her to learn a man she was with was so deceptive.

And yet, the more time she has had to sit with this knowledge, especially after meeting Lori for herself, Edie's not so certain of her mother's innocence. Her mom had sounded more worried—scared, even—after learning her daughter had gone to see Lori. It surprised Edie. She expected anger for not telling her first, or some reprimands of chasing things she had no business going after. Instead, her mom seemed concerned, as if Lori Meyers might be of harm to her. It puzzled Edie.

But it was done, her truth in her quest revealed, and with that, Edie relaxes her shoulders, unaware of how tense they had been. The hard part was over.

She tries to concentrate on work, but her mind is still obsessing with even more questions she wants answered. She wonders how long her mom and Richard had been together, or whether or not her mom had been lying when she said she didn't know about Lori at first. *At first,* those were her mother's words. Meaning there was some relationship that went a whole lot further than a simple sperm donation.

And then another alarming thought occurs—what if Lori and her mom had met? Did Lori find out about Richard and Erica, Edie's mom?

If that's the case, could Lori's supposed ignorance of Edie's existence be a lie? Edie wonders if Lori Meyers is holding deeper secrets of her own.

ten

. . .

lori

"HERE, TRY THIS one," my mother says as she hands me a completely hideous dress of a green that can't decide if it's lime or mint. I should have gotten rid of this thing years ago.

"This color is an insult to the rainbow, Mom," I say, holding it up with a frown. Why I ever bought it in the first place, I'll never know.

"It's in *your* closet," she points out. "It brings out your eyes, and it's tasteful."

On second thought, it *did* make my eyes pop. Maybe if it was just a bit shorter. I slip off my robe and try it on, relieved to find that it still fits, just barely. It's long sleeved, fitted and knee length. Simple and classy, though something's not right about it.

"It's a beautiful contrast with your hair," my mom admires. "I'm amazed you've not gotten any gray." I see her glance at herself in the mirror, inspecting her own gray shoulder-length hair.

"Think I should try and squeeze in a quick haircut before tomorrow night?" I ask, not really looking for any particular answer.

"No," is all she says, and I decide I might try to anyway.

I look in the mirror and examine the green dress. "It's better than I thought," I tell her with some reluctance, "but I look a little like I'm going to a Ladies Who Lunch. In fact, I think that's exactly what this was for. Some charity luncheon for the new library." Which opened about twenty years ago, I might add. That's saying something.

"Well, I don't know, Lori. When your father died, I never dreamed of attempting to date again. One man was more than enough."

I slip off the dress and reach for another one—this one a deep purple with small pale pink flowers scattered along the hemline. Ahh, now that's more like it.

"It's too short," my mom mutters.

"So?" I twirl around in the tri-fold mirror tucked in the corner of my room. I meet eyes with my mom, perched on the padded bench beside me. "What's wrong with being a little sexy?" I lift the hem and flex my calves in the mirror.

"Leave something to the imagination. That, and the fact that you'll freeze to death."

"I'll wear tights. Think black tights could match? There's black in the flowers."

My mom sighs and tosses me a cropped black jacket sitting over the armrest of the bench. "Add this."

I grab the jacket and eye her, wondering what's on her mind. "You're awfully unenthusiastic. What's up?" After sliding my arms through the sleeves, I give it a little tug. It's cute, I admit.

My mom rises to a stand and pulls the strands of my hair out that are stuck beneath my jacket. She pats my shoulder gently. "Dom Francesca, Lori?" Her voice is soft, but her eyebrows raise. I can practically see the judgment oozing out of her.

"I thought you liked Dom."

"I do."

"So why not be thrilled with this date for me?"

She pinches the bridge of her nose and closes her eyes. "You can be so naive, Lori Raina. My daughter with the eternal Peter Pan syndrome." She drops her hand and meets my eyes in the mirror. "Think about it, how can you possibly trust a man that rubs elbows with celebrities on a regular basis, tell me that?"

"Oh, stop. There's nothing to worry about there."

"It's foolish."

"Mom," I say, my voice stern. "*Ruby* is the one in show business. Not him. You're being paranoid, Dom's a good man."

"You thought that once before," she mutters.

I have the urge to slap her. I don't, of course. I'm not a monster. But my blood is beginning to boil at her insinuation. I'm so excited for this date, it's the first one in a very long time that I've felt like could be the start of a really good thing. I'll be damned if I let her ruin this for me.

I try and keep my voice calm, turning around to face her. "I was young and naive then, maybe. But not now, alright?"

Her pale eyes dart between mine, and I can see the motherly concern in them.

"If you say so."

I attempt to calm my irritation. We've come a long way, she and I. Roommates after all these years, my fellow pool house cottage buddy. If you had told me that would be the case back when I was a kid, I would have laughed in your face. Strange the way the world can shift.

I smile and give her a hug, her aging body feeling frail in my arms. "Don't worry about me." I pull back and give her a kiss on the cheek before turning back to the mirror.

"No matter how old you are, as a mother you will always feel two things," she says.

"What's that?"

"Worry and guilt." She looks at me and the corner of her mouth crinkles up in a small smile. "That never goes away."

eleven

. . .

edie

THE NEXT DAY at work, thoughts of her confession with her mom still obsessively repeating in her memory, Edie mindlessly scrolls through Lori's Facebook page. It's private, the friend request still pending, so the only thing she can see are any posts shared from her daughter, Reggie's, physical therapy clinics. Edie decides to click over to the clinics' business page, and she leans closer, sucked into the world presented before her.

There's the sweet banner photo of the team out front of one of the sites. She spots Reggie right away, a beautiful woman in her thirties, maybe. A younger and fairer version of her mother, with light green eyes and strawberry blonde hair. Edie scrolls down to a post about the difference proper posture can make when sitting in front of your computer screen. Edie instinctively straightens her spine, adjusting herself in her seat. Another post hails a "Best of Philly" award, followed by a photo of Reggie herself, accepting a crystal plaque. Edie narrows her eyes to get a better look. She's curious about Reggie, the girl that knew a childhood with Edie's very own father acting as Reggie's own in his stepfather role. She wonders what kind of presence he was in her life.

After longer than she cares to admit of this scrolling, Edie hears a car in the gravel driveway in front of the trailer. An unexpected visitor, meaning her downtime has reached expiration.

She rises to glance out the window, spotting a gray SUV and a man stepping out. He has golden brown hair cut short and is sporting a long black coat covering what looks to be a suit. An air of arrogance and money. Very attractive face from what she can tell, despite his sunglasses. Men in suits aren't something Edie's used to, and as she watches this man, she feels slightly intimidated.

Edie hurries back to her desk just in time to hear the door creak as the man walks in with a quick burst of cold air. Suddenly the tiny trailer office feels about a thousand times too small for the two occupants inside, though a part of her is happy for the distraction to keep her from obsessing over all things Richard, Lori, and her mom.

Sunglasses still on, the man closes the door behind him, spinning his keys around his finger, the jingling sound breaking the silence. He steps up to Edie's desk. "Who's in charge here," he demands more than asks.

Edie releases a small laugh, willing herself to not get caught up in his presumed authority. "Hi...Um, can I help you?" Her heart beats nervously and she folds her arms across her chest. If she's not mistaken, she notices the man reacting with the smallest of head tilts down, then up again. Was he checking her out? She can't tell since he's left on his sunglasses, the type where not even a glimpse of the eyes beneath are revealed.

"I'm short on time," he says, head swiveling around to scan the desolate temporary office. "Is it just you in here?"

"Yes. Yeah. It's just me in here." She searches the depths of her vocabulary for a better string of words beyond "yes" and "yeah." She unwinds her arms and adjusts the strap of her overalls. "I guess you could say I'm in charge. Who are you exactly? And maybe...

um, would you mind taking off your sunglasses?" *Because I kind of want to see if you're as hot as I think.* Edie hopes she's not obvious in her blushing.

He seems to consider her request momentarily, but eventually obliges. Honey brown eyes stare back at her. He looks younger than she'd have initially guessed, no more than thirty, maybe even mid to late twenties.

"I'm looking for Louise Sako, when does she get back?"

"Oh. I see. So you really are looking for the woman in charge. Um, your name, sir?" Edie lifts the corners of her mouth in her sweetest smile possible. She knows she's not the most beautiful of twenty-something-year-olds. Her face is too angular, smile too wide. But what she lacks in movie star looks, she more than makes up for in brains, friendliness, and tenacity.

"What's *your* name?" he counters.

She opens her mouth to answer, an instinctive reaction to the question, but then thinks better of it. "Actually, you walked into my office."

"Aren't you the observant one. Your point?"

"I...well," she gulps. "My point is that you should probably tell me *your* name." Edie sits up as straight as she possibly can, hoping her voice doesn't reveal the fluster of her rapidly beating heart. She's committed to holding firm on getting him to say his name first, a silly little gameplay move that she nonetheless wants to win. Something about the suit makes her feel like she needs to portray her own authority. In a world of casual office attire and video meetings, who wears suits anymore?

His brown eyes glance down to the plastic name plate on her desk, then back up to Edie. With a smirk he says, "Edna Mackenzie." *Dammit.*

Edie crosses her arms again, unsure what else to do with her hands, and notices his eyes glancing over her chest, ample bosom on display in the square-neck sweater beneath her overalls. Yes, he's definitely checking her out, but in a good way or a bad way? "Edna

Mackenzie is your name? What a coincidence," she says, feeling pride in her quip.

He narrows his eyes. "Do I know you from somewhere?"

"Ha!" she laughs a little too loudly. "Doubtful. I'm from Florida, only been here a few months." He nods his head as if absorbing the information. "Seriously," she tries again. "You need to tell me your name. Or else leave," she blurts out. Edie's acutely aware of how utterly alone and isolated they both are. She's torn between feeling how erotic that is or wondering if she really is in fact about to be kidnapped by an opposing force. Although who would oppose a community agricultural operation, she's not sure.

"Trenton Wroe. With Turner & Tan Law Firm. I'm supposed to meet Louise here at two-thirty and by my estimation, it's," he lifts his arm, pulls back a sleeve to reveal a gleaming silver watch, "two-thirty on the dot."

Edie inwardly groans. Of course her boss has blown off some attorney meeting, leaving Edie to deal with it. At least she gets a little eye candy out of it.

"Well, Trenton—"

"Don't you mean Mr. Wroe?"

"I—what? No. You planning on calling me Ms. Mackenzie?"

"I wasn't planning on calling you at all. Though Edna does seem like an old lady name for someone..." his eyes move up and down Edie's body, and she suddenly feels completely on display. Despite a slightly revealing neckline, her outfit is far from sexy, so what is Trenton Wroe doing checking her out? Judging her, maybe?

"Yes? You were saying, someone..." Edie prompts.

He smiles, though it comes across more suggestive than genial. "Under the age of seventy."

Edie debates how to respond to this. This guy is clearly one of those beautiful assholes who knows he's gorgeous and thrives off making girls uncomfortable.

Good thing she's not easily shaken up. Mostly. Too bad her

mind can't stop slowly undressing the man in front of her, but he doesn't need to know that. She tries to push down the alarming image popping in her mind, fearful of a telltale blush creeping up her neck.

She goes for an attempt to look bored and uninterested, leaning back in her chair with a heavy sigh. "You may sit and wait if you like," she says with a flat expression. "Though I can't say Louise will be back any sooner than an hour."

Trenton nods once, then moves over to another folding table that, like her own office space, serves as a desk. He pulls out the chair and takes a seat, and she half expects him to put his feet up on the table and cross his ankles. He seems like the cocky type to make himself at home like that. Instead, he merely leans back and pulls out his phone. His eyes remain firmly on the screen. Apparently, their conversation is over.

Edie allows her eyes to roam over his body, noticing the way the hem of his coat slowly slides off his thick thighs before dropping to his side. A pale purple dress shirt covers what looks to be a flat stomach. His silver belt buckle catches her eye, and she imagines yanking it off. She blinks away the thought before her mind gets carried away any further.

Edie feels torn about what to do with herself now with this unexpected visitor. No one will be back for at least another hour, if not more, and it's not as if the phone is ringing off the hook with multiple tasks to keep her busy. She's already completed most of today's to-do list, and normally at this point she'd whip out her Chromebook and study, but she's painfully distracted.

And realizing she really needs to consider the casual hookup lifestyle to release some pent-up energy.

Her last boyfriend was a fellow tree hugger from undergrad. Zeke is a sweetheart, fun and kind, much like Edie's very own soul —but boring. He wanted them to stay together when Edie left Florida, but she knew in her heart she wasn't into the relationship. So they had amicably parted ways, Zeke telling her he loved her and would always be there for her, and she had smiled and briefly wondered if she was making a mistake.

Still wondered it from time to time. Does she have Daddy issues? Does she not know a good thing when it's standing right in front of her? Her moms assured Edie that, "When you know, you know." As if that was any solid comfort to her.

Although something about this man sitting here now tells Edie there's definitely more to know.

Even if he is an evil lawyer.

"OH YES, THE TALL DRINK of water," her boss Louise says with a wink a solid two hours later. She places her scarf on the hook beside the door, fluffing out her sleek cascade of black hair, silvery streaks of gray accenting.

"He stayed in here for a full hour, Louise. Silent the whole time, just fiddling on his phone." Is Edie disappointed and feeling slightly rejected that Trenton hadn't uttered another word to her? Definitely not. Good riddance. Not like he would see anything in her anyway. He probably liked tall women. Sexy brunettes. Women with powerful careers and a love of designer clothing. Who thought children made nice accessories and animals were a dirty nuisance.

Louise sits down at the "desk" Trenton had previously been occupying, dismissing the two volunteers who had been working with her today. They say their goodbyes and walk out, leaving Edie to give an uninterrupted glare to her boss.

"Don't give me that look," the petite Louise says, opening her laptop and busying herself with connecting her camera. "I had no interest in meeting with him, thought you'd handle it. It's just pushback on the grant we're about to secure. Some upset over the tiniest little increase in taxes it'll cause that he's been tasked with trying to sort out. It's all a scare tactic, they have no leg to stand on since the community support is largely in our favor."

"So why even set up the meeting then?" Edie asks. Her screen pops up with a notification. "Got the pics, you're good."

Louise nods and unplugs the camera. "Thanks. Let's see, I took the meeting because we need the assistance, and I get such pleasure in wasting the time of these goons. We play along like we're all on the same side and they can look good by 'helping out' the non-profit. Plus, I knew they'd be sending Trenton, figured maybe you'd make a friend your own age." She raises an eyebrow in Edie's direction. "What happened? I set you up perfectly."

"You're unbelievable! I can't believe you let him stroll in here under the guise of a meeting you never meant to attend." She sighs in exasperation. "And I resent that you think I need a friend my own age. I have all of you guys, what more do I need?"

Louise's face falls in disappointment. "Apparently nothing. So you really said not a word to him?"

"After informing him the person he was thinking he'd be meeting was a no-show? No, we weren't exactly sweet pals after that."

"What about when he left?" Her brown eyes widen in hope, as if Trenton had potentially pulled a romantic move and pleaded with desperation asking Edie when he could see her again. Which most definitely did not happen.

Edie stars her three favorite photos from today's project, then opens the newsletter she drafted, sliding the three photos into their designated spots. "He got up, then walked out, leaving behind a gust of cold air because he left the door wide open. I legit thought he was just getting something out of his car, then next thing you know, he's driving off."

Louise laughs at this. "No, he didn't. Wow, that's so..."

"Petty?" Edie offers. "Childish and borderline toxic in an attempted power play?"

"In a door left open?" She shrugs. "Maybe he just didn't realize it wouldn't swing shut behind him."

"He's not my type anyway." *At all.*

"I just meant make a friend, not that you needed to marry the guy." She arches an eyebrow, as if Edie had been misreading the intention.

Edie knows full well that her boss would love to see more than just a blooming friendship form. The woman thrives off potential office romances, with multiple attempted set-ups, but she has yet to facilitate a successful match.

Still, Edie lets her comment slide. "Louise, why would I be friends with some suit? Can't imagine we'd have anything in common. He's probably all Scotch and cigars and ruthless attorney maneuvers. I'm a free-spirited hippie with an old soul."

"Opposites attract."

"I thought you said you didn't mean for me to marry him."

"Have you eaten? You're irritable when you're hungry. Go home and get some food. I officially release you," she says, waving a hand in dismissal.

Edie flips her glasses up, pulls on her prescription sunglasses and grabs her bag. "Fine, fine. I'll see you Friday," she says as she walks toward the door, bracing herself for the blast of cold air.

"And will you please get yourself a coat? You're looking at several more weeks of cold," she hears Louise cry out behind her.

"I have one, I just don't like feeling so constricted in it," she explains with one final goodbye.

As she pops in her car and makes her way on the short drive to campus, she thinks about Trenton Wroe. The sexy lawyer that possibly likes her breasts. Maybe. Which should be insulting to her, a disgusting glance at her chest is so very...*expected*. And yet?

Edie kind of wants to see if it's possible to entice the evil stooge.

twelve

. . .

dom

DOM OPENS THE door to the restaurant for Lori and watches as she slips in, her slender body and chestnut hair mesmerizing. The tinkling of chimes in the door and the gentle purr of soft music offers just the right ambiance, and he's committed to showing this woman a good time this evening. He'll enjoy himself with Lori Meyers, why the hell not? When she texted him, asking for a drink, he immediately texted her back before he had time to overthink it. While a little flighty and not his usual type, there was no sense in denying his attraction to her.

Then a strange number of questions settled in his nerves. Was he stupid in trying to entertain something with her? After things ended with Jules, Ruby's PR manager, he had resolved to not mix business and personal. Not that Lori fit that rule exactly, but she certainly fit the "too close to home" one.

Next, he needed to decide where to take her. She wanted romantic, so that made it a bit easier. But should he make a reservation for a formal dinner? Or would it be better to sit at the bar for a drink? He wanted to find a spot that would not be too crowded, so he could hear that gorgeous light and airy voice of hers. Yet he didn't want a spot that would be dead either. Too awkward. He debated calling Xavier to ask him if he had any suggestions, but then realized that might be odd given that Xavier is Lori's son-in-law. Revealing this date wouldn't be appropriate; some things are better left private.

Instead, he called Joey, his soon-to-be son-in-law who's also a restaurateur. He kept quiet on who the date was with, and without prying, Joey directed Dom to what is looking to be the perfect spot. A small restaurant on the outskirts of Philly that's got the warm ambiance he had hoped for. As he follows Lori in, he notes the stone pillars, dark wood paneled walls, several small electric fireplaces dotted throughout. It almost creates a bonfire feel but encapsulated in mellow walls as opposed to the great outdoors.

"It's perfect," Lori says, swinging her head over her shoulder to meet Dom's eyes with a beaming smile.

"I'm happy you think so," he says, searching her expression for signs of genuine satisfaction and not the dreaded pleasantries of politeness. He places his hand on the small of her back, fighting the urge to wrap it around her waist. He directs her over to the bar, pulling out a chair for her to sit before taking his seat beside her.

Lori slips off her coat and drapes it on the back of her chair, and Dom does the same. She leans forward, rests an elbow on the bar with ease that he both admires and envies, the charm emanating on her face as she flags down the bartender, a young redhead covered in tattoos. He recognizes the bartender from somewhere, realizing he's met her at one of Joey's Philly restaurants.

"You must be Dom and...oh, you're Lori! Am I right?" she says as she places two water glasses in front of them. Dom inwardly groans. Of course the bartender knows them both. He hopes she has the decency to keep her mouth shut, as a "Dom and Lori" narrative isn't exactly a story he's ready to create just yet.

"Yes!" Lori says, exuding sunshine with the one simple word. "Are you Katrina? We've definitely met before."

"We have, yes. At The Guilty Olive, Joey Conti's restaurant. He gave me the heads-up Dom would be here tonight. I have been given very strict instructions to take good care of you. Didn't realize you'd be joining him though, Lori," Katrina says with a wink. "How you been?"

Shit. Dom realizes they're now exposed and a wave of panic sets in. It must be evident on his face because as soon as Lori answers her, stating, "Great tonight," with a nod in his direction, Katrina mutters out something about how their secret's safe with her.

"Well, what will we be having, Dom?" Lori asks with a sparkle in her eyes. "Or do I need to be the one to select, given that *I'm* the one that had to finally ask *you* out. Not something I usually do, you know."

"I'll leave you with this," Katrina says as she slides a drink menu between the two of them. "If you want to sample anything, just let me know. I recommend any of the Rural City beers."

"Thank you, love. My God, you are just gorgeous, aren't you?" Lori gushes to Katrina. "I love your tattoos. One of these days when I finally get the courage, I just might find myself on the receiving end of one."

Katrina raises an eyebrow at Lori with a side smile and a shrug. "If it feels right, why not," she says before bringing a beer to a neighboring patron.

Dom takes the opportunity to dive into this line of conversation with Lori. "What would you get?"

Green eyes scan the menu. "Hmm, I'm thinking a Pinot Grigio, you?"

"I meant for a tattoo."

"Oh!" She laughs in a chuckle that sounds like bells. "Right! Oh, I don't know if I'd really have the guts, just fun to dream."

She's leaning in close to Dom to examine the singular menu

between them, and he catches a whiff of her perfume. Sweet, just as he'd expect.

"Do you have any tattoos?" she asks.

"A few acquired over the years while in the Air Force, yeah. Nothing like Katrina's there."

Lori stares at him with hooded eyes. Seductive, if he's not mistaken. "I'd love to see them. Any in naughty places?"

Whoa. He tries to contain a startled response, though he's pleased to know they're on the same page. "Ahh, not exactly. Just an eagle on my shoulder, a flag on my chest. Another with some dog tags." He thinks of the fading old ink in places that would require de-robing to see. Which is exactly what he wants in time, but he'd rather be thinking with his head and not his dick right now. He tries to shift gears. "Speaking of dog tags, I've actually been on an odd mission, thanks to Ruby."

"Oh?"

"Yeah, trying to find out more information on something." He starts to give Lori a quick re-cap of his letters research but is interrupted as Katrina makes her way back to them for their drink order. "Pinot Grigio for Lori, and the Rural City IPA for me."

"Great choice, coming right up."

When Katrina walks away, Lori returns her attention to Dom, turning her body and he feels her knee softly pressed against his. "You were saying you needed to find out information for Ruby," she prompts.

He clears his throat. "Right. Years ago, we found old letters hidden in our house, uncovered during a home renovation. War letters from the 1940s, written by a German girl to an American soldier. They all were written as 'To Dog Tags,' and signed, 'With love, Lace.' No names, just that."

Lori's eyes go wide at this. "Ruby's album, incredible," she beams. "That's where she got that from? Old letters?"

He nods, thankful to be on this easy train of conversation. There's something about this woman that feels foreign to him.

She's got an air of youthful enthusiasm that is fun to be around, yet Dom feels almost apprehensive of her in a way. As if she's far more delicate than she lets on, and he's afraid of breaking her.

"Yeah, old letters that, because there aren't any envelopes or any other identifying information, we've never been able to find out much about. No idea who exactly they're from or who the recipient was. We've traced back to the homeowners from that time, have a name of the soldier that might have been the recipient, but apparently, he has no more surviving relatives."

Disappointment fills Lori's face. "Oh. Well, that's not as fun. So now what, why do you need more information on them?"

He sighs. "It's not that we really *need* it, per se. Ruby wanted me to try to dig more just to get some inspiration for her next album. Also makes for a good PR story, and her publicist, Jules, is heavy on that kind of thing."

"Well, the tactics seem to be working. Ruby's bigger than ever."

He nods his head to the side. "I know. Terrifying."

Lori places a hand over top of his. "She's in good hands though, right?"

"She is, yes." He clears his throat, and Lori pulls her hand back to lift her water for a sip. "You know, the more I think about it, the more I'm suspicious that this letter hunt was more about Ruby being worried I'm in need of a project since I'm no longer as active in her career as support. I used to handle her financials but she's, uhh, outgrown me now and has the real deal professionals on that kind of thing," he laughs. He runs a hand through his hair, itching to do something with his hands. Katrina saves him as she places down their drinks. Dom raises his glass to Lori. "Cheers," he says with a clink, then curses when his beer sloshes over the glass.

"Cheers, whoops!" she says as she grabs a square cocktail napkin and wipes down the cinnamon wood of the bar, accosted by his spill. They take their sips, and Dom tries to ignore the restlessness he feels in the following silence. He's not sure what's got him so on edge around her. It's a simple happy hour between two consenting adults, nothing more.

"How's your drink?" he asks.

Small hands and nails decked in red polish hold out the white wine in examination. "Buttery and delicious," she says, dragging out the "s" in a sinful hiss, the full pout of her lips threatening Dom's focus.

Dom realizes his discomfort around Lori—she's different than other women he's used to. He tends to go for the more direct and straightforward types. Career-driven and focused. Lori, on the other hand, is warm and nurturing, dynamic and magnetic. She's the type of woman that can get along with anyone. But is she truly interested in him? Or is he, as he assumes, merely a convenience in her life as a single man of similar age?

"You know, the strangest thing happened to me recently," she says between small sips of her wine. "Part of the reason I reached out to you, actually. I'm dying to talk to someone about it. You wouldn't happen to know someone by the name of Edie Mackenzie, would you?"

He pinches his brows together, rolling through his memory banks before shaking his head no. "Doesn't ring a bell, why?"

"Well, listen to this," she says, leaning forward and placing a hand on his arm. He likes the way Lori's red polish looks against his crisp white shirt. "This girl pops up on my doorstep a few days ago. Says she's my late husband Richard's secret daughter."

A spray of beer shoots out of his mouth. "Jesus, what?"

"Oh yeah. Edie is her name. Sweet girl as far as I can tell," Lori replies, smirking at Dom's spray. Once again, she's wiping beer from the bar.

Dom takes the napkin from her hand and continues cleaning, feeling a little embarrassed by his reaction. "I didn't see that coming. Secret daughter?" He absorbs the last droplets and neatly folds the napkin before placing it aside.

"Yup. No idea she even existed," Lori murmurs. She sips her

wine and he searches her green eyes, peering at him over the rim of her glass.

Dom is vaguely aware that Lori had been married twice, first to Reggie's father, a man that died in a car accident many years ago, along with their three-year-old son, Reggie's twin brother. Then Lori married another man, who died of cancer or a heart attack or something. "Do you believe her?" he asks. "How'd she find you?" He's both intrigued if not a bit concerned at this unexpected revelation, though he notes the relief he feels at having an interesting subject to talk about. The pool of questions and conversation starters he had pre-arranged now feel like a comical effort.

Lori nods enthusiastically, raising her eyebrows in a look of excited wonder. "Edie looks just like him, it's hard not to believe."

"How old is she? The daughter, I mean?"

"That's the thing. Twenty-two or twenty-three, I believe?" She rests her chin in her hand and glances at him from the corner of her eye. Her voice is quieter as she continues. "Meaning Edie was conceived while Richard and I were married, though I already knew he wasn't faithful to me."

Dom sips his beer to buy himself a moment before responding. When he sets the glass down again, he opts for transparency, though he leaves out his gut reaction of disgust for her ex. "Christ, Lori. Are you okay? That's a lot to take in."

He wishes he was better at comfort or the right words, but with Lori, he finds it difficult. His troops? No problem. Clear mission, clear goals and obstacles to be aware of, the backing of America to conjure up motivation.

A beautiful woman revealing an encounter with a secret daughter? Dom's at a loss.

Lori waves a dismissive hand. "It was so long ago, no big deal, it's not worth anger or upset. Old news."

While he may not be the most intuitive, Dom is not ready to fully buy her cavalier response. He gently reaches for her hand on the bar. Her skin is soft, her hand warm within his. "Lori, a secret daughter showing up is hardly no big deal. Are you sure you're okay?" He's concerned her attitude over this means she's still in shock over the surprise. Not that he can blame her.

Lori squeezes his hand in return and mindlessly spins a strand of hair around her fingers, nodding. "Don't look at me like that, Dom. Really, I'm fine! Richard didn't know about her, as far as I know. I think. And he died when she was still little. What's there to be upset about?" she says with a grin that doesn't match the gravity of the situation. That, or she really is truly gifted in the art of optimism.

"Alright. So what was she doing showing up to see you? Does she want money?" A protectiveness over Lori fills his chest. Some girl's sudden presence doesn't sit right with him, and he knows enough about Lori from their interactions and from Xavier to know that Lori can be a bit naive.

"Not that she's stated so far. She's originally from Florida but moved up here to PA for her master's degree. Social work. I think she just happens to be nearby now and was really just genuinely curious to meet me," she says with a casual shrug. "I'm the closest thing she has to answers, apparently her moms never told Edie who her biological father was."

"Okay," he says tentatively. "Be careful, Lori. You don't know anything about this girl. How exactly did she find you?"

"That's the thing!" The wild excitement returns to her emerald eyes. "She said she's good at researching things, then hands me a business card." Lori reaches for her purse, rifles through before pulling out a card, handing it to him. He scans it and registers the words "Heirloom Hunter" above the girl's name, Edna Mackenzie. He makes a mental note to do his own research and see if he can find anything nefarious about this girl.

He hands the card back to Lori. "I've heard of this, they link up old things with surviving family, right?"

"Yes. Actually, the other day when I quite literally ran into you," she says with a laugh, "I watched and saw you walk into the historical society office. For a moment I thought you had something to do with her showing up."

He shakes his head, feeling eager to squash that notion. "No, no, definitely not. Never heard of the girl before. That was a meeting Ruby had set up for me to find info on the letters, but they were no help."

"Well, maybe Edie can help you?" Something crosses over Lori's eyes, though he's not sure what. "It's what she does, and she's got the youthful energy that I bet could help find out more information with these letters. Maybe I could help you too."

Her whole expression lights up with this proposition, a new energy in the excited tap of her finger on her lips. Her red nails are drawing his eyes to her mouth, and call him selfish, but now all Dom can think is that if he indulges Lori in this, it will give him an excuse to see her more. With the added bonus of something to focus on. While he's far from ready to join in on Lori's blind trust of this mysterious Edie, he can't deny the incentive in Lori's suggestion of joining forces with him on this fool's errand. He can cross-reference that the girl is who she says she is, and if that all tracks and no alarm bells sound, then letting her help is in fact not a bad idea. At the very least, if Lori's going to continue talking to the secret daughter, Dom can be a supervising force in case the girl is after something more than friendship from Lori.

He nods tentatively. "Alright. It's worth a shot, I guess. If you're comfortable with that and have the time, that is."

Lashes flutter back at him with excitement, and his chest warms at seeing her so hopeful. He thinks how beautiful Lori is and wonders why he's never paid her much mind beyond basic pleasantries before now. This woman who has been through so much, and yet can still sit here and look forward to working with the illegitimate child of her late husband, all to help in what is more than likely a dead-end task.

"Let's do it," Lori nods. "I need a project. Reggie and Xavier have James and Ronnie in pre-school now, meaning I have entirely too much time on my hands since I'm no longer watching them."

"You teach yoga too, right?" he asks, knowing that Lori also works at Reggie's physical therapy clinic.

"A whopping twice a week. It's mostly a hobby. Though I do love my group, I have the sweetest elderly yogis. You should come to one! It'd be fun." At the look of horror on his face, she adds, "No need to be scared, you don't have to be some flexible master, I promise. Only thing you'd need to fear is the little old ladies who would have a field day flexing their seductress skills on the likes of you," she says with a surprising kiss to his cheek.

He admires her fervor. It's hard not to join in and feel it too, out of his comfort zone as he is.

Yoga and heirloom hunters. Old letters and secret daughters. Dom wonders how he's ended up here, though he realizes if he wants to push past his own frustrating barriers, then this might be the best way. He has a feeling Lori could be worth a little further exploration.

AFTER ANOTHER ROUND OF DRINKS and some light bar food that exceeded expectations, Dom and Lori wrap up their date in what was a slightly rushed attempt on Dom's part to end on a high note. He drives her home in far more comfortable spirits as they talk about everything from favorite times of year to the tentative game plan for tackling any info they can on the letters.

When they pull into Lori's place, Dom's discomfort begins to rise as he thinks about how to say goodbye. A kiss on the cheek? A quick hug?

Or will she go straight to asking him inside for a nightcap?

The air is mild and comfortably cool as he walks Lori up to her door. The guest cottage is dark, no lights aside from the ember of the sconces flanking the front door, and he wonders if her mother, Kathryn, is inside.

Lori must sense his question because she turns to peer inside the window beside the door, then back to Dom. "Mom's asleep already, I'm sure. Who knew she would be my roommate all these years," she says with what he thinks is forced brightness. Her eyes dart down to his mouth, and she takes a step closer to him. The sweetness of her perfume fills his nostrils, and her hand grazes his arm.

This is the moment of truth. He wants to kiss her. Lori's full lips look inviting as hell, and based on her multiple arm touches and collarbone caresses she'd been teasing him with all night, he feels reasonably sure she's expecting a kiss.

Yet Dom's frozen, his feet firmly planted in place. He's completely locked up with no idea why. *Lean forward, dammit, and kiss her,* is all he can think.

But he can't.

"Well, Dom. Sure am glad I got John Stamos to finally take me out on a proper date. I'd invite you in, but with my pesky roommate and all—"

"It's fine," he says, cutting her off. "Had a great time, call you tomorrow and we'll figure out a day to go over the letters?" He starts walking backwards, and stumbles slightly at the unexpected small step in the sidewalk, just as Lori starts to call out to warn him about it.

He turns and walks away, leaving Lori standing at the door, not even checking if she makes it in okay. Which is not the gentleman approach he'd like to take, but for some reason his feet seem to be working beyond his control, and now here he is abandoning the glorious Lori Meyers completely.

But not before he vaguely hears her sing-song voice mutter in the air behind him, "What in the hell was that?"

He pauses mid-step, looking around and willing himself to do something. He looks up and sees the warm glow of outdoor lights illuminating the big house on the property, where Xavier and Reggie live. The home sits up on a slight hill, a sturdy symbol of family and sanctuary, and Dom reminds himself that those things aren't obtained without opening your heart now and then.

Before he can overthink it, he turns back around, quickens his steps, swiftly popping over the surprise unevenness on the pathway, and he grabs a startled Lori by the shoulders.

"I want to kiss you," he says, and he barely registers her responding nod and closing of her eyes before he drops his mouth to hers, to finally taste the soulful sweetness of Lori Meyers.

thirteen

. . .

edie

WHEN TRENTON WROE walks back into the trailer office the following week, Edie is more prepared. Louise had given Edie the heads up that he'd be coming in, that she should play nice, that he was just doing his job, and to help him with whatever he needs.

It's a warm fifty-five degrees today, March having officially rolled its way in and offering some semblance of hope for spring temperatures to come. Edie watches as Trenton makes his way up the gravel drive in yet another luxury suit, this time no coat. With a burst open of the door, Trenton steps into the office, closing the door behind him before gliding over to Edie's desk.

"Ah, how nice of you to close the door behind you today," she says, hating that her heart is instantly galloping in her chest. She tries to breathe deeply and stay cool.

Trenton looks behind him to the closed door, then back to her. "I generally always do."

Edie scoffs. "Sure. So last time when you were here and left it wide open, that was just an accident?"

Confusion fills Trenton's face. "What? You think I left the door open?"

"I know you did. The chilly air informed me, though you didn't need any symbolism of the chill you naturally exude." She pushes her glasses up the bridge of her nose, now questioning her recollection of the incident. She worries she's sounding incredibly rude, especially if she got that all wrong. She seems to only have two tones with this man—bumbling or stony.

"I truly have no idea what you're talking about, Edna. If the door swung open, that wasn't on me," he says with a hand to his chest.

She sighs, unsure if she should apologize now or what. She tries for something along the lines of indifferent. "Fine. Blame it on the wind, I guess. And carelessness of the operator. Come on, let's get this over with," she says as she rises, not sure why she's acting so salty. She smooths out her sweater dress as she steps out from behind her desk, walking around to the front.

His eyes graze over her body in very clear appreciation, if she's not mistaken. "You look...dressed up." He steps closer and takes a seat in front of her desk, propping an ankle up to his knee. "You dress up for me?" he grins.

"Ha! Really? Yes. Yes, I did. All for you, is that what you want to hear?" *Though he's not wrong.*

Trenton shrugs. "Well, I liked the overalls and sweater combo from the other day too, but this presents a whole other side of you." *He remembered my outfit?* is all she can think.

"Are you...are you trying to flirt with me?" Edie perches on the front of her desk, then immediately jumps up as the flimsy card table leans forward with her weight. With cat-like reflexes, Trenton jumps forward to steady the table with opposing weight. He's leaned forward, his torso nearly touching hers, both of his arms on either side of her to avoid what would have been a horrifically embarrassing mishap. She can smell a citrusy aftershave on his neck with him so close like this.

He looks down at her, pupils dilating in his whiskey eyes. He's still for an agonizing few moments. "Whoa, easy, now," he says, and she catches a hint of mint on his breath. He pulls away from her to stand. "Maybe a chair is a better choice," he says as he sits back down. "Or a sturdier desk. And no, I'm not trying to flirt with you. Trust me, you'd know if I were." A cocky grin fills his face, and Edie is taken aback by Trenton's shift in mood, different than his abrupt mood from the other day.

With a sudden urge to hide, Edie moves back around to her original seat across from him on the other side of her desk, straightening the things that had been jostled. Her cheeks flush but she refuses to let him unsettle her. "What are you doing here, Wroe? Word on the street is you're here to find holes in our spending so that this grant slips right through our fingers." Her tone is clipped, which she decides she's fine with. Better than the gushing schoolgirl she feels like in his presence.

"On the contrary," he says with a commanding index finger. "I'm tasked with trying to help avoid any mishaps so that you guys don't find yourselves in trouble."

Edie narrows her eyes. "That's not what I heard. I heard there's been pushback due to the potential for tax raises in us dipping into certain funds."

"That's always an issue with non-profits," he says, smooth in his reply. "The ripple effect—the grant to the do-good community agency looks all shiny, but those that hold their wallets closest to them know the funds come from somewhere."

"Sure. It's called government support for a reason. Equity means stabilizing, though, right? Win-win?"

He shrugs. "Social structure isn't exactly much of my concern. I'm just here to help make sure you all are categorizing your funding properly."

Edie huffs out a laugh. "So, you could care less about helping out those in need? That's what you're saying?" His devil-may-care attitude is sickening. Revolting. Defiant. Sexy. Nope, not sexy, revolting.

"As captivating as you berating me with your snap judgment is, I'm on the clock. And here's what I need," he says, sliding over a file folder with a list of requested documents stapled to the front. "Should be pretty straightforward, to start."

With a sigh Edie flips through the folders on her computer that Louise had prepped her with. Apparently, the fun banter is over, and Edie hates that she's disappointed by this. *He's just here to work,* she reminds herself, willing her blooming crush to burn away.

They spend the next several minutes examining the files, Edie confirming with Trenton on which to print out, which need to be sent via e-doc for further examination, and what is still missing. He tells her what he's focusing on for today and she prints the corresponding documents.

They both get to work, the quiet silence of the otherwise empty trailer office feeling awkward, and Edie wishes she had put on some music, but now she's uncomfortable with the idea of starting some and unintentionally conveying a mood she's trying to set. So they work in silence.

After several minutes, Edie glances up and notices the concentration on Trenton's stern face. He's moved over to the neighboring makeshift desk, eventually slipping off his suit jacket and rolling up the sleeves of his dress shirt. She smiles slightly to herself as she notices his habit of nibbling on the end of his pen before typing something on his laptop keyboard. They continue to work, Trenton asking the occasional question, with Edie happy to be able to inform him. She wonders if he has a girlfriend, maybe even a fiancé, or what his type is.

Not that she's looking for or expecting anything from him. They're simply two unlikely workmates for the time being. Temporary.

And still, Edie can't help but admire how sexy Trenton is, here like this, working alongside her, brown hair catching the sun from the window behind him in a golden glow. Watching him focus with seriousness on his tasks humanizes him in a way, and she's torn between frustration with the feelings of attraction bubbling up, and the reminder that there's no harm in looking and admiring.

A stretch of time passes in their co-worker silence, him focused on his job, Edie focused on her own list of emails to follow up on and previous sponsors to touch base with. She'd eventually gotten more comfortable in the space with him and had finally been able to more fully focus on her own job.

She jumps when she's in the middle of typing up yet another mundane email, and feels his hand unexpectedly on her shoulder.

"Jesus, you're like a ninja. When did you even get up?" she asks, flipping her glasses onto her head and rubbing her burning eyes.

"Come eat lunch with me." His voice is hoarse from lack of speaking for the better part of two hours.

"What? Why? No."

He smiles. "But we've come so far today. Solving the world's problems," he says with a gesture to their adjacent workspaces.

She raises an eyebrow. "I have a feeling I'm solving the world's problems, and you're over here dismantling them."

"We need balance in life. Come on, my treat," he says as he grabs his suit jacket and swings it behind his shoulder. "The phone hasn't rung all morning, I doubt you'll be missed."

Edie leans back in her chair, contemplating. Trenton remains firmly in place with a hand in his pocket, waiting for her next move. "I'll leave the door wide open if you don't join me," he finally says.

"It's strange that you're actually more friendly today, even when saying things like that," she says, shaking her head as she rises out of her seat. She walks over to Trenton, still hovering in the doorway, but he remains a statue. She studies his face for signs of what he's doing. Or thinking.

Something passes over his eyes—sincerity, maybe—as he says, "You caught me on a bad day the other day. I'm really a decent guy.

Mostly." There goes that grin again. "Cross my heart." He's looking at her like he wants to eat her alive.

"You *did* leave the door open on purpose," Edie breathes out, mouth gaping. "I knew it!"

"I'm an ass, I'm sorry. My uncle put me up to this job, I had zero desire to be here, and I...handled it poorly." He drops the suit jacket from behind his shoulder and slides his arms in, giving it a tug before opening the door.

Edie shakes her head in amusement as they walk out, relief at seeing him admit to a chink in his armor. So, he really did have himself a mini temper tantrum the other day. A misplaced one, she notes—he was mad at his uncle, and shouldn't have taken it out on her with that silly little door-open move. But still, she feels a little more comfortable with him admitting his mistake and apologizing.

Trenton motions her to the passenger side of his SUV, opening the door for her. She slides in and watches as he glides around front and over to his side. He slips in and starts the car, reaching an arm behind her as he reverses out of the gravel drive with the ease of a professional driver.

She tries to ignore her disappointment when he removes his arm from her behind her seat as he grabs the gear shift and puts the car back in drive. "Your uncle? So it's a family law firm?" she asks as they make their way out to the main road.

"Unfortunately. I mean, it's corporate law, so the money's great. When we're not doing gigs with non-profits, that is," he says with a glance in Edie's direction. He's kept his sunglasses flipped up on his head, and she's thankful to be able to see his eyes. There's a kind of mischief in his expression.

"God forbid," she says with a roll of her eyes.

"That's what I'm saying." She sees the corner of his mouth raise and she knows he's teasing, a playful attempt to grate on her nerves.

"Oh lord," Edie whispers. She can't help but be slightly amused.

"Some people save the world," he says as he points in her direction. "And some people keep the economy going so that the rest of you have the option to work to save the world."

"Aren't you the suited-up hero." She shakes her head before asking, "Well, do you like it? The usual work, I mean?"

"I do, yeah. I resented the hell out of my parents pushing me in that direction at first, though."

They hit a bump in the road and Edie grips onto the edge of her seat. Trenton softly apologizes and she turns to look at him, unable to help the feeling she's having of warming to him. "I can relate," she finally says.

"Yeah?"

Edie nods. "Yeah. My moms are very...persuasive, I guess you could say. Generally speaking, I agree with their viewpoints. I just wish they'd give me a bit more credit that I actually know a thing or two on my own."

"Exactly," Trenton agrees. "They mean well, it's just hard to get a chance to put your own opinion in, especially if it doesn't align."

Edie hums in agreement, surprised at this relatable side of Trenton she's seeing. "But ultimately the career direction did align for you?"

"As much as I hate to admit it, yes. It's just long hours when you're bottom of the totem pole like me, and the obligatory community aide gigs get old."

"At least you get to right the wrongs of helping all the rich stay nice and rich though, right?" Edie asks hopefully. If Trenton Wroe could at least pretend to have some semblance of a heart, maybe her attraction to him wouldn't bother her so much.

Or maybe he'll be quick with his work here and she won't have to see him again.

"I'm not that selfless," he says with a smirk. *At least he's honest.* "And what's so wrong with liking money? I work hard, it's not like I'm stealing candy from babies."

"And others don't work hard? The janitor in a school doesn't work as hard as you then?"

"I think custodian is the appropriate title for that, Edna. And here I thought you were the virtuous one."

"It's Edie," she says, staring out the window at the endless expanse of fields. She feels like they're worlds away from civilization. "Everyone calls me Edie," she explains more to herself than to him.

"Who's everyone?"

Edie sighs, turning to face him. "Everyone that's not my moms? Although even they call me Edie sometimes."

"Okay," he nods. "So uh—Moms? Plural?" he asks in confirmation.

She smiles, loving to see his clear discomfort at this tidbit of information. "Yes indeed, Wroe. I have two moms. Yes, they are lesbians. And wonderful."

He throws a hand up in the air. "Okay, understood. Two moms. Very happy for you. And them."

Edie fully laughs at that. "I'll be sure to let them know they have your blessing." She's joking, naturally. Her moms would hate lawyer-guy Trenton, but she keeps that to herself. "Actually, my mom named me after her favorite book, *The Awakening*. Kate Chopin. Edna is the name of the main character. Both my moms love the book."

"Is it any good?" he asks, drumming a thumb on the steering wheel in beat to the music playing in quiet waves of rock. She looks and sees the song title displayed on his screen— "Schism" by Tool. A bit eerie and intense, but she likes it. His other hand is drumming on his thigh, though she tries not to let her eyes linger there.

She lets out a soft laugh at his question. "You want to know if the book is any good?" Edie loves the opportunity to share this answer when people ask. Then she thinks better of it, stopping herself before giving her usual response. "See for yourself. Let me know," she says with a casual shrug.

"Nah, I don't read."

"Ever?" She gapes at him in surprise, wondering how someone as educated as he is refrains from reading a book once in a while.

"You just said 'ever' like I said I don't shower. Which I do, by the way," he says with an eyebrow raise and glance in her direction. He gives another scan of her chest, this time very obvious, and Edie rolls her eyes.

"My eyes are up here, you jerk." The bluntness of her words surprises her. She fights the urge to pop a hand over her impulsive mouth.

Trenton looks back away, out the windshield to the approaching town ahead, but not before adding, "Stop wearing sexy-as-fuck sweater dresses then."

At first Edie thinks she didn't hear him correctly. No way he just said that. But the lift of the side of his mouth confirms he said exactly what she thought he did. Her breath catches at his candor, but she can't help but smile too. Which is all wrong, she should be insulted, should be putting him in his place for such obvious objectification. She starts to open her mouth to say something to that effect, but he beats her to it.

"Don't even give me shit for saying you're sexy, Edna Edie. I caught you checking me out on more than one occasion back there, you know."

She feels the heat of her embarrassment of being caught travel right up to the tips of her ears. She places the knuckle of her clenched fist between her teeth to contain a laugh, but fails, her shoulders shaking with her laughter despite herself.

Trenton looks at her in confusion. "What's so funny?"

Eyes held firmly out the window to the sprawling stone of a high school passing by, Edie shakes her head, laughter still erupting. She raises her eyebrows. "Nothing, it's just...I'm not sure I've ever had a guy talk to me like that before."

"That's a damn shame. No one's ever called you sexy?"

"No! I mean yes, of course they have. My ex-boyfriend Zeke did." She thinks. Zeke called her sexy, right? She blinks rapidly and tries to focus on the road in front of her. "Just not when I don't even know them. The guy calling me sexy, I mean," she says, attempting to recover. "It feels—"

"Rude? Forward? Panty-soaking?" Trenton offers.

At his last words, an instantaneous heat hits between her legs.

Why am I not disgusted when he says this stuff?

Edie thinks about the way guys usually approach her, not that she's ever really had to bat many away. But generally speaking, they exhibit a nervousness in asking her out, all three or four times it's ever happened. And certainly no one has commented so forwardly on her apparent sex appeal or even general attractiveness before ever even confirming that kind of talk would be accepted. No—the guys Edie interacts with tend to be respectful. Polite. Very committed to consent to the point of being overbearing with it. Every fiber in her knows this is a *good* thing, that respect in that way is something to be expected and appreciated.

It's then that she realizes why she's okay with Trenton's forwardness. Edie drops the fist that had been the victim of her teeth. "You know what? My dress is sexy. And I *was* checking you out." She was, she can admit that. She realizes that in her circles, the commitment to respect has gone so far that it's diminished the art of flirting. Even when she herself has tried to make it clear that she's interested.

"I knew you were. Naughty girl, canoodling with the enemy."

"Oh my God, did you really just say that?"

"Sorry, you're right." He raises an eyebrow in her direction. "You're definitely not naughty."

He's baiting her, she knows. She contemplates how to respond but decides she's not going to do the obvious and fight with him on this.

No. She's in a new town. New job. She's not a kid anymore, and she can't deny how much she is loving this car ride interaction with the hot-as-hell Trenton Wroe. So, Edie shrugs a shoulder. "Oh, I can be, in the right circumstances. Now what, do we go fuck or something?" The words bumble out of her mouth before she can stop them, and her pulse quickens. She tries her absolute hardest to keep her cool, fighting the urge to retract that last statement. She rarely ever even curses, let alone says things like, "Let's go fuck."

To her utter delight, it's Trenton that now looks like the one caught off guard. "I mean...yeah. Uh...Fuck, yeah, you want to?" he glances back to her hopefully.

Edie studies his face, deciding she's going to be unafraid in shamelessly admiring him. She leans back in her seat, folding her arms across her chest. "I could be persuaded. Though I'd still prefer to be taken out for a meal first. And not some work lunch."

Trenton nods, fingers now furiously drumming on the steering wheel, and Edie wonders what those fingers would feel like on her body. "So that's your deal?" he asks. "A dinner date before we fuck?" She sees a little flush of red on the tips of his ears.

Edie can't help but smile. She's a little high off the unexpected power she feels here, with Trenton and his forwardness that she should find infuriating, but instead finds it turning her insides to lava. She turns back away, returning her attention to the busy town outside her window as they approach what she assumes is their destination. "Sure. But just dinner and the fucking. Don't go falling in love with me after. You're not my type."

"Those sound like famous last words," Trenton mumbles beneath his breath, sitting straighter in his seat. Edie wonders if that means he's up for the task.

AFTER WHAT PROVED TO BE an enjoyable lunch of continued arguing back and forth between the very conservative Trenton and the very liberal Edie, followed by a far more chemistry-filled working afternoon, Edie walks into her studio apartment humming.

Trenton is everything she's not used to, and he himself

admitted much of the same thing to her over the course of their workday together. She had teased him about bimbos and future trophy wives. He retorted with admonishment of her feminist betrayal in referring to her fellow young women as "bimbos." They discussed politics with obvious opposing views, yet he listened with interest and asked pointed questions regarding her stances. Then countered with his own focus on economic concerns and the perception that in a more socialist economy—one she might view as equitable—couldn't that lead to complacency and lack of innovation?

It was the most refreshing exchange she'd ever had.

And when the tiny office was later occupied with Louise and two volunteers, their exchanges morphed to quiet glances in one another's direction. Not-so-subtle touching masked in reaching over the other for a pen, or a tissue, or a dropped item or anything else they could creatively concoct.

It had become a fun game, and Edie was a downright giddy participant.

When she finally plops herself down on her couch that evening, head buzzing with the small moments from her day with Trenton, she's all but forgotten completely about the recent contact with Lori Meyers. So, imagine her surprise when Edie tucks her feet beneath a blanket to scroll through missed texts and emails, and notices one with the subject line: Try again? sent by none other than Lori herself.

Edie immediately goes into action mode, furiously typing up a response before Lori can change her mind. Edie writes back with her personal cell number and is even more surprised when, within ten minutes, her phone is ringing.

"Hello?" Edie answers with hope, sitting up straight in a fight against the swallowing forces of her old and worn sofa.

"Edie, sweetie. Haha! That rhymes. Edie, it's me, Lori. You have a minute?" Edie can hear some soft tranquil music in the background followed by a muffled, "Hold that stretch, drop lower with each exhale."

"Hi, I do have a minute. Although, do you?"

"Not really," Lori quietly laughs. "I'm in the middle of teaching my yoga class, but I saw your email and figured I'd strike in hopes the iron was still hot. I have an idea for a project for you."

Edie nods, then realizes Lori can't actually *see* her nodding. "Oh, really? You mean... the interview?" Edie's surprised to hear this, and confused, as she'd really prefer to forget about the whole thing and focus instead on getting to the bottom of the mysteries regarding her father.

"Oh, that," Edie hears disappointment in Lori's voice. "Not exactly, that's not the project I mean. Though maybe we could warm into it. There's something else I was wondering if you could help with."

Disappointment and confusion fill Edie's chest, but she prompts Lori to go on anyway, listening patiently as Lori describes some letters and the necessity for tact and privacy. Her interest is piqued, though, despite her preference to meet with Lori in hopes of learning more about her father—and more importantly—the mysteries of his relationship to her mother. *It's a way in,* she reminds herself as she scribbles some notes to what already sounds like a futile cause. Letters with no identifying information? Unlikely to go anywhere, but she'd take whatever opportunity she could get. Maybe it was the universe telling her she was doing the right thing. Maybe this was a sign.

They end the call with plans to meet next week, and Edie hangs up with a little hope.

If not a little trepidation.

fourteen

. . .

lori

"GREAT CLASS WE had tonight, right? Sweetie?" I ask my daughter, Reggie, as we're closing up her physical therapy clinic for the night.

She pauses her bustling around the front desk to glance my way. Green eyes that mirror my own blink back at me. "You're in a good mood," she says with suspicion. "It's always a good class, Mom. This crew loves you, you're a natural with them." I see her examine my face for a moment longer before giving up and resuming her duties, turning off lights and rearranging the day's clutter from the desk.

When she faces me again, I finally reply. "Thank you for saying so. I think I just felt exceptionally in tune with everyone tonight. New moon perhaps."

"Uh-huh," Reggie responds with little inflection. She slips back a sleeve and checks her watch. "I want to get home before Xavier puts the kids down. You about done?"

I scoop up my personal yoga mat and nod but remain frozen in place.

Reggie studies me again, then sighs, dropping her purse down and pulling out a seat. I smile, victorious. "Go on," she prompts. "Obviously something is on that spirited little mind of yours. What's up? Talk to me."

I walk over to her and pull out the chair beside her. "How's Lucy doing?" Reggie's childhood best friend, Lucy, has been having some marital problems, and now she's pregnant.

Reggie narrows her eyes at me. "Fine. Getting close to the end."

"And I heard Lila is back in town to help out?" Lila is Lucy's little sister. It's funny to think of these kids I've known since they could barely ride a bike, all grown up now and having adult lives.

"Yes, Lucy and Lila are doing fine. Lila's new show comes out soon, so that should be cool."

"How exciting, can't believe she's acting now."

"Mom, get to the real point of what you wanted to say," she prompts. I see her patience dwindling.

"You know me too well. Fine," I say.

I had already horrified Reggie with news of Edie several days ago, and attempted to temper it with the exciting news of my new thing with Dom. Naturally, Reggie had been both shocked and suspicious of Edie, but after doing her own digging and seeing her social media accounts, even Reggie couldn't deny that our girl was undoubtedly Richard's mini in female form.

Today, I have another favor. "I'm hoping you'll want to meet Edie." I scan my daughter's face to gauge her reaction.

"There it is. I figured this was coming," she says, but she's smiling a little, so that's good.

"Okay," I say tentatively. "And? Your thoughts on it? She'll be helping us with hunting down information on the letters. Maybe you could join in?"

Reggie shakes her head. "I'll leave that to you guys, I got enough on my plate," she says, scanning her eyes around the office.

"But some other time?" I ask hopefully.

I watch as she fiddles with the hairband on her wrist, pulling it back and forth in a miniature resistance band stretch. "Yeah," she nods. "I'd be okay with that."

I grin. "Thank you! I'm so glad to hear that. You'll like her, you really will." I hate to ask, because I want Edie to feel as comfortable with our family as possible, but now I'm curious. "What made you switch from skeptical to...interested?"

Reggie shrugs. "A mix of curiosity and wanting to make sure you're not in over your head with something. But also because I've been thinking about it, and realizing that I'm like a strange step-sister to her in a way." I'm taken aback by Reggie's observation. It's rather optimistic for her sensible mind. "I mean, I'm the one that got to grow up with her dad."

Then understanding dawns on me. Reggie has no living siblings, so maybe she likes the idea of this potential sister-like relationship? I ask her.

She smiles. "Maybe. It's hard to explain. I'm not ready to dive full-fledged in, I'd like more solid proof of her biological connection or who her mom is. But I'm intrigued, I guess, yeah. If she doesn't have siblings either, maybe she's looking for a family connection."

"Maybe."

I feel an odd twinge of jealousy. For some reason I want Edie to be *my* thing, even if meeting Reggie was my suggestion. I feel a confusing mix of emotions regarding the whole situation. "I may even let her do the interview thing on me. For her grief class," I blurt out.

Reggie's eyebrows shoot up to the far-off heavens above. "You'd be okay with that?"

I cross my arms and look directly at her. "Of course. Why wouldn't I be?"

She shrugs and looks at her watch again. "Because you're like a vault with all topics of Dad and JJ. You don't even have pictures up, for God's sake. Only the one of you and Dad at prom, next to me and Joey at homecoming with me wearing your old dress."

My mind floats back to the photos she's referring to, the twin frames that sit on a shelf in my little cottage. James and I had been crowned Junior Prom King and Queen, a magical moment not just because of the beauty of a night that's drenched in traditions of rites of passage, but because of how far I had come in convincing my overbearing mother to let me do anything with James at all. She couldn't exactly deny me prom with my crowned king.

When Reggie's high school boyfriend and she were going to their own homecoming, I had given Reggie the same lilac dress I had worn that beautiful night all those years ago. I had hoped Reggie and Joey would follow in the high school sweetheart steps that James and I had taken, but her heart had gone another way.

"Well, you know what?" I say. "It's been nearly thirty years now. Maybe now's the time. What's one little harmless school interview project going to do, anyhow?"

Reggie rises from her seat and grabs her purse again. "If you're up for it, I actually think it could be good for you, Mom. Give you a chance to process, revisit, maybe. It comes up for me in therapy now and then, and it always amazes me the things I had been holding onto in my subconscious that needed a little dusting."

"It does?" I'm surprised to hear this. She was so young when we lost them.

"Sure. Like when I opened the first clinic, and I had to hire a handyman for certain things. Call me old-fashioned, but I couldn't help but wonder if Dad or JJ were here, if they'd be the ones helping me install the new light fixtures and whatnot."

"I hate thinking about things like that," I mutter. I'm officially over this conversation.

"Exactly my point." She grabs our coats from the hooks on the adjacent wall and puts hers on after handing me mine. "Come on, it's late and I really do want to catch the kids for story time."

I rise to join her, slipping my own coat on before grabbing my yoga mat. "Alright, so I'll set something up for the three of us. A lunch or something."

"Sounds good."

"You know you haven't asked me about how things with Dom are going," I point out as I follow her out the door.

She slips the key in to lock up, then gives me a mischievous smile. "I'm all ears if you're willing to share." She pulls the key out and double-checks that the door is bolted before dropping her keys in her bag. "But come on, you're a romantic. And Dom's a good guy. I'm sure you both are falling so very madly in love already." Her voice holds a mock dream-like tone. She grins at me. "No one ever could resist the charms of Lori Meyers," she winks. "Xavier and I have had bets going on when that would finally turn into something."

We take a couple steps to head toward the parking lot, the wind picking up and the chill biting on my exposed ankles. "You have?"

Reggie laughs. "Yeah, we have. You two are perfect together."

I find my daughter's approval on this a relief. She's smart. Careful. Observant with a good and logical handle on things. "Caught me," I say. "It was only a matter of time."

lace

. . .

February 1946 ~ South Germany

Dear Dog Tags,

I live with no regrets. Not even now with the loneliness crippling me and the future so uncertain. I shall instead choose to remember as much of our time as I can.

Those moments that passed between us were charged, right from the start, would you not agree?

Perhaps it was living in the tragedy of war. Human connection in those times feels like glimmers of a dream in an otherwise painful existence. It is these small moments that feed the starved soul.

I remember being so pleased when your wounds finally were clearly healing. I found such great pleasure in being the one to nourish you and bring you back to health. The tender touches we would exchange as I fed you, changed your bandages and nursed you back to health—they were caresses that I had been starved for in those days on the run and in hiding.

Do you remember the first night you kissed me? Of course you do, how could you not?

I didn't know much about desire then. Such talk was not allowed before a woman was married and ready to have children, but I knew I desired you. I decided early on that I was going to live for today, our future so at risk that nothing else seemed to matter. Only today. I pushed aside all doubts and let you kiss me, let you touch my breast and glide your hands under my dress, desperate to feel as close to you as I possibly could. Even if I knew that in time, I would have to let you go.

Soon after, when you first made love to me, I thought I could die then and there and would feel nothing but peace. The feel of you inside me, my legs wrapped around you as you rocked above me—so gentle at first. I looked up into your eyes and saw so much love in your gaze. As your movements quickened and my own hips found their natural rhythm, it was as though all the anger and torment of the months and years prior were no longer of any concern. We would carry on and survive, I believed it most right then. I thank God I was right.

With love,
Lace

fifteen

. . .

lori

nineteen years old

P REGNANT. THAT'S WHAT the twin blue lines on the test meant. Pregnant. I looked up at James with wide eyes, and the grin on his face melted away any worries I'd had on how he would take this news. He scooped me up and spun me around, planting kisses all over me before dropping me back down again, his gaze shifting to one of concern.

"Here, here, have a seat," he said, pulling my hand to the nearby worn leather recliner in our apartment.

We were attending a local college together, me studying art and basking in all the creative expression, and James studying finance. When we had been selecting majors, I told him he should be doing journalism or something for his writing. You know what he said? He said there couldn't be two artists between us. That one of us needed to have security in a job that would pay, and that he loved math anyway and that my art needed to be shared with the world.

He never admitted it, but I think he was just hell-bent on leaving behind his roots. Moving on and moving up and taking me with him.

"You need to be taking it easy now, baby," he said to me, and I knew I was going to love the way I was about to be doted on while carrying his child. "Shit, I know this isn't exactly what we planned—"

"Sure it is," I said with a smile. "We always knew we'd have a big family. It's just a little sooner than we thought."

The love and relief pouring over his face squeezed at my heart. He dropped down to his knees in front of me, taking my hands in his. "I hate that I have to leave you for the next few weeks." I could see his eyebrows pinch and the turmoil on his face. "Maybe I should get out of it."

"No," I insisted, and I put a hand to his chest. James had landed a fantastic internship for part of the summer down in Georgia. "Actually, I think it was when we were down there for your final interviews that we conceived," I smiled.

"Oh yeah?"

"Yeah," I nodded. In fact, I knew that was when it happened, and it was utterly perfect.

WE HAD MADE THE ROAD trip together a few weeks prior, and walking into our hotel room we felt like we had won the lottery, as the program paid for his stay. I had been grinning ear to ear as we entered, feeling like there was something so fantastic about the excitement of a hotel room. Like an enchanting escape, with surroundings certainly far nicer than our crappy apartment. I had lifted the eucalyptus-scented mini bottles of shampoo and lotion to my nose in appreciation. I wandered to the bed and basked in the crisp white sheets and fluffy pillows.

Pillows on a king-sized bed. We had both sunk into that bed in wonder, imagining all we were about to accomplish there.

The next day, both of us a bottle of nerves, I helped him get dressed for his day of interviews. I wrapped the tie around his neck and fumbled my way through, pretending I knew what I was doing. He took my hands and laughed at my failed efforts, looking like the trail-blazing professional I knew he was going to be. He was so sexy.

"You're sure you'll be okay in here waiting?" he asked, coffee on his breath and nerves in his voice.

I nodded. "Yeah. Maybe I'll check out the pool or something." I kissed him goodbye and wished him good luck and tried to busy myself for the next few hours, anxious at the thought of how he was doing. It was amazing how much I missed him, as if he were still back in PA and it was only me there in Georgia. I felt ready to crawl out of my skin at times.

By the end of the day, nearly mad with my anticipation of his return, I lay waiting on our beautiful temporary bed. I had dressed myself up in a short, racy baby doll nightgown, determined that no matter how his day went, he was going to return to his girl and feel like none of it mattered. I heard the latch on our door and the flutter of anticipation flickered in my belly.

And there he was. I looked up at him, at my James, looking like a man wearing the hell out of his new charcoal gray suit. He sauntered in, his face serious as he dropped his bag and leaned a shoulder on the wall, placing his hands in his pockets. His face gave away nothing, as he only held his eyes on me. I watched as he scanned my scantily clad body with the slightest nod of approval, but still no smile. I gripped the blankets under me in nerves and questioning, wondering what he was thinking. God, he looked so handsome standing there like that. But I started to worry that the interviews hadn't gone well. I wanted so badly to make him feel better.

I released my hold on the soft linens and crawled over to the edge of the bed, kneeling and sitting back on my heels.

That's when I saw the flicker in his eye, and the slightest lift at the corner of his mouth. I knew it then. He killed it. His serious face was one of victory, absorbing his day. And he was looking at me like I was the dessert to cap it all off.

I skirted my fingertips along my collar bone, slowly and seductively, feeling the rise and fall of my chest beneath my touch.

"You're beautiful," he whispered. He remained standing in his spot, watching me. "So fucking beautiful."

A wave of heat traveled through me at hearing the raw hunger for me in his voice. "I'm all yours," I murmured.

He nodded. "Drop the strap down."

I did as he asked, slowly pushing one strap from my shoulder, feeling the gentle graze of fabric on my skin, now buzzing and sensitive to all touch. I slipped my finger over to the other side and pushed that strap down too. The top fell away and dropped to my waist, exposing my breasts. I could feel the air hit and my nipples perk. I heard him groan in approval and my eyes grazed down to his pants, seeing him harden as he stood and watched me. I felt a mirroring ache between my legs.

Still, he made no move to come closer to me. We were in new territory, as our usual lovemaking was always a frantic clawing at one another, not slow and torturous like this. I was in the spotlight and determined to do it right. I grazed my fingertips over each of my nipples, feeling the small bumps as I was so turned on by this new level of manly confidence I could see in him. My belly was tight with wanting him to touch me, but loving him watching me like this.

"Lift the dress. I want to see you," he said, his hazel eyes growing dark.

I bravely pulled up the bottom of the hem to meet his request. I had on no panties, and I was soaked already. I spread out my knees to give him a better view, wondering what he could see, and he rumbled a groan in response. "Perfect," he whispered. He tilted his chin toward me, pure lust and hunger in his eyes. "Now touch yourself."

I smiled, taking one last look at his obvious erection to give me some courage before closing my eyes and pressing my fingers into myself. I felt shy, but I pushed past it and rocked my hips and glided along the silky slickness. I tried to focus on the feeling as much as I could, worried now that he would want me to make myself come. I wanted to do that for him, but I was faking a confidence at that point that wasn't quite within my reach.

Eventually, I heard him shift from the wall. My skin was tingly, my senses on fire and I caught a whiff of his cologne, knowing he was now in front of me. When I opened my eyes, he was staring down at me with intensity, his eyes dark and dilated, and I removed my fingers from inside me and lifted them up to my mouth, sucking. I had never done something so erotic before, and he groaned and pushed me back down onto the bed, hungrily landing his mouth on mine. I slipped my fingers through his hair and grasped with all my might, needing him as close to me as possible.

"James," I whimpered.

"I need to feel you, I need to be inside you," he was saying with kisses up and down my neck and my breast. His tongue flickered on my nipple, and I squeezed his hair harder. I could smell his shampoo and wanted to bury my face in the soft waves.

"Yes," I whispered. I reached down and felt around for his belt buckle to set him free. He pulled away from me, kneeling and slipping off his suit jacket, racing to undo his tie, then his dress shirt. I reached up and greedily helped him work faster.

When he was undressed, I ran my hands down his smooth torso, feeling his breath hitch with my touch. Even after four years together, it was like I still couldn't believe all this was mine. I could remember the boy he was when we first met and loved the way he was filling out into the man he was becoming. The rounded shoulders, corded with the ripple of muscles. The biceps that had been steadily growing in the hours of manual labor at his part-time job. I loved every inch of this body I had watched transform.

After allowing my exploration, he pushed me back onto the bed and hovered on top of me, gaze held on me and fire in his eyes. I could feel as he moved his cock up and down my slit, and I arched my hips up to him, urging him to enter, begging him.

"Wait," he whispered in a strain, closing his eyes. "Condom."

I leaned back in defeat as he rustled around the table next to us, then over to the one on the other side. "Fuck. We out?"

I looked at him and smiled at his naked body and the erection springing out between his thighs. I lifted my calf to press into the side of his torso, pulling him back over me. "It's fine, James, I need you," I pleaded. "I need you so badly."

I was on birth control but notorious for forgetting it, so he'd reluctantly use backup as often as possible. When we had self-control, at least. Which was far from every time.

He leaned back toward me, grabbing my legs and sliding me back under him, wolfish grin and dark haze in his eyes. I looked up to him and placed a hand on his cheek, clean shaven for his interview but already feeling like light sandpaper. Anticipation flipped in my belly, and I lifted my hips to slide myself along his length, loving the feel of him on me like this. He closed his eyes with a groan rumbling through his chest. I closed my eyes too and could feel him reach between his thighs, guiding himself to my opening, pressing.

"Baby, look at me," he said, and I opened my eyes to see him staring at me. "I love you, Lori." His eyes were so tender, and he stroked his hand on the side of my head, in my hair. "And I'm going to give you everything you deserve, okay?" His expression was determined. My chest ached with how much he loved me, how important it was for him to give me the world.

"You already have," I said. I needed him to know just how sincerely I meant that. I kissed him and told him how much I loved him, how he was my everything, and when he pushed into me, stretching me, I felt so complete, so right.

I wrapped my legs around him and laid mostly still at first, wanting to allow him to enjoy his thrusts of being bare inside of me, his growls telling me his ecstasy. When I couldn't help myself anymore and started arching my hips in rhythm to his, it was only mere moments until I came undone around him, and he stilled inside of me. I could feel his pulses as I clenched around him, and I knew he was trying to hold out for me to have another. But I rocked into him again, locking my hands on his back, saying, "Take it, baby. Take it," as I rode him from below, and he gave one final push deep inside me, nearly too much for me to stand.

"I'M GOING TO LOOK INTO taking classes over the winter, so that I can try and graduate early," James said, kneeling down in front of me. I leaned forward in my seat and scanned his face, seeing the concern in his eyes as he processed this news of our baby.

"Don't stress," I reassured him. "We'll figure it out." I hated the idea of him thinking he needed to pressure himself to rush things and jumpstart his career. I knew how hard he could be on himself, and I needed him to see that no matter what, whether he was in his dream job or not, none of that mattered. He himself would always be enough.

He nodded. "I'm ahead of schedule anyways, so if I do that, then classes next summer, I'll be able to get a job that pays something real." I watched as his eyes looked around our microscopic apartment, the walls dingy with a border running along the top in gray waves, markings of the smoking habits of previous tenants. We worked our asses off day and night to be able to afford the place, completely against the will of my mother, of course. But we had it, and it was ours. "I'll get us out of here and into a place you deserve," James said with a kind of sadness in his eyes. "A place you and the baby deserve. It won't even know any of this by the time it can remember anything."

How could I possibly make him understand that with him, I had the world? My heart was so full in his determination to do right by me. By us. I grabbed his cheek in my palm. "James. We could live in a cardboard box, and as long as I'm with you, I'd be as happy as Tinker Bell."

He tilted his head to the side. "Tinker Bell was a fairy too tiny to hold more than one emotion at a time, and she was jealous of Wendy and any other girl that got close to Peter Pan."

I threw my head back in a laugh. "Well, that's perfect then. The only emotion I hold is happiness, and I'd kill any girl that tried to get their hands on you."

"That sounds like anger." He leaned back on his heels and crossed his arms in mock judgment.

"Alright, fine. I'd be angry, get rid of the girl, then return to happy." I threw my hands up in surrender. "See?"

He shook his head. "You wouldn't hurt a fly. I'd love to see you try."

I smiled and ran my hands through his hair. "How did we get so lucky to find each other so early on?" I asked.

"Nope, I'm actually pissed. Hate that I had to wait until I was fifteen to meet you. Robbed," he laughed, and I pinched his shoulder.

"Don't be so greedy."

But then an unwelcome sadness swept over me. I had a sinking feeling in the pit of stomach. Was it the news of the baby? I didn't think so. Maybe fear of telling my mother? Actually, if anything, I was looking forward to the shock and reprimand I'd be given. I had a feeling she'd suggest an abortion, and I would later be proven right.

No, my sadness in that moment was something else.

"I think you're too good to be true," I whispered.

James rose up from his kneeling position in front of me. He

lifted me slightly so he could scoot under me in the chair, pulling me close to him in the cradle of his lap.

"I know what you mean," he said with a kiss to my temple.

We sat there like that for a while, absorbing the magnitude of how our lives were about to change, James rocking us in that old recliner. He placed his hand on my belly and made me laugh with his introduction of himself and me to our baby, calling us "The reckless teens that got lazy and didn't use protection." Warning the baby that he or she made the wrong choice in parents, and that the baby was surely in for trouble.

sixteen

. . .

dom

OF ALL THE times he's recently imagined opening the door to something real with Lori Meyers, Dom certainly didn't expect this.

"This" being hanging out in his house, papers spread out on the dining room table. Old World War II love letters, with Lori and him on a hunt to find out all they can on two people long gone, a story tucked away in the quiet depths of history, along with countless others.

Correction—Lori, Dom, and a third party by the name of Edie.

He can see why Lori likes and trusts Edie, as she does in fact seem to be a good egg with a passion for this kind of thing. Edie shows them how to get organized, mapping out dates and little indications of the progression of the end of the war, potential locations for the farm the girl mentions in them, that kind of thing. She even came armed with protective sleeves for each of the letters, sparking some guilt in Dom's acid-free folder attempt. Dom was practical and structured by nature, but something about the idea of old love letters just didn't spark the same kind of interest that it clearly did in the two women before him.

He watches with something akin to admiration as Lori listens intently to the young Edie, nodding and jotting down her own notes. Lori has on black-rimmed reading glasses and her hair is in a messy knot on top of her head, little wisps of chestnut hair slipping out and falling on her neck. In a way it makes her look like a student, eagerly drinking up the knowledge of a wise instructor. It stirs something in Dom. He finds her sexy and beautiful in her passion and excitement, even if his own mind remains far less hopeful or enthralled in this whole endeavor.

"I'm going to put out a social media campaign to see if we can get somewhere with this," Edie explains to them.

Dom passes out some waters to his guests, careful not to place them too close to the papers, even in their new homes of protective sleeves. "What kind of campaign?" he asks.

Edie takes her water, thanking him, and explains, "Well, without names, we really don't have anything to put into online databases or anything, so linking to a family tree is out. But if we do a blast to anyone that might know anything about loved ones referring to one another as 'Dog Tags' and 'Lace' in old letters, we might get some bites. Might be some false alarms, so don't get your hopes up too much. But you never know. We'll leave out some details just as a way to vet through in case we get people that are only looking to collect and resell."

"People do that?" Lori asks in alarm.

Edie nods. "Oh yeah. There's money in this, sadly. People looking to find gems to auction off. But don't worry about that," Edie says looking over to Dom, assuming he would be just as alarmed by this as Lori. "I won't let that happen."

He takes a seat and watches, unsure of exactly what to do to be of assistance and feeling more comfortable on the sidelines. Ruby had been excited to hear of this project, her own creative juices apparently flowing not just in the idea of finding more about the letters themselves, but in the very nature of the hunt for answers and the commitment to doing justice for the potential loved ones the mysterious Dog Tags and Lace may have—their children or grandchildren or even nieces and nephews. She hopes this could help them find a new level of awe for their family from a generation plagued by war, her mind swirling in some fantasy of admiration and pride in learning of the details of a true love erupting from the ashes of turmoil.

Dom just liked making his daughter happy.

His own belief in true love was rather shaded. He'd foolishly married a woman he thought was a good match, only to later be the victim to her own unhappiness, blamed on Dom as the man forcing her to live all over the world in pursuit of his military career goals. Here he thought he was giving Pearl the world. Pearl, on the other hand, thought he was robbing her of it. He felt not just heartbroken in the aftermath of their divorce, but also guilty. With reluctance, he sent Ruby to live with Pearl back in the States once Pearl left him, feeling torn between wanting to be an active fatherly presence in Ruby's life, but believing a daughter should be with her mother.

He learned the hard way that Pearl's own depression sent her down a rabbit hole of alcoholism and dangerous decisions. Ruby lived with her mother for only a few years, but the damage was done, and Dom felt a new wave of guilt upon learning of Ruby's struggles in those years. He's spent every waking moment since trying to ensure his daughter has everything she deserves to make up for her suffering as a result of her mother's neglect. The only relief Dom has felt is in knowing Ruby now has Joey, a man Dom knows to be good, with a clear and pure devotion to his daughter. For Dom, love isn't about some fairy tale, it's about stability and protection. Care in the form of meeting needs.

He looks over to Lori and watches as she zeroes in on one letter in particular, squinting as she makes out the handwriting and accompanying translation. "It's so sweet. You can see how Lace starts to fall for him, even though it's all risky for her. Can you imagine?" she says, dropping the sleeve and looking up at Dom as she pops her glasses up in her hair. "Still feeling love even when in hiding, fearful of your life?"

A thump of something stirs in his chest as she says this. Without thinking, he reaches over and squeezes her hand, saying, "I have a feeling you can imagine it, Lori." They lock eyes for a moment, and he smiles as he sees a flicker of something pass over her. "You find light in anything."

The clearing of a throat breaks their exchange, and Edie cuts in. "Well, I've taken pictures of everything I need and know where I'm going with this, so maybe I'll leave you two and get started on what I can find on my end." She rises and grabs her jacket from the back of her chair. "Memorial Day is what—eight weeks away? How sweet would it be to figure out who they were and make a big splash about it by then?"

"I love that idea," Lori gushes as she rises to give Edie a hug.

"I'll be in touch if anything comes up. Nice to meet you, Dom," she says, and he shakes her hand. "These are really awesome, and it's cool to have a front row seat for the mystery."

"Appreciate your help. Ruby thanks you too," he adds. He knows dropping Ruby's name on a young woman like Edie can get a fun reaction. Hell, even old Sis at the historical society was a Ruby fan.

"I just admire that Ruby not only writes her own songs, but she has a passion for finding such meaningful inspiration." Edie nods her head in approval. "Pretty cool," she adds, and Dom's respect for her goes up a notch that she didn't get fangirl flustered like he would have expected, and she instead focused on the quality of Ruby's artistry. His dad-pride flares up in his daughter's work, and he appreciates that Edie can recognize it as well. He finds it refreshing to see someone so young care beyond the chart-topping stats or media gossip that most people ask him about.

Lori and Dom walk Edie out with one final goodbye and a plan to stay updated on any potential leads. They stand at the door and watch as Edie makes her way to her car with a wave.

As she pulls away and Dom closes the door, he's thankful to have a moment alone with Lori.

She turns to look at him with mischief in her eyes. "So, Dom, about that kiss the other night."

She's referring to the one from their most recent date, where he all but stripped her down right out there by the pool area, with far too many people on the property who could potentially see. He had been dangerously close to a "fuck it" moment. He really needed to stop picking her up from her house—zero privacy there.

He smiles. "Yes, well. Can't just give a show for free. Would be wrong."

"Very wrong," she agrees. She steps closer to him, and he thinks she's going to reach up and kiss him. He wills himself to shift gears with her, to enjoy this moment alone with her, and he starts to lean his head down to hers, only to feel Lori grabbing his shoulders with an exciting shake. "Oh, these letters are amazing, aren't they? I feel like I'm there with those two, falling in love right alongside them. I can't wait to read through them all. You've read each one?"

He tries not to tense as he feels her hands slide down his arms with a slow tenderness before grabbing his hands, giving them a squeeze that's more like the comfort for an ill patient than the kind of squeeze he'd prefer from her hands. But he returns the gesture, giving his own grip to her hands in return, unsure what to say next. Does she really still want to keep talking more about the damn letters? Wasn't the past hour or so enough? As thankful as he is for the help, futile as it might be, he'd really rather try and get to know Lori better. Sure, they've known each other for a couple years now, but pleasantries at parties is far from real connection.

"Why don't we go have a seat in the living room, somewhere more comfortable?" he suggests, then instantly regrets how that came out, worried it sounds like he's luring her in just for sex. Which, okay—he most certainly is. But he's finding the seeds of feelings starting to take root for Lori. While he's not sure a long-term relationship is necessarily on his radar, he would like to give her the respect of solid conversation before he resumes what they started the other night.

He racks his brain for something else to say, but she beats him to it.

"Or you could show me to your room?" Large, green eyes stare at him with very clear seduction.

"Oh, I mean. Now?" *Shit.* That's not what he meant to say.

She raises a questioning eyebrow. "Are you on some sort of schedule I'm unaware of, Dom?" She lifts a hand to his chest, leaving it there for a moment before slowly grazing up to his neck, pulling him down for a kiss.

He obliges and kisses her, because she's a stunning siren and he wants to, but alarm bells are going off in his head. She tastes so good, she feels so warm and small in his arms and this kiss is making it hard to think straight, but he wills himself to think with his head and not his dick, which is literally getting harder with every moment. In every sense of the phrase.

He pulls back but keeps his arms around her. "Fuck, Lori. You're exquisite."

"And those baby blue eyes of yours keep me up at night, Dom." She reaches up and runs her hands through his hair. "Black hair and blue eyes are a very sexy combination, you know."

It would be easy, so incredibly easy to take this woman up to his bed and make this happen. He's tempted.

Very tempted.

But this is Lori. There's something a whole lot more fragile about her than there was with Jules, the career-focused mastermind that he felt more secure in engaging with sexually. Dom knew Jules could handle it. With Lori, he's not so sure.

"Lori, I...fuck, you are irresistible, I hope you know that." He doesn't mean to curse so much in front of her, but his mouth is having a hard time behaving given his clouded thoughts.

She gives an adorable little half shrug. "Still is nice to hear."

"But don't you think we should get to know one another a little better before we dive into," he darts his eyes upstairs, "that?"

Disappointment fills Lori's face. "Dom. We do know each other. We've had several dates now. You know my kid, my mother, for God's sake. I've known your soon-to-be son-in-law for most of his life." She starts to pull away from him, but he gives her a small squeeze, wanting to reassure her that his resistance isn't in a lack of want for her.

"Right. We know everyone else, but I want to know more about *you*." How does he explain this better? He wonders if he's nuts to be trying to take this slow.

She sighs and gives a dramatic eye roll that he thinks is meant to be silly. "Let's see, I don't have a favorite color because I love them all, movies often bore me, but I'll sit through one if I really have to. I like to paint, draw, do yoga, read romance—oh wait!" she says with excitement. "I do like watching romance movies!" He laughs at her revision. "I love food and cooking, though I do wish I could cook better, because I'll always need a recipe."

"Why's that?"

"Without one, my creativity runs a little wild and I ruin the whole thing. There, happy?"

And then her lips are on his neck, and he groans at the igniting contact, realizing his original intention is becoming very difficult to stick to. "Fine," he whispers out, distracted by what Lori's mouth is doing. "For me it's action movies and good beer and...I can't think what else, so I'll go ahead and shut the hell up," he says before succumbing to the very powerful draw of everything Lori Meyers. *Fuck it, don't overthink it*, he reminds himself for the hundredth time.

In a trance, he lets her lead him up the stairs, lost in the way her ass shimmies up the steps and realizing he feels like a guest in his own house.

Moments later, as she does a shocking and intoxicating strip-tease for him that's got Dom feeling like a kid all over again, he tries to squash down the feeling of concern that's creeping in somewhere in the back of his mind, warning him to take this slowly.

But she's right, they do know one another already. So what is he afraid of? Nothing worth any concern, he hopes, because with her naked body now in front of him, he loses all sense of control and dives right in.

seventeen

. . .

edie

SEX WITH TRENTON Wroe turns out to be a very enjoyable thing, Edie notes as she lies naked and wrapped up in his sheets, sweaty and admiring the satisfied grin on his face as he circles her nipple in a move that's just post-sex fun and not even meant to be erotic. Yet it still makes her belly tighten, and she wonders how quickly he'll be ready to go again. Edie stares at his body, feeling like he's been carved to perfection. His shoulders are rounded with muscles—muscles that proved able to lift her with ease, hovering her mid-air against a wall while he slammed himself into her, filling her with dizzying ecstasy. Nothing like Zeke and his far narrower shoulders that often struggled to carry more than a six pack of beer and a bag of groceries. Certainly hadn't been able to lift her to straddle him the way Trenton had.

As promised, Trenton took Edie out on a dinner date. He had been incredibly gentlemanly about it, much to Edie's surprise, even showing up with flowers when he picked her up. Then he opened her car door for her, and actually waited until she was settled before closing it, like it was 1955.

But that's about where the politeness ended.

It was fun to be so direct with their intentions, Trenton shamelessly checking her out during their car ride, or rubbing a hand up her thigh while they sat at the bar and waited for their table. She was exploring a whole new side of herself when around him, and Edie fell in the rhythm with ease, shifting in her bar stool to spread out her legs, placing each thigh on either side of his. She had rubbed her knee up against his crotch, feeling his growing erection and loving the groan and look of torment on his face.

All for her.

Edie wasn't a prude or anything, but she was also never one to explore casual sex. Generally speaking, she had a two-week minimum dating rule before she ever let anyone get to the coveted prize. This equated to only two sexual partners, both being guys with values very much in line with hers. Kind guys. Sweet guys committed to saving the world, just as she was. They would talk prison reform and support for inmates and pride themselves on what *good people* they were, how they were going to ensure the future of their beloved country would continue to evolve, how they'd right the wrongs of injustices.

And this is still the type of guy Edie hopes to end up with one day, make no mistake. There's so much love her heart can feel in someone with values near and dear to her own.

It's just—tension can sometimes be lacking in that scenario. At least that's what she's found so far.

Not here, though. Not in the uber bachelor pad of Trenton's apartment, complete with navy blue walls in the entire place, dim lighting with far too many LED fixtures glowing. There's a low leather couch and massive TV screen in his living room, and music pulsing from a sound system Edie imagines tech junkies would envy. He first turned on Chris Isaak's "Wicked Games," and she had to suppress a giggle. He had lit candles as if an expert in the art of seduction. Trenton even has old muscle car art on the walls, for

Christ's sake. Could he be more cliche? It was laughable how perfectly she had pegged this guy.

And she doesn't even care. She's going to explore this idea of a fuck buddy for all it's worth. Her hippie soulmate can wait.

"What's so funny?" Trenton asks her as he slides his hand through his hair. She watches the bulge of his bicep as he does so and leans forward to bite it.

"Nothing," she mumbles on his skin before pulling back and settling on his pillow.

He drops his arm beside her and rolls on top of her, peering down into her eyes. "Lies. Wicked lies." He drops his mouth down to her nipple and bites as she squeals, shimmying her hips up to him and noting with satisfaction that he's hard once again. "Holy fuck, you're so sexy, Edna. I love your hips," he says as he moves down her body, planting kisses down her belly in a trail as he moves lower, eventually finding the coveted spot between her legs.

And then he pauses. "Do you want my tongue here?" he asks before inflicting a teasing lick.

"God, yes, I do." She grabs his shoulders, then glides her hands to his hair to grab in fists, loving the silkiness. "I'm so glad you don't use hair gel," she whispers out, remembering the way Zeke combed his hair to the side with precision, and the meticulous way he was sure to purchase more gel before ever running out. She tries to squeeze the image out of her mind. Why did she keep thinking about him, especially now?

"I'm not trying to think too much about why you're talking about hair gel," Trenton says as he nibbles at her inner thigh. "But if you want my mouth here," he says with another teasing lick, "then tell me," lick, "why," lick and a nibble, "you're laughing." His mouth returns to the soft skin of her thigh and sucks. Hard. Marking her.

She moans between a reflexive giggle. "Your apartment. It's just so..."

He releases his grasp on her and moves to the other side, sucking and marking her there as well. "Yes?"

Edie rises up to prop herself on her elbows, peering down at him. "Those hickeys are going to be awkward for tomorrow night's date. Poor guy might feel some kind of way."

"Tomorrow night's date better be me then," he says, and Edie drops back her head as he fully buries himself between her legs, relentless in his mix of teasing tongue strokes. The cool air on her torso is in complete contrast to the heat of his mouth on her.

After he starts to slip two fingers inside her, he stops again. "Tell me about my apartment, Edna. You don't like it?"

She struggles to concentrate as he slowly resumes his movements, his fingers slipping in ever so slightly, his tongue maneuvering through her with precision. She grinds in response to the rhythm, feeling her breasts bobbing across her rib cage with his movements. "I like it. I do. It's a really nice apartment."

"Lies again," he says as he abruptly stops his movements, and she feels the vacancy between her legs. She pops open her eyes in disappointment and sees him rise up and lean back on his heels. In the darkness she can just barely make out the flicker of light in his eyes as he grabs her hips and lifts her with a twist to turn her onto her stomach. She feels the softness of the sheets beneath her followed by the sharp slap on her ass, and she giggles reflexively through the radiating heat of the sting.

With her fists clinging onto his pillows, Edie squeezes her eyes shut and feels Trenton's grip on her ankles as he yanks her down and spreads her out wide, then pulls back on her hips to prop her to her knees. She feels deliciously exposed to him positioned like this, and he rubs a finger onto her clit, soaking wet and slick, and she whimpers out, "Oh God, yes, Trenton," in a lust-filled haze.

"Fuck, baby, you're so fucking hot when you say my name like that," he says, and her insides clench in hearing the raw lust in his husky voice. "I can't get enough of you," he breathes out in a barely audible whisper. His cock presses against her in teasing torment.

Edie is in heaven, loving all of it. How rough and raw he is with her, the way he slips out little phrases like it's *her* that's *his* undoing. Little old Edie bringing frat-boy-turned-cocky lawyer to his knees.

Trenton continues to slide his fingers on her swollen clit, slipping them between her folds, then back up further on her ass. She hums out a moan in appreciation, then startles as he glides right past the opening she would expect. Is he heading where she thinks he's heading? Do people do that? She certainly hadn't had contact there before. He's hesitant, eventually pausing, she assumes waiting for her to stop him or resist. But her senses are on fire and her pleasure has her inching her hips back to him, needing to get as close as possible.

Before she has time to think, he pushes a finger in, just a bit, and she jolts at the surprising and new sensation. She buries her face into his pillow as she feels this erotic invasion, and she feels the head of his penis return to her clit with gentle strokes. Her head swims with the feelings flooding her between her legs. She says nothing, no attempts to stop him, too curious to ride along with him in this, because it amazes her how incredible it feels.

"Do you like that, baby?" he asks, and Edie surprises herself with the appreciative moan she lets out. "I'll be damned," he says with gentle rocks to press the head of his penis against her. "You really did turn out to be—"

"Don't say naughty," she mumbles out, her voice husky. "Don't ruin it." She's aiming for serious, but a smile escapes her. Whatever is happening between her legs is too exquisite not to. The pressure of his finger combined with the presses of his dick up and down her clit are a sensation she can't get enough of. "Please, just shut up and fuck me," she says. "Not back there, though!" she rushes to add as her eyes pop open in sudden panic.

She feels him back up and off of her and she looks over her shoulder to see him smiling. "Relax, I wasn't going to," he says. "Though who knew Edna Mackenzie was so naughty," he says before leaning to the side to the nightstand beside her, reaching for the pile of condoms.

She wants to say something smart in return, but she's too lost in the sight of his beautiful torso, bronze and toned, the shadows caused by candlelight catching divots of muscle just right. *He might be the hottest guy I've ever seen*, she thinks to herself.

And a machine.

Edie closes her eyes and feels as he trails the corner of the condom wrapper down her spine, and her skin erupts in chills. Then she hears the enticing sound of the foil ripping, imagining Trenton rolling the condom onto himself. All of his movements are so commanding, and often unexpected, leaving her constantly guessing.

She feels him tug her legs to prop her further up on her knees, her ass in the air and all laid out to him. She's sure she's soaking in anticipation. And when she feels his cock, slow and steady this time as he eases into her to the furthest depths he can, leaning over her to torture her nipples, she can't help but think how wonderful this man is. How wonderfully he can fuck, how uninhibited she's been able to be with him, and how happy she is to be having this experience.

When her next orgasm rips through her at the feel of his strokes in and out of her, she screams out his name into his pillow, louder than she's ever screamed in pure ecstasy before.

eighteen

. . .

lori

W ELL, IT'S HAPPENED again. I'm in love.

With Dom Francesca. A man who might be a quiet spirit on the outside, but is a most dominating force in the bedroom, and I'm loving every minute of it.

Let me run you through the past couple of weeks. It's been great sex, ordering takeout and roaming around his house naked as much as possible, something I like to think I introduced him to.

I told him I have a strict No Shirt rule in the house, because his tanned torso adorned with his faded military tattoos really are an addicting and beautiful sight. He joked that my rule was quite the coincidence, because he has a No Pants rule.

One morning when Dom was pouring us our coffee wearing nothing but a pair of boxer briefs, I slinked up behind him, my naked skin gliding along his, breast pressed into his back. I slipped my hands in the waistband of his underwear, reaching down and running my fingers through the black hair surrounding what I find to be a truly beautiful cock. I grabbed ahold and whispered in his ear, "It should be illegal to hide this," and I reluctantly removed my hand only so I could slide off the briefs, down his muscular thighs, his calves, removing them completely. His groan was my reward.

When I stood back up, he turned around, his ocean blue eyes turning dark as he took in the naked sight of me. "You are nothing but trouble," he said, and I gasped at his delightful pinch of my nipples. I threw my head back, feeling the ache between my legs, and I gasped at the sensation of the pinch of his fingers now being replaced by the feel of nearly burning heat from the side of the coffee mug he was pressing into my breast. "Careful, now. Can't move or this coffee is going to spill all over you," he warned, his voice low. I had no idea Dom had such a wild side, but I'm never letting go.

Then he moved his fingers down along my slit, the other hand still holding the hot mug against my breast, and he began torturous strokes, warning me to hold still, but that was impossible. My hips rocked with his movements, the hot coffee spilling on me in delicious stings, and he dipped his mouth down to drink in the mess right off my skin. I could feel his erection pressing against me, my skin buzzing with desire, needing to feel him inside me yet again.

I've barely been able to walk. It's been heaven. Lovely heaven.

OF COURSE, THERE ARE ALSO the letters. Oh, these letters have so much beautiful love in them. Their journey leaps off the pages, yanking and catapulting my romantic soul into the depths of their fears, their hope. I'm finding that images of my early days of young love with James keep creeping in as I read. Not just the sneaking around, but the worry I would feel for him whenever a painful stretch of weekend passed and I knew he was at home in his own dark environment, fighting the demons of his father. I've been close to tears on more than one occasion, the plight of Lace and her love for Dog Tags feeling so familiar. Survival in one's turbulent childhood home may not hold the same gravity as survival in war, but there's no denying the squeeze of fear I feel all over again as I read the letters.

Now that I think about it, it was as if I knew in those days that tragedy was ahead of us, one way or another.

But that's the past, and thankfully, I have my gorgeous man Dom Francesca in front of me to distract me from those memories.

Today, we're ice skating. My idea, naturally. He's a bear in these skates, and he calls me his tiny dancer as I spin around him in easy glides, laughing at his discomfort.

"I hate you for this," he teases me.

I skate over to him, press against his chest as he grabs my arms to steady himself. "I'll make it up to you," I whisper.

He growls before attempting to release his hold on me, slipping and falling down hard on his ass. I wince for him—I know that hurt. I reach out my hand to help him up, but I fall right down with him, and we're both laughing like little kids on the cold ice, watching the annoyed skaters that now have to dodge us.

"Are you very angry with me for choosing this excursion?" I coyly ask with a flutter of my eyelashes as we carefully hold hands to help one another up.

Once standing, his expression turns surprisingly serious. "No."

"No?" I try and study his face, but his eyes have a distance to them, the blue a bit darker.

He shakes his head, then looks away and stares off into space. "My ex-wife, Pearl, never liked doing anything out of her comfort zone, and it was like walking on eggshells with her."

"That's terrible."

He nods, his gaze still distant. "It was." I see his chest rise and fall in a heavy sigh. "And all I was ever trying to do was make her happy." He looks down at me, finally. "Never did succeed, though."

I grab his hand and guide us over to the wall to help him steady himself. I spin myself around and smile at him. "That's a damn shame, love. Because I find myself positively floating in your presence."

A FEW DAYS AND COUNTLESS orgasms later, I'm standing in Dom's doorway, reluctantly heading out for yoga class. I hate leaving the bubble we've been escaping in. I scan his body for one last appreciative look, loving the casual side of him I now get to see. His sweatpants hang low on his hips, and I yank the band playfully and let it snap back.

"Looking for something?" he asks.

"Always." My eyes meet his and I expect to see a smirk or something, but instead I see something more like hesitation on his face. I kiss him on his cheek and ask him what's wrong.

He reaches his hand up to run through his hair, a move I love watching him do, though I'm also jealous of his hair, wanting his hand on me.

He drops his hand and looks away, not meeting my eyes. "I have to leave for a few days."

I grip my yoga bag and press it to my chest, pulling my head back. "Leave? Leave where?"

"Out to LA for Ruby."

I absorb his words and note my disappointment, but I try not to show it. "Oh, when?" I ask as I turn to grab the doorknob. I know it's silly, I can't expect the man to never leave the house, yet I can't help but feel hurt.

"Tomorrow. I'll be gone less than a week, hopefully."

I snap my head back at him and try to read his face. "Tomorrow?" I'm sure the surprise is clear in my tone. I open the door and step backwards into the frame.

"Yes," he says as he places a hand in his pocket. That's all he offers in explanation, just that one simple word. I wish he would say something more, explain the sudden trip.

I try and plaster on a smile to erase the tension my obvious disappointment is causing. "That should be fun." My gaze drops to the ledge below me, and Dom pulls his hand out of his pocket to gently grab my chin.

"I meant to say something sooner." He smiles with a little mischief. "But I've been very distracted by a certain woman."

I try to allow the words to soothe me, even though whispers of hurt at him waiting until the last minute to tell me echo in my mind. I'm about to mumble out generic well wishes on having a great trip, how the warmth of LA should be a fun change, but then I get an idea. "Here's a wild thought…how about I join you?" Actually, yes, now that I think about it, it's perfect! Ruby already knows me, it could be our first blended family adventure.

Dom frowns. "Join me in LA?"

I nod vigorously. "Sure," I say, leaning my elbow on the doorframe as I twirl my fingers through my hair. "I'm not exactly swamped around here. I could get away for a few days." I look for his reaction, a little nervous at putting myself out there like this, but knowing Dom, he'd be too shy to ask if it was something he had considered.

"I hadn't thought about that."

Oh. Apparently, he has *not* considered this.

I drop my arm and slide my hands up his chest. "We could get a place with a jacuzzi, and I'll tease you in ways I think you'd love to punish me for." I give my best suggestive eyebrow wiggle, but the look he gives me is not the one I'm expecting.

He removes my hands from his chest, and it might as well be a slap to my face. "Lori, I'm not sure that's a great idea."

"What? Of course it is. Not everything has to have a structured plan, you know. Find your spontaneity." I'm trying to keep the conversation light, but there's a little desperation in my chest, an unwelcome shame at having suggested this, given his reaction. I feel a need to have this end favorably. A fun, spontaneous trip! He can see that, right? "I haven't been to the West Coast in years," I add.

He shakes his head. "I'll keep that in mind. Another time." I don't say anything, I just nod. "Look," he says with a stroke up and down my arm that feels condescending. Like I'm a child. "I like you very much, Lori."

Like. How romantic. Here I am falling in love with the man, and he's telling me he likes me.

"You like me," I repeat.

"You make me feel like the inept fool that managed to land the dream girl," he says with a smile.

Dream girl—I've been called that before. I nod and smile in return, though there's sadness in it. "Dream girls have high expectations, I guess."

He pulls me into a hug. "Honey, don't do that." I hesitate to return it at first, but then the soothing feel of his arms around me is irresistible, and I wrap my arms around his waist. "We've spent pretty much every day together," he says, his voice rumbling in his chest by my ear. "Maybe a little time away is a good thing."

"Ouch."

Dom laughs a little at my pout and I breathe in the clean scent of laundry detergent on his chest. "Haven't you ever heard of too much of a good thing?" He unwraps his arms from me and tucks a strand of hair behind my ear. I try to focus on the tenderness in his eyes, despite rejecting the words coming out of his mouth.

"That's a stupid phrase invented by cynics," I say.

"You calling me a cynic?"

"Did you invent the phrase?"

"No, but I fear the man that did, given the wrath of Lori," he says, and I can't help but smile.

"It's been heaven, all this time together, hasn't it? Like we've been making up for the years before that we've missed."

He takes my hands and lifts them to his lips in soft kisses. "It has been, yes. But it's also borderline unhealthy, we've hardly even left the house." His tone is playful.

I smile lazily with heavy hooded eyes, thankful at having regained some of the magic of our bubble. "Mmm, how perfect.

Forget sliced bread, it's DoorDash that's the real gift, don't you think?"

Dom gives my fingers one last kiss before dropping my hands. "Seriously, a few days," he says. "A week, tops. Ruby and Joey are sorting out their wedding plans, and when you play the role of both parents, that apparently means I'm tasked to chime in on floral details. Wish me luck."

Ugh. He pulled the "both parents" card. I know that card, can't exactly argue with that. Or can I?

"Hi, hello! Mother with a female touch, here," I say, raising a hand and arching an eyebrow. "I'm guessing you wouldn't know the first thing about floral arrangements, would you?"

"Relentless, aren't you?" he says with a smirk. "Listen, it's not only wedding things. I'm also going to join Ruby for a few meetings. I need to check in on my daughter and offer moral support, make sure she's still in good hands with her team." His eyebrows crease and I see the genuine concern on his face. "It's tough when you have a kid so glaringly in the public eye. I worry about her, and I like to be there when I can to ensure her team is doing the best *they* can to not only support, but keep her out of harm's way. When you're on top of the world, there's plenty of people that would love to see you fall down, sadly."

I nod and try to hide my hurt, logically knowing that it's unwarranted. "I understand. You're a good dad," I add. "She's lucky to have you. Send her and Joey my love."

"I will."

I step backwards and out the door. As I drop my gaze down to the ground, I read the large black lettering of the "F" on the door-mat, a reminder that this is the Francesca house, and I'm just a guest in Dom's world.

But I'm an optimist. So he'll be out of town for a few days, no big deal. I conjure up some courage and smile my brightest, step-ping back up for a last kiss on his cheek. I whisper in his ear, "I'll be sure to text you a few little gem photos. Just don't go opening them in public now. Might be embarrassing for you." I'm rewarded with his growl of a groan as he pulls me into him for one last kiss. I run my fingers through his hair and squeeze, wanting to soak up all of him I can in these last couple of moments together before he gets on a plane to cross the country.

And I try and push away the fear I have in knowing he's about to leave me, that he didn't want me to join him, and that he chose not to tell me until just now. Until I was on his doorstep and walking away.

nineteen

. . .

lori

twenty years old

JAMES AND I had a shotgun wedding before I was even showing. We eloped with no one there but the judge at the courthouse and the witnesses they provided for us. James figured before we went to my parents and disclosed our little situation, he'd better at least have put a ring on my finger.

My parents were mad as hell, just as expected. His parents were indifferent. James's little brothers were teenagers by then and, much like their older brother, were in the midst of their own path to get out from under their parents' misery and do their own thing. Their mission in distancing themselves as best they could meant our news wasn't of much interest to them, though I have a feeling James was disappointed by that.

So it was just me and James. Ultimately, we were perfectly fine with that, especially because we soon found out that we were expecting not one baby, but two. Twins, our own little group forming. We didn't need anyone else since we'd be doubling our family in due time.

I quit school—the student loans just weren't going to be worth it. I waddled around our apartment and scoured every thrift shop I could find to create the perfect space for our babies. Never in a million years did I imagine my life would turn out this way, but I suppose it's the unexpected twists and turns of life that offer up the best surprises.

Most of the time anyway.

I remember the day I sat in a wicker rocking chair, back aching with my growing belly as I watched James work to put together the babies' crib. It was the space they would share as two attached creatures, just as James and I were. I couldn't help but think over and over again how lucky we were as I soaked in the sight of the divot between his brows, concentration and determination in every twist and turn of his screwdriver. He was committed to providing safety for our soon-to-be-met twins, and it amazed me that someone who had such a rough childhood could still find it in him to be a man with integrity. I was grateful to have such a wonderful person to do this with. Not just be the father to our children—though I couldn't have picked a better man if I tried—but to share life in general with.

You would think I would have been nervous in those months of the pregnancy. I was barely twenty in the days leading up to their birth. I should have feared the struggles of being young and broke, raising two unexpected children.

Instead, I felt nothing but giddy excitement at the adventure. I couldn't wait to see what the future held for us, me as Mrs. Lori Blake, and James as the loving and doting father. Something neither one of us knew a thing about.

"They're asleep," I whispered one evening, and James and I grinned at each other in victory. Our babies were here, though it felt like they'd been with us the whole time. At seven months old, we were beginning to see tiny glimpses of their budding personalities. JJ was the adventurous one, Reggie was more cautious. James and I smiled with relief at the two sleeping cuties, each of us patting the fuzzy sleep sacks enveloping our little miracles.

"Shh, don't jinx it," James said with a finger to his lips. His eyes glanced above the babies' crib, and I followed his gaze to the swirl of letters I had painted above, a poem James had written.

Wander in fairy lands before the promise of dawn
Let my wings fly. Your courage, our march along
Twinkle bright as tiny stars, create dreams bespoke
For only in the wake of glittering repose, can we be made awoke

I always felt such comfort in James's words. I needed them, as I had a surprisingly rough start to motherhood. James proved to be my life raft.

In the early weeks with Reggie and JJ, James and I knew nothing but exhaustion, and we were navigating the cranky tempers brought on by new parenthood, experiencing more fights than we'd had in the entirety of our relationship. The first time I threw a nearby object at his head, a coaster—If I correctly recall—before collapsing on the floor in a fit of delirious tears, we knew something wasn't right. And in my postpartum torment, I caused my amazing James suffering.

One evening was particularly bad.

It should have been a quiet and easy night. The babies had been sleeping in their two mismatched swings, the quiet swoosh of the motors nearly inaudible beneath my shouting. James had made some benign comment, asking if I had done some chore or another, no animosity in his tone whatsoever. Yet all I heard was whispers of *you're not doing enough, not good enough for this,* and I had hurled a rattle at him. He snatched it just before it made contact with his head.

The next moments happened as if in slow motion. Him snatching the rattle. Face twisted in contorted lines. Slamming the counter beside him. The counter falling short of fulfilling his fury of fiery needs. Him turning, two steps to the nearest wall, fist meeting drywall in three solid punches, still with the rattle in hand. White revealing black in the hole left behind, and the spill of the beads within the rattle cascading down as if fleeing the fury.

"God *damn it*, Lori!" he had shouted.

We both stopped then. Just stared at each other, stunned.

You see, while I might have been known to have an anger episode that involved an object or two, James certainly did not. He was the calm one. Always. Until now.

I saw the instant regret on his face, saw him glance down at his still-clenched fist before jerking it open, then storming out the front door, leaving me. I heard the rumble of our car turning on, heard the rev of the engine outside of our apartment building, and I rose up in a rush to the window to see him drive away.

When he returned an hour or so later, I could tell he had been crying, and it broke my heart. The babies were awake by then, and I was on the floor with Reggie on the blanket in front of me, and JJ was at my breast. James crouched down to join us, picking up Reggie, and we laced our fingers together and leaned side by side back against the couch.

We sat in silence, and the only sounds accompanying us were the suckling of JJ and the intermittent coos of Reggie. My feelings were numb at that point, but the love of my family was never far, despite the daze I was in.

After a while like this, James finally spoke. "I never want to be my father," he said softly.

Guilt washed over me, and I squeezed his hand, raising the joint bundle to my lips, kissing his knuckles. "You could never be." I wished there were better words to convey how much I meant that. I could feel the torment in his body at having lost his temper, even though I had lost mine countless times before. It killed me to see him hate himself like that. I wanted so badly to stop his hurt, to be able to control myself better, but the whirlwind of emotions in those first breaths of motherhood were an unstoppable blanket of lava.

I felt shame and a loneliness I hadn't expected. I had everything I could have wanted, and yet I longed to sleep, and not because of middle-of-the-night feedings. This sleep was a tomb with a spell that was calling out to me, luring me in with the promise of darkness, and I felt hopeless in the loss of my way. I had become a brittle shell of my former self. Postpartum depression wasn't something you heard much about back then, and I hated what I was doing to my family. It's a strange thing to feel a love that runs oceans deep, yet you're at the water's edge, completely unable to dive into its sweet abyss. I was trapped on shore beneath the suffocation of sand, threaded with shrouds of unworthiness.

Along with this mental torture was the pressure to successfully breastfeed not one, but two infants—not just because formula was a luxury, but because we wanted to give the best nourishment for Reggie and JJ. My nipples were cracked and bleeding, and I'd lay with a blank stare, zombielike in a nest of pillows on our marital bed while James tenderly draped warm washcloths on my chest. These babies felt like leeches, and my husband was the savior sent on a most unfair assignment. I was in a daze, resentful to these foreigners wreaking havoc on the previous bliss of love that James and I had.

There were days I even wondered if I should be their mother at all, or if it was all some divine mistake.

But the rattle instance aside, James was there to carry us through. When our fights reached a peak and my anger would explode into a torrent of tears absorbed by the rough carpet of our apartment floors, James would soften. His own fuel from whatever stupid squabble we had been in would quickly evaporate, and I'd feel his hand on my back whispering soothing lines of one poem or another, knowing they unlocked my calm. Those first months felt like hell, but we survived them.

In time, as days and nights found their distinction within my existence once again, I felt my motherhood role slip over my skin like a silky robe, finally. The relief I felt once that cloud had lifted was like the first breaths of fresh air after being without oxygen. We were finding our rhythm as parents. James had carried me when I thought I'd never see light again. He marched us through our darkness until we found our dawn.

As JJ and Reggie got older and took their first wobbly steps, chubby hands grabbing hold with tentativeness to anything within reach, I felt the real glimmers of the future within our own reach. James graduated early and landed a banking position at a company with plenty of opportunity to grow. As a father and husband, he was committed to working hard and giving us everything he had promised, but he never failed to come home with a smile. I'd steal glances at the clock all day, willing the hours to pass to when he'd return to us. It felt like a gift every time he'd walk through the door, and I'd watch as he'd throw JJ and Reggie in the air, their giggles and squeals a sound that to me equated pure fairytale bliss. Then he would pull me to his chest for an embrace, his fingers running through my hair in a gentle scalp massage, thanking me for my own hard day at work taking care of our little love babies.

We were young. We were scraping by. But we had everything.

AND THEN ONE DAY, THREE years later, thieves of fate came into our world and dismantled all of it. My entire life as I knew it. The existence I loved and thrived off of—gone in the cruel joke of life.

It was a wintry December evening, shortly after we had finally bought our darling starter home, and I couldn't wait to decorate it for the holidays. The air had the sharp crispness that promised future snow angels and the iridescent hue of a wintry landscape, but the sun still shone low in the sky. We had been Christmas shopping, and afterward had treated our little family to an early dinner out.

My heart was the fullest it had ever been on that car ride home. I had been admiring my husband as he whisked us up and down the hills of the back roads, three-year-old Reggie and JJ squealing with their belly tickles.

An ice patch in the road. So simple. That's all it took to snatch away the very life I knew and loved.

James was dead, and he brought the final breaths of our baby boy into the afterlife with him.

I always thought about that. I wondered if James needed JJ there by his side, or if James died *for* our sweet boy, because in some transcendent way James understood our son would be gone. That James knew his fate and couldn't stand the idea of our boy up there in the heavens lost and all alone, with no grandparent or aunt or neighboring friend to welcome him, and so James decided he would ensure JJ would have his father.

Was that possible? Is that why James left me here to be a prisoner on Earth with our Reggie, an innocent baby girl now banished to care from a broken-hearted mother? Maybe that was it. James left us in a moment of sacrifice.

And I wondered and dreamed if my two loves were walking together out there in the great unknown, golden halo surrounding them with hand in fragile hand through fields of wildflowers, perhaps. Laughing in painless bliss. James keeping watch on our baby boy for us.

Waiting for the day his other half joins him.

lace

. . .

Dear Dog Tags,

An abused dog will stay with its owner so long as there is food. The dog believes, even through its suffering. It is torn down to skin and bones, yet will still eat the meager sustenance provided by its abuser, its desperation for survival taking over.

It saddens me to admit this, but for a long time I felt true hatred toward the citizens of my country that followed along quietly as oppression raged through our beloved lands and stole the very essence of one's rights of humanity. How could they stand by such cruelty? But in time I realized they are like the abused dog.

My country was weak when those abusive forces took over, and wanted something to believe in. When a commanding presence appears with promises to lead to a better future with prosperity, and when that leader uses fear as a tactic to cease questioning, then people will listen, won't they? What choice do they have?

Or so one may believe they have no choice. Not all can be strong, and for that I am grateful to have been born with courage—a *manic obsession—as it often need to be, to dream of more for myself and the suffering surrounding me.*

While I can never forgive the monsters that thrived off their power that killed so many, today I choose to forgive the silent bystanders. In the wake of this war, that is what I am trying to learn. You have taught me that, my love.

In fact, without your inspiring guidance, I fear I too would have lost the shreds of hope that kept me moving forward. I now pray with compassion in my heart for those that have fallen into the arms of abuse, blind hope in the fantasy of what could be. May they awaken in time, for then their journey of healing can begin.

And may you and I be one day united again. How or when, I can't be sure. But I can hope.

With love,
Lace

twenty

. . .

edie

HER GRIN STRETCHES across her face, and Edie untucks the hair from behind her ears to hide that grin from her present company, Lori and Reggie. A quick glance shows the two distracted in their inventory of a stack of cardboard boxes all labeled "Richard." Edie's thankful for the low lighting of the basement storage area and turns her body slightly to look down to read Trenton's latest text—a string of thoughts of all the things he was apparently dreaming about doing to her body. She flushes in anticipation for another one of their "dates" later tonight, and she types back her response.

> E: I'll wear something scandalous under your beloved overalls. Teach you all about the fun things birth control allows me to do.

Pleased with herself, she hits "send." The text is a jab after their most recent argument on women's health and reproductive rights, something Edie thoroughly enjoys engaging in when she can point out Trenton's own hypocrisy in his stance on "letting nature do its thing."

"If you believe that, then what about condoms? Birth control? Vitamins, for that matter—where do you draw the line?" she had asked. At the time, she had been standing completely in the nude in her bathroom under the blaring lights of her vanity. The small space showcased an almond-colored fiberglass tub and shower, an ancient vanity, and peeling linoleum flooring—all far from the modern shine of Trenton's place. She was getting ready to brush her teeth, throw on some sweats and kick Trenton out for the night, as her mind was occupied with all the things she wanted to accomplish the next day. There was the paper she needed to finish, final assignments to turn in, as it was April and nearing the end of the semester. A lead regarding the letters had her intrigued as well, and she wanted to follow up. Someone had reached out claiming to have letters written *to* Lace from Dog Tags, and she needed to do some investigating on who this person was and their credibility.

But she couldn't let Trenton's comment slide without calling him out on his own benefits of the wonders of modern medicine within their very relationship, or whatever it was they were doing.

He came up behind her wearing only his jeans, and Edie admired his sculpted bare chest before locking eyes with him in the mirror. She watched as his eyes moved down the reflection in clear appreciation of her naked body. Normally, post-sex she would have covered up by now in self-consciousness, but Trenton had a way of making her feel like her body was something to be worshiped.

With a wicked grin, he snaked his arm around her waist, twisted her around to face him and he pulled her into his chest, whispering, "I'll show you where I draw the line." She felt the ridge of the vanity counter press into her ass as he proceeded to slowly drag a finger along the back of her neck, down her spine, then around the arch of her hipbone to her front. She laughed and flinched at the ticklish spot provoked, but he continued in slow movements, stopping just before her slit.

"I like the line from here to here," he said as he made his way up to her breast, his mouth now trailing behind his finger in warm kisses that threatened to make her lose her focus.

"That's awfully selfish of you," she breathed out. "It's my body, those aren't lines for you to draw." Was she talking about women's rights anymore? "You shouldn't have a say," she whispered, throwing her head back as Trenton continued painting "lines" all over her skin with the teasing touch of his hands and the warmth of his tongue. She slipped her hands through his hair, loving the soft pop each gentle suck of his mouth made on her body.

"Fine then," he said as he removed his mouth from her and rose to a stand. His eyes darkened as they looked back into hers. "I have no say." Edie opened her mouth to respond, but then saw the tension in his jaw. "None at all." She expected him to continue, but he remained still.

"Alright then," she responded and started to turn back around to resume her nightly routine, but his hand on her hip stopped her. She looked down at it, as if she needed confirmation of its existence despite the blanketing warmth of his palm. "Yes? You have more to say?"

"Edna," he whispered as he placed his other hand on her back, and he pulled her into a hug that felt far more tender than the playfulness from moments ago. Her body stiffened as he held her to him.

"So very serious, Wroe. What's on your mind?" she asked, her head pressed against the smooth skin of his chest, her gaze focused on the purple towel hanging on the plastic rack beside them.

His voice was quiet. Strained. "I want you to know I'm not an asshole. Okay?"

Edie couldn't see his face, but she could hear the vulnerability in his tone. She gulped and let out a light laugh. "Sure you are. It's what makes you so fun to do all this naked rolling around with."

She was uncomfortable with his switch in attitude. And intention—she had been loving the soft touches of him drawing on her body.

"I'm serious," she heard him say above her, but her eyes remained fixated on the grooves of the lilac terrycloth. "I care about you. A lot, and I...I don't like the idea of you thinking I'm some heartless prick that doesn't..." his voice trailed off before completing the thought.

"Oh, no shame in being a prick. Especially when I like this one a whole lot," she teased with a stroke on his jeans, down his shaft before pushing her palms against his chest to disentangle herself from his grasp. He slowly withdrew his arms with reluctance, a look of confusion and something else etched on his face. "Now go take that and your ass home so I can get some beauty rest."

Edie scurried between Trenton and the doorway, grabbing the hoodie that was draped over an armchair and slipping it over her head. She pulled her arms through as quickly as she could, then grabbed a pair of underwear from her dresser drawer, rushing to balance herself as she stepped in and shifted them up her legs.

She glanced over to her bathroom to find Trenton's hands on her vanity, his torso leaning over slightly, his head hanging down, muttering what she thought might be, "I like you," but it was too soft to be sure.

Edie blinks away the memory and image from her mind, taking a deep breath in, inhaling the mustiness of the old memories and locked-away dreams surrounding her. She looks down at the phone still in her hand and sees Trenton's response.

> T: You teach me a lot of things, you know.

> T: I'm serious about that. I like it. All of it. I like
> you, Edna Mackenzie.

Edie shudders her shoulders a little, not used to hearing—or seeing, rather—someone call her by her full name. Saying they like her.

"You cold, honey?" she hears Lori ask, the sound muffled by the faux Christmas tree between them.

Edie shakes her head and keeps her eyes glued to the phone, saying, "I'm fine, just got a chill."

"It feels damp in here, doesn't it?" she hears Reggie say, but Edie is fixated on coming up with the right response to Trenton's text.

> E: Mr. Wroe, I'm very smart, you know. You could learn a whole lot from me.

She bites her lip in debate for what else to add before finally landing on something.

> E: My classes are hosted 9pm to midnight, in bed. Nudity strongly recommended.

She hits send and waits for his response to come in, but it takes a little longer than expected. Just as she's rethinking her phrasing, her phone vibrates, and she smiles.

> T: Can I get a preview photo, please? I'm anxious and like to be prepared.

> E: Surprises are more fun.

> E: But for real, I'm at Reggie and Lori's and can't right now.

> T: Right now?? You're looking through your dad's things while standing there texting me dirty things? Naughty girl.

With a smile and another glance to confirm that Lori and Reggie aren't watching, Edie squeezes her arms together to enhance her cleavage, quickly snapping a photo. She looks down and laughs to herself at the dark and blurry image before sending it.

T: Okay, I think those are your tits. Sign me up
for hot teacher class time and again. I'm
addicted.

T: See you tonight.

With a relieved grin, Edie pushes her glasses back on her face and places her phone in her pocket. She looks up to find Reggie and Lori no longer behind the faux tree, but now here and watching her.

"Someone looks happy," Lori notes as she drops to the floor to the box in front in her, slicing through tape with the stretched-out leg of a pair of scissors. A plume of dust rises as she lifts the flaps, and Lori coughs.

Edie walks over to the new treasure. "I'm just happy to be here resurrecting the only way I can get to know a man I'll never know, that's all."

Reggie scoffs. "Oh, there's more to that particular kind of smile, Edie. Come on now, who's the guy? Or girl," she adds as she drops down to the floor and curls her legs up to her chest. She rests her forearms on her knees like she has zero intention of moving until she hears what Edie has to confess, and she leans her head back on the exposed two-by-four framing behind her. "We all know the look of being smitten. And you, my darling, have that look." Edie laughs in appreciation of Reggie's candidness.

"Caught me."

It's been a fun couple of weeks, meeting Reggie and her kids. There's something to be said about the people that enter your world and feel instantly familiar, like a new song you hear for the first time, but the words and the beat settle into your soul with ease. Edie had met Reggie first over lunch, Lori introducing them and gushing that now she has two daughters. Reggie had scolded her mom for being so aggressively unhinged in her welcome, to not scare Edie away, and Edie had laughed at the backwards dynamic of spirited mother and caregiver daughter. Over salads and sandwiches, Edie had observed their relationship with a kind of soft envy. Reggie and Lori appeared more like equals—friends, even— as opposed to Edie's own relationship with her protective mothers. Even now at twenty-two years old, she barely feels like they see their daughter as a true adult.

Then earlier today here in the main house, Edie finally met Reggie's husband Xavier. At first the man was slightly intimidating to Edie, with his long hair tied back in a messy bun, and thick beard covering his face. He reminded her of Aquaman. It wasn't until Edie observed him on the floor with their two small children that Edie felt more comfortable. Xavier was going back and forth between zooming Hess trucks with their son, James, and "planting" wooden vegetables in a toy garden box with their daughter, Ronnie. Edie felt a tug at her chest to see the fatherly interaction displayed before her.

"Hey, um…" Edie says, looking at Reggie, "how old is Xavier?

Reggie laughs. "He's forty-five to my thirty-three."

"He's actually closer in age to me than Reggie," Lori chimes in.

"Oh yes, mom. You could have been a real Mrs. Robinson in another life." Reggie looks over to Edie and rolls her eyes, but she's smiling. "So?" Reggie asks, emerald eyes staring up to Edie with playful curiosity. "Care to share?"

"Share what?"

"About your person you were very clearly enjoying talking to?"

"Oh. It's a guy," Edie confirms. "His name is Trenton—"

"I love that name," Lori says, and Reggie shushes her.

"It's a perfect name for a snobby corporate lawyer who happens to be doing a little pro bono work for the non-profit I work for."

"Can't be so snobby if he's doing that," Lori offers.

"It's not exactly his choice, so don't go giving him too much credit." Edie crouches down to look inside the box Lori is rustling through. She's torn between wanting someone to talk to about Trenton and being unsure how much to share with women she's only just recently met. How do you navigate a new family that's not *really* your family, but have made it clear she's been accepted as a member, nonetheless? Especially when there's a bond between them that feels so right?

"So, are you dating this Trenton guy or just working with him, with after-hours weekend texts because you're both terribly committed to the job?" Reggie asks with a sly smile.

"We are…having fun." Edie's unsure how to describe the "fun" that is mostly just sex, and overall unchartered waters for her in the situation-ship status as a whole. "Not quite dating, there's zero future there. He's polar opposite on the values scale to me, so I have no interest in anything serious. But we're having fun."

"Good for you," Reggie nods like she understands exactly what Edie means. "Use protection, of course."

"Oh yes, we always do," Edie says with a blush. *Is this what having a sister is like?*

"But explore and enjoy. Take it day by day without over-thinking it."

Lori pulls out a few old articles of clothing, t-shirts with band names and a crumpled cream-colored suit jacket. She lifts one to her nose and inhales before frowning and pulling it away, discarding it to the side with disappointment. "Don't close off your heart, though, if you feel a connection to Trenton. Sometimes we never know what the heart really needs until we're introduced to it."

"I'll keep that in mind."

"Your father was that for me, you know. At a dark time in my life." Lori has a dazed look on her face as she says this, and Edie's interest is piqued. Lori tends to keep things at surface level, Edie has learned, but then she remembers her first meeting with Lori and the surprising mention of the car accident. It's as if she sprinkles in things when she happens to have forgotten to close the window of her inner thoughts.

"Because of your loss, you mean?" Edie looks over to see Reggie, who is looking down at the ground, quiet.

Lori looks directly at Edie. "Yes. Because of my losses. Plural."

"R-right," Edie stammers.

Reggie meets Edie's eyes, a gentleness evident. "Your dad was full of surprises, as you well know," she adds with a half smile. "I always remember him doting on my mom, though I felt more like a little fan in the stadiums, watching their love."

"I know the feeling," Edie says, thinking of her own moms.

"Yeah, well...he pulled my mom out of a deep depression. That's what I think my mom is trying to say. I don't remember that time well, I was only five or so, but I remember feeling like my mom had come to life, in a way. The first time I met your dad, my mom was actually laughing. That, I remember very clearly."

"You do?" Lori asks.

Reggie nods. "I do, yes."

"And I hadn't laughed before?"

"Mom, of course you laughed. But I mean my kid brain just has this image of watching you lean into him. And me thinking he was a giant," she adds with a laugh.

"Wish I got that height," Edie mumbles in reference to her five-foot-three frame that is one of the only significant traits from her mother.

"You're perfect," Lori and Reggie say in unison, and all three of them dart eyes between one another before laughing. It's a welcome moment that breaks up some of the tension that Edie feels she's standing on the outside of, trying to understand. There's a frustration in feeling the whole world is making grave efforts to keep things from you, and you can't get anyone to say a damn thing of real substance.

Lori hands Edie a leather album, and Edie receives it like a gem to be handled with care. She opens the cover and finds pages of faded photos of a young Richard in his teens or twenties. It's clear it's him based on the pale blond hair and sheer size—he was apparently well over six feet—and Lori often refers to him as her "mountain of a man."

Edie flips through with fascination at the young life of the father she always longed to know. There's Richard at the beach, or on a hike with a sweeping valley view behind him, another photo of him perched on the roof of a copper-colored car, feet resting in the open window and his forearm on his knee. There's one with a group of friends, Richard laughing with his arms around a girl that's definitely not Edie's mother, but has a similar brown hair, small and feminine features and overall look of amused annoyance. In every photo, Richard has a commanding presence and seems to fill the space not just in size, but in confident body language and easy smile. Edie looks at the photos and can see her father come to life in each one. She can see the way he would have moved to raise that hand to his hip or perch his elbow on that tree beside him. The sepia tinge over each colored photo offers an almost eerie feel, and a wave of goosebumps passes over Edie's arms. She swears she hears a whisper of a man's voice saying, "I was there and everywhere," and she shuts the album with a thump as a swell of emotion rises in her chest.

"Not everywhere," she mutters under her breath. She looks up to find Reggie watching her curiously, and Reggie rises and wraps an arm around Edie's waist in a small side hug.

"You alright?" Edie's bizarre variety of a stepsister asks. "It must be strange to finally be able to see all this."

Edie nods and wipes at her eyes, surprised at her emotion. "I didn't think it would be so hard. I think I was solely focused on knowing something, *anything* about him. These photos make it more real, I guess. He was a real person, not just a theory."

Lori places the clothing back in the box and rises to join them, embracing Edie from the other side in a shoulder squeeze. "Your father was as real as they come, a wonderfully intense force that instantly dominated any room. I loved that about him," she says, her last words almost dreamlike. "But we're here for you, sweetie. And what I lack in memorabilia, I can at least make up for in stories." Lori swivels her head, scanning around the basement.

"Looks like most of these boxes are just the clothes I had packed up years ago. I should probably free up Reggie's basement and donate them."

"Add it to the to-do list," Reggie jokes.

"I'm sorry there aren't more albums and whatnot. His ex-wife might have more. We could always try to reach out to her," Lori offers.

Edie shakes her head. "No, my half-siblings can find me if they want. This is enough for now." She inhales a deep breath and smiles. "More than enough, really."

"You know, I think I needed this," Lori muses quietly. "A little glimmer of light in the wake of darkness after Richard."

A stillness settles among the three women. The hum of the heater rumbles softly in the air, and they can hear the muffled squeals of laughter of James and Ronnie in the family room above them, Xavier's deep voice bumbling indiscernibly in between the youthful bellows.

"There's more to your story with Richard than just love after loss," Edie quietly says. "Isn't there?" She glances back and forth between the two women—Reggie with her strawberry blonde hair in thick waves, her mother Lori with nearly matching reddish hair and green eyes, only both darker.

"Yes," Reggie eventually says, and Lori clears her throat loudly. Reggie crosses her arms over her chest and snaps her head toward her mother, emphasizing, "Yes, Mom. Edie deserves to know all she can."

"I agree, Raina Georgia, but maybe think about your words wisely." Lori wipes her hands on her jeans and Edie can sense her nervous energy.

"Of course, I will," Reggie annunciates each word before whipping her head back to Edie. "Edie, what I mean is, your dad could be very extreme. Either crazy happy and the life of the party, or very—"

"Intense, and I was great at helping him keep that at bay," Lori interrupts. "We'll leave it at that for today." She turns her body and starts busying herself with tidying up the disarray of opened boxes.

A heaviness sits in Edie's chest, as she has the sinking feeling that "intense" is a kind word for something much worse. There's something about the photos of Richard that feels chilling, in a way. Not just in their age, or their representation of a man long gone. It's another layer she feels, an intrinsic warning deep in her belly of a man she wonders if she was better off not having in her life after all.

It dawns on Edie like a crash. An image of Richard hovering above her mom in anger flashes before her eyes. Is it a memory? A true recollection, or merely a phantom vision? A swirl of images float in her mind of the man in those pictures, a man that could be laughing one minute, but then a shift in the wind would happen. Sunshine evaporating and replaced by an impending storm. She sees it in her mind as if happening in real time.

Edie braves stating the realization that has just pressed its weight onto her shoulders. "He was...he was violent, wasn't he." She does not lift the statement at the end. This is not a question. The unblinking eyes in front of her confirm her suspicions.

It's a fact.

***

"THOSE MOMENTS WEREN'T THE REAL Richard," Lori blurts out in a rush.

Those moments. So Edie's right. Her father was a violent man.

"No, of course not," Reggie says. "Not the whole of Richard, at the very least. He was a good man, I do believe that. I mean he was good to me, and I wasn't even his kid." Reggie nods as if the gesture has the ability to lock in the statement. "He just had his demons. They came out now and then." She shrugs and grabs Edie's hand for a squeeze. "We all have them. But I didn't even know about Richard's abuse toward my mom until a couple years ago, until—"

"You know I really hate that word, 'abuse,'" Lori interrupts, her back to Edie and Reggie as she yanks at a strip of tape to close the previously opened boxes. Edie jolts at the sound of the tape separating from its spool. "Our marriage was not some statistical category to be defined by a couple bad fights. Fights I often helped provoke."

"*Mom*," Reggie says with warning. "That's not what I'm saying." Edie watches Reggie as she seems to consider saying more to her mother, but she opts instead to turn toward Edie. "Look, Edie. I hate not knowing things. There was a lot kept from me through all that, and you strike me as someone inquisitive like me."

"I am," Edie confirms, thankful for having Reggie here to be a voice of reason and truth in a world hell-bent on keeping alive the Truman Show. "I like answers. And I'm so sick of the dance of deception."

Reggie scoffs. "Girl, I know just what you mean. There's power in facing truths head on, right?"

"Absolutely," Edie agrees. She glances over at Lori, her back rigid but remaining silent.

"I wouldn't bullshit you, okay? I'd tell you if I thought he was some monster. He wasn't. Your dad was good to me. Distant, not entirely present. He traveled a lot," she explains. "But kind." She shrugs. "Lots of men have done a lot worse to the daughters of their new wives, know what I'm saying?"

"I hate that I know what you're saying," Edie responds, and at the frightened look on Reggie's face, now Edie feels it's her turn to give a half hug of comfort. "Not like that, not directly, I mean. But yeah. And I'm just glad he was good to you."

"He was."

"Very kind to her," Lori cries out from afar.

"Okay, Mom. Kind of a thin line we're walking between bragging about Richard, the temper-laden jerk, the stepfather who doted on me, and the biological father who wasn't there for our girl, here," she says, her eyebrows raised to accentuate her point. Edie finds herself smiling in gratitude for the succinct way Reggie can spit out some much-needed bottom lines. If only everyone in the world could be so upfront and honest.

Edie stifles a giggle, laughter threatening to bubble up.

"What?" Reggie asks, matching Edie's smile.

Edie shakes her head. "It's so funny, you know? Here I've spent my whole life wishing I had him, and you two did, but it wasn't all roses, was it?"

"Nothing ever is," Reggie says with a tilt of her head to the side.

"I think I'm just more thankful than anything to have found you two, which I know might sound strange, but it's true." With a shoulder lift she adds, "Makes me think I moved up here for a reason."

"Agreed. Just curious, why *did* you choose this area, what was the draw?" Reggie asks.

"Wanting to be close to so many cities, Philly and New York and DC and Baltimore. Although, I'm thinking that maybe it was to meet you two."

Did she sound crazy to say so? Edie's not sure, but her worries are quickly assuaged when Lori turns to rejoin them, and Reggie and Lori murmur that they agree in the swings of fate, that you just never know the mysterious reasons for something, and that on another day, Reggie would blow Edie's mind with an even crazier story of the whims of fate.

In fact, the two ladies standing here now by Edie's side confirm to her that they absolutely feel Edie is in this ghost-riddled basement of the home formerly belonging to her father, right here and now, for a reason. One she hopes she discovers soon, if she hasn't already.

twenty-one

. . .

lori

twenty-five years old

TO SAY I was barely functioning after the accident would have been putting it mildly. My bed was my sanctuary, and most days I stayed in it for as long as possible. Reggie would wander in and out to bring me water or frozen waffles, or her favorite blankie. She'd crawl up in bed next to me in the small house James and I had just bought, and Reggie would turn on the TV and watch cartoons most of the day or drag books into my bed to flip through. I'd listen to her sweet little toddler voice babbling on and making up the story to match the illustrations, or she'd recite the ones from the books she had memorized. I wanted to be better for her, I really did. She deserved a mother that could make her daughter a damn waffle, for Christ's sake.

But I was completely numb.

Eventually, my mother had to move in with me and Reggie, which was the last thing I ever wanted to have happen. James and I had been relocated to PA by his job at the bank shortly before his passing. I loved our darling starter home we had just purchased, and there was no way in hell I was leaving it. It was as if by us staying there, maybe I could one day wake up and hear James walk through the door once again, with JJ on his hip and promises that it had all been a tragic nightmare.

Of course, that wasn't the case. I had no real friends in the area, no help that I could trust. The idea of selling the home James and I had dreamed of for so long was out of the question. So my mom moved in, and I felt a strange shame, like I had proved her right after all these years of my fight for my love for James.

A FEW MONTHS AFTER THE accident, I had reluctantly gotten a job as a bartender. I was miserable with the way my life had turned upside down, all my original hopes and dreams vanished away right along with my boys. But it was necessary; I needed the money. I went through the motions of all of it as if partially detached. I was there in the flesh, but not really awake.

Then came the day that Richard Meyers walked in during one of my shifts, and he changed everything. He was handsome in a pale gray suit, and he slid his arms forward on the bar to lean closer to me. His broad smile and ice-blue eyes melted me into an instantaneous puddle. Some spark of life started to stir within me as I allowed his easy charm to whisk me up and away. He provided the lifeline to pull me out of the prison of my grief, and he floated me onto a cloud of a new dream come true.

Richard was older than me by eighteen years, and at twenty-five, that age gap felt pretty significant. But, my gosh, Richard was a silver fox. That's what I called him, my silver fox, and he called me his little lady, his angel.

He worked in insurance and was very successful. He made friends easily and had all the best connections. You wanted tickets to see the Eagles play Dallas? Done. The hot new Philly restaurant everyone's talking about, but no one can get into? We'd be there in style. He'd get these impulsive ideas to jet to some island somewhere, as he was always looking for the next exciting thing, and his energy was an atmosphere-breaking rocket that was exactly what I needed. The only force capable of yanking me out of my debilitating grief. I jumped on full steam ahead, and Reggie and I moved in with him in his massive house, leaving my mom to live in the house that James and I had bought. After Richard, I hardly ever went to visit her. Before, I clung to that house like it was my escape —the place I could pretend I was still in my happily ever after with James—after Richard, I visited only out of necessity.

thirty-four years old

AS THE YEARS OF OUR marriage carried on, my addiction to Richard had become my everything. By the time we were nearing a decade together, I felt like he was my only form of oxygen.

"Close your eyes," he said to me one day while standing in our bathroom. I was in a lacy white nightgown, a perfect contrast to the dark wood and black granite of the space around us, and I could see my nipples peeking through the sheer fabric. I knew Richard went crazy for me when he saw me in it. I smiled and obliged and could smell his crisp cologne behind me as he placed his hands over my eyes and pulled me into his chest. "I'm sorry about yesterday," he whispered, and the flash of him slamming me against the wall, his massive hands squeezing my shoulders in rage invaded my skull, but I pushed it down.

I could feel his gentle caress on the bruising below my color bone, and I focused on that touch and ignored the throbbing I could still feel pulsing in the back of my head.

"I'm sorry too," I said. "I shouldn't have snapped like that."

"Shh, my angel," he whispered, and his other hand scooped up my hair, the chill of his breath blowing on my skin before he dotted light kisses to my shoulder blades. "My little lady, my beautiful angel." I hummed in appreciation and leaned my head back in the cradle of his arms, felt his hand covering my closed eyes. Nothing existed but the enveloping warmth of him wrapped around me.

I craved Richard's love and his intensity, and would do anything to get it back when he'd withdraw from me. The fight the day before had been my fault, and I knew better than to provoke him. He'd been traveling so much for work recently, and I had the sneaking suspicion that there was someone else he was seeing. But when I'd let my mind obsess over it, I'd lose all control. Men like James didn't exist, and I knew better than to expect more from Richard, my silver fox. I was determined to do better, to be sexier for him, to lose those couple pounds I had allowed to creep on. I could be enough for him—I just had to try harder and watch my mouth, contain my emotions. Be his little angel because that was who he married. That's what he deserved, and I wanted so badly to give that to him.

When his ex-wife left him years before, it had crushed Richard. He was insecure and I'd see glimpses of that now and then within the safe confines of our home. The world saw the captivating and gregarious variety, but I knew the real him. My heart ached when I'd see him in moments of vulnerability, and I felt shame in letting my emotions get the better of me when I did. The times I snapped and lost it on him, slapping him across the face like I had the day before—in those moments I was doing nothing to help him. He needed me to be my charming and sweet self. That's all he ever asked of me, and I could give it to him. Then I'd get the best of Richard, my mountain of a man that had saved me. As much as it scared me when my hurt and anger flared, causing his temper to balloon to epic proportions, it scared me more when he left and took all his energy with him. The silence was always far more threatening to me than any force Richard ever had shown.

At least within the hurricane of his force, I knew he felt just as intensely about me as I felt about him.

He dropped my hair into a cascade down my back, and I could hear him rustling behind me. My belly did a little flutter, knowing he had something for me. I heard him put something down on the counter in front of us, and then I felt his hand guide mine to touch the mystery object. I felt a box below my palm and wondered what kind of surprise he had for me. Jewelry, I suspected, as was often his way.

"You don't need to do that, Richard. You know I don't need anything. Just you," I whispered.

He removed his hand from my eyes and told me to open them, and I fluttered my lashes to adjust to the light after the moments of darkness. I looked down at the box in front of me.

"A phone?" I asked. I already had a cell phone—it was only a few months old. Why was he giving me another?

"This one's a BlackBerry, much nicer." He stepped away from me to take the box and pull out the new device, handing it to me. "With a new number. I already had all your contacts transferred."

My heart sank. I knew what this was about. I already knew that by "all contacts," what he really meant was all but one. My stupid trainer at the gym—he had called me the other day while Richard and I were out to dinner with some of his colleagues and their wives, and I made the mistake of answering. It was only to reschedule, but one of Richard's buddies had cracked a comment about a young and beautiful wife like me being dangerous to allow in the hands of some male trainer. I had seen Richard's eyes narrow, the ice crossing over his easy smile, and I instantly wanted to reverse the previous three minutes.

But he never mentioned it, not yesterday during our fight when I complained about him traveling so much, and not even right in that moment of handing me my new gift. He didn't need to, I knew. I had already canceled my training sessions, knowing my mistake.

"Richard, I—"

"And I got something else for you, too. Another new treadmill for here in the house. I know Reggie said she wants to start running, that's great for a teenage girl. Now you'll have two. My girls can do their workouts here at home together."

I turned around to face him and slipped my arms around his neck, running my hands through his wisps of hair. "That's perfect. Thank you," I said, and he kissed me with an intensity that erased all my fears that he wasn't going to move past this. I hated the idea of hurting him and I knew that his jealousy could eat him alive and crumble his confidence. That's the last thing I wanted for my husband.

I felt his erection pressed against me and the grumble of a moan in his chest. I moved my mouth over to his cheeks, kissing and loving the prickle of stubble against my lips. I kissed his neck, his chest, and began unbuttoning his dress shirt with eagerness.

He grabbed my wrists to stop me, and I looked up to see the dark hunger in his eyes. "Oh no, you little slut. You're not getting off that easy."

My belly flipped, knowing his anger was far from gone. I nodded and stayed mute, desperate for whatever he had in store for me. His fighting anger could be terrifying, but his anger in his love was ecstasy. I focused on the tightness of his grasp on my wrists, and my belly fluttered in anticipation.

His eyes scanned down my body and I could feel my nipples scratch against the lace of my nightgown as they hardened. "God, my little slut's wearing white, but how can that be?" He dropped one hand from my wrists, keeping his hold with the other while he gently rubbed the lightest caress of circles on my nipple over the fabric.

"Richard," I breathed out in a whimper. I needed more of his touch. I needed his roughness, and he knew it. The tease of lace against my skin was torture.

He dropped his hand from my wrist and slapped me across the

face. I resisted the instinct to raise my hand to my cheek, instead closing my eyes and basking in the bloom of the sting and the hardness of Richard's erection pressing into my belly.

"You may not speak," he said, and I nodded eagerly. "Open your mouth," he commanded. I squeezed my eyes shut and relaxed my jaw as he asked. I felt the cool hard rectangle enter my mouth and I clamped down on it. My flip phone, the phone my new one was replacing. I adjusted it with my tongue as best as I could to get a firm hold on it. "Now slip off your nightgown. Sluts don't wear white."

My breath was coming in fast as I reached my hands up and slipped the straps down my tender shoulders, one at a time. I pushed the fabric down from my waist, stretched it over my hips and felt it fall to the floor. I kept my eyes closed as I heard him move away. Saliva was pooling in my mouth, stuffed with the hard device, and I carefully swallowed, shifting my tongue around to readjust once again.

When he returned a moment later, I heard the yank of duct tape as he tore off a piece. "Arms up," he said, and I lifted my arms over my head while he taped my wrists together. "Keep them raised."

I stood there like that, phone in my mouth and more saliva filling with each passing moment, my arms already sensing the tiredness I would soon feel of being held directly above my head like this, bound together with the sticky tape. I heard him unbutton his shirt and could imagine him slipping it off, then the t-shirt underneath. I playfully opened one eye to steal a peek of his glorious chest and shoulders and was rewarded with the lift of the corner of his mouth.

"You just can't resist, can you, little slut?" *Slut.* He stretched out the word and tapped the t at the end like the last eerie note of a song in a minor chord. I slowly shook my head. "You like what you see?" I nodded my head.

He stepped forward and roughly inserted two fingers inside me, and I closed my eyes again and garbled out a moan. "Fucking soaked just from looking at me. Open your eyes, little lady." I opened them and stared at the wall of chest in front of me, the curl of chest hair twisting around as I rocked my hips into his hand, his thumb on my clit, and my insides twisted in knots. I wanted to moan out how good it felt, how good his fingers felt inside me and how I wanted him all inside me. But all I could do is choke back the saliva and my moans, my arms starting to tremble above my head with ache, but I was loving the torture of not being able to touch him.

He got me close to the edge, but I knew better than to expect him to let me come yet. He pulled his fingers out from me, and I looked up to watch him put them in his mouth, the hollow of his cheeks forming as he sucked on the taste of me.

When he removed his fingers, he grabbed both of my nipples, pinching. Hard. He could pinch as hard as he wanted, I wanted all of his strength anywhere on my body. The pain that rippled through was nothing in comparison to the pleasure he would give me. "No one, *no one* tastes as good as you do, little lady. You know that?" I looked into his eyes, dilated, the black now nearly blocking out the startling blue. I nodded. "Sweet," he whispered. "Like a cherry."

He was forgiving me. I could feel it. He couldn't help himself.

"Come, follow me," he said as he walked out of the bathroom and towards our bed. "Leave your arms up."

My arms were tired, but not so tired that I couldn't do as he asked. I followed behind with my arms raised, watching the ripples of his back muscles as he walked. Down by his side he held the duct tape in his hand, and my belly summersaulted in excitement of what was to come. He stopped in front of one of the slender poster columns at the end of the bed, and he reached for my hip to guide me in front of it.

"Close your eyes, just for a moment," he said, and I did. He pressed me back and I felt the hard column behind me, heard the snap of the yank of tape once again. I felt him wrap the tape around my wrists and the wooden pole of the bed frame, relieved at now having assistance in keeping my arms up. He ripped off another piece, and I felt it press against my breasts as he tightly wrapped my torso around the pole. I'd be tortured with no nipple play. No feeling of his mouth on them, sucking at their hardened peaks, no squeeze or pinch anymore.

"Now open your eyes, and see how beautiful you are like this," his gravelly voice instructed. I opened my eyes and looked in the massive mirror hanging on the wall in front of our bed. I took in the sight of me naked and taped to the frame like this, the phone still stuffed in my mouth and drool spilling out the sides. My hair looked wild in its chestnut waves, pieces of which were trapped in the tape around my breasts. It would be hell to take off, but he'd do it gently, I knew. Those were the moments I looked forward to the most, Richard's soothing, gentle tenderness as he'd put me back together after gloriously ripping me apart. In those moments with Richard, there was no pain or grief. There was no loss of a child. Of a first love. Of a life I once knew and a heart that had been left broken. None of it existed in my most tender moments with Richard.

He walked away and I inhaled the scent of him left in the gentle gust of air in his wake. I stared straight ahead into that mirror, wondering what he'd do next. I was completely soaked and starved for the feeling of him inside me. I needed him pressed against me, his cock filling me, the need was so strong it was making me weep. I watched as a tear rolled out from the corner of my eye and felt it roll down my cheek.

I could hear water running from our bathroom, and when Richard returned a moment later, completely naked and cock springing forward from the nest of gray and blond surrounding it, he was holding a small bowl filled with water, and a washcloth. He saw my tear and gently kissed it away before dropping his mouth to my shoulder and biting. I watched through the mirror as he set the bowl down beside me on the bed, and he dipped the washcloth in. With his other hand he returned his fingers inside me, saying the little slut was still so wet, then he dropped to his knees and pressed his mouth against me, the swirl of his tongue on my clit moving in warm strokes. He sucked hard, and I jolted at the feel of his fingers inside me once more, my legs quivering on the brink of an orgasm before he pulled back and returned to a stand.

"Not. Yet," he smiled before gliding his tongue along my lips, still wrapped around the hard metal of phone. I swallowed again and attempted to wipe the drool with my shoulder, but the tape around my torso made it impossible to reach. My lips were quivering with the effort of keeping the phone in my mouth. "Close your eyes," he whispered, and I did.

I heard him move beside me, heard the splash of the water, the drips of the washcloth being pulled out. I felt his knee on my inner thigh as he pushed apart my legs, then jolted at the freezing cold washcloth now between them. He scrubbed with roughness, and I popped my lids open to find him staring into my eyes, his expression stony. I thought he might tell me to close them again, but he didn't. He only watched my expression as the cold of the washcloth scrubbed against me. "I need my angel back. You understand? I need this slut clean so that I can have my angel back," he said, his voice low and almost pained. I nodded and blinked away another tear, wanting so badly to hold his face in my hands and tell him I loved him, and that I was sorry. He could do whatever he needed to me to feel safe again. I could do that for him.

When he was finished scrubbing, he pulled the washcloth away, and I was raw with the cold and the friction of the rough texture. I watched in the mirror as he tossed the washcloth to the side, and it landed on the edge of the bowl, causing the bowl and the water inside to spill out onto our bed.

He yanked my legs up to straddle him and slammed himself into me, pain searing with the movement from my freshly cleaned and completely unlubricated area.

But he was inside me, he was finally inside me. I felt nothing but relief as he pulsed into me, and I grabbed what bit I could hold onto of the pole by my hands, feeling his cock up to my hilt with each and every thrust. I was dizzy with the feel of it and with trying to stay wrapped around him with the upper half of my body having no give, the wood pressed into my spine with a sharpness. My breath was hot and fast, and I felt like I was choking on the metal in my mouth, but my Richard's face was etched with pleasure, his eyebrows raised slightly and his eyes closed, finding his own relief in his possession of me. I made my Richard happy again, and my own pain and discomfort were slowly moving aside to allow for another rise of pleasure.

After several minutes of this, I could feel his cock swell even more inside of me, but he pulled out and gently dropped my legs down. I scanned his face and saw the sweat beads forming on his temples. He removed the phone from my mouth and before I could even readjust my aching jaw, his mouth was on mine, and I tasted myself on it as his tongue invaded me with hunger.

"Richard, I love you," I said when he pulled away from me.

"I know," he said. "My angel, I know." He removed the tape from my wrists as tenderly as he could, then did the same with the tape around my torso, plucking away the strands of hair just as I knew he would. A few stayed with the tape anyway, tiny pricks to my scalp with each one, but I didn't care. "Such a good girl for me, aren't you?" he asked as he pulled me away from the pole. I nodded and pressed my palms to his stomach, then around his waist. He kissed the top of my head and then grabbed my arms from around him to free himself, walking away to the bathroom. I caught a glimpse of his erection stabbing the air, and I smiled, knowing he wasn't done with me yet.

When he returned, he had with him my white nightgown. I raised my arms as he slipped it over my head and draped it down my body. "You'll always be my beautiful angel."

He turned me around and pushed between my shoulder blades

to fold me over the bed. My face landed in the cold wetness from the spilled water, and I felt him lift my nightgown up to my waist. He spread out my legs, then my cheeks and I felt his tongue stroking up and down, eventually making its way around the sensitive rim of my rear.

I whimpered out, "Richard, please," and clenched my hands in the blankets beneath me. "Yes, please. I need you."

"How do you need me, angel?" he asked, rising and pressing his chest against my back, the tip of his cock teasing my clit.

"I need you back inside me, please," I cried out. "I need all of you. As deep as you can go."

When his cock slipped back inside me, slow and gentle this time, I nearly wept with the relief of feeling every inch. He reached his hand underneath my stomach, grabbing the lace fabric of my nightgown and pulling it down to rub against my clit.

"Move, little lady," he instructed. "Move those beautiful hips and feel this on you." He kissed my shoulder. "You've been such a good girl for me. You're all mine."

"Yes," I whispered. "I love being your angel. I'm yours, Richard." Tears streamed down my face as I struggled to move faster against the fabric of my gown, the texture so exquisite.

I could hear him chuckle behind me. "Slow down, little lady. Enjoy this. We deserve this, don't we?" I nodded and clutched at the hand he had beside mine, pulling it down and under me to cover my breast. We moved together in slow and tortured thrusts, his one hand firmly holding the nightgown over my clit, the other rolling my nipple around in his fingers, and the weight of his body on my back.

From deep in my belly, my orgasm started and ripped through me, and I screamed out his name with each wave that rolled. He pinched harder on my nipple and my fists clutched at the blankets. I wanted to freeze this moment. I wanted to ride this wave of pleasure forever and ever. As good as it felt, it almost maddened me to know I could feel this and then have to feel when it ended.

I held onto my orgasm for as long as I could until my knees gave out and I sank completely into the mattress. Richard's cock started to pulse inside of me with his own orgasm. Then he pulled back and out of me and shoved up my nightgown, and I felt the warm liquid of him on top of my ass as he trembled behind me. I loved when he came on me like that. It felt like a gift.

When he had stilled, he reached for my hand and pulled it behind me, stretching my arm so I could feel the liquid on my fingers. He guided me to taking as much as I could, instructing me to close my hand and I held his semen as he rolled me over onto my back.

I stared up at my mountain of a man. "Beautiful," he said. He pushed my nightgown away from my breasts and instructed me to rub myself. I lifted the hand that was holding the sticky liquid and rubbed as best as I could across my chest, bathing myself in him. "Now lick," he said, and I put my fingers in my mouth and tasted him. He had claimed me once again. I was his, and I was forgiven.

When we made love again a while later, he held me afterward and begged me to never leave him. As if I ever could.

In the end of the day, about a year after the cell phone incident, it was Richard who left me the day that his heart stopped working. I always wondered if it was my fault. I worried I had killed him, because loving me was too much for his heart to bear.

twenty-two

. . .

dom

DOM HOLDS THE phone up to his ear as he steps outside to Ruby and Joey's poolside oasis, taking a seat in a lounge chair and stretching out his legs. The elevated space offers sweeping panoramic views of rolling hills and lush greenery of southern California trees, complete with a crystal clear blue sky. As much as Dom hates having his daughter living across the country, he can't deny the tranquility offered here. He keeps his residence in Pennsylvania to offer Ruby some sense of normalcy when she needs to escape the celebrity world, but every time he visits, he can't help but be tempted to move here as well.

Although maybe he has more reasons than ever to stay on the East Coast.

"Edie did it!" Lori cries on the other end of the line. Her voice is as high-pitched as he's ever heard before. She's rambling on in an excited rush about the lead Edie followed up on that proved to be legitimate.

"That's incredible," he responds, loving hearing her enthusiasm. "I thought for sure this was a lost cause."

"No, not lost at all. I just had a feeling she'd figure this thing out." Dom can imagine Lori's eyes shining in her optimism. Ever the believer.

He drags a hand along his jawline, not wanting to break her excitement, but still wanting to be careful before they dive fully in with blind hope. "How does she know these people are legitimate?"

Lori quiets. Whatever fidgeting she had previously been doing comes to a pause. "Oh, well, easy. The dates coincide, and the details do too, apparently."

"Encouraging."

"Yes!" He hears her movement resume and he can imagine her pacing around her small cottage. "They had sent a few photos to Edie, and there's things in there that match up to Lace's letters."

"Photos of the letters?" he confirms, leaning back in his seat and settling himself into the backrest.

"Yep! Can you imagine? The family must be so thrilled to have these answers."

Dom looks up to see his daughter walk out to join him, adjusting her own lounge chair with a book in her hand, her dark curls spilling forward as she takes her seat. He leans closer to her and pulls the phone away from his mouth, whispering, "Edie solved the riddle of the letters."

Ruby's startled look tells him exactly what he'd suspected—she had no real belief in finding answers. She pops up from her seat before ever even fully settling into it, rushing back in through the wide sliding glass doors of the mid-century modern house, leaving him alone once again.

Dom smiles to himself, wondering what she's up to before turning the phone back up to his mouth. "Just be sure to keep Ruby's name out of it. Until we can be one hundred percent certain."

"Yes, yes, of course! I'll send you their info when we hang up. And maybe a little something else," she adds, her tone shifting from excited girl on Christmas morning to seductive temptress.

He clears his throat. "While I'm not going to say I don't want all I can get, just uh...make sure it's not too revealing. You never know who can get their hands on something." Dom had already received several photos from Lori, each progressively more scandalous than the last.

"Oh, I see," Lori purrs. "Is that why I have yet to get something in return? Scared of where it might end up?"

Dom leans forward in his seat and lowers his mouth, aware of the sliding door behind him opening once again. "Something like that." He glances up to see Ruby return with a notebook, and his heart warms knowing that even with all the luxuries his famous daughter now has, she hasn't lost some of her girlhood signature habits, like carrying around a good old-fashioned journal for writing her songs.

"Listen, I have to run. I'll call you soon," he says, wrapping up his conversation with Lori and ending the call.

He leans back in his lounger again. "Feeling inspired?" he asks Ruby. She's already furiously scribbling something down, the thumbnail of her free hand between her teeth in concentration.

"Shh," she says quietly, and Dom waits patiently for her to finish.

When she finally drops her pen, she looks out toward the hills with a satisfied smile and a nod.

"Got something good? I haven't even given you any info yet."

Ruby leans on her side to face him. "The hunt for answers/the quest to soothe the question marks/the hunger to seek/And for what? In my search, I no longer weep/Remember to weep is to be free/and to be free is to leap." She gives a casual shrug. "Not amazing yet, but something."

Dom grins. "I truly have no idea how you do that. Do you hear something with it too? A tune to go along?"

"Not right now, or I wouldn't be out here sitting with you. I'd be at the piano or strapped to my guitar. But most of the time, yeah." She closes her eyes as if trying to capture the process in her mind. "The sound will come and inform the lyrics," she continues, opening her eyes again. "But I find I stretch myself more when I focus on the message before getting caught up in the sound."

"Interesting. Meaning?"

"Think about it. The sound is the razzle dazzle. That's the easy part to cling to because there's such a clear feel that is very tempting and enchanting. But sometimes in doing so, I risk missing a deeper and more meaningful thing."

"Sounds like life," he notes. "Or a bumper sticker."

Ruby nods, laughing. "A little, I guess, yeah. But it's true that you have to challenge yourself to pay better attention to what's beneath the surface and look beyond the initial shimmer. I did that with my nightingale song. I felt the words of that first and zeroed in on it before I let the sound join in. I have no doubt that the sound that came is ten times better for it."

Dom looks at his daughter and her blue eyes that sparkle with a fire he long ago recognized as a passion and determination he'll never quite get used to. His little girl, always so precocious, now a mega music star, but ever the businesswoman as well. Her million-dollar home he's currently staying in is blaring evidence of that.

He smiles at her and asks the question he's been quietly contemplating these past few weeks. "Daughter of mine, did you send me on this letter hunt just to keep me busy?"

"Why, Father!" Ruby gasps with doe eyes and mock hurt. "I would never!"

He shakes his head and returns his gaze out to the view beyond the black iron railing. "I knew it. I'm just fine, you know," he says with a side glance in her direction.

"No, it wasn't all just to keep you busy, though that was an added bonus," she says, smiling briefly before turning serious again. "I just felt like it was a box I hadn't properly sorted through. I wrote the 'Dog Tags & Lace' album as a breakup anthem assortment, imagining that Lace never did get reunited with her Dog Tags, and I left it at that. But now," she says with a smile and head tilt to the side, and Dom can practically see the image of her fiancé Joey floating into her mind. "Now I want to know the rest. See what kind of album I can create around it. Maybe the music will be inspired by the missing half of the letters, or maybe even just seeing them be reunited with the descendants will inspire something. We'll see."

His chest fills with pride. "Can't wait to see what you come up with."

"Me too. Though I have no doubt Jules will be nudging me in some kind of way that can churn up a narrative fans will love," she says through a grin.

They both laugh, knowing the fearless determination Ruby's PR manager has. Jules and her ferocious approach has been a huge part of not only Ruby's success, but also her ability to teeter along a precious line. She's able to remain visible and engaged with her fans, while Jules works to protect Dom's daughter from being carted around to interview after interview, which always runs the risk of words getting twisted and new rumors being concocted from story-thirsty outlets attempting to read between the lines.

In truth, it's part of what made Dom feel attracted to Jules in the first place. Her incredible business sense, and her ability to look out for his one and only daughter. Thankfully, Jules has remained back in the strictly professional zone these past few days in the meetings Dom has attended with Ruby. They hadn't spoken on a personal level since their brief fling ended several months ago, and Dom had been apprehensive about seeing her again. Jules looked great, as always. She's a leggy blonde that seemed to be born in a skirt suit, but Dom was relieved to realize the flame of desire he had for her has simmered down for the most part.

His mind wanders to Lori, to the nurturing and warm woman that she is. Dom recognizes her to be more his speed than he initially thought, though he still feels a hesitation holding him back. Maybe it's his way of not falling for the enchanting sound, like Ruby said. It's better this way, as he had been feeling uneasy with the amount of time he and Lori had been spending together. He recognized that that were diving in hot and heavy over the course of a few short weeks.

This trip now seemed like a good opportunity to slow things down a bit. He hadn't been out to LA since the holidays, and he liked to check in every couple months to lend Ruby support, although recently Dom has felt less inclined to do so as frequently. Ruby has Joey, and Dom knows Joey is a good man that would move mountains to ensure Ruby's well-being. Still, Dom figured he'd use this trip as a chance to grab a little healthy space from the aggressively romantic Lori.

He understands Lori's somewhat histrionic tendencies—she's suffered losses he couldn't even imagine, but Dom couldn't deny the allure he finds in Lori's bubbly and exuberant spirit. However, he also knows, thanks to his ex-wife Pearl, that that level of emotion can have a dark side. Very dark. So dark that Ruby and her mom no longer talk and haven't in years. It's just been Ruby and Dom since the time Ruby was fourteen.

But is Lori different? His gut tells him she is, though he can't be sure. She has a kind spirit, and there's enough mutual people in their lives that would say the exact same thing about her. He tries to focus on that.

Dom also knows that Lori is the type of woman to expect something romantic during this time apart, though that's never been his thing. Maybe he could send a quick photo of him poolside out here, with the gorgeous view in the background. Adding in, "Missing you," in the text. It might not be the most original or sexy, but it's something. He could at least give Lori that.

dog tags

. . .

November 1946 ~ New York

To my beloved Lace,

To receive word from you after all this time is such a relief. Yes, of course, I remember those first moments when I was nearly at my last breaths. I thought you were an apparition, that this was most certainly the end. An angel sent down to whisk me away to the afterlife, and God help me, they sure did send me Aphrodite, didn't they? I would have devoured you if I weren't fighting for each breath. I hope you are laughing now, knowing the scoundrel heart of mine that you have captured.

But you also looked so young and innocent, a frightened little bird. I thought of you as delicate as lace, yes. Not only was I pointing to my chest to show you my identification, but I uttered those words "dog tags" because that's what I thought of myself in the presence of you. Nothing but a dog.

Someone had started using that term in reference to our identification plates, likening our treatment during the war to the treatment of dogs. And here I was with you, just a dirty and battered dog in the presence of grace. The words "dog tags" slipped out, I chuckle now to remember. Yes, I was delirious, my dear Lace. But I would go through that again and again if that's what it takes to be with you.

Of course, you turned out to be quite the opposite of all that innocence I perceived, didn't you? A fierce woman that was going to survive no matter what. People can surprise us, and I'm not one that is easily surprised.

Until we meet again. My love beats on all these miles away, waiting for you.

Love always,
Dog Tags

twenty-three

. . .

edie

"**W**ELL, THAT'S IT, then. The last of our work," Edie says, handing over a file of documents to Trenton with a smile. "It's been a pleasure working with you, much to my surprise."

Louise comes around her own desk to where Edie and Trenton are standing. She embraces Trenton in a hug, and Edie watches with curiosity. "Thank you for all of your help here," she says as she pulls back and grabs his shoulders.

Edie rolls her eyes. "Please, as if he had volunteered out of the kindness of his heart."

She sees the flicker in his eyes as he glances her way momentarily, some thought that passes, though she tries not to read into it. Today is his last day here, and likely the next time they need help, it'll be someone else's turn to step up to the task. Trenton's "good deeds" box is officially checked.

Louise releases him and folds her arms over her chest, looking at Edie with a glare. "When did you get so sassy? He saved us from mishaps that would have surely disqualified us from this grant. You should be thanking the man."

Trenton slips into his coat and lifts the corners of his mouth in his easy smile, and Edie looks away. "It's alright, Mrs. Sako. Edna's right, I wasn't the most pleasant to work with at first."

"For the love of God, call me Louise," she says, unwinding her arms to playfully swat his shoulder. "I'm not my mother-in-law."

"Maybe you should have kept your maiden name," Edie chimes in.

"Have you eaten?" Louise asks, snapping her head to Edie. "Awfully cranky again."

Edie laughs. "You blame every little thing on someone being hungry."

"So let me take you out," Trenton offers. "A last lunch, to thank you for not making my job harder for me." He turns to Louise. "Can you spare your gal for an hour, Louise?"

The smile that slowly creeps across her boss's face has Edie inwardly groaning. Of course, she's going to kick her out and have her do this lunch. Other than the first lunch out and the one dinner date they've had, Edie and Trenton haven't been out on any other occasion, choosing solely to meet at one another's apartments instead. Edie insisted on it. One horrifying time, Trenton had asked her to come to a friend's house for a Phillies viewing party, some big baseball opener or something that, for one—Edie had zero interest in, and two—felt entirely too intimate. A risk to the very firm boundaries Edie had established. He had looked hurt when she balked at the offer, but to his credit, he quickly backed off.

Her moms knew she was seeing someone, and Edie kept it all very light when mentioning Trenton, making sure they understood that he was a corporate lawyer, which naturally they both hated. They gave much of the same advice that Reggie had, to use protection, although they added in the warning of being careful and not falling for him. Edie laughed and assured them he was the last person she'd have in her sights for anything serious.

And then Zeke came up in conversation. "He misses you, you know," her mom Erica had said.

"You're talking to him?!"

"Relax, it's not like we invited the kid over for dinner. We ran into him at the store, that's all. He looked handsome. Like he's found his groove, maybe."

Edie could hear her other mom, Jessica, in the background, shouting, "He was wearing a backwards baseball cap! Said he was coaching Little League for his nephew!"

Both moms had giggled. "I didn't know he played baseball once upon a time."

"He didn't, Mama," Edie muttered. "They must have been short on coaches or something."

The interaction had bothered her for some reason. She had hung up the phone feeling confused.

In fact, she had to admit, the idea of Zeke out in the field with a bunch of seven-year-olds *was* rather appealing. Does she miss him? Yes, Edie can say with honesty that she does. Zeke is kind and good, and things were always very comfortable and friendly with him. They want the same things out of life.

The tall drink of water standing before her now by the name of Trenton Wroe most certainly does not. He told her that, during that very first work lunch. "No kids, no marriage, not for me." Case dismissed.

"Hello, Earth to Edie Mackenzie!" Louise says as she waves a hand in front of Edie's face.

"Sorry, I spaced out for a minute." Edie glances up at Trenton to find him staring at her, a hopeful look clear on his face.

"I said you're done for the day. Go enjoy your lunch, I'll see you tomorrow." She turns her head to wink at Edie before giving her a literal shove toward the door.

"Well, then. Looks like I get you all to myself," Trenton murmurs, and the look in his eyes he's giving her goes straight to Edie's core. She silently curses her betraying hormones. He leans against the door and pulls his coat aside to place a hand in his pocket, like he has zero intention of leaving without her no matter how long it takes.

"Fine," she grumbles as she grabs her things, throwing her phone in her purse with a little more force than is necessary. She shuts down her laptop and shoots Louise a glare. "You sure you don't want me to bring you back something to eat?"

Louise shakes her head. "Nope, I'll be grabbing something on my way to my next meeting, all good. Have fun!"

Edie heads toward the door, and Trenton grabs her sweater from the rack and raises it for her to slip on. As she glares at him and slides into her sweater, he leans down and whispers, "I told you we're not over yet."

Edie can't help but feel relief in hearing that, though she doesn't dare to explore why.

WHEN SHE PULLS HER CAR in the spot next to Trenton's, she scans the building of the place she followed him to. It's a large structure that looks like a hybrid of a strip mall and a house. There's an arched roof and raised elevation sitting in the middle, with gingerbread siding made to look quaint in an otherwise industrial space. The parking lot is about halfway full, no major lunch rush here, apparently. It's a curious spot that feels in the middle of nowhere, as there are wide open fields surrounding it, though it's not too far from the center of town.

Edie startles as Trenton appears in her driver's side window, and he smiles and opens her door for her, draping an arm on the frame and twirling his keys while he waits for her to step out. He has on his sunglasses, but the smirk on his face is evident.

She steps out and he closes her door before grabbing her hand to hold. "Come on, I'm taking you on a proper date," he says, and she numbly follows along, wondering about this strange restaurant he chose.

One last date. Fine. She'll enjoy this, a nice meal to celebrate their parting ways.

"What is this place?" she asks as they make their way toward the building. She breathes in the enticing scent of charcoal cooking and her stomach grumbles in anticipation. She squeezes Trenton's hand without thinking.

He glances down at her and she sees the slightest lift at the corner of his mouth before returning his gaze toward the restaurant. He lifts his chin in its direction. "It's a little bit of everything. Good old-fashioned American bar food."

"Naturally." Her mouth waters at the thought of crispy fries drowning in a pool of ketchup.

"Plus games like virtual golf, archery, giant Jenga setups if that's more your thing."

"Jenga? Alright, you're going down," she says as they step up onto the sidewalk out front.

"Oh yeah? Jenga does it for ya?" Trenton pauses, releases her hand and turns toward her, grabbing her face in his hands. She looks up to see her own reflection in his sunglasses, wishing she could see his eyes. She expects him to kiss her, but he only holds her there.

"Edna Mackenzie," he says.

"That is my name, yes."

He sweeps a hand through her hair, and she can't help but sigh at the feeling of his fingers lacing through. "I will show no mercy," he says seriously. "I am a Jenga master."

"You are not," she laughs.

"No, I am not," he whispers before leaning down to kiss her chastely. He grabs her face again, and she can't help the grin that doesn't seem to want to leave her face. "But the fact that you apparently are makes me want to be a better man."

"A better *Jenga* man."

"Yes," he confirms, briefly dropping his hand to his heart before returning it to cradle her face.

"Dream bigger, Wroe," she says, then realizes she's clutching his coat, fighting an instinct to slip her arms beneath the fabric and wrap them around him.

"I already am. In fact, I'm looking at my dream this very moment." Her heart flutters at his words, even though she knows it's a joke. She reaches up to his face and pulls off his sunglasses. Warm brown eyes stare back at her with intensity, and he licks his lips. His full and beautiful lips that have been all over her body, that have led the way in doing things to her that she'll forever fantasize about, locked in her memory like a treasure. She's sad to be letting him go, it's true. But you can't build a relationship on pure lust, she reminds herself.

"What do you see?" he asks.

"What?" she asks, unsure of what he's getting at.

"On my face. You pulled off my sunglasses." He drops his hands from her cheeks and takes a step back.

She scans the sight of him, all six-foot-something corporate lawyer in his suit, going into a gaming restaurant to play Jenga with her, but looking at her intently like he could hang on each and every word she ever has to say.

"Well?" he prompts.

She smiles. Hands him back his sunglasses and pulls her sweater over her chest. "I see what I think might be your breath in the air because it's absolutely freezing. It's April, when does it start getting warm around here?"

He's silent at first, then he nods once and places his sunglasses in an inside pocket of his coat. She looks and sees the flare in his eyes from a moment ago now gone. "Not soon enough, I guess. Let's get you inside." He places his hand on the small of her back and turns to lead her in.

EDIE HAS ALWAYS LOVED THE idea of snowy weather. As a kid growing up in Tampa, the closest thing she had experienced to "snow" on a regular basis was cutting up sheets of paper to be threaded through yarn and hung around various places throughout the house. Her moms were warm weather people, through and through. Edie often wondered if her father was the northern influence of her heart.

To say she was disappointed to not have snow here this winter would be a lie, however. As she and Trenton walk back out to their cars after a somewhat awkward lunch and Jenga date, she realizes how ready for warm weather she is. The temperature seems to have shifted a bit during their time inside, thankfully, the sun no longer hiding behind a sheet of gray, and Edie looks longingly at the digital temperature displayed on a sign by the parking lot entrance, willing it to creep up even further.

"You uhh, you want to head back to my place?" Trenton asks her now. She pulls her sweater tighter around her chest and considers him. He throws his hands up. "Nothing naughty, I promise."

Edie smiles a little at this, tempted to blurt out, "Disappointing," but instead she remains silent. Her mind whirls back to their most recent "naughty" escapade, the slow and gentle build-up that had led to that moment. They had been at her apartment, the one and only time she let him spend the night, and the next morning Trenton had been joking that he liked being allowed in completely, teasing her that staying the night was a big deal and next she'd be begging him to marry her. They were lying naked in her bed, and she pinched his nipple and gave it a twist, telling him he could dream on.

"I'm just saying," he chided, his fingers gliding up and down her spine as she nestled into his chest. "You're in love with me, I know it. I've locked in."

"Please, hardly," she had said with a sly smile crossing her face.

She pulled herself up to lean her forearm across his chest. "Although..."

He pinched his eyebrows together as he looked at her. "Although what? What's on that mind of yours?" He tucked the falling strands of her hair behind her ear.

"There's one place you have definitely not locked in yet," and she darted her eyes down to the rounded curve of her exposed ass. "Just saying," she emphasized with a lift of her eyebrow when her gaze returned to him.

He sat up, his face serious, and she lifted herself to her knees and sat back on her heels. "I'm willing to try it."

A grin swept over his face. "Naughty, naughty. You sure?"

She nodded eagerly. "I'm sure, yes. I want to try it. With you," she added, as if that were in question.

He leaned toward her, parting her lips for a tender kiss, and her pulse quickened with the anticipation of what they were about to do. When he pulled back, his eyes searched hers. "It might be uncomfortable at first, okay?"

"I know."

"I want you to tell me if you want to stop." She nodded, assuring him she would.

With sunlight pouring in over her bed, Trenton stood up and guided her to her hands and knees, her eyes held steady on the swirls of light and shadow intertwining in the divots of her pillow. She closed her eyes and felt as he gently pressed his knee into hers to spread her out wide. His tongue was on her lower back next, teasing circles as he trailed his way down, soft kisses and strokes of his tongue all along her skin, her ass, then the backs of her thighs, and she repressed a ticklish giggle.

He slowly moved his way back up until his tongue was on her clit. Gentle little flicks at first, and she focused on the sensation to bat away her nerves, focusing on the feeling of him pleasuring her. She inhaled a deep breath, the smell of fresh linens comforting her, and as his movements intensified, she hummed and shimmied her hips, loving how good his mouth felt so intimately between her legs like this. She couldn't believe she was getting ready to do this, couldn't believe how at ease she felt with this man that she never in a million years would have thought would be anywhere near her apartment, let alone in her bed. In her body, a most welcomed guest.

When his tongue went from playful and sporadic to steady and determined, working to bring her close to the edge, he stopped, pulling back and she whimpered out for him, his name falling as a whisper from her lips. She kept her eyes closed and her belly was tight with the torture of being denied her orgasm. She listened as he got up off the bed and rustled around in something. She heard the sound of soft music come on, her small speaker coming to life, and she smiled, realizing he had gone into her phone to find a playlist to connect. She was happy for the surrounding noise to fill the previous silence.

When the sinking of her mattress indicated his return, she opened her eyes, peering back to him. He was rolling on a condom, then she watched in fascination as he spread lubricant all around. Next, he picked up a small vibrator, pressing it on briefly before turning it off again. His face held a look of concentration, as if he were a doctor preparing for surgery. She imagined a stethoscope around his neck, and she giggled into her pillow, not wanting to break the moment.

Trenton moved behind her, and she closed her eyes again. "Are you sure?" he asked one last time, and she nodded. When she felt the head of his penis up against the tight opening, her breath hitched. He gently pushed forward, just a little, but she was tight. Edie could feel his resistance and she worried this wouldn't work somehow. As if maybe there was something anatomically wrong with her and she'd made a mistake, this wasn't a fit that could happen. Nerves and the threat of disappointment washed over her.

"Breathe, baby. You have to try and relax, okay?" She nodded and tried to do as he said, taking deep breaths to allow for the new sensation. His palm stroked her back in soothing circles, and he tried again, pushing forward with more force. She released her grip on her pillow, trying to loosen her body as completely as possible despite her apprehension mixed with nervous excitement. Still, she struggled to focus and relax the tight space he was trying to enter.

Trenton pulled back completely, and she raised her head and looked back at him. "I'm okay, really." She didn't want him to stop, especially now after how far they'd come. They had started this. She'd be damned if that was as far as they would go.

He lay down on his side behind her, pulling on her hips to lay her down as well. "Here, let's try this," he said. "Might help you relax," and she allowed him to ease her down and back to him. She felt the warmth of his chest on her back and then his knee in between her legs, spreading her once again. His palm pressed on a cheek, and she felt his tip as he pressed in once more, this time sliding in the slightest bit. She went slack into her pillow as he whispered, "Breathe, baby," into her neck before giving gentle kisses to her shoulder. Edie focused on the sensation and willed her body to open up for him.

Slowly, methodically, he moved further inside, deep and she sucked in a sharp breath as she felt him consume her. Trenton was in, nearly completely in. She loved the sensation. Each inch he moved into her exploded a new feeling of fullness she had never before imagined could feel so good. His hand covered her breast, and she heard his groan as he began his gentle thrusts. She reached for his hand and covered it with her own, a small gesture of assurance that she was okay.

"It feels wild," she breathed out, getting more comfortable with the sensation with each passing second.

"Holy fuck, baby," he said as he bit down on her shoulder. "You feel so fucking good." He rocked behind her for a minute more, and she leaned back into him, molding her body to his.

Then he paused. He reached for the vibrator and turned it on, bringing it to her front, and she cried out with the exquisite mix of stimulation, him inside her in this new way combined with the fire of the gentle vibrator on her clit. It was as if every crevice of her had reached a new level of charge, and her orgasm was clear on the horizon. She twisted her leg tighter around his, rocking in rhythm with him and crying out as the sensation from within her body radiated into an orgasm that ripped through her from deep within, every nerve ending in her body seeming alive and explosive. It was too much, yet everything she craved, and Trenton shuddered behind her too. She reached back and clawed at his hair in rough tugs, hanging on for dear life, unable to stop her screams of ecstasy from escaping in loud cries out of her mouth. She heard her own name fall from his lips to be lost into her hair as he held her tight against him, allowing his pleasure to pulse inside her.

"Edna," he whispered. "My God, Edna." Trenton's voice dropped off in a low and barely audible grumble.

They lay still for a while, stunned and high and drinking in the slow descent of their mutual waves. Her breath slowed and he pulled out of her, and already Edie knew she'd be sore for days.

And yet she couldn't wait to play repeat and try that all over again.

Afterward they showered, and she looked in his amber brown eyes as he held her face in his hands and swirls of steam spilled around him. "Are you okay?" he asked, so much tender concern on his face.

Edie nodded and smiled. "I've never done that before," as if that were news and he didn't realize. Of course he already knew that.

He pulled her into his arms, whispering, "Neither have I," and she thought she might die of the surprise at the statement, and the vulnerability in the man here in her shower, Trenton Wroe.

"SO EDNA, EDIE. DO YOU want to go back to my place? Talk or something?" Edie shifts her weight as she considers.

During their Jenga round, Trenton had been surprisingly quiet. She expected a shark ready to play dirty. Instead, Trenton was pensive. Mechanical in his moves. Quizzical as he watched her, as if this were a quiet game of chess requiring intense concentration, not some meaningless tower of blocks bravely defying the laws of physics for as long as possible, holes within its structure threatening its demise.

She pushes her glasses back and shifts her weight. "I don't know, I think we should end on a high note, don't you?"

"Fuck, Edna," he says, running a hand along his jaw, turning away from her. She stares at his back momentarily, waiting for him to respond. When he turns back, the spinning of his keys in his hand makes a surprising impact to her belly—the jingle eliciting a flip of desire. "What are we doing here, what is this?" he finally says.

"What do you mean?"

He drops his head to the ground and huffs out a laugh. She sees the reflection of the pavement in his sunglasses. "End on a high note."

Edie steps away from him and leans back against her car, crossing her arms over her chest. "We want different things, Wroe."

He raises his head to look at her, and she notes how small her reflection looks. He steps toward her and leans his forearm on the roof of her car, encasing her, his hand dropping near her head and snaking through her hair. "What do you want?"

Edie fights the urge to close her eyes and lean her head back to fully enjoy what his hands are doing to her scalp, to her body.

"I want..." she starts, words fumbling. Eventually she has to tear her eyes away from her own reflection captured in the golden-green of his glasses.

"Yes?" he prompts. "Tell me."

She steps to her left and out of his lingering stature over her, unsure how to answer without sounding needy. To list the things she wants feels like she's asking too much, and the idea of him rejecting her requests is a difficult reality to potentially face.

Edie decides to be honest anyway. "I want a husband and children one day. I want that husband to be somebody who doesn't laugh at the humming from an electric vehicle, and who will vote in support of the school referendums, even with the tax increases."

"What?" He stares at her as if looking for understanding.

She continues. "Or one who wouldn't be upset if I were pregnant, and there were complications, and I decided to terminate for safety."

He drops his arm from the roof of her car and steps closer to her again, but this time he stops before touching her, shifting his hands to his coat pockets. She sees the clench in his jaw, then the way his teeth pull in his bottom lip and his nostrils flair. "You think I'm some shithead who would force you into decisions you weren't comfortable to make, is that it?"

"I don't—no, I don't think you're like that."

He smirks. "Sure, you don't. Then why are you saying stuff like that?"

"Because you asked what I want!" she says, unwinding her arms and throwing them in the air. She pushes herself off her car and starts walking around toward the driver's side, with Trenton following after.

"What the hell?" he calls from behind her. "Is it too much for you to see me as an actual human being with feelings and not as the fucking heartless jerk you keep telling yourself I am?"

"But it suits you so well," she blurts out, and instantly slaps her hand over her mouth in regret. "I didn't mean that," she mumbles through her palm.

"No, you know what? I know you didn't mean that. Because I *mean* nothing to you, right? Just a toy you get to mess with and throw away. Isn't that right?"

"Me?!" she stops and turns to face him. "I'm just messing with you?" She laughs in disbelief. Never in her whole life did Edie think she'd be called out for essentially being a player.

He throws his arm out to the side, gesturing toward the restaurant. "You won't even let me take you out! You need your boss to force you into having a damn meal with me. You won't introduce me to this new family you've found and love. No interest in meeting my friends. All just sex."

"Isn't that what you wanted?" She meant to put more heat and anger into her words. Meant to drive in the point, but her voice comes out soft.

"Don't do that," Trenton says, shaking his head.

"What?"

"Don't make me out to be the jackass that started some friends with benefits thing. Don't peg me like that, I've done nothing to deserve that."

"Other than having no problem with the proposition of just sex?"

"Yeah, okay," he nods. "I think I should remind you, that proposition started with you." He flips his sunglasses to the top of his head, rubbing his eyes, his temples.

"You didn't seem to mind it too much."

Trenton pauses his movements to look at her, considering her words. "No, Edna. I didn't mind it. Because if that's all you wanted, then at least it meant I got to spend time with you."

"Please. Great line. Bet you use it all the time."

"Listen to yourself, Edna. Use that line for what, exactly—falling into my arms forever and ever? Because we both know it's not to get you to fall into bed."

"Right. Been there, done that." She glares at him with resolve. Doesn't he see that there's nothing else for them here? She wonders what his end game is exactly, because if he really believes they could continue a relationship based purely off sex, he's wrong.

Edie huffs out a sigh, her irritation stubborn and persistent.

"You know what I want to know? Actually, yeah. I got a question for you. Wanna hear it?"

"I'm sure I don't, but please. Go on. Let's see how else I can fumble in your presence."

"Why do you always call me Edna, why not Edie, like everyone else?"

Trenton pulls his head back in a frown. "What? That's what you want to know?"

"Yes," she nods, feeling a little silly for asking as she registers his surprise at the question.

He shakes his head and looks away, then runs a hand along his face. "Fine, alright," he finally says. "Let's think about this. I guess it's because we're never with 'everyone else' for me to experience you as Edie," he says, facing her now with air quotes, frowning in confusion laced with frustration. "When we met, I saw your name was Edna." She thinks about several weeks ago, when they first met, and he saw her name on her desk. "And you said your moms call you Edna, so," he shrugs. "That's who you are to me."

She nods, feeling silly now for bringing up such a ridiculous point.

"Is that okay? Do you not like being called Edna?" She scans his face and sees the genuine concern in his eyes, as if all this time he might have offended her by simply using her real name. It didn't even occur to her that, other than Louise now and then, the two of them aren't around anyone else.

She sighs. "Of course it's okay."

"You're sure?"

"Yes," she nods. "Definitely yes. You're the only one that uses my name."

"Other than your moms," he confirms.

"Right, though they slip in Edie here and there too. But Edna feels more grown up, in a way." She lifts the corner of her mouth. "It's especially cute when you call me Edna Edie. Like a hybrid."

His face softens and he steps closer to her, grabbing her hands.

She slips into his warmth like an old and worn blanket wrapping around her. While she had felt like an idiot for bringing up her name, she's now thankful, as it seems to have offered a little escape out of their fight, or whatever this altercation is. She doesn't fight in relationships, not even when ending things with Zeke where it was all rather amicable. This feels like odd territory for her, though not in a bad way. Just an honest way.

"Well, good," he finally says after a moment. "And, Edna Edie, I need you to know that while I may not see the world the exact same way you do, I'm trying to."

She looks up in surprise. "You are?"

A smile sweeps across his face as he nods. "Yeah. Because I love that about you. I love how positive you always are, and how you want to make things even better." His thumb rubs over the back of her hand in gentle strokes. "I've loved spending every single minute with you I possibly could. At work, they offered me help on this project, and I jumped so fast to say, 'No thanks,' they all thought I was nuts. And, yes, you made it clear this was nothing serious, but I've stuck around clinging to hope that it could be. Because I'm far from done with you, and I don't want to just mess around anymore, okay? And I definitely don't want some horribly awkward Jenga game where I was too nervous about this being the last time I'd have with you—I don't want that to be the *high note* of us."

Her thoughts feel chaotic as she takes in everything he just said. He's not done, he wants something serious. Does she want that too? "Trenton, I know you're a good guy."

"You do?" He raises his eyebrows in what looks to be either hope or skepticism.

She nods. "Yes. And I'm sorry about what I was suggesting earlier."

"I forgive you," he says, the edge of his mouth lifting. "If it means you'll give this a real shot."

Edie sighs, sadness mixed with frustration. "Trenton, no," she says softly, trying to force the words out. They're the words she knows to be the right ones, but they feel all wrong. "No," she repeats with more firmness.

He pulls his hands back, dropping hers and looking away. "No," he scoffs, shaking his head.

"I'm sorry."

He looks back at her, and her pulse quickens with the look of hurt in his eyes. "But why? Baby, why, when we're so good together?"

"Because you..." she stammers, fighting a bubbling of tears. "You think you like me now, but...but you'd get bored of someone like me eventually," she whispers, emotion heavy in her voice as she looks down at her now-lonely hands. *Because there's no way I'd be able to keep your affection.* The thought is crushing, but it rings loudly in her head, much more so than the thoughts that make her want to believe everything he's saying and go running into his arms.

"Jesus, is that what you think? You really think that low of yourself?" He steps closer and lifts her chin up to look at him. "How is it possible that someone as smart as you doesn't see how —" his voice trails off, and his chest rises in a sigh. "There are no words. Amazing? Incredible? I think I need a goddamn Hallmark card. I'm no good with saying the right things. Fuck, Edna. You must know how *everything* you are."

Edie lifts her mouth in a half-hearted smile. "How everything I am?"

She watches as he crouches down slightly to meet her gaze at her level, telling her "Yes" before pulling her in for a soft hug.

"Those are good words," she whispers, leaning into him. "You're doing alright. And I do know those things."

"Good. You better."

A car pulls into a nearby spot and Edie glances at the intrusion, wondering where to go from here. It would be so easy, so incredibly easy to go home with him right now, let her body melt into his and throw all caution to the wind. With Trenton Wroe, the lawyer who waltzed into her office and had an instant impact on her heart.

But who also waltzed back out, leaving the damn door open in a temper tantrum.

"Trenton," she starts, "I just worry you're being shortsighted in how—I don't know—how sustainable your interest in me would be."

"Sustainable? Edna," he says, releasing her from his embrace to trail a thumb across her cheek.

"What?"

He kisses her lips once before pulling her back into him once again, this time more firmly as he wraps his arms around her body in a tight squeeze. She lets him, thinking how never before has a scratchy coat on her cheek felt so comforting. She feels the rumble of his voice in his chest. "I really want to know who the fuck hurt you so badly that you think I could ever just walk away from you."

dog tags

. . .

January 1947 ~ New York

Dear Lace,

I think I have now fallen in love with you a little more after hearing of your escape. It hurts my heart to think of what you went through. Then again, I'm selfishly happy, because otherwise we would have never found one another, and our time in hiding was such a beautiful thing, wasn't it? Yes, we must be able to find moments of tenderness, and hold onto them for all we can, even when scared. Even when the future sits within so many unknowns.

But the desire I felt for you, I was greedy with it. Was I a fool to act on it? Perhaps. Yet nothing could stop me, I was helpless under your spell. I fear I still am.

Please forgive my selfish ways, my darling. I know I should feel guilt for taking your innocence, however such regret never seems to reach me. How can it? No, the only regret I feel is in the distance we now hold.

The war may have ended, but the war I feel now in our separa-

tion feels cruel. May God forgive me in having to leave you, and may fate lead us into one another's arms once again.

Love always,
Dog Tags

twenty-four

. . .

dom

ONE WEEK IN LA turns into two weeks, then three, and Dom finds himself settling into a rhythm that feels increasingly more comfortable. One of the hardest parts about having a daughter in the spotlight is having to share her with the world. Not the persona, which naturally is a carefully curated enterprise, one that Ruby works to make as authentic as possible, while the rest of her team drags her back in an effort to keep her safe and sane.

No—the hard part is the day-to-day pieces that Dom has to watch from the sidelines. To see his daughter living her dream is more than he could have ever asked for, especially given the couple of years she endured living with her mother while Dom was still active in the military after their divorce. He's happy to see his daughter not only come into her stride despite the childhood abuse she endured under Pearl's so-called "care"—all unknown to him at the time—but to come out on top. At the very top, in fact, as a Grammy-winning artist with zero plans on slowing down. Ruby deserves every ounce of success she has earned.

However, the price they both pay for it is a life where they do not get to be in one another's worlds in the same way Dom would like. They don't get to do routine Sunday dinners surrounding a big table spread with pastas and anecdotes of the latest silly work endeavors, or the chatter of a grandkid's recent elementary school art award. Dom had always imagined a life of having these kinds of interactions. In his early days of marriage with Pearl, he had wanted more children, with hopes for one day having a house full of open doors and grandchildren filling their home with scratched knees, ruddy faces, and the laughter of youth. Pearl hadn't wanted more children though, and that might be the one and only selfless decision his ex had ever made. She didn't have the mothering instinct. Dom only wished he had known that sooner.

It occurs to him that Lori does in fact have that life he had once dreamed of. She has the grandchildren and the Sunday dinners with Reggie and Xavier. Dom momentarily imagines the possibility that he might join in that vision. He can see Lori now, smile radiant while she holds a birthday cake for little James or Ronnie. There's a brief guilt he holds in his desire of the prospect of that life, as if it's a betrayal to his commitment to stand by Ruby's side as the makeshift bodyguard while she navigates the precarious world of fame.

But being with Lori promises so much of what his family-driven heart truly wants. Lori offers even more than just the steadfast affection she so unabashedly holds in her heart, on her sleeve. Being with Lori could also mean those very kinds of experiences, and he can't deny his interest in that. Not that he doesn't feel immense pride and fulfillment in the path Ruby has been on—though he still holds out hope that she'll change her mind on the decision not to have children. Ruby has remained adamant that she's career-focused, and that bringing a child into her world of fame doesn't feel like the right choice for her. Joey maintains that as long as Ruby is by his side, he's the happiest man alive—his words, verbatim. Dom wonders, though, if, like him, that's Joey's own sacrifice. He knows Joey would make a great father if given the opportunity.

Dom shakes away his wandering thoughts and the life he has put on hold on the East Coast. He straightens the bowtie of his tux and drains the last of his whiskey. His eyes scan the ballroom they are currently in, finding Ruby smiling and shaking hands with a few people as she makes her way through the crowd, finally landing at their table.

"Thirty more minutes, tops. Then we can leave," she assures him as she slides into her chair. Her blue eyes sparkle, though, and Dom can see the hum of satisfaction in her role for this evening. They were at a charity gala supporting the building of a new wing at a pediatric hospital, and Ruby had sung her heart out to a crowd of enthralled music enthusiasts and wealthy donors. Dom had glanced over at Joey, his love for his future son-in-law growing even more as he saw the pure awe in Joey's eyes, watching his love up on stage. It was as if Joey's affection never dulled, it only grew. It gave Dom comfort to know Ruby was in loving hands.

"I'm in no rush," Dom assures her.

Ruby swings her dark curls over her shoulder, and they bleed in with the black sequins of her gown. "Well, I am. The fun part's over, I'm ready for sweats and a good movie now," she grins, sipping her water.

Dom laughs and nods to the waiter as he offers him another whiskey. "Sure. One more, why not?"

Jules makes her way over to the table, long legs slipping through the slit below each hip of her emerald evening gown. Dom keeps his eyes above waist. She's been increasingly flirtatious this evening, and he doesn't want to give the wrong impression.

"Darling Ruby, one more request, if I can whisk you away," Jules says to Ruby as she leans over the table. Ample breasts spill over the low cut of her gown, and Dom looks away, straightening up in his seat.

"Fine, fine. What is it?" Ruby asks, already shimmying out of her seat to stand again. Dom watches as Ruby rises and glances behind her shoulder in the direction of where Jules is pointing.

"A bigwig donor. Dying to meet you," Jules directs. She looks down at Dom. "Actually, I'm sure he'd love to meet you too. Come with, it'll make him feel like he's part of the family," she says, hand out to Dom to join.

Dom rolls his eyes and grabs Jules's hand. "I don't know how you ladies do this. I'm exhausted already."

"A quick conversation, laugh at the old man's crude jokes, then you're free. Promise," Jules says with a cock of her eyebrow.

The three make their way through the crowd to the robust man in question. He's red faced and clearly intoxicated, and Dom glances over to what he assumes to be the man's date, though the young lady looks about three decades younger. She smiles tersely with a soft handshake to each of them before excusing herself. Dom imagines there's a line of coke somewhere waiting for her, and he feels a twinge of sympathy for the poor young woman and her affiliation with this man.

Within seconds of his date disappearing, the man reaches in for Ruby as if to attempt a hug, and Ruby startles back.

"Oh, hi!" his daughter says, and Dom instantly has his hackles up in her stiffened body language. Ruby throws out an elbow. "Sicknesses and all, am I right?" she says as she taps the man's elbow.

He barks out a laugh. "Nonsense. In fact, I'm hoping for a private party with you."

"Not sure you could afford it." Ruby's voice is firm despite her smile.

"Please, I've got more money than God," he says, leaning forward. "You sing like the most incredible of performers, sweetheart. Come on. Entertain me." The look on his face reveals his clearly disturbing thoughts that have nothing to do with a love of music.

"Careful, now, Henry," Jules purrs. "Show our girl some respect."

"I just love her voice," he insists.

Dom takes in the man's awkward lean, and he clenches his jaw, not wanting to cause a scene but very much wanting to set this guy straight. Is this the kind of thing his daughter has to endure? How many interactions like this must she have to deal with in the name of keeping face? It sickens him to think of it.

Ruby smiles her best fake smile. "Gotta take that up with people other than me, I'm afraid." She darts her eyes over to Jules.

"That's right," Jules says as she steps in between Ruby and the man, and Dom admires Jules's ease in attempting to diffuse and protect his daughter. "Easy, Henry," she murmurs to the swaying man as if talking to a child. "My Ruby here is not someone you just summon in hopes for a private party." Dom's grateful for her intervention. The man needs to be put in his place.

Henry's grin is smug. "I'm sure we could work something out."

Dom sees the entire interaction of the next twelve seconds as if outside of his own body. He sees Henry's hands—one slipping just below Ruby's chest, and another on Jules's ass, fingers splayed out. He hears Henry slur out, "How about I summon you too then, to chaperone. Name your price," and Dom shoots forward and presses his arm into Henry's throat, slamming him against the wall.

Dom's nose is inches from the man's, and he fights a gag at the tequila-infused breath. "Watch your fucking hands, you little shit." Dom gives a hard press, and takes in the sight of Henry's face, now creeping from red to purple. Soft jazz hums in the background, the party guests swaying and chattering, completely unaware of the altercation happening. "I don't care if you're the fucking king, you don't touch any woman like that."

"Dad, let's go," Ruby says as she grabs Dom's arm. "Now. Before a goddamn camera flashes."

Dom gives one more shove to old Henry before releasing, a

final death glare to solidify his threat before he breaks eye contact with the man, now hunched over and gasping.

Dom turns and rubs a hand down his face as he follows the quickly shuffling Ruby and Jules. He watches Ruby catch eyes with Joey, off charming a group of elderly women in his own circle of fans, and Ruby snaps her head to the side, toward the exit. Joey nods at her, then turns and flashes a grin to his ladies, placing his hand on his chest in apologies before breaking away from his octogenarian fan club. He jogs his way over to them.

"We leaving? What's up?" he asks, meeting eyes with Dom.

Dom shakes his head as he leads the ladies out, dropping his head down at the flash of bulbs blinding them upon their exit.

"The world is filled with fucking scum and perverts, that's what," he spits out through clenched teeth.

"But Dom sure did save the day," Jules says with a hand linked in his arm as they leave. "Our hero."

DOM GRABS A SEAT OUT in the sunken sitting area to the side of Ruby and Joey's pool deck. An electric fire pit glows in front of them, and Dom stares at the blue iridescent rocks beneath the flames, willing the disgust he feels to dissipate. It's hard to see people you care about—people you recognize as vulnerable to muscle, wealth, and power—be treated like playthings. Violated so carelessly.

On the drive back home, Jules had been apologetic for the whole thing, as if she was the one to have done the groping, and Dom hated that she felt the need to do so. She was just as much a victim in it too, and it infuriated him to see her attempt to take responsibility.

When he said as much, she surprised him by throwing up a middle finger. "That guy can go fuck himself, I'm in no way apologizing for him. I just wish I hadn't forced the introduction in the first place. I knew he was a pervert. That, mixed with drinks, was bound to not end well."

Dom had laughed, admiring her fire. It's what drew him to her in the first place, especially when that fire had done so much to aid in his daughter's career.

He smiles at the thought and looks up to see Jules now, making her way down the couple steps to join him, her gown glittering in the fire light. She nestles herself next to him. "Hey there, handsome."

He shifts uncomfortably, gaze held firmly forward, but Jules drapes an arm around him, crossing her legs and leaning into his body. His eyes glance down to her thighs, skin exposed through the slits of her gown and looking more inviting than he'd like to admit. There was something so raw, so openly sexy about Jules. She's a fearless woman who knows what she wants, and he's keenly aware that right now, she wants him.

"Nice night," he says. It's a pleasantries phrase, but he's hoping to temper the chemistry and attraction for one another they still clearly have. Especially given the affection he very much holds for her as a woman so central to looking after his daughter's career interests.

"Don't be modest. You made it a great night, didn't you?" She's trailing her fingertips along the back of his neck, and he wills himself to not focus on it, as good as her touch feels.

"I don't know about that. I hope that doesn't cause any problems when the prick wakes up tomorrow and remembers the man slamming him against a wall."

Her fingers make their way into his hair, and she scratches his scalp in gentle strokes. "Don't worry about that. He's a drunk that's known to black out, chances are he won't even remember. And even if he does, I control the media, remember?" She hums, her face now inches from his. She smells like honeysuckle and desire, and Dom leans forward and rests his arms on his thighs in an attempt to create some space. It's not her fault; Dom hadn't told her he was seeing anyone. He contemplates how to formulate the words, but he's struggling.

"Hey," Jules says, hands on his shoulders to try and pull him back. Dom remains firmly in his position. She nuzzles up closer to him again. "Hey. Just so you know, your little hero stunt turned me on."

He huffs out a laugh, dragging a hand along his jaw. "Oh, did it? That sounds like trouble."

She lifts a slim ankle to graze over his shin. "Only if you don't still find me attractive."

Before Dom gets the chance to respond, he hears light footsteps on the pool deck above. When he looks up to see who has joined them, his pulse quickens.

Lori.

twenty-five

. . .

edie

"HONEY, IT'S JUST worth a general reminder that you need to watch out for men like him."

Edie is standing just outside her classroom, waiting to step in and take her final. "I know. Trust me, I know." She pulls the phone away from her cheek and peeks in to see the students hunched over desks, flipping through index cards and scanning screens, trying to get in the last minutes of studying, as if answers and enlightenment will suddenly come to them now.

Though who is she to judge, she's about to do the exact same thing.

"Listen to me," her mom says. "Men like that, the power-hungry, money focused types—they're great at sucking you in. It's easy to fall for them, I get it."

"I'm not falling for him, Mama. Have you been listening to *me*? I told him we're done. That's it, it's over." It's not a total lie, Edie reminds herself. She had told Trenton she needed time to think, but her mom doesn't need to know that. Even as she thinks about that last interaction with Trenton, she can't help but feel a twinge in her chest at hitting pause with him. Something in her gut that feels like—well, like grief, in a sense. She pushes down the feelings, reminding herself that it's just the chemistry they shared, nothing more. It was the best sex of her life, but now she can take that and explore it with someone else. With her true match.

Maybe even Zeke.

"I'm glad to hear that. Listen, I have to run, there's a protest happening not too far from us. We're getting ready to head over and join."

Edie nods, thankful to be wrapping up their conversation. "Alright, good luck. Be safe."

"I should say the same to you. This Trenton guy? Block his number."

"Mama, stop," Edie groans, dropping her head down in defeat. "I don't need to block his number, he's not dangerous."

"That you know of. Not yet, maybe. The last thing you need is some narcissistic stalker on you. You want to know more about Richard?"

This catches Edie's attention. She snaps her head up, eager to hear where her mom's going with this. "What about Richard?"

"That was him, through and through. A narcissist. Sick."

Edie's heart sinks. It's a tough thing to hold a space between wanting to believe the good aspects of a man in the way Lori tries to present—especially when it's a man that assisted in your creation —but then hearing the obvious disgust for him laced in her mother's voice.

"I don't need to hear that, Mama."

Her mom sighs. "You asked, Edna. Remember? This is exactly what I had been trying to protect you from."

"From what, exactly? A man that was dead anyways? There was nothing to even protect me from!" Edie glances around the hall, aware that she's raising her voice. She walks down a little further to attempt some semblance of privacy.

"You don't understand," her mother says.

"How could I if you never talk to me about it? I don't get it, what's the big deal? You could have just spun up some stories about what a wonderful man he was, too bad he's gone now, and called it a day."

"I didn't want you trying to find his family, alright!?" her mother blurts out.

Edie blinks, stunned into silence. She pulls the phone away and looks around her as if someone in the hallway could help her confirm what she just heard. Her mom's unexpected little confession. Edie huffs out a laugh, absorbing her words as she slowly raises the phone back to her ear.

So there it is, the reason behind all the secrecy. Part of it, anyway. She suspected her mother had worried about that, but up until this moment, she never said so outright.

"Are you happy now?" her mom continues, her tone exasperated. "I didn't want you reaching out, trying to find your half-siblings and opening up that whole thing."

Edie's heart beats faster as she thinks about how to respond to that. "But why not? I could have had..." Her sentence drops, because she's not sure how to fill in the blank. Could have had siblings? A connection? Answers to lifelong questions? It's all those things and more.

Her mom sighs. "Honey, listen. I don't want you getting caught up in what this Lori woman is telling you, because believe me when I say that Richard was not a good man. And forgive me if my choices hurt you, but I wanted nothing to do with him, and so I shut the door on it. It was what was best. Safest."

Edie feels an overwhelming sadness rush over her. She thinks about the small snippets her mom finally shared about her interaction with Richard all those years ago. How he had wooed her when she was twenty-eight, and her mom was a secretary for a place that was one of Richard's accounts. He'd waltz into town and wine and dine her, and she ignored all the red flags. The late-night phone calls because of his supposedly long days. The way he'd be reaching out to her several times a day, then disappear with zero contact for days on end. Her mom knew he lived in Pennsylvania, and she justified his inconsistencies on the distance. Until the day her mom asked him point-blank if he was married, and when he admitted he was, her mom ended it, but by then she had the parting gift of Edie. She never told Richard.

But Edie knows there's more to the story. There always is. If it was that simple, why hadn't she told her that right from the start? Surely she knows Edie would have respected the decision to not try and find Richard's family. Not as a kid still living under her parents' roof, anyhow.

"Fine, Mama. Fine," she says, her voice firm. Slow and steady so she can clearly make her next point. "I get it. I may not agree, but I get it."

"Thank you. That's all I'm asking for, just to try and see my perspective. It came from love and protection."

"I know." Edie chooses her next words carefully. "But that was Richard, alright? Richard who was not a good man. That's not all men, though." *That's not Trenton*, some little voice inside her says. "You can't just go around assuming someone's a narcissist, especially when you've never even met them, Mother. It's not a diagnosis to throw around."

Her mom sighs. "Edie, you're young. But you'll learn."

"Uh-huh," is all Edie says, thinking she never wants to learn a level of cynicism like that. Never wants to close up her heart and belief in people's innate goodness the way her mom has.

She worries a part of her already has.

twenty-six

. . .

dom

"I HAVE A surprise, look who's here," Joey says as he steps out the sliding door behind Lori. Dom does a double take, sure his eyes are playing tricks on him. *Lori's here*, is all he can think, with a swell of warmth and relief flooding over his chest. She looks breathtaking in a floral sundress and sandals, and Dom stammers at the unexpected sight of her.

"Lori, what are you doing here?" he says, quickly removing himself from Jules's grasp and rising to walk up the couple steps out from the fire pit area. He sees Lori's smile fall, her glance between him and then back to Jules, still seated on the bench below.

"Hi," is all she says. *Shit*. She saw all of that. Maybe heard, too. How long had she been out here?

Oblivious to the subtle tension of the situation, Joey grins. "I couldn't resist, I had to grab this gal of mine a plane ticket out here. She just got in," he says, wrapping an arm around Lori in a side hug.

"I um, I thought I'd surprise you," Lori explains, looking sheepish. Dom sees her glance once again over to Jules, and he looks behind him to watch as Jules rises and joins them, her legs slipping through the slits of her evening gown. "I feel very underdressed," Lori says as she glides her hands nervously over her sundress.

Joey flashes his grin, dimples doing nothing to add their usual brightness to the exchange. "Stop, you're gorgeous, as always." He winks at Lori. "We just came back from an event, and you *know* the first thing I did was change. These two just enjoy being uncomfortable, I guess."

"I see," Lori nods.

Jules offers out a hand to Lori. She's probably only and an inch or two taller than Lori, but in her heels, Jules appears to tower over her. "I'm Jules, Ruby's PR manager."

Ruby walks out to the deck holding glasses and a champagne bottle, dressed equally casually to Joey in sweatpants and a t-shirt, and Dom reaches out to grab the items out of her hands. "How fun is this?" she asks.

Joey crosses his arms over his chest and nods in Dom's direction. "You should have seen the look of shock on your dad's face, baby. Like he couldn't believe his eyes."

"Joey's idea, naturally. But what a great idea, right?" Ruby's blue eyes shine up toward the sky. "We can explore our letters angle here under the gorgeous full moon. Should we go sit?" She takes a few steps forward toward the fire, then spins around, walking backwards. "Actually Joey, do you mind grabbing me my water from inside?"

Lori scans around the outdoor space, the flicker of lights dotted among the hills, then down to the fire pit area where Dom and Jules were just sitting in what Dom knows was far too intimate a position. She looks back to Ruby. "I can get it for you! I'd actually prefer water myself," she says, hand placed over her throat. "I'm dehydrated from the plane, it feels like it's been forever since I traveled! Forgot how it can just suck the moisture right out of you." She does an exaggerated gulp. "My mouth feels like the desert."

"I'll help you," Dom rushes to respond, and he walks past a still-beaming Joey. He looks at Ruby, who now has her eyes narrowed in some kind of inquisitive glare. Dom never did reveal to his daughter his brief Jules fling, but his far-too-smart daughter seems to be reaching a light bulb of understanding. She looks over to Jules, who has been uncharacteristically silent.

"Right," Ruby says. "Well, we three will just be out here. No rush on the water. Dad, maybe you could show Lori around, show her to your room?"

He nods, so thankful to his daughter for being the keen observer that she is, with a knack for intuition. "Sounds good."

Far better than his own anyhow.

"SO ARE YOU GOING TO tell me what exactly I walked in on back there? You have history with that woman, obviously," Lori asks, hurt clear in her voice as they step into Dom's room, his designated suite here in Ruby and Joey's LA home. "Is that why you came out here? To make comparisons, see which one you'd prefer? Me or her, is that it?" Dom drops her bags on the bed and turns to face her. The burnt orange on the walls shines around her in a soft glow that's amplified by the low light of the bedside lamps.

He runs his hand down his face. "No, Lori. I mean yes, Jules and I had...a brief thing. That ended months ago."

"Right. Not that there's any competition, of course. I'm just the housewife with no babies left to mind. And that woman is," she says, thrusting her arm out as if Jules were standing in the room with them. "Well, she's the genius sailing your daughter through the seas of success!" She laughs, but Dom sees the wetness in her eyes.

He steps over to her, reaches behind her to close the door to the room, then back to look at her. "Stop. Please, hit rewind, let's try this again," he says, his voice soft in hopes to calm her.

Lori covers her face in her hands. "I feel so stupid. I shouldn't have come here, you *told* me not to come here. I should have listened."

"No, Lori." He swears softly, unsure how to placate her. "I love that you came here, I love that that's the kind of woman you are." He says the words because they sound right, and he thinks there's truth in them, but he struggles to feel them fit in the presence of Lori's emotion. He thinks back to Joey and Ruby and how the three of them must have been planning this surprise. Is that what dating looks like? Surprises and gestures like flying across the country to see someone?

"Well, that was one hell of a way to show it," she says softly. Her eyes glisten with the threat of tears.

"Christ, look…I'm just an idiot who doesn't know how to navigate things with someone I care about, that's all that's happening here," Dom says, grabbing her in a hug. Her body is stiff in his arms, and he wishes he could take away her hurt. *Fuck*, why did he have to let Jules talk to him like that? Lean in on him in that way? He should have stopped her, should have put distance between them right out of the gate.

But he didn't.

"No. If you *care* about me, then what about what I saw out there?" she asks, pulling her body out from under his grasp, her voice wobbly. "Don't make me feel like I'm the crazy one here. You two were awfully chummy. In fact, if I were to take a guess, I'd say you were close to kissing, if you hadn't already."

"We were *not* kissing, that I can promise you." His voice is raised, indignant at the idea that he would ever cheat. He steps closer to her but stops himself before attempting to pull her back into him.

"What, then? Because I can tell you that if that woman hadn't kissed you yet, she sure was about to." Lori scoffs. "Not that you're off limits, I guess! We haven't exactly defined this," she says sweeping her hand back and forth between them. "Guess I'm the fool who thought we had something more than just fucking. Shame on me. My first *clue* should have been you leaving town without informing me until I was walking out your door and your plans were already made." She grabs her temples and starts massaging in rough circles. "When the fuck will I learn?" she mutters, a tremor in her voice.

Dom winces. "Stop. Lori, please, we are something more, you know that. Can we just take a minute and talk?" God, he hates this. If he could jump in a machine and be out of this room and this whole interaction, he would.

Lori drops her hands and snaps her head up to him. "Fine. Go on, talk then. Not like I have a choice but to sit here and listen, do I?" She wipes a tear from her cheek.

He sits down on the bed and drops his head in his hands, attempting to find the right words. The faint sound of muffled laughter from outside interrupts the silence in the room. He looks up and sees Lori's face turn in the direction of the noise, and she closes her eyes. The steady rise and fall of her chest slows after a moment, and he wonders what she's thinking.

"I'm not great at this," he finally says. "I don't know what the rules are of starting a new relationship, alright?"

She opens her eyes and looks at him. "Does anyone?"

"No, I guess not," he agrees.

Dom tentatively reaches out to grab Lori's hand. "Please, come sit down. You've come all the way out here, and I need you to know how happy I am about that. Really, I am."

"Do you actually mean that?" she asks, and he sees such raw innocence in her expression behind the anger of a woman scorned.

"I do, yes," he says, reaching forward further to grab her hand, pulling her toward him.

With a sigh she sits down next to him and looks down at her hands clasped in her lap. "I want to believe that."

"Good, please do. Because it's true," he says softly.

"Why do I get the sense that you're trying to convince yourself of that just as much as me?" she whispers.

Lori looks at him expectantly. When Dom remains silent, unsure how to respond, she looks away, out toward the window and the darkness beyond, quiet muffles of chatter still floating in.

"Look," she says. "I've been through this kind of thing before, remember?" She looks back at him with the most gorgeous dark green eyes, and for a brief moment Dom feels he could stare at only them for the rest of his life and be content. It's a thought that catches him off guard, and he feels a new sense of urgency in needing to make this right with her.

"Lori, I'm not Richard." He may not know much, but that's one thing he knows for sure.

"No, you're not. I know that." She shrugs.

"I'm sorry about what you saw up there. I knew she was trying to make a move—"

"So you admit what I saw wasn't nothing?" He looks in her eyes to study her expression, and he sees more hurt than anger in them. Sad disappointment.

"Lori, no line was crossed," he says, shaking his head. "That's not me, I wouldn't do that."

She sighs in defeat. "I guess I know that. You're better than that, a good soul."

He wishes he could think of something to say, but moments like this aren't his strong suit. To thank her feels ridiculous. He goes for honest. "I'm not sure what to say to that."

Her eyes dart between his, and he sees the divot form between her brows. "This is hard for you, isn't it? Us in general, I mean. So you've been avoiding," she says quietly, dropping her gaze down to the floor as she runs her fingers through the bottom edge of her hair. "That's what's been going on. You're running from this thing between us, whatever it is. Aren't you?"

The question hangs between them and Dom considers how to

answer. He doesn't want to lie, but he knows it will hurt if he admits the truth.

He does so anyway. "Yes."

Lori nods. "I can't say I blame you. I can come on strong, I know that."

Dom leans closer to her in an attempt to placate her, but Lori stops him, raising a hand up. "Let me just talk, alright?" She leans herself back and lies face up on his bed. Her eyes are unblinking as she stares up to the ceiling, her body completely still like a corpse. Dom's unsure what to do with himself, so he drops his own body back to lie beside her, and together they stare up at the swirling fan above.

"You know, there was a time in my life not too long ago when I would have stormed out of here. Or been throwing things just now," she says. "Just snapped. So easy to do."

Dom suppresses a groan, remembering similar fits by his mother. She had a heart of gold, and pipes that she gifted down to Ruby. But when his mother felt wronged or disrespected by someone, she too could snap and surprise all those around. It's as though the women with the kindest of intentions, the ones that do and give for everyone around them, they feel the biggest hardships of emotion when their feelings get hurt.

"So what stopped you then?" he asks, though he's almost tearful of the answer.

"It's not my house," she says with a small laugh. "Not my things, and I respect Ruby and Joey too much. But I don't think that's the only reason."

"What else?"

She sighs. "I'm not sure, exactly. It's been an odd couple months since Edie showed up. I think having her around has been resurrecting all these old things for me, things I've stuffed in a box in a cave so deep, I didn't even know it was there. It's forcing some reflection."

"Life is funny that way," he responds. He reaches for her hand, and she squeezes his in return, to his relief.

"And then starting things up with you, whatever we are. Maybe it's not just you that doesn't know how to go about it. Maybe it's me too. I mean, I was fifteen when I met James, and that all seemed so natural and *easy*. We were everything to each other, you know? The urgency of young love. And then it was gone."

He remains silent, because once again, no words seem good enough. To say "I'm sorry" would feel generic, and to say he can't imagine would feel disconnected somehow. Because while he can't exactly imagine the pain of losing the love of your life—or worse, your child—he can relate to the pain of losing someone he *thought* was the love of his life. But is that even fair? Probably not. And at the very least, Ruby was the reward for all of his pain.

"I was numb and barely surviving after the accident. Until Richard came along, and the more I talk about him with Edie, the more memories that float up for me, and I can see how dysfunctional it all was. I hate to admit that. It feels like it does a disservice to what we had, and I don't like that. But I know it was, right from the start."

Dom releases her hand to lie on his side and face her, torso propped up by his forearm. This is good. These are the kinds of conversations he had been hoping to have.

Lori turns to face him too, and she rests her cheek in her hand. "There was love there. It was very real love. But it was poisoned by our own demons. His, I guess I'll never truly know the depths of, and mine was me running away from my own grief. And the more that's coming up for me in thinking about that, the more I feel this very strong urge. It's hard to explain. But with it comes the need to run into someone else's arms."

"Mine, with any luck," he says with a smile, reaching out to grab a strand of her hair.

"Lucky indeed. Look at you," she says, poking him in the chest.

"Two women fawning over you, those blue eyes sure do know how to capture."

He closes his eyes. "How about now?" Dom waits patiently for her to answer, but instead he hears her rise, the mattress shifting beneath him with her movement. He opens his eyes to see her sitting on the edge of the bed again.

"When I saw you and that woman out there like that, her leaning in like she was seconds away from straddling you, it dawned on me."

Dom runs his hands over his face to cover his grimace and lays flat on his back again. "What's that?"

"That you were running away from what we had been starting. I guess I had felt it in many ways but chose to ignore it."

"I'm sorry, I should have communicated things better with you," he says, meaning it whole-heartedly. She had done nothing to deserve his sudden withdrawal.

"Yes," she says quietly, and he rises to sit next to her. "So now what, what do you want?" she asks. Her voice is soft. Meek, even, and Dom is once again aware of the delicate nature of Lori Meyers. This woman that captivates everyone around her with enchanting charm, a woman that takes in the secret child of her late husband, that commands a classroom of elderly yogis that literally bend to the singsong lilt of voice. The mother that lost a child, that lost her first love. The hopeless romantic that planned a surprise, with his very own daughter and her fiancé assisting, to jump on a plane to see him. All just to walk in on him allowing another woman to get far too close to him, the romantic flicker of a fire before them.

Lori deserves better.

"I meant it when I said I care about you, Lori." He reaches for her chin and pulls it toward him. "Hey. More than care, alright? I want to be with you. Completely. Only you." He brushes her hair back from her face before pressing his lips to hers softly.

When he pulls back, he sees her closed eyes and the furrow of her brow. "Do you mean that?" she asks.

"I mean that. But...maybe we just slow it down a bit." She opens her eyes with hurt, and he presses a kiss to her forehead. "I don't mean that in a bad way. I mean to get a chance to get to know each other on a deeper level, maybe work through the baggage we clearly carry." He attempts a smile to reassure her. "Side effects of dating past the age of forty." He's relieved when he sees her nod, and he pulls her into his chest and kisses her head. "Is that okay with you?"

She sighs into his chest, and he makes a silent vow to treat her with better care, to fight past his own hurt from his past and see Lori as she is without entangling the mistakes of his ex. Lori is different, she's not capable of the monstrosities committed by Pearl. Pearl's demons caused darkness. Lori's, in her amazingness, bring light.

He leans away to grab her face and again kisses her lips tenderly. Lori returns his kiss with a feverish urgency, fingers clutching onto the collar of his shirt, her mouth soft and warm on his. He slips his fingers through her hair, his cock stirring and making him lose all sense of his words uttered mere moments ago.

Slow down.

The words ring in his head, but with Lori's mouth on his, her hands grabbing hold of him, her sweet and floral smell of delicate femininity, Dom feels his control slipping, and instead of the vow to go slow, he's pushing her back onto the bed, hovering his weight over top of her. She whimpers and he feels her knee gliding over his arousal, and he groans into her mouth.

"Dom, please," she whispers. "I missed you so much," and he feels her reaching for his belt. She unbuckles it, then undoes the button, the zipper, and now she removes her mouth from his and he feels her slip down the length of his body, dropping herself to the floor beneath him. He keeps his eyes closed, his feet pressed into the floor on either side of her hips, and his palms pressed into the mattress, hovering over the bed. He feels her mouth as it finds his cock and she sucks in urgent pulls. God help him, he pulses his hips into her head, fucking her soft mouth with reckless and selfish abandonment. Her hands grab his ass, and he quickens his thrusts into her, his pleasure rising.

"Lori, fuck," he breathes out, and she tugs harder onto him, taking him in deeper with each pulse.

When he's close, he reaches a hand down and fists her hair, guiding her head onto him, knowing he's pushing her to the limit, but he's helpless to stop, the feel of power in doing so too addicting to hold back.

He comes in her mouth with a shudder, his legs suddenly weak. He feels her tongue on him as she swallows, massaging him before pulling back to suck him clean.

Draining him of all resolve.

twenty-seven

. . .

lori

"THIS FEELS SO exciting, doesn't it? Like we're investigators of a crime or something." I look over to Edie and grin, but she's awfully quiet for being the entire reason behind this impromptu road trip.

"Hopefully it's more sweet reunion than dead body," she mutters as she stares out her passenger window.

"Now where's the fun in that," I chide.

Despite a rocky start when I first arrived in LA, Dom and I ended up having a glorious few days. I can see the California appeal. While spring is finally fully in bloom here in PA, the weather is still very much hit or miss, and that Cali sunshine sure did bring some much-needed warmth.

But I'm back on the East Coast now, and we're fulfilling our letters mission. I return my attention back to the road, glance at the GPS and note that we're about halfway to our destination, a small town just south of Buffalo, NY. It's a six-hour drive, and so far, our victorious heirloom hunter companion has proven to be most disinterested.

I dragged Reggie along with us, though she was resistant due to her best friend, Lucy, recently having her baby, and her little sister, Lila, has gone to London where she lives. I assured Lucy I'd be whisking Reggie away for only two days, and I opted in my own mother for backup support.

So here we are, a sweet little trio, off to retrieve the other half of the Dog Tags and Lace letters. Thankfully the family didn't seem too interested in keeping them, and while we couldn't exactly disclose that Ruby Francesca was behind the hunt, Ruby has stated that when the time comes, all will be revealed, and the family will get to hold onto both sets of letters for their own generations to come.

I glance in the rearview mirror and see Reggie passed out, snuggled with some massive kitten stuffed animal/pillow combination on loan from my granddaughter Ronnie. My mind flashes back to when JJ and Reggie were infants, sleeping in their car seats. In some ways it feels like yesterday. In others it feels like a dream that never existed in real life at all.

I run my hand through my hair and try again for conversation with Edie. "Alright, spill. What's on your mind? You're entirely too quiet."

Edie drops her arm from the door frame with a heavy sigh. "I ended things with Trenton."

"No! Oh, you seemed to really like him!" I never met the guy, but I could tell Edie was falling for him. She had a new pep in her step. As much as I'd like to take credit for it in having been able to provide a newfound family and information about her late father, I know better. Edie had a kind of glow to her, the glow of young love, and a reddish aura, though now as I look at her, I fear it's turned muddy.

"It was just sex," she says, waving a dismissive hand. "That's all it was."

"No, it was not," I say, picking up my fountain soda from the cupholder between us. I wave it in Edie's direction, asking, "What makes you say that?" before taking a sip.

Edie pushes her glasses back and I put the cup down to lower the radio so I can hear her better. "It's how we defined it right from the start. He's very conservative, he's all buttoned-up lawyer with zero regard for the environment."

"Well, that can be changed. Pop a recycling bin in his apartment or something."

She laughs at that. "He has one, actually."

"Great! What more is there to really do, anyway?"

"That's not the point. It's a belief in the science, Lori." I smile at her passion. I love that about her. "Besides, my moms would sooner disown me than see me end up with a guy like that."

She crosses her arms over her chest with a huff. I reach over and pinch her leg playfully. "Are they dating him, or are you?"

"As of right now? None of us are dating Trenton Wroe." She gives me a pointed look.

I wait a minute, debating how to respond. I know she felt more than just a casual thing for this guy, so I ask, "You seem unhappy with that. Are you?"

I can see her in my peripheral vision, and if I'm not mistaken, she wipes a tear. "I am unhappy with that," she says quietly. "I miss him. I can't believe how much I miss him, and it's only been like, a couple weeks."

"You haven't talked to him at all?" I glance in the rearview mirror again and see Reggie shift in her seat.

"Stay out of it, Mom," she mutters, eyes still closed.

"It's fine," Edie waves her off. "It's actually nice to get a devil's advocate perspective."

"So you haven't seen him in a couple weeks, but have you talked to him?"

Edie sighs and turns her head to look out the window. "He texts me every day. Things like, 'Good morning, beautiful,' and 'I'm not giving up on us.' It's...sweet."

"Persistent," I note approvingly. "Do you respond?"

She nods. "Yes." The word comes out like a confession.

I think about my own mother and her disapproval with James in those early days. She eventually learned to tolerate him, I think once she finally saw the way he stepped up when the twins were born. But I wasn't as close with my mother back then. Lord, if someone ever told me I'd be living with her in this stage of my life, I'd have laughed in their face.

Edie, on the other hand, seems to have a much different relationship with her moms.

"Let me ask you this," I say tentatively. "If your moms approved of him, would you be giving it a real shot?"

She groans. "I hate that I think the answer to that is yes. But they're such good women! Smart! I value their opinions."

"Sweetie," I say gently, "if we do everything exactly by our parents' rules, then we're living their life, not our own."

"Like you're one to talk," Reggie mumbles. I see her stretch out her arms and straighten up in her seat. "You've not been shy with your motherly opinions in the past."

I know where my daughter's going with this, and I'm eager to shut her down. "I thought you wanted me to stay out of it," I remind her.

Reggie leans forward, draping an arm on the back of my seat. "I've changed my mind. Because I very clearly remember a time when you pushed and pushed for me and Joey to stay together, and what do you know? In the end of the day, I followed my heart." She settles herself back and readjusts her seatbelt. "Which lead me to Xavier, and now Joey has Ruby. Just as it should be."

"Is that true?" Edie asks, wide-eyed. She turns behind her to Reggie. "You and Joey Conti were together?"

"High school sweethearts, yeah. And my mom, the romantic, loved that. Thought we were destined to be just like her and my dad. But I always had this nagging feeling, if that makes sense."

"Like what?" Edie asks, and I can't help but feel the tiniest guilt in rehashing this. I see Edie perk up at Reggie's disclosure.

"Joey and I were always better as friends," Reggie says with a solid nod of her head. "That's how it felt with him. And that can be confusing, because we were good together. It's just...the passion wasn't really there. The raw chemistry, deeper connection."

"And you feel that with Xavier?"

"Oh yeah. Right from the start," she says, and I glance back and see Reggie smile.

"Listen, speaking as a mother," I explain, "I can tell you that we want our children to be happy. I know each and every time my mother warned me about James, as much as I couldn't see that as a kid, I know now that it came from her own place of feeling like she knew what was best for me."

"True," Reggie adds. "I'm sure I'll screw up with my babies at some point, all in the name of thinking I know what will make them happy. I can feel that, as much as I hate to admit it."

I smile and do a little internal victory dance. My ever-wise daughter still can learn a thing or two. Maybe even from me.

"So?" I ask. "What do you think you'll do? You're obviously still talking to him, even if you haven't seen him."

Edie leans her head back and closes her eyes. "I may have already screwed up."

"Why's that?"

I glance back in the mirror to Reggie, and we meet eyes and share a curious and concerned look.

"My ex-boyfriend from Florida, Zeke, has been reaching out to me," she says, her tone flat. "He's sweet and a good guy. I should be happy he still wants a chance with me."

"You can be flattered, but that doesn't mean he's right for you," I point out.

"Let me guess," Reggie chimes in. "Your moms love him?"

"Yup." Edie shrugs, and I can't help but notice how young she really is. Smart as can be, but naive in so many ways. "He's an environmental engineer," she continues, "and my moms ran into him at the store not too long ago and have been on me about what a great guy he is, how he apparently looks fantastic, he's coaching his nephew's baseball, all these things that check every box."

"I see," I nod. "So how did you screw up?"

"I invited him up for a week now that school's out. He'll be here Wednesday."

"Oh, shit," Reggie blurts out.

Edie nods. "Yeah. Shit."

FIVE HOURS LATER, THE THREE of us are right back in the car again, leaving the home of Lace's granddaughter, silently holding our collective breath.

Reggie is driving now, I'm in the passenger seat, and Edie is in the back, snuggled up with the kitten pillow. We're heading to the hotel, the Dog Tag letters written to Lace now in hand, a victory on that account, yet I don't think a single one of us feels that way.

Apparently, the family Edie found feels that the entire love affair from their grandmother was just that—a sordid affair. Dog Tags—real name, Edward Cook, was a married man when he went away to war. And the German girl—Anna Weber, had been seduced by good old Edward.

The mystery of how civilian letters would have been sent to the US during that time is also solved—they weren't. Instead, Anna wrote the letters as a kind of diary, initially, and once air mail and overseas correspondence was possible at the end of 1946, Anna sent that first diary/letter as a test. And the response letters from Dog Tags to Lace are few, and nothing of major interest.

It gets worse. Sweet Anna wound up pregnant by Edward during their time together in Germany. Her dream had been to find her way to the US and be reunited with her love in New York. Imagine doing so and finding that Edward was *not* the unattached gentleman with the heart of gold that she had thought. Nope—he was married, and had just recently started a family of his own. After her arduous journey overseas, Anna was broke and alone.

At four years old, the child became ill, eventually passing away. Anna herself barely survived in those first months here but had managed to secure a job and roof over her head working as a housekeeper.

Turns out the Dog Tags & Lace love story we had all grown so fond of was really a tragedy.

Anna turned out okay, thankfully. She eventually found her real love and married a fellow refugee. They went on to have six children and lived happily ever after to the ripe old ages of ninety and ninety-two, dying just days apart. But Anna had kept all of the Dog Tags letters neatly in a box, with their original envelopes and all. Stark contrast to the carelessly stuffed-away letters with no envelopes that Edward had kept in his last home in Pennsylvania, a home that eventually was purchased by Dom Francesca.

Anna's family was helpful and kind. They sung their praises of their strong-willed and righteous Oma Anna but felt at a loss with what to do with the letters. The three of us half wondered if they would mention Ruby Francesca and her famous album named after the nicknames, but the connection didn't seem to be made. It's up to Ruby and her team to decide where, if anywhere, to go from here.

Who knows, maybe her next album can be all about the poisons of deception.

We drive along in silence, the world passing by me in a blur as I process the whole encounter. A lonely woman. A small child. No one to turn to and the pains of her child falling ill. Losing the child, the one thing she had left in the world. The torment she must have felt at that time, I can't imagine.

Only I can, can't I? Yes, I very much can imagine what that must have felt like. The emptiness in your heart and the "what ifs" and the torture of the pain that can only be described as relentless.

My crying starts softly, and I attempt to stop the tears, but they seem to have a mind of their own.

"Mom, are you okay?" Reggie asks with a hand on my shoulder.

I groan and rub my eyes. "No, sweetie. I'm not okay."

"What's wrong? I mean I know it's not quite the happy story we thought, but it was a long time ago. At least we got the other half of the letters," she offers.

"I just can't stop thinking about that poor woman." My throat is tight. There's a muffled strain in my voice.

"Who?" she asks, looking confused. "You mean Lace? Anna?"

I nod. "Yes, Anna. Risking so much, risking her very life to take care of that man while she herself was in hiding."

"I know, she must have been pretty incredible," Edie murmurs from the back seat.

"Right. Suddenly she's caring for two instead of one. All to be completely deceived by the man. The risks and sacrifices she must have made, then he returns home and leaves her pregnant."

"Mom, it was war," Reggie says, her voice attempting to be reassuring. "They were in hiding, probably doubtful of their survival. Swept up in all of it."

"He lied to her!" I cry as I pound a fist into my thigh.

The warmth of Reggie's hand catches my attention as she gently wraps her fingers over my fist. "*Maybe* lied. That we know of." She gives my clenched hand a small squeeze. "Remember, we're far from getting the story firsthand. And he wrote her back, right? He must have cared. If he didn't, he wouldn't have written her back at all."

That, for some reason, reignites me. "Right! He wrote her back! As if he really did love her, so she thinks she's finally getting this incredible reunion." I shake my head, my mind spinning all over again. "I mean who knows what she went through to make it over here, how excited she must have been to have her child meet her father, only to learn he's happily married to someone else?" I can't stand the thought of it—how heartbroken she must have been.

"I'm sure there's a lot we don't know," Edie says.

"Right, exactly. This was literally a lifetime ago," Reggie agrees with one final squeeze of my hand before pulling away.

I can't let it go, though, and I continue. "As if the universe isn't mean enough, she has to suffer through—" my voice catches, and I take a deep breath. "She has to suffer through the loss of her child too?" I can barely even speak the last words out loud.

The car is silent for a moment, no one sure what to say to that, I suppose.

Reggie glances over at me. "Look," she starts, her voice soft. "It was war."

"I'll say."

"They clung together for survival in a time of tragedy," Reggie presses. "Maybe it was a real kind of love, we don't know the details."

I look over in surprise at the tender optimism my usually pragmatic daughter is showing. Given her husband's former military status and tales of his time in war, maybe she has a soft spot for that kind of thing.

"It's so unfair," Edie says quietly.

"So unfair," I agree. "Can you imagine how distraught she must have been, maybe blaming herself for coming here?" I whisper. "For believing in something, and then her child is taken away from her like that. The ultimate punishment when all she did was give."

I suck in a deep breath, my lower lip trembling. "No one deserves that," I whisper through my tears. "How cruel the world can be."

twenty-eight

. . .

dom

IN A RUSTIC courtyard of what will in a couple months be the Francesca/Conti wedding venue, the crew walks across the pale orange tiles, taking in the view of mountains beyond. Dom can imagine what the space will look like once flooded with guests and soft music, the stillness of the desert oasis coming to life. It really is a perfect hideaway spot.

They go to take their seats at the table lined with white linen, a centerpiece of creme flowers punctuating a fresh eucalyptus garland cascading over a brass vase. Small votive candles surround the display.

Dom and Joey both reach for the back of a chair to pull out for Ruby, laughing at one another as they do so. Dom steps back and lets his soon-to-be son-in-law do the honors, and they all take their seats as a round of waters is poured for them. Grayson, Ruby's best friend and fellow musician, places an order of appetizers for the table to nibble on.

Joey swings an arm over the back of Ruby's chair. "Please just try and keep in mind that the wedding is for us, with all the photos for the fans. That's the deal, right?" Joey gives Ruby's shoulder a squeeze. "Don't let it stress you, babe."

"I know, I just want to make it feel like they're a part of it too. My fans are my everything."

Dom's fiercely loyal daughter is committed to making her fans feel as included as possible, which to her means having live stream stations set up. To everyone else, that means a paparazzi nightmare when the location is inevitably figured out, not to mention the diminished value in selling photos to magazines.

"No one even knows the exact date or location yet, we have all the non-disclosures. What's the harm in a little live stream here and there?"

"Lunatics storming in, that's what. It's a no, Ruby," Dom says in the firmest voice he can muster.

Grayson, who will be Man of Honor to Ruby, chimes in. "It's a nice idea, though, love," he croons with his soothing British accent.

Joey meets eyes with them both and mouths "Thank you" before grinning and planting a kiss on Ruby's temple.

"Fine. I'll just have a couple quick video clips to post afterwards, disappointingly generic, and we'll call it a day." Ruby leans back in her chair with a huff, but Dom can still see her wheels turning.

Joey clears his throat. "Moving on—so Dom. Your wedding date?"

"Oh yes," Grayson grins. "The dazzling Lori Meyers and you are an item, I hear."

Ruby nods. "Indeed, they are. And I imagine Lori will be more than a mere guest in attendance, right, Dad?"

"Does that make a difference?" he asks.

"Oh yeah!" Joey beams. "We'll do it up right. Make sure she's included in some of the more intimate family things, right, babe?" Joey glances to Ruby.

"I'd like that," she nods.

"You would? I mean, we've only recently started dating." Dom can't help but feel surprised at how readily they both are accepting Lori as Dom's serious someone.

Ruby cocks an eyebrow at him. "Dad? Am I sensing a little commitment phobia?"

"Uh-oh," Grayson chides. He leans forward on the table. "You know, from my vantage point, I have to say. You Francescas can be too sensible for your own good at times."

Dom glares at him. Grayson's a good man, but Dom doesn't like how accurate his assessment feels.

Ruby rolls her eyes. "Ignore him."

"Will do," Dom nods.

She continues. "I'm just saying, remember that this is Lori we're talking about. The woman that just flew out here to visit you. And Xavier's mother-in-law, not some new girl you met online."

"Your point?" Dom asks, smoothing out a nonexistent wrinkle in the linen before him.

"My point is that you either care about her and feel like it's serious, or you don't. Because I can tell you that *she* feels it's serious. Unless..." she says, cocking an eyebrow.

"Unless what?" Joey asks, looking genuinely confused.

Ruby shrugs. "Unless you still feel something for Jules?"

"Ahh," Joey nods. "Forgot about that." He looks up and thanks the walter that has just placed down multiple plates of food. Dom's stomach rumbles in hunger, but he can't get past what his daughter just said.

"You knew about me and Jules?" he asks in alarm. He leans his elbows on the table and drops his head in his hands. "Is nothing private anymore?"

"You get used to it," Grayson offers.

A staff member comes and refills their water glasses, and Dom greedily downs his, suddenly parched.

"Yes, Dad. We knew. And in my humble opinion, Jules isn't it for you."

"And here we go," Joey smiles before stuffing a bruschetta slice into his mouth with an approving nod.

"I had no idea you had all these opinions. Enlighten me."

Ruby sighs and pushes her fork through the arugula on the plate in front of her. "Remember how I was talking about writing my songs, and the sound is the razzle dazzle that's easy to get swept up in?"

Dom nods. "Yes. Where are you going with this? Lori is the razzle dazzle?"

"No, Dad," she says, dropping her fork. "Jules is the razzle dazzle. Lori is the real deal, she's the deeper meaning." She widens her eyes at him in exasperation. "That's what I'm saying."

"Deeper meaning?"

"You know what I mean."

"I really wish I did." He fights a smile, knowing exactly what she means but feeling less than thrilled at her need to discuss it.

Ruby sighs and leans back in her chair. "Look. Jules is the easy thing to cling to because she's very direct and straightforward, she's no-nonsense. She views the world as pieces of a puzzle that she can rearrange to make whatever picture she wants. It's what makes her great at her job, and why Grayson and I love her."

"So why shouldn't I?" Dom asks with a smile. He's not serious, but he can't help but poke the bear. Ruby can be very opinionated on certain matters.

"Because you already do that!" she cries, briefly throwing her hands up. "You're also straightforward and no-nonsense. You need the other stuff." She drops her hands and fiddles with a trail of vine from the centerpiece before her.

"Reggie and Xavier appear to be no-nonsense," Grayson points out. "Very sensible, those two."

"You're not helping my case," Ruby glares, pointing the edge of the vine at him. "And Reggie is funny in a dry sense of humor kind of way."

"True, she's hilarious," Joey agrees, nodding his head side to side in consideration. "But you're funnier," he grins to Ruby.

"I'm not jealous, if that's what you're getting at. I adore Reggie." Ruby turns to her father, draping her elbow across the back of her chair. "But Dad, what I like about Lori for you is that she's all about the whims of taking things moment to moment. She's lighthearted and that's good for you. Kind of like me and Joey, really," she says with a glance over to her fiancé. She smiles and keeps her gaze held on him. "He does that for me too."

Joey flashes her a wink and reaches for her hand on the table. Dom notes the sweet interaction between two people so comfortable with one another, and it makes him think how comfortable he feels with Lori. Moreso than he's ever felt with anyone.

Yes, she compliments him. She's fun and lighthearted, the couple days she had spent here with them were easy. She had no agenda or demands, and they had strolled around LA exploring, walking the streets hand in hand. Lori would light up when she saw something that caught her eye, and Dom had loved seeing her unabashed excitement over the smallest of things.

In fact, one moment in particular had him feeling a little like he more than simply cares for her.

They had been out to lunch at a street-side cafe, and a young family was sitting at the table beside them. Their toddler was reaching that point of restlessness, and kept coming up to Dom and Lori's table, ignoring his parents' requests to stop. You could sense their rising stress, and Lori had assured them it was fine, she loved the entertainment. To Dom's initial horror, she ended up scooping the child right up onto her lap, pulling out a notebook and crayons from her purse, explaining she keeps a whole bag of goodies with her for emergency activities for her grandchildren. He looked over to the couple, certain they were going to demand their child back, but all they said was, "You sure he's not bothering you?"

Lori urged the couple to relax and enjoy their meal together, laughing and bouncing around her new mini friend on her knee, and the couple thanked her profusely for the borrowed time. She made it all look so easy and natural.

Dom had felt a strange warmth blossom in his chest at the entire interaction.

He smiles to himself as he remembers the way he felt in that moment, and he looks over at Ruby. "How did you get so wise?"

"Please—I create music," she says with a dramatic wave of her hands in the air, conducting an invisible orchestra. "In order to do that, and do it well," she says, dropping her hands, "I need to understand what speaks to people. What makes them tick, what emotions I can evoke and how someone can identify with something."

"It's a gift."

"A gift that also tells me you're letting Pearl stuff cloud your head." Dom startles at the sudden and unexpected accusation, and Ruby raises her palms out to the side. "There, I said it."

"Yes, you did," murmurs Grayson affectionately to his best friend. "And having been around for my girl, Ruby, here through some of the aftermath of Pearl," he says with a knowing eyebrow raise her way, "I can imagine you're onto something."

Dom thinks about it, knowing somewhere in his gut that Ruby is right. Pearl felt like a giant "fuck you" of deception, and he hated the feeling of helplessness in never once seeing it before it was too late. And he wasn't the only one hurt in that—Dom blames himself for putting Ruby in harm's way with her mother's neglect.

But he also knows that moving through life with a lack of trust would only be allowing Pearl to hold a continued power over him. And Lori deserves his trust, just as she's given hers to him.

"Fine. You're right," Dom finally concedes.

Ruby widens her eyes. "Holy hell, can I get that in writing? That's it, you admit that you're being kind of an ass to Lori, hiding out here with us pretending to love wedding planning, all to avoid what could possibly be a really fantastic thing?"

With that statement, Dom starts to worry he's been overstaying his welcome. Ruby's right, though—it's time for him to go home. If he's honest with himself, he misses Lori. A realization that both scares and excites him.

Grayson darts his eyes between the two of them. "Alright, easy now, tiger. Give your dad a break, he's trying to open his heart here. It's a tough thing to do."

Dom nods. "A man who understands."

"It needed to be said," Ruby insists. "Because as much as we love having you here—"

"Which we do," Joey interrupts.

Ruby continues, "—your ass needs to get back to your real life. To Lori. Who is a good woman that quite honestly, deserves better than what you're giving her at this point."

"Christ, I know. Message received," he grumbles.

Joey looks at Dom with seriousness, a quality he rarely exhibits, and he takes in his earnest expression. There's something on Joey's mind, clearly, and Dom braces himself for whatever he's about to say. "You know, seeing as I've known Lori most of my life, I feel like you should understand something about her."

"What's that?"

Joey shrugs. "Well, she was the neighborhood mother hen growing up. The one with the best cookies, or the biggest poster board sign at my football games, all that stuff."

Dom laughs, picturing exactly that. "I have no doubt."

"She's good people. Trust me on that."

"I sense a but coming."

Joey nods. "But—she also gets her feelings hurt easily. It's not always pretty when she does."

Joey's words sound like a warning, and the same alarm bells that have gone off in Dom's head before when it comes to Lori start ringing again. Only now, the ringing isn't fear for himself anymore. No, these bells are fear of hurting her.

He nods. "As fun as all your input is, you don't have to

convince me." He exhales with a sigh before continuing. "Initially, I needed some time to clear my head because we dove right in and it was a lot, and fast. But truth be told..."

"Yes?" Grayson prompts with a smile that looks far too much like he's enjoying watching Dom in the hot seat.

"I miss her," Dom admits. He rubs his hand over his jaw. "A lot."

And I'm pretty sure I love her.

The thought pops in his mind, the small flicker of a flame he'd been trying to ignore, now showing itself in full force. But he's not about to share that with his daughter, her best friend, and his soon-to-be son-in-law.

"Good," Joey says. "We approve," and he lifts his glass in a salute before taking a sip.

Ruby stretches her arm out to Dom and pats him on the shoulder. "And from you? I think that's about as big a love declaration as we can expect."

LATER THAT EVENING, SITTING POOLSIDE back at his daughter's house, Dom starts to feel an unease in his chest. The wind has shifted, and the lounge chairs start inching themselves across the patio toward the pool. He jumps up to save them before they drown themselves, telling Ruby he's going to stack them up and tuck them in the storage area. She nods, helping him do the same. They rush to secure everything before escaping back in the safe confines of the house.

"That came out of nowhere, thanks for the help," Ruby says, taking a seat at the marble kitchen counter. She grabs her phone, saying she's going to check the weather, but she frowns. "Oh, shit," she says, typing something furiously.

"What?" Dom asks, hackles up.

His mind goes to the worst-case scenario, and he hates that he has to ask what he's about to ask. "Did your mother reach out to you?" She was known to do that from time to time, though it had been a while since the last contact attempt when it was clear Ruby wanted nothing to do with her, and that was in no way ever going to change.

"Worse," she says. "Here, look at this." She tosses her phone over to him.

He catches it and turns it right side up, his pulse quickening as he sees the photo.

Of Dom and Jules, the night of the charity gala. It's of them leaving, right after the altercation with the pervert. Jules is leaning in, whispering something to him. The photo looks like two lovers caught in an intimate moment. Just like Lori had caught them the night she came in to surprise him.

Only this moment is online for the world to see, with a headline reading, "Can We Expect Two Weddings from the Francesca Family?" and a story to follow on the secret relationship between Ruby Francesca's father and her publicist.

"She wouldn't have. Do you think she did this?" Ruby asks, now up from her seat and pacing.

They both know the answer, though. This is Jules's job, her world.

"Fuck, fuck. If Lori sees this, it will crush her," he says, grabbing the back of his neck.

"I think you better get back home, Dad," Ruby asserts. "If you really care about her. It's time to make that clear, wouldn't you say? Enough avoiding."

He nods. She's right, he knows his daughter is right. God help him, the idea of screwing this up with Lori has him twisted in knots of panic. He thinks about what Joey had said earlier, about what happens when Lori's feelings get hurt. He feels physically sick to his stomach at the idea of being the cause of that. His fear of her reaction is not for his own consequences, but out of his concern for her. And if that doesn't tell him something about what he wants, about his love for her, then nothing will.

twenty-nine

· · ·

lori

thirty-five years old

WHEN THE DOOR slammed that evening, I knew it was going to be a rough night. It was early summer, Reggie was fifteen and at the beach with her best friend, Lucy, and their family, so I was all alone in the house. Richard was always more tame when Reggie was there. He knew she wouldn't tolerate any violence, that my spirited daughter would never stand for him hurting me. He could be careful and controlled when he wanted to be. I clung to that knowledge.

I also knew that any moments of his rage were like an escape room I was in, and I just needed to figure out the riddles to unlock and be free. Not just free myself, but work to free the hurt man that was trapped inside this aggressor, disguised as my Richard. We were both victims in those dark hours when his anger would get the best of him.

I could always tell by his eyes. Richard's eyes were a bright blue, with a warmth behind them.

Not when the violence happened, though. Then, his eyes would show a kind of blank, robotic stare. All ice, as if no living human actually occupied the space behind those eyes. And I would look at my Richard and feel pain that he was trapped inside there, knowing he would hate himself later, realizing that this thing had taken over him and hurt me. I just had to survive the spell, and do whatever I could to pull Richard out, and all would be okay.

But that last fight we had, shortly before his heart attack—it was our worst one. In fact, it was the first time I thought I might actually die by the monster's hands, and all I could think was how guilty Richard would feel afterward. That I had to survive, because I couldn't let Richard feel that.

WHEN THE MOON IS FULL, it's because it's positioned in such a way that it can reflect all the light from the sun. As it makes its way around the earth again over the next several days and weeks, the moon appears to shrink, until the darkest point of a new moon, when the light is gone and it's impossible to see.

That's how it was with me and Richard. If our balance was off, it made him feel threatened. He would be in darkness, empty, and it crushed me to know it.

Something had been off with him around the time of that last big fight, but I didn't know what. He had been just a sliver of his full self for a while now. I suspected he had another woman some-where, but instead of feeding him light like I imagine he wanted, the affair was taking.

I had come to understand that he and I were both addicted to falling in love. Whereas my addiction came certified with loyalty, his did not. I give my whole heart and then some to the person I'm with. I could never imagine cheating. But Richard was different. In time I learned that Richard was the kind of man who saw what was in front of him, and he lived completely in that moment, with a tunnel vision that blocked out the rest of the world. And if that meant he was standing before a beautiful woman who was falling prey to his easy smile and allure, then he would live in that moment and allow himself to love her. Not the same kind of love he had for me, but a different kind, maybe. One that was a quick rush that would just as quickly fall, as opposed to the rush that was our connection—ours only grew and became more layered and complicated.

I do believe he was faithful those first few years with me. Those were the good years—I had saved him from his hurt caused by his ex-wife, and the hurt from their now-grown children who wanted little to do with him, aside from the plea for money now and then.

But that slammed door that evening told me we were in a vacuum, and no love would exist for the next who-knew-how-many hours. I braced myself. We were in the darkness of a new moon.

I tried my best to look casual when he came into our bedroom that evening. I was in bed and reading a magazine, tucked under the thin sheet and wearing my favorite lacy nightgown, this one a pale purple. I looked up and smiled my brightest when his body filled the doorframe, though my heart was pounding. My next words needed to be chosen carefully if I wanted to help us both escape.

"My silver fox, I missed you," I said, putting my magazine down and swinging my legs over the side of the bed to rise and greet him.

He smiled, but it didn't reach his eyes. "I should think so. I've been gone for three days."

I wrapped my arms around his waist and hummed into his chest. He smelled like his usual cologne mixed with something else, I wasn't sure what. Something stale, probably the remnants of the plane.

"I hate when you leave me." I was trying to keep my voice the perfect combination of light and playful, with undertones of pleading to let him know he was wanted, but not in a demanding way. My performance here was everything.

To my relief, he caved, and I felt his arms wrap around me just as fiercely as mine were around his. "I'm going to make a drink," he said, and I pulled back from him and rushed out to our mini bar, wanting to beat him to it. If I made his drink, I could water it down with ice. If he made it, he'd prepare it neat.

"Make two," he said. "We're celebrating." Another wave of relief flooded me. This was good, maybe I'd jumped to conclusions when I heard the slammed door. I was being paranoid.

It was dark outside, but we sat by our pool in two lounge chairs. The water was calm as all the jets were off, and the glow of light radiating blue created an electric feel, topped with the small swirls of steam as the water's heat collided with the cool air. I watched the phenomenon and was transfixed during our silence. The occasional firefly flickered in the woods beyond, and a harmony of crickets provided our soundtrack.

"So, my love," I said. "What exactly are we celebrating?" This is where my riddle-solving attempts started to fail. I shouldn't have brought it back up. I should have kept quiet, let him take the lead. Maybe the evening would have ended with nothing being said at all. We would have gone to bed, had a good night's rest and avoided the whole thing.

He looked over to me, and I could see the ice in his eyes. A chill swept over me with his intensity. "Curious, are you?"

I tried to act nonchalant. If I overshot my enthusiasm, he'd question my sincerity. "Of course."

He looked away and out to the trees again. "We're celebrating new beginnings." He raised his glass to his lips for a drink, and I did the same, mind rolling through all the things that might mean. Did he lose a big account? Were we in financial trouble? Because while his words conveyed something positive, everything else about him did not.

"Good," I finally said. "I like new beginnings."

He chuckled. "Oh, I suspect you do."

I glanced over to him. "What does that mean?" Another misstep.

He reached over and squeezed my hand. "I was your best new beginning, wasn't I? You had nothing before me. And then you hooked your talons in. Got exactly the new beginning you needed." He smirked and raised his glass as if to cheer. "Smart girl. Fooled me."

"I fooled you?" There was so much more I wanted to say, and my pulse was buzzing through my veins. But those three words were all I could manage.

"You women are all the same, aren't you? Calculating. Just like my ex."

I was frantic with trying to understand what was happening. Did his ex-wife reach out to him? Did he think I was being unfaithful to him? Was he in trouble with work, and he somehow thought I had something to do with it? If I could just figure out where this was all coming from, then I could crack the code and set him free.

I slammed the rest of my drink and quickly grabbed the bottle sitting on the small table between us, pouring another. I needed the courage. Yet another misstep, because within half an hour I would soon learn that all it did was give me the wrong kind of courage.

At that moment, though, I still had my wits about me, and I rose to join him, lifting my nightgown and straddling him. "Richard," I purred. "It's me. Your little lady, remember? I'm nothing like your ex." I kissed his cheek, scratchy with a stubble of needing a shave. "Yes, you were my new beginning. But even if you had nothing, I'd still be helpless in your arms and hopelessly in love." I nibbled his ear and rocked my hips against him, willing an erection to form so we could make love and move past whatever was troubling him. "I'll always be hopelessly in love with you."

But instead of giving in and letting me take us both out of this trap, he grabbed my hips and threw me off him. I stumbled backwards and dropped hard on the slate stone beneath us. I bit my lip and closed my eyes, willing his rejection of me to not cloud my thoughts. There was no room for my disappointment or anger here.

I placed my hand on the table beside us, the one holding my glass and the bottle of Scotch, using it to steady me as I rose to my feet. Instead, it crashed down under my weight, and I stumbled again. He snapped his head down to me and the mess of glass from my drink, eyes darting over to the bottle that had survived the fall and was still intact. He snatched it and took a long pull from the bottle before removing it from his lips, then wiping his mouth with his hand.

"Clean that shit up," he spat out before rising and moving back inside, leaving me.

My body started trembling then. On shaky legs I rose up, lifted the small table back to its position, and I started gathering the broken glass as carefully as I could. For a moment, my mind imagined taking a piece and slicing myself with it. I couldn't be sure if it was out of hurt from his words about the blanket of grief I had been in when we met, or if it was out of wanting to hurt myself so that he'd see it and feel sympathy for me. Maybe it was both.

I didn't cut myself, though. I took a deep breath, still holding onto hope that this would pass and all would be okay. He had left me alone, and that was a good sign. I gathered as much as I could and walked back into the house, knowing what I would do. I'd throw away the glass and head upstairs. Our bedroom was on the main floor of the house, so I'd hide away for the night up in a guest room, and all would be okay.

If only I had followed my own plan.

thirty

. . .

lori

I BLINK MY eyes as a sharp slice of sunlight pokes through the curtain of the hotel. My eyes are puffy, I can feel it, and I dread looking in the mirror to see the damage.

It had been a long night in the hotel. The three of us had shuffled in, throwing our bags down and collapsing on our beds, Reggie and Edie sharing one, leaving the other to me. My eyes were burning from my tears mixed with mascara, and Reggie offered to run me a hot bath. I shook my head no, not wanting to soak in the tub of a hotel. I showered instead, willing my emotions to wash away with the heat of the water.

I had tossed and turned all night. I wished I were back home in my little cottage I shared with my mother, in my own bed. I felt restless and uneasy, though also ridiculous for letting this whole stupid letters nonsense affect me so much. Eventually, I fell into a dreamless sleep, so now as the sun makes its appearance through the sliver of curtains this morning, I'm thankful to know it means we can make our way back home.

We eat the meager hotel breakfast and pack up to head out. As we step outside, I hear the birds chirping and note that the May air is warm, though my mood still feels frustratingly flat. We all feel the heaviness of it based on our glazed-over stares, and I feel a bit at fault for my mini-breakdown yesterday. It's like I've made the girls feel like they aren't allowed to be happy, and I'm determined to shake away this cloud.

As we head out of town, my head still foggy but my mood slowly finding more light, I get a hare-brained idea.

"Turn off here," I direct Reggie. "This exit."

"Huh? Why?" She looks at me with confusion but obliges. "We just left the hotel, you need to use the bathroom already?"

"Did you forget something?" Edie asks.

I lean back and look out the window to the passing greenery. "Maybe I did," I say.

"Mom, what the hell does that mean, did you or didn't you?"

I turn back around to look at Edie. "I think I'm ready for that grief interview now," I say with a small sad smile. "We're going to my old hometown. Where James and I first met."

"Oh," she says with a look I can't quite read. "I already turned that paper in."

"You did? Who did you use?" I ask.

Edie shrugs guiltily. "I may have fudged my way through it a little. Kind of pieced together my own thing."

I look over to Reggie and see her stifling a laugh. "I didn't know you had it in you, Edie."

I lean back and smile too. "Guess we're all rebellious sinners now and then, aren't we?"

"Sometimes you gotta do what you gotta do," Edie mumbles.

Reggie reaches over and grabs my hand for a squeeze. "Small ways of surviving."

We drive off in silence to the little lakeside town where it all began.

WE WANDER AROUND THE BEACH with shoes in hand and our toes sinking through the cool sand. It's a gorgeous day with crisp blue skies and a mild breeze to break the heat of the sun. Warm for early May, but if there's one thing I love, it's being by the water.

"I haven't been back here since we left," I say. It feels like a confession. James and I had left town for his job, and we never looked back.

"You haven't?" Edie asks. "What about your old friends, or to see your parents?"

I lift my shoulders. "Didn't really have anyone worth visiting. And my parents came to us when they wanted. And then after the accident, it just felt too painful to return."

"How about now?" Reggie asks. She sets herself down and hugs her knees to her chest.

Edie and I join her. "It's easier than I thought it would be," I say as I stretch out my legs and lean back on my palms.

"It's so beautiful here," Edie murmurs. "I'm spoiled with Florida beaches, but there's something so peaceful about a lakeside beach." She's dragging a finger through the sand in a small wave pattern, and my mind flashes back to myself doing the very same thing here with James years ago.

"You know I lost my virginity right over there," I say with a mischievous smile, lifting a hand and pointing to a spot tucked between two large trees, the canopy of greenery providing a shaded cocoon. "I was seventeen, and your dad was so gentle about it. He took some convincing, you know."

"Mother, you exhibitionist, you!" Reggie says with mock offense.

"Quite the contrary, it was after the park closed, we snuck in. It was actually the only real privacy we had. Nana was strict as all hell."

"You've mentioned that before."

"Oh yeah?"

She laughs. "Yeah. Usually, when I was a kid and mad if I couldn't go somewhere and you'd tell me I didn't know how good I had it," Reggie says, knocking a shoulder into mine.

Edie nods in understanding. "My moms were so strict with me. Very protective. I was a good kid, too. They didn't need to worry so much."

"Well, I wasn't quite so perfect," I say. I lean back again and watch a flock of birds circle the water overhead. "I meant well, but I was often bored and restless. I snuck the car out before I even knew how to drive, I was known to break curfew. Loved stealing from the liquor cabinet."

"That doesn't surprise me," Reggie says through a smile.

"It was actually your father, the school bad boy, that leveled me out." I tilt my head to the side. "He was incredibly smart, and we were good for each other. It was like our recklessness was just us searching for someone to finally understand us. And when we found one another, we didn't want to be so reckless anymore." I smile. "Mostly. We were still a little rebellious at heart."

Reggie scoops up a handful of sand and slowly drops it through her fingers. It catches the wind and floats on a mini journey before settling. "You're a lot like him, you know," I tell her. "You look like me, but your mind is all James."

She pops her head up with a smile. "Really?"

"Sure, I've never told you that?" I ask.

Her smile drops. "Maybe you have, but not often. Dad and JJ have always felt like forbidden topics."

Edie pauses her wave pattern and looks at Reggie. "I think people prefer to lock in the memories that hurt. I think it's why my moms never told me more about Richard. There's something there, I can tell. I just don't know what."

I gulp, unsure what to say. My hunch is that he may have... pushed Edie's mother. Her conception may not have been consensual. It pains me to think so, and I don't want to believe he would be capable of that. But then again, I'd had my own fair share of questionable encounters with him. He was a man who got what he wanted, when he wanted it.

"You know what," Reggie says, clapping her hands together to brush off the sand. "If Dog Tags and Lace taught us anything, maybe it's that some questions are better left unanswered." She glances over to me, and I can tell her mind has been following the same line of thinking mine has.

"I guess so," Edie says half-heartedly.

"So, Mom...how is our boy Dom doing?"

"Good!" I say brightly, thankful for her change in subject. "He's coming home the day after tomorrow, actually." My chest warms as I remember the text he had sent me earlier. It was an unexpected and long-winded one, and I can tell he put some time and thought into it. He apologized for his distance, saying he misses me and admitted to being taken aback by how strongly he feels about me, but that he's committed to pushing past his head-in-his ass ways because I'm worth it. I had laughed and wrote him back that it was fine, and to look forward to coming home to a new roommate, that I'd already begun painting and rearranging things in his house. It feels good to be able to openly talk about and laugh over our differing emotional tendencies. It's far more honest than any of the relationships I've muddled through in recent years.

"I still can't believe you guys know Ruby freakin' Francesca," Edie chimes in. "And you're dating her father, that's amazing. She is a true artist."

I laugh, because it's the first time I've heard Edie gush in any way about Ruby. I have to hand it to her, she's remained very professional throughout the letters hunt.

We hang for a little while, mostly in silence, and enjoy the scenery. I'm not entirely sure what exactly made me have Reggie make this detour. Maybe it was knowing that we were so close by. Maybe it's feeling like something has finally shifted with Dom, an honesty that's been reached in talking about an "us" in a more real way that's not just superficial. Who knows, but as I sit here now and watch the handful of other people wandering and exploring, surf fishing in hopes of a good catch, I feel some serenity settle in. Yes, this is a place that held memories for me, but it's also a place where new ones are constantly being made. Little moments of connecting with nature that feel very continuous, in a sense. Life moves on. It's not a time capsule, this small stretch where land meets water. Nothing is frozen or locked in here. This place has continued to provide an earthly playground for its visitors, and I can feel the beautiful moments that have taken place, time and time again right here.

I find comfort in that.

AS WE GET READY TO head out, Reggie's phone buzzes with a text. She rises to a stand as she pulls it out to see. "This is probably Xavier, dying to know what we're doing here and not on the road to rescue him from the kids."

Edie and I stand to join her, shaking off the sand as we head back to the car. I take one last glance over to the shady cove where my sexual adventures all began, and I kiss my fingertips to blow a kiss to the area. A quick wave of emotion bubbles up, though it's brief. I can't bring myself to walk over to the spot, it's as if I don't want to tarnish it with the person that I am now, but I also can't tear my eyes away from it.

"Oh. What the..." I hear Reggie whisper.

I say a silent, "Until we meet again," and reluctantly look over to Reggie. She's stopped walking and is staring at her phone.

"What is it, sweetie?" I ask, glancing down at her screen. I see a photo on it, but she quickly clicks out and then fumbles, accidentally dropping the phone in the sand. I bend to retrieve it, and she beats me to it, grabbing it and clutching it to her stomach.

"Nothing, just something from Xavier."

"Is everything okay?" Edie asks.

"What was the photo?" I say, a chill sweeping over me. Something's off, I can feel it. Reggie's face has gone stiff, though, and I'm annoyed with her silence. "For the love of God, speak up!"

"I need a minute, I'm not exactly sure. Just hang on," she says, turning her back to us as she looks down at her phone.

Edie and I glance at each other in confusion. I nod my head over to Reggie in a silent command for Edie to try and look, but she remains frozen. As silently as I can, I peer over Reggie's shoulder. She's reading something. It looks like an article, but without my glasses I can't make out what it says.

After a moment she turns to face me. "Okay. It's just a dumb rumor, that's all. Someone snapped a photo of Dom with another woman, and there's an article suggesting that they're together."

"Is it your mom?" Edie asks.

But I know better. "Who is the woman, Reggie?"

"Ruby's publicist, Jules Arnold."

I nod silently until I huff out a laugh. "Of course it is." I start to walk to the car, eager to be moving my body. Then I stop and turn around. "Let me see the picture," I demand, hand held out.

Reggie slowly hands the phone over to me, and I scroll up through the article to the top of the page. And there it is, a photo with Dom and Jules. I recognize her gown from the night I came into town and walked in on her up against him. This photo mirrors her close body positioning of that night, but in this one they're walking and she's leaning into his body, with a hand slipped into his tuxedo jacket. Looking for what, exactly? His car keys? Unlikely.

My breath starts coming in short and I try and collect my thoughts, tossing the phone back to Reggie.

"Mom, it's a stupid gossip-hungry site."

"Mmm hmm," I say. "With a woman that controls that type of thing, imagine that!" I'm hurt and confused. What did I ever do to this woman? What's her end game here, to push me out?

My mind thinks back to Dom and his admission of running

away from us when he left town. Did something happen with them when he first arrived? Am I a fool to believe nothing did? My mind is spinning in a wave of emotions. Confusion. Hurt. Sadness. Anger.

But it's the disappointment that feels the most crushing. Yes, disappointment is what is sitting heavy in my chest right now and threatening tears.

I've been so *hopeful* in something good happening between us. Even feeling like I was in love all over again. I've been so patient because I know Dom has been through his own hurt and hell. I've justified his actions in an attempt to offer him grace and *respect* despite his pulling away, making me question whether or not he found me good enough for him. I've tried to sidestep that, logically knowing it's not about me, though every insecurity I have has been raised in the process, and it feels awful.

I'm disappointed to realize that I seem to never receive the same grace and respect that I put out there for him. For everyone, all the goddamn time. When do I ever get that? When is it my turn to be put first?

My own phone buzzes, and I scramble in my pocket to pull it out. It's a text. From Dom.

> D: Hi, can we talk when you get a minute?

Ha! Typical. He needs to talk. Yet another need someone has placed on me. I look up at Reggie in question.

"I texted him. He knows you saw it," she says guiltily.

"Well, that was fast," I spit out.

"I'm sure there's an explanation," Edie offers.

I stare at them both, eyes darting back and forth between the two. "Yes, I'm sure there is. Only you know what? I just don't feel like hearing it right now. Why do I *always* have to be the one to hear the explanation? To have to be soothed? I'm feeling rather sick of it!"

I turn on my heels and march over to the trees. To our spot. The sand is kicking behind me and I stumble on a small drop, but I find my way over to it, willing it to offer a time portal to take me back to that magical moment all those years ago. The moment my one true love and I finally connected. James and his pretty girl. Two kids with nothing but hope and love in our hearts. Thinking we had the whole world ahead of us.

And we did. For those blissful few years, we did. I rub my hands against the rough bumps of the bark, closing my eyes and inhaling deeply. It smells the exact same, just as I remember, a mix of sea air and lush green. The perfect combination. I can see James's nervous smile, see his eyes as he holds me afterwards, concerned that he hurt me, and me running my hand along his bare torso and ensuring him it was worth it. Knowing so completely that this was right, the beginning of something beautiful.

I drop down to the ground and wait for tears to come, I can feel the sting behind my eyes, but they don't. Even that feels like its own kind of betrayal. Let me cry, at least. I cried for Anna, for God's sake! A woman long gone with zero connection to me! Let me cry now and unleash and bask in *feeling* something for a person that actually matters, for the memories, right here in the place that once belonged to me and my love.

I sit and rock back and forth, waiting for this block to clear and for the tears to rain down and work to heal me. But none ever come.

dog tags

. . .

March 1947 ~ New York

Dear Lace,

You remind me of such incredible bliss, that first night we made love. Nothing else mattered then—only having you. Trust me when I say that my sole intention was to love the woman that had been my savior. I was blind and ravenous with the need to do so.

I had told myself I would not touch you. I told myself it was wrong to do so.

I was lying to myself, right from the start. Forgive me, darling, as I was helpless in your presence. I took advantage of you, I'm afraid, but I thank God to hear that you live with no regret.

I should like to say that I feel the same way, but I know that I am a selfish man. While I feel apologies might be in order, my selfishness keeps me from doing so, because my regret is not for our time together. No, the only regret I can seem to hold is for our separation afterward. To love you and leave you has been cruel, and I reflect quite a bit on the choices I've made that have made leaving you that much more heartbreaking.

I believe I'm confused within the confines of my mind. I'm tasked with having to make sense of our memories together, and the alternate existence of my world now. You said that I have taught you forgiveness, and I'm holding onto that lesson as I myself am struggling with its application on my actions.

Though to have our actions be judged in the times of our crises is surely unjust. Perhaps the path forward to healing can be paved in reminding ourselves so.

I pray you are well, my darling Lace. And I selfishly pray that one day, our paths may cross once again.

Love always,
Dog Tags

thirty-one

. . .

dom

HE STEPS UP to the guest cottage in a quick jog. It's an overcast day, a stark contrast to the eternal sunshine he left behind in California, but it feels like a relief. The property is quiet, and Dom notes the return of the patio and pool furniture dotting the slate. The pool has been opened and the filter hums quietly behind a small hedge of bushes.

With a deep breath, he knocks twice. Lori had been ignoring his calls and texts, so his last hope is to see her in person.

When he hears the footsteps, he's hopeful. He had given Lori a heads-up that he'd be coming over, so he feels this is a good sign that she's willing to hear him out. While Jules had worked to have the article and picture removed, Dom already knew the damage had been done. It killed him to think that Lori had seen it and read anything more into it, and he needs to fix this before he loses her.

But when the floral wreath before him jostles with the swinging of the door, it's Lori's mother, Kathryn, who appears before him.

She's a tall woman with a proud stature, even in her old age.

Her gray hair lays straight in a tidy bob around her shoulders, and Dom has the feeling he's in the presence of a scolding nun.

"Kathryn, hello. Good to see you," Dom says. Her arms are crossed, and she makes no attempt to move past the door frame, or offer a handshake or a hug, not that he'd expect one.

"I'm only the messenger here," she says. "But the message is that she'd rather not see you right now."

Dom drops his head in defeat. He feels like a kid having to face off with a disapproving parent. He grabs the back of his neck and thinks what he can possibly say to get through this gate. When he meets Kathryn's gaze again, he thinks he sees the tiniest flicker of sympathy in her eyes, but he questions his judgment.

"Do you know if she's at least read any of my texts?" he asks. All the words are in there, the apologies and explanations that nothing happened with Jules. That he's falling for Lori and that a stupid photo shouldn't be a hindrance to what they've started.

"She has, I believe."

"Good, that's good," he says, with the slightest bit of relief.

Kathryn sighs. "I know my daughter, and she's a spirited fighter."

Dom smiles a little at this. "That she is."

Kathryn stares at him, eyes darting back and forth between his, and Dom gets the sense he's being studied. "She's been through some tough things in her life."

Dom nods. "I know." *God*, he knows, and he hates thinking about all Lori has been through, and the way he's jostled around her heart. It's his own fear and pain that have led to those actions, but Dom knows better than to try and justify his mistakes. Doing so only escapes accountability, and he's determined to take a more honest look in the mirror than that.

He shrugs, unsure what else to say. "She's incredible. I hope she knows how incredible she is."

They continue to stand there as if waiting for something to

happen. Dom glances behind Kathryn, wondering if Lori's listening, but all he sees is the small and empty kitchen.

He looks back at Kathryn and decides to go for his moment of truth. Maybe Lori's in there somewhere. Maybe she could hear the sincerity in his voice. "Could you just tell her that...tell her that I love her."

Kathryn's face remains impassive, and Dom's gut twists at the vulnerability of having spilled out these words to the woman in front of him, hoping that there's a woman behind her to hear them.

"Just give her time," Kathryn finally says. "She'll come around."

"How do you know?" he asks. His tone is soft, but even he can hear the desperation in it.

"Because," Kathryn declares. "She always does." With that, the old woman unwinds her arms and steps back, closing the door.

thirty-two

· · ·

lori

thirty-five years old

I HAD BEEN tossing and turning in the guest room upstairs, trying to keep my distance from Richard, but my mind was reeling from the interaction by the pool. The liquor was kicking in, and with it came a wave of emotions. I felt like I could burst right out of my skin with all of them. I was hurt, I was angry, I was sick with a lust for wanting to understand, or wanting to win this argument and make *him* understand how twisted he was to suggest I was anything less than the angel he once believed me to be.

I rose up and paced the room, locking my fists in my hair and twisting strands in knots. I was wild with booze and grief and torment. And then rage, because I was sure this was about some whore he had been sleeping with. Yes, that had to be it. Some affair with a whore he had in another city, and she had put an end to things, robbing him of light. Only that was his fault—not mine. If he was broken right now, I'd be damned if he was going to blame me.

Eventually, I flew down the stairs and stormed into our bedroom. The smell of soap hit me, and I noted a cloud of steam stretching around the corner. I made my way down the small hall and into our bathroom. Richard was in the shower, I could just make out his body through the fog on the glass doors. I threw open the door and pushed against him, the water now pouring down on me and soaking my nightgown.

"Who is she, what did you do?" I cried, fists slamming into his chest. It was the wrong move, of course it was. But I didn't care. I was too hurt to care what price I would pay for this. He couldn't talk to me like that. He couldn't dismantle my pain as if it was a worthless ploy to obtain some fortune of his, a thing I never even knew about when he first captured my heart.

He snatched my wrists from his chest and slammed me against the tiles of the shower wall. I was used to the crack of my head by then. By that point, a move like that happened in steady cycles.

But when I looked up at him, I saw that his eyes were red. He had been crying. My Richard had been crying, and it broke something in me. He stared at me, and the pain I saw in his eyes brought on my own tears. The shame swept over me, and I began to cry. "Richard, talk to me, what happened? What's wrong? Tell me, please," I begged.

The pain in his eyes pulled back, swept right back into his mind, and the ice replaced his gaze. He pushed me again, softer this time, then released me, turning off the shower and stepping out. I stood there on the pebbled shower floor, soaking wet and dripping as I watched him take his towel from the hook on the wall, and he began to dry himself off. I gasped deep breaths and tried to find air in the stifling humid heat surrounding me.

Carefully, I stepped out of the shower. Richard was still damp, and I was mesmerized watching the roll of his muscles beneath his skin. He wrapped the towel around his waist, and I clenched my nightgown in fists by my thighs. I lifted it up and over my head and flung the wet ball of fabric into the sink, reaching for my own towel, wrapping it around my chest without any attempt to dry off.

His eyes darted over to the sink before snapping back to me. "You're disgusting, get that shit out of there." He marched over to the sink and grabbed the nightgown, shaking it in front of my face. "This is how you treat the things in your possession, isn't it?" A smile snaked across his face, but I could see the rage in his eyes. I didn't understand what was happening. This didn't feel like our other fights. In other fights, I'd be explaining myself somehow, trying to make him forgive whatever indiscretion he perceived I had committed.

This fight felt like something else. As if he were slipping away from me, and I wanted desperately to get him back.

"Tell me what's wrong, Richard," I said, my voice unsteady. "Please, let me help you." I quickly wiped a tear from my face and looked back at him, stepping toward him and placing my hands on his chest, willing him to come back to me.

"You disgust me." He raised the balled-up nightgown to my face, shoving me with it, robbing me of air as he backed me up against the wall. "You're sick, you little cunt. Sick and selfish, and you want to help me! You think I need help!"

The wet fabric was pressed to my face, and I was seeing spots, grabbing hold of his wrists in attempt to pull his arms away so I could breathe. My face was completely covered, and I couldn't see anything. I couldn't see his eyes, I couldn't do anything to try to get through to him. His body was completely pressed against mine and I was helpless, my legs locked. I tried to move my feet anyway, but it was pointless. They slipped, wet on the tile floor, and he pressed into me harder to keep me from falling.

I was dizzy and suffocating, and I thought this is it. This is the moment I'm going to die, and I had no idea why. I thought about how guilty he would feel afterward.

Then my mind went to another place—to Reggie, and what

would happen to her. She'd move in with my mother, I hoped. She'd be okay. She was a smart and strong girl, and she'd be okay. I believed that.

And then I saw James and JJ. My body went still, and I could see them, their backs facing me as they walked ahead of me, hand in hand in the glowing field of wildflowers. I felt my body floating to them and I internally smiled, knowing our time had come to be reunited. This was it. I could see James turn to me, looking over his shoulder. He smiled at first, and I tried to run to him, but I couldn't. I was still locked.

And then I heard James's voice. His smile fell, and his mouth didn't move, but I heard James's voice in an echo all around me. "No, my love. Not yet."

I tried to reach out to him and explain that I was ready, that I wanted to run to them and drop down to hold JJ. To turn JJ around so I could see his face, his chubby cheeks and his grin, that it would give me strength as I suffered through this torture to make my way to the other side.

But James refused. He was telling me not yet, not yet. To fight through because it wasn't time. "Fight, pretty girl," he said. "Fight and see the dawn of another day."

Keep fighting, keep fighting…

I begged him to please, please let me see JJ. Please turn around our baby boy and let me see his face. But James kept repeating his phrase, *keep fighting…*

Keep fighting.

His voice became quieter, and eventually I was hurled back in my body again, fighting to breathe. I released my hands from Richard's wrists and reached beside me for something. My hands searched and found the counter, then a glass, and I lifted it and slammed it with all my might into his head.

Just like that, the fabric was gone from my face and I gasped in a desperate gulp of air. I blinked away the splotches and stumbled my way past Richard, running out of the bathroom, down the hall and through our room, then up the stairs.

He didn't follow me—not at first. I crawled my way to the top of the stairs before collapsing on the floor of the catwalk, gasping and coughing in fits. I heard him downstairs after a moment. I could tell that his movements were slow. I hoped that meant he was out of it, that the monster had left him when I knocked the glass on his head. I peered through the rails of the banister and saw him below. He was clutching his head and slowly making his way toward me, climbing the stairs and crying, his shoulders convulsing.

Even despite my fears from mere moments ago, I could feel my heart soften ever so slightly. This one was bad, but I had provoked him. He would feel so much guilt for hurting me. I didn't do what I was supposed to do to help him when he clearly needed me.

I could hear him saying his apologies, and I held onto the rails to pull myself up, my legs feeling weak. When he finally reached me, he stopped, making no attempt to touch me. It was as though he was scared of me in that moment.

But when I looked in his eyes again and saw his pain, it didn't thaw me like I thought it would.

Instead, his tears felt like mocking. I found them to be hideous. I hated the sight of them. It was *him* that was now disgusting *me*.

Maybe it was seeing James and JJ in what I thought were my last moments. Maybe it was a sick anger that I had survived, instead of being allowed to reach and hold my baby boy. And now I was stuck here with Richard, tasked with constantly mending him and fighting his demons. I slammed hard on his chest, screaming, "You bastard!" He reflexively grabbed my arms to pull me off him, pushing me.

I stumbled backward at the top of the stairs, losing my footing, instantly panicking at the inevitable fall I knew I would not be able to stop. I fell down in a spiral, one hard thump felt on my ribs and shoulder, the world spinning upside down, and then going black.

thirty-three

. . .

lori

THE INKY DARKNESS of the sky above me offers the mysteries of an abyss, holding souls and secrets in the great beyond, and I drink it in as I let the sting of cold water roll over my naked body. I'm floating in a sea of chlorine and the salt of my very own tears, my hair snaking around me like serpents threatening to wrap around and strangle. I'm willing them to do so, but they remain stubborn in their own free-falling journey. How selfish.

My breasts feel weightless. A counter to the heaviness in my heart. I glance down at them and see my nipples, erect given the seventy-degree pool water, the heat of warmer weather not yet reaching the depths of the concrete below. I allow my legs to drop, followed by my torso, my shoulders, and eventually the slip of air disappears completely as I submerge into the water, heaving out yet another fantastic sob.

How long have I been out here doing this? I can't say. I had been lying in bed and willing sleep to find me, but it never came. I had snuck into the big house, creeping my way down to the basement and finding the corner I was looking for. The sole box I had saved for JJ, my baby boy who, were he alive today, might have had his own baby boy by now. Might have made me a grandmother not just twice, as Reggie had, but maybe three or four or even five or six times over. I had pulled out the hat and blanket we bundled him in that cold February day when James and I first brought home the twins. I held the hat to my nose, as if doing so might reveal some magic spark of his scent, but it was gone. I smelled only cedar from the trunk that had been housing my box saved for JJ.

With shaking hands I had opened an album, one made for me years later by Reggie. The few photos she managed to scramble together, enlarging some so that whole pages were filled with hazel eyes and the sloppy, wet grin of my boy. I looked back at the young woman in the photos, holding her young toddlers, one on each knee. Grinning like a fool who had no idea what the future would soon bring. I barely recognize her now. Not from the effects of age —except for fuller cheeks and smoother skin, the facade is not all that different than now. No, what I barely recognized was the sparkle of life in her expression, the pureness of her grin. I could feel her, though, and still can as I imagine the smiling face. Seeing her then is a reminder that she lives within me still, and I'm able to feel a flutter in my chest of the woman that always loved so fiercely, even when unwell and in despair. She's helped inform who I've now become, and for that I'm thankful.

When I think about looking at those photos of JJ, of holding his blanket and his hat, looking at the lock of golden-brown curls from his first haircut, I'm amazed by the pull I feel toward some other life that must exist *somewhere*, locked in a universe I'm not invited into. I feel less raw anguish in bravely facing my grief head-on than I might have expected. Instead, I feel something more like sorrow and hurt—wrapped in a despair for an existence I've not been privy to, but I know in my heart is out there. It feels like a cruel joke. A party where half of my family are the guests of honor. I can see it through the window, but I'm locked outside, standing in the freezing rain.

I pause my sobbing and pop up for a breath of air, cool and burning in my lungs, and then I sink back beneath the surface again, screaming out with my voice being carried in the water, "Why, why, why won't you let me in?"

Why won't you let me in...

...the water echoes, carrying my screams in muffled waves of a sound beyond my comprehension

What have I done to deserve this refusal

Where is the secret, the other place where we could all exist...

...another gasp of air before my next descent

Some mistake made

Someone, make it right

I have no more air left to give

Let me in, let me in

But I'm here

I'm not supposed to be let in

Not yet

My thoughts are a jumble, making little sense. But they are what materialize as I sit in my visit with grief. I sink lower and lower, waving my arms around for as long as possible before I brave the surface again. I breathe and repeat, dropping below as if one more submersion will be the one to empty my despair. I sink lower, hoping to dispel of the remaining questions of why them, why did it have to be that way, and how do I sit with the guilt of my continued existence here.

My quest for understanding is interrupted by the deep rumble of a splash, something making contact with the water and joining me beneath the surface, disturbing me. And I feel an arm snake around my waist as I'm yanked backward, up toward the surface.

***

XAVIER PULLS ME TO THE stairs, and I'm suddenly alarmingly awake and aware of my son-in-law holding my naked body in strong arms that firmly place me down. My bum hits the concrete of the top step of the pool with a scratch, and I look up to find Xavier soaked in a t-shirt and boxers, long hair loose and dripping, his eyes avoiding looking at me. He stretches a finger to me as his voice booms, "Don't move."

I pull my knees into my chest and wrap my arms around my legs, chattering as the damp night air meets my cool skin. I'm vaguely aware of Xavier rummaging through the outdoor storage cabinet. After a moment, he returns with two towels and a blanket. He drops the blanket and one towel on a lounge chair, and whips open the other towel before draping it around my shoulders, lifting me to a stand to avoid the towel getting in the water.

We both say nothing. I let him wrap the towel around me, allow him to chastely pull me into him as he uses strong hands to bring on friction in warming me up.

When my chattering finally seems manageable to the point of being able to talk through it, I speak. "You found the biggest beach towel you could for this, didn't you?" My voice is scratchy and nasal. I'm aware of the pressure below my eyes.

"Yes," is all he says, and I can't help but smile, tears pouring over my cheeks at the kindness my son-in-law is showing me, even with how uncomfortable he so clearly feels at having found me naked at the bottom of the pool.

"Thank you."

He leads me over to the lounge chair and sets me in it, draping the blanket over me as well and tucking me in like a baby being swaddled. He peels off his soaked t-shirt, bare chest and charcoal shoulder tattoo revealing themselves, and I turn away to offer him some privacy as he dries his torso before wrapping the towel around his waist. I'm sure he'd feel more comfortable if he removed his wet boxers, but I know better than to make that suggestion.

He settles himself in the lounger next to me, and we stare up at the sky. I focus on my breaths and will my emotions to settle themselves as we sit in strained silence.

Xavier finally speaks. "Are you going to tell me what the hell you're doing out here at 3 o'clock in the morning, in a pool that's only just been opened and completely freezing?" He turns to me, beard and long hair dripping. "Which one was it—trying to drown yourself or die of hypothermia?"

I furrow my eyebrows at him. "Neither."

He holds my gaze for a moment as if to challenge me. When I remain quiet, he eventually turns and looks away. "Could have fooled me."

XAVIER AND DOM WERE IN the military together once upon a time. It's how the Francescas have come to be in our lives. The rest of us had our own kind of history. Reggie, Lucy, and Joey were in the same grade, rode the same school bus together since kindergarten. They'd pop down the street to one another's houses, their mothers and I all feeling safe knowing we only needed to look for the bikes out front to know where our children were. In a neighborhood of giant houses and even bigger properties, it was an unexpected comfort to have that kind of village.

When Xavier and Dom both retired and found PA to be their common home state, Ruby and Dom joined in our circle as well, which felt like a natural addition. But it makes me think about the deployments both Xavier and Dom have experienced. What that must have been like, what they saw. And for Dom, what being away from his daughter must have felt like. I think about how fiercely protective both men are of their children, an innate volition to safeguard that I tend to think of as primarily falling on mothers, but that's not always fair or accurate.

I softly cry new waves of tears here with Xavier, silent beside me as I think about all of this. So much love and honor and fight, yet so much pain. I cry for my own fallen boys, the wound I've recently re-opened in digging out the emotional graves of their existence in the form of photos and fuzzy blankets.

At one point, Xavier rises and walks quietly into the cottage, then back out with tissues, handing them to me before taking his seat once more. We continue to sit and watch the stars, more prominent now that our eyes have adjusted.

When it finally feels that I have no tears left, and only the occasional quiet sniffle accompanies the crickets and rustles of the night, Xavier breaks our silence.

"My own mother was nothing like you, you know." I look over to him and see his profile as he stares up to the sky. "I always imagined what it would be like to have one that could do the things I saw other moms do."

"Like what?"

He smirks. "Cook a warm meal, for one."

"She didn't cook?" My voice croaks with the question. Xavier's countenance remains impassive.

"No. I learned early on what I could."

I drop one final tissue on the small table between us and readjust my blanket around me. "That's too bad. I mean, I'm not a natural with cooking, but I like feeding my family." I smile. "James was actually the better of the two of us. He'd go to work and still come home and cook most days. I'd try and protest, but he insisted I did enough with being home with the twins."

"A good man," Xavier murmurs.

I smile. "He was."

After another few moments of silence, Xavier eventually swings his legs over the edge of the lounger, feet on the ground and facing me. He leans forward and props his forearms on his thighs, forming a steeple with his hands. "Reggie thinks a lot has been coming up for you recently. Not just because of what happened with Dom, but because of Edie's arrival and forcing you to take a look backwards."

I scrunch up my nose, face twisting into in a frown. "Something I don't like to do."

"Exactly." He looks up to me, a strand of hair dropping in his face, and I have a motherly instinct to tell him to get a damn haircut. I don't verbalize it. "How are you doing, Lori?"

I raise my chest in a heavy sigh, and slowly exhale. "I'm okay," I say, and I realize it's true.

"You sure about that?" His eyes dart over to the pool. "Because that looked an awful lot like you not being okay."

I resist the urge to cover my face with the blanket. "That was me doing what I needed to do to start being okay. That's all." I look over to him, willing my eyes to speak for me and let him know that I mean what I say.

I attempt to further explain. "My wise daughter is right, I've been struggling a bit. So many memories, some pleasant. Others not. I couldn't sleep. I wandered into your house tonight to look at what I still had from JJ. Photos with all four of us. Things I haven't looked at in years, and probably should have a long time ago, but," I shake my head, "I just never could."

"It had to have been hard," Xavier offers.

I nod. "It was. But...necessary. They're always on the edges of my mind, no matter what. It's better to face them, I know that."

"I agree. So then what happened?"

"You mean why'd I lose it, strip off my clothes and plunge into the freezing pool?" I say with a small smile.

"At three o'clock in the morning," he reminds me. But I see the hint of a smile at the corner of his mouth.

I widen my smile. "Because, Xavier. Sometimes you just need to feel something like that to remind yourself how alive you are. And that you want to stay that way. To accept that others aren't so lucky, but that it's okay."

He nods and drops his head, and I recall knowing of some of his own painful memories of his time at war, a combat medic out in the field doing who knows what. "Yes," he says, eyes fixed to the ground. "It's unfair, but okay. We sit with our painful memories, but can still enjoy today." He looks up at me. "So, you're sure that's all that was? Not some attempt to find the light of another side?"

"No. Definitely not, no. The fantasy is there from time to time," I admit. "But I have too much to live for right here and now. Too much I don't want to miss."

He nods. "Good."

After another moment our eyes meet. His seem to be contemplating his own pains, combined with a concern for me. "Thanks for jumping in anyway," I say meekly.

He cocks his head to the side. "You were at the bottom of the pool, hair floating around. I thought you were dead."

A soft and sympathetic groan escapes me, and I lean back and look to the sky as I imagine what that must have been like for him. "I'm so sorry, Xavier. Oh, God, I didn't even think about what that must look like for someone to see. I thought I was alone." I turn my head slightly toward him. "Lucky for us both, though, I'm not dead, nor was I planning to be."

He runs his hand down his face, then back to pull his hair out of his eyes. "I believe you. But try and warn us before you need to feel so," he looks pointedly at me, "alive again."

I assure him I absolutely will before getting up to stand, tightening my layers around me and lifting the blanket to keep from dragging. I carefully pop a hand out through an opening, giving him a pat on the head. "Good night, Xavier."

"Good night," he says, heaving out a long exhale.

I start to pad my way to my cottage, but then stop and turn back to him. "Hey, uhh, could you please not tell Reggie about this?"

He looks at me and then leans back in the lounge chair again, lifting his arms behind his head and stretching out his legs, crossing one ankle over the other. "Secret's safe with me."

"Thanks."

I'm nearly one-hundred percent positive my son-in-law is lying to my face. Still, I appreciate it.

thirty-four

. . .

edie

"**I** STILL CAN'T wrap my head around the whole thing," Zeke says, shaking his head. "A pseudo stepmom and sister."

"Are you nervous to meet them?" Edie asks. They're on their way to spend an afternoon poolside with Lori and Reggie and the kids.

"A little. I don't know, it feels like you have a whole other life here. *You're* different here."

They're at a red light and Edie takes the opportunity to turn to him, dropping her hand from the steering wheel and giving him a little shove. "Quit making such a big deal out of it, it's freaking me out."

"How so?" he asks, genuine confusion etched all over his face.

The light turns green, and she returns her attention to the road ahead. "I hate feeling like I'm locked into some perception you have of me, and that I'm not allowed to change."

"Oh God, babe—that's not what I mean."

Her skin crawls at the sound of him calling her "babe," and she tries to shake off the feeling, reminding herself that he's here because she invited him. It's just one week. She can do this for one week. She glances over to him and notes his new look—he's traded hair gel for baseball caps and has apparently learned the benefits of a push-up. He's lost the remaining boyishness and climbed his way into looking a whole lot more man than she remembers.

Still, he's no Trenton.

Edie sighs, frustrated with herself, and tries to soften her tone. "Sorry, I know. I guess I'm a little defensive because I do feel a little different. But in a good way."

"The northeast suits you?" Zeke offers, and Edie merely nods her head, knowing it's more than that, but having little desire to discuss it with him.

She realizes she's come to think of Lori and Reggie as pieces of her life she can't imagine not having. They've formed an easy bond, and on more than one occasion, she has found herself fantasizing of an alternate course of meeting them. What if Richard had known about Edie right from the start? Sure, she would have only had four years with him, but she would have had Lori and Reggie in her childhood as well. Would they have continued contact with her after his death? It's a pointless question, of course, but one she can't help but wonder, although Lori has already made it clear they would have. There will always be a twinge of disappointment and sadness that her mom had chosen the path she did in keeping her existence a secret from Richard.

"You don't mind the cold up here?" Zeke asks. "Did you get snow?"

"Just some flurries," she murmurs. His question reminds her of how uneasy she felt exposed to the chill of winter, though not just because of a climate she was unaccustomed to. It was something else, a piece that was missing. And then she stepped into the last home her father had lived in, and a piece of the puzzle seemed to slip into place.

Edie thinks about Trenton as well, and the changes she has felt within herself in the wake of the Wroe Era. How could someone stir up so much in her, yet hold none of the same goals in life that she does? He'd said right from the start that marriage and settling down weren't for him. Edie had found their other differences increasingly alluring. But ultimately, Edie wants a family. That much is for sure, and apparently, Trenton Wroe has no plans for that kind of thing.

But Zeke is here now, and it's familiar and comfortable with him. Sensible.

Regretful.

Edie shakes her head as if doing so could chase away the last thought. It stubbornly lingers anyway, and she realizes she needs to figure out what she really wants. Zeke hadn't forced anything, hadn't expected some magical reunion upon his arrival in town, but still. Edie knows it's only a matter of time before he pushes the subject.

They pull into the circular driveway and step out in front of the massive brick home she has come to love. As they walk up to the front door, Zeke grabs her hand to hold. It's a small gesture, she reminds herself. She fights the urge to let go.

"Introduce me to your new family, babe," he whispers in her ear.

And with that comment comes another wave of regret, because all Edie can think is how she wishes she had done that very thing with someone else.

EDIE STRETCHES OUT HER LEGS to the rattan ottoman in front of her, pleased to be earning a bit of the tan she had kissed away when she left Florida. Her white bikini finally has a bit of contrast behind it. She smiles as she watches little James and Ronnie, begging her to watch them for the hundredth time as they waddle in their swim vests and jump with gusto into the pool, the splashes doing nothing to muffle their fits of laughter. The smell of coconut sunscreen and lime from her margarita give her a sense of familiarity, and while she's learned to love the crisp cool of winter, she can't deny she is a summer girl through and through.

"You want to get in?" Zeke asks her.

"No. Still a bit too cold for me. Maybe in another couple weeks when summer's truly here."

Zeke's face turns serious, and he leans back in his chair with a sigh. "Too bad I won't be here then. I was kind of hoping to see you wet."

At this Edie laughs. It was the first truly flirtatious thing he's said since he arrived two days ago. "Straight to the point, I see."

"Just being honest."

It's a perfect afternoon with a clear blue sky that mirrors the pool water. She scans around the pool area to Lori and Reggie who are sitting on the slate and swinging their legs in the water. Xavier is off by the deep end, skimming some invisible debris and tinkering with any maintenance he can. Kathryn, Lori's mom, is safely tucked beneath the shaded porch area by the guest cottage, eyes closed beneath a pink sun visor as she reclines on a lounge chair.

"This is the life," Zeke notes, as if reading her mind.

"It is."

"Thanks for bringing me here."

"Yeah, of course. It's nice having you here." She means the words, she realizes. Zeke has always been sweet and easygoing, and she's felt comfortable with him despite her strange reaction to him grabbing her hand earlier. But the overall friendship with him has always been their strong suit.

He clears his throat. "Have you uhh, have you dated anyone since being here?"

She looks over to him and sees the corner of his mouth lift as he tentatively asks his question.

"No," she responds. It slips out easily, the lie. And it very much is a lie, Edie can admit that. Sure, she never allowed her and Trenton to label anything. But at the end of the day, what Zeke is asking is if there's been anyone of interest, and Edie is one hundred percent aware that telling him "yes" would crush him.

Zeke nods, looking relieved. "Yeah, me neither. Since you left, I mean."

Edie smiles but remains silent, turning her attention back to the kids splashing in the pool.

THE TIME INEVITABLY COMES WHEN Lori and Reggie join them, ready to pounce and get to know Zeke a little better. They're sitting on the other side of the L-shaped sofa, and she laughs to herself at how alike the two women look, both in halter top one-piece suits, though Lori's is floral and Reggie's is plain black. They look effortlessly stylish in wide-brimmed hats with similar wavy reddish hair. Reggie's is lighter, more of a strawberry blonde as opposed to Lori's chestnut, but their resemblance is striking. It's funny to see it, as Edie looks nothing like her own mom.

"So, Zeke," Lori says in between sips of the massive margarita in her hand. She licks her lips and nods approvingly before placing the drink down. Edie can see the distance in her expression, her usual bubbly self not quite reaching her eyes. Her heart squeezes for the hurt she's going through, but she appreciates her being here now. "Any fun plans while you're in town?"

Zeke sits up straight, cupping his knees with his palms. "Checking out Philly, for sure. I've never been."

"Lovely history," Reggie offers. "If you like that kind of thing."

He nods with enthusiasm. "Oh yeah, you kidding? I couldn't be with this one if I didn't," he says, hooking a thumb in Edie's direction.

She tenses, and Zeke seems to freeze up as well, realizing what he implied. No one says anything, and Edie gathers everyone is probably happy to have the shield of sunglasses to hide wide eyes. She is, at least.

"Edie, watch this!" Ronnie squeals, her two-year old voice pressing out the statement, so it sounds like, "Edie, whachiss!" She spreads out her limbs and leaps like a starfish into the water.

"Beautiful, honey," Edie beams when Ronnie pops back up, chubby hands smearing the mess of red hair from her eyes. James has made his way to the stairs in the shallow end and is pushing a boat around him in large circles. But Ronnie is non-stop on her mission to jump.

"My kids have come to love Edie," Reggie explains to Zeke. "You'll have to excuse them for stealing all her attention."

Zeke grins. "They're cute. And I'm glad to know Edie's got people up here. When she told me about you guys, I thought she was nuts for reaching out."

Lori waves a hand. "Are you kidding? It's felt like a missing ingredient has been added. I only wish we had met sooner." She smiles sadly at Edie.

"Any more insight from your mom on that?" Reggie asks, tucking her legs beneath her and turning toward Edie.

"No. I'm done prying. It is what it is. She says she just didn't want me reaching out to find his family, and maybe I don't need to understand the full reasons behind that. I finally know who my father was, I've got you guys, and maybe some things just aren't my story to know."

And she means that. After the disappointing truth behind the letters hunt, she had reflected a lot on the things people do when in times of struggle. She can understand the reasoning behind keeping tight-lipped so that Edie wouldn't go searching, but she's still hung up on her mom's secrecy from day one of her pregnancy with Edie. Was it that her mom really did know about Lori the whole time she was with Richard, and didn't want to ruin a marriage by revealing she became pregnant? Whatever it was, it must have been a hard decision, Edie can recognize that. Her frustrations and anger over the secrecy of it all have slowly subsided, replaced with general gratitude that she's here now, and has formed such a strong bond with the women before her. That can be enough. It has to be.

Lori pops forward in her seat. "What if I talked to her? To your mom, I mean?"

"Why would you do that?" Reggie frowns.

Lori takes the sunglasses off her face, and Edie sees a little glimmer in her eyes. "It's a great idea. I'm the woman that would stand to be hurt in all this, right? So maybe if I reach out, I could put her at ease, maybe see if there really is more to the story."

Reggie shifts in her seat, looking uncomfortable. "Is that appropriate?" She looks back at Edie. "Would you even be okay with that?"

"Actually, yeah. That would be amazing." It was something Edie had already debated, in fact. She felt a need to have them meet, especially given how close she had come to feel to Lori. Edie felt too shy to suggest it, not sure how Lori would feel.

Reggie still looks unconvinced. "I don't know, Mom. Edie's parents are clearly private. They might find that a bit invasive."

"I doubt it," Zeke chimes in. "Edie's moms are cool, and I bet they'd love to talk to you."

There's a guilt Edie feels in how much she'd like to make that happen, as if it's a selfish thing to ask. But then again, Lori is the one who brought it up, right?

Could having the two women meet   the women that all those years ago had both fallen for the charisma of Richard Meyers— really be such a bad thing?

thirty-five

. . .

lori

I STARE OUT the oval window next to me and take in my bird's-eye view of the city of Tampa. It's smaller than I would have thought, but I'm already looking forward to the palm trees and a couple sultry nights, touring around. When Erica and I spoke on the phone, she was hesitant, unlike Zeke's insistence that she would be more than fine with the interaction. We danced around a topic of conversation that had been a regurgitation of what she had already told Edie. A quick Richard fling, she learned he was married and dropped him. End of story.

But I know better.

I suggested I fly down there, meet face to face, attempt to get to know one another since we've been snatching up Edie right into our lives with no plans on stopping. It pains me to think of the years we could have had with her. If we had known right from the start, it would have been tense, sure. Call me stupid, call me a coward, but I know my thirty-something-year-old self would not have left Richard, even if I had learned about Edie back then. I was too consumed with him, too broken in my grief still. I felt like a hollow shell in those days, and Richard filled me, what can I say? Yes, I knew he cheated on me. Yes, I still I stayed. Anguish and fear are a dangerous cocktail, squatters that sneak in, protected under the shroud of darkness and you're completely unaware of the way they've settled in and taken control. Those squatters rob your capacity to see clearly, and you end up doing things under the guise of thinking there's no other way. I'll be damned if I'm judged on the choices I made while victim to that plunder.

Today I'm a different person, I can confidently say. I think about Dom, and the pull I have to throw my hurt aside and dive right back into his arms. It would be so easy, I could slip back into the relationship we had started and blink all my worries away. He says nothing happened with that calculating woman Jules? Sure! I'll believe! No problem, just tell me where to sign and I'll trust you to read the contract and ensure all is right.

But I'm done with that. Enough is enough, because I'm flat out *tired* of always being the one to give the benefit of the doubt. I'm tired of it. My feelings were so hurt when I first arrived in LA and saw them together, I felt like a fool. And I was functioning off of delusion when I chose to believe him that he wanted me there, despite literally telling me in the breath before that he had been running away from us. And then seeing that photo, his arm protectively around her and her hand on his chest, tucked beneath his blazer like it was a car parked comfortably in its garage. Seeing that all while standing in the very place that held some of the best memories of my life, with the only man that ever did truly treat me with honest and pure love.

I'd had enough.

I laugh to myself, realizing that here I am now, once again chasing down some truths. Only this time it's for Edie.

I'll admit that I want to know who this woman is for myself, though. If she really was unaware of my existence at first. How long did it go on once she found out? Did she truly kick him to the curb, or did it linger on further?

Then there's my other, darker thought—was my husband truly capable of rape? This trip is, in many ways, a sick quest to prove that something sinister had taken place. If I can do so, maybe then I can close off my heart from all the foolish hope I so often hold, and free myself from expectations that come crashing down in pain. Maybe it's finally time for me to wake the hell up and see people for who they really are.

AFTER CHECKING INTO MY HOTEL and taking a much-needed shower, I hop into my rental car and head over to the home of Erica and Jessica Mackenzie. I'm nervous as hell as I ring the doorbell to the bungalow, and I scan around to distract myself as I wait. It's a cute neighborhood of ranch homes bathed in warm shades of stucco. The garden is tidy with a mix of hibiscus in large pink blooms flanked by mini palms. The house next door reveals a small pool surrounded by a screened lanai, and I wonder if Erica and Jessica have one too.

The door opens and I take in the two women before me—one with shoulder length jet black hair and a sundress—Jessica—the other with long brown waves and sprinkles of gray. She's petite in flowing pants in a floral pattern with a simple white t-shirt. The elusive Erica. She has tiny features, like a doll, and is a good inch or two shorter than I am. I can see how Richard would have fallen for her, she's beautiful in an innocent-looking way.

Her tone, however, is not.

We all bumble our way through terse introductions, with me blabbering on about what a lovely home they have, how long they've lived here, and all those expected and completely forced conversation topics. Erica gives clipped answers, though Jessica is slightly more friendly.

Eventually, they lead me over to the pool-lanai area I antici-pated, and we have a seat at the wrought iron table. A decorative standing fan perches next to us, offering a little breeze and relief from the heat, and I strip off the linen blouse I had over my tank top.

Jessica excuses herself, saying she'll leave us to it, and Erica pours me lemonade from the pitcher between us. I grab it, wishing it was something stronger to calm my nerves. My excitement I had leading up to this seems to have quickly vanished given the surly presence of Erica, and now as I sit here sweating and uncomfortable, a strange slice of anger sweeps through me. I try and keep it at bay.

"So, Lori Meyers," she starts, and my head whips up at her purposeful use of my first and last name. Of Richard's last name.

"That's me."

"You've insisted on coming all this way to solve the mystery, is that right?"

I huff out a laugh. "Mystery, alright. You make it sound like a crime was committed." *Was one?*

"Crime? Nothing that sinister, no." Her eyes are locked on mine, and I can see that she's trying to study me. She's not sure if she can trust me, which is rather infuriating, considering I'm the scorned woman here.

"Well, you agreed, so my hope is you're willing to share."

At long last, she finally breaks eye contact. "I agreed because I know my daughter likes you." Her tone is bitter, and she's looking away as if facing me while she says this statement is too difficult.

My mother brain understands this pinch of jealousy. I, too, could feel that when Reggie would seem under the spell of Joey's mom, Isabella, when they were kids—a woman that seemed to have a sensibility similar to Reggie's.

I set my glass down and drape my arm on the back of my chair. "So you figured you better get to know the woman that is spending all this time with her."

"Exactly," she nods.

"Well, what do you want to know?"

Erica seems surprised by this. "In all honesty? I'm wondering what kind of woman stays with a man that she knew cheated on her. Edie told me you knew of his infidelity."

Oh, my. No, this woman is not going to sit here and judge me. "Wow," I breathe out. "You've got some nerve."

She shrugs. "How so? It's a fair question. If my daughter is hanging out with you, you can understand that I'm concerned you aren't the best influence on her."

"Can I understand that?" I say in disbelief. "What, you think I'm going to cloud her head with forgive and forget and she'll go running around and making bad decisions, all with my blessing?" I scoff. "How little you think of Edie's own judgment."

"I know my daughter, and she's an optimist. And young and impressionable."

I try and find empathy here, I really do. Clearly this woman has been hurt in the past. But my patience for calm understanding for everyone has been wearing thin.

"You know what?" I say, my voice icy. "It should be *me* that's judging *you*." I lean forward and point a finger toward her. "Don't you think? You're the potential homewrecker here. For all I know, you knew damn well Richard had a wife and stepdaughter at home. That's what I'm wondering."

"And yet I wasn't a homewrecker, was I? Because you stayed. With a man you knew was unfaithful, and I want to know why."

"Please, you couldn't care less why. This is about you being able to prove that I'm a mess, that Edie shouldn't continue talking with me and Reggie, all so you can keep her to yourself like you have all these years. That's what this is about, isn't it? And you know what? I resent the hell out of that, Erica. The way Edie came to be in this world may have been a mistake, but yes, I would have forgiven my husband, because I knew he loved me, and I know he would have been filled with remorse. Call me crazy, maybe you can't understand that, but there it is. I'm loyal that way, so sue me.

"And I would have welcomed that baby girl from day one if

Richard knew he had a daughter. She could have had a dad at least for a few years, and we would have continued to love her even after his death. But you never even put that out there as an option, did you? And that's fine, I imagine I may have considered the very same move if I were in your shoes, I'll admit. All I ask for is the same courtesy of understanding that I'm trying to give you. That's it. We may not understand or agree with other people's choices, but we should show respect for someone doing what they think is right for them. So don't you dare sit here and judge me when I've done nothing, *nothing*," I shout, "but show kindness and warmth to a young woman trying to find answers, even if it hurt. Even if those answers revealed a layer of betrayal to me."

My chest rises and falls rapidly, tears stinging my eyes, and I hate that I might fall apart in a minute here. I don't want tears in this moment. They feel weak, and I want to be strong. "Satisfied?" I ask, wiping a tear. "Did I give you all you need to know to successfully prove to yourself what a mess I am?"

Erica looks at me, her tiny doll face unreadable. I look up to see Jessica step out, and Erica looks over her shoulder to her.

"Is everything alright?" Jessica asks. I glance at her, half expecting to get thrown out of here, and I take a gulp of my lemonade to distract myself so that I'm not walking out of this house in a puddle of tears.

Erica looks back at me. She tucks a long strand of hair behind her ear, revealing a series of small silver earrings. I take in the contradiction of this sweet and delicate-looking woman that has proven to have a fierce side I would not have expected.

She finally speaks. "What do you say we get some stronger drinks?" she asks. The smallest of sad smiles forms on her face, and I see her expression shift. The accusatory stare is gone, replaced by something else.

I lean back in my chair and nod. "Probably a good idea."

thirty-six

. . .

edie

WITH HER BARE knees pressed into the grass, Edie watches as Zeke's paintbrush bleeds into hers, and he presses to fan it out, the bristles spreading wide to create a half heart shape.

He nods his head to her. "Press yours in. Let's make a heart here."

With her shoulder, Edie shrugs to wipe a drip of sweat pouring past her temple, the warmth of early summer catching up to her in spite of her Florida blood. She leans back on her heels, looking over to Zeke as he sits on the grass, forearms resting on propped up knees. His gym shorts glide down his legs and expose the stark white of his thighs. "Zeke, a heart is not part of the design."

They're at one of her community project events, painting the fence surrounding the newest school garden. Edie had told Lori about the project, and she had suggested a colorful floral design. Edie shared the concept and Lori's design with Louise, who loved it, saying she wishes they had done so on other outdoor classroom set ups.

Too bad Lori is down in Tampa now, having who-knows-what kind of interactions with her moms.

"Just a little one. No one will ever even know. It'll be like a sweet secret, just for us."

Edie looks into his blue eyes, so tender and warm and filled with endearing hope and love for her. She smiles. She still hasn't given him any kind of commitment, but she told him she was willing to consider a Take Two on things.

"Okay," she says, and she presses her own brush to fan out, mirroring his. But she pulls back too fast, and the paint smears out and away, making it look like a heart from a cartoon in a runaway motion.

Footsteps approach and the sunlight slips away in someone's shadow. "Uh-hem," booms a voice from up above, and Edie's heart quickens as she hears the distinct jingling of keys she has come to know so well. The motion that stirs an automatic flutter in her belly, her very own Pavlov experiment.

It can't be.

"Edna," he says, and Edie closes her eyes, sure she's not hearing correctly. It's the heat, it must be getting to her.

She's vaguely aware of Zeke's voice beside her as his hand grazes her shoulder. "Edie, hey. I think this guy wants you."

"What?" she says with a whip of her head in Zeke's direction and instant guilt. "He doesn't want me!"

Zeke frowns in confusion, an uncomfortable smile lifting at the corner of his mouth. "I mean, he's trying to get your attention."

On her other shoulder she feels another nudge, followed by a hand sliding down and grabbing her arm, pulling her up. "Edna, can I talk to you, please?" Her paintbrush accidentally swipes up Trenton's chest as she stumbles into him.

"Oh God, I'm so sorry," she cries out, stifling an embarrassed laugh at the spray of pink paint, a startling mark made very obvious against the black of his suit vest.

She hears the rumble of a groan in his chest. "You marked me," he whispers so that only she can hear him. At least, Edie thinks only she can hear him. Her eyes had been held firmly on his chest, refusing to meet his gaze. But with his comment she looks up to see his eyes and her favorite sunglasses covering them, the ones with the mirrored lenses.

"Hi," is all she says.

"I didn't know you could paint," he responds.

"You don't know a lot about me."

"I know enough." They both remain frozen, locked in an impasse.

Edie registers the body popping up beside her. "Hey, I'm Zeke, nice to meet you." Edie looks over to see Zeke smiling idiotically.

She looks back up to Trenton in horror. But all he does is smile, slow and slick, and she knows that smile is really a mocking smirk. She sees his eyebrow raise above his sunglasses before he slowly turns his head to Zeke, jutting out a hand to shake in return. "Hey there, Zeke. I'm Mr. Wroe," Trenton says, and Edie rolls her eyes, not just at the formality he's going for, but how unnecessarily firm his handshake to Zeke clearly is.

Zeke pulls his hand back, shaking it out. "Mr. Wroe, are you one of the sponsors for this awesome project?" Edie's cheeks flush.

She starts to respond for him, tell him no, that this evil Adonis is not a sponsor, or something along those lines, when Trenton answers.

"In fact I am, Zeke. Sure can't thank you enough for all your... assistance with putting the final touches on here." Edie notes the cocky head tilt Trenton adds in. "Couldn't have done it without you. Now if you'll excuses me, I need to talk to Edna here."

She feels his hand on her elbow, beginning to pull her away. But then he pauses, grabs the paintbrush out of her hand and hands it to Zeke. "Would you, man?" he asks, and Zeke eagerly grabs the brush from him with a nod and a "Sure, man!"

With a sharp pull, Trenton grabs Edie and she bobbles behind him, aware of the various other painters stopping to look at the spectacle of a man in suit, minus the jacket, sticking out like a sore thumb amongst the casually dressed volunteers. She catches eyes with Louise just in time to see her grin and wink, and Edie flushes with embarrassment.

Trenton pushes Edie around the corner of the building and down a few steps of an alleyway before stopping. She wonders what he's going to say, waiting for his words to explain himself and his presence here, but all he does is release her and pace, keys jingling in the nervous energy of his hands.

Edie points a finger in the direction of the garden. "Were you serious back there? You're behind this, that was true what you said to Zeke?"

Trenton pauses, then turns toward her slowly.

And smiles.

"So that's Zeke the Geek, huh?" he says, crossing his arms over his chest. He looks down, remembering the paint smear, but shrugs and resumes his sly grin, focused on Edie.

She rolls her eyes. "Yes. That's Zeke. I can't believe you just made him think you were the big boss behind all this."

His smile remains smug. "I donated, doesn't that count?"

"Hardly."

Edie scans her eyes over Trenton. His sunglasses are still on, his arms crossed over his suit vest with that pink streak of paint popping over his forearms. "What's he doing here?" he asks, his friendly tone from a moment ago now gone.

"He...uhh," she stammers before huffing out a breath. "He came for me, Trenton. He flew up here, through a fear of flying and everything, because he loves me and wants to be with me."

Trenton unwinds his arms and extends one back in the direction of the fence painting. "That guy?! Seriously, you think that guy is the one for you? Zeke the Geek," he says, bringing his hand to his chest and laughing.

She wants to slap the smug grin off his face.

"Stop it, you ass," she says, giving his stomach a small shove. It's a move she quickly regrets. Touching Trenton is dangerous, the familiar buzz of attraction now amplified with the contact. She drops her hand, turning away from him slightly. "Don't act all high and mighty."

He rests his hands on his hips. "Please, high and mighty? I could snap that kid in two like a twig. I don't need to be high and mighty with him. Just...average. Very average would suffice."

Once again, as she seems to love to do with this man, Edie sidesteps the bait. She doesn't fight him and tell him how petty he is, or how he's a bully or that he doesn't even know Zeke and can't pass judgment.

No. Instead, Edie smiles sweetly and says, "You're jealous of Zeke? How adorable."

And it's Trenton that falls right into her trap. He gapes back at her, rips his sunglasses off his face and steps forward, stopping just short of pressing against her body. "Do you love him? Tell me, do you love him?" His amber brown eyes search hers frantically, and she sees the hurt in them.

But she resolves to remain strong. "I love and care for him very much." Even she can hear how flat her tone is.

"But you're not *in* love with Zeke the Geek," he counters.

"I...I could be in love with Zeke the Geek," she insists. "I mean! Goddamnit, don't call him that!"

They lock eyes in a silent staredown, Edie breathing heavy and feeling the buzzing of her body as she stands so close to Trenton like this. In a quiet little alleyway, just the two of them.

He reaches a hand up to her cheek. "He's not for you, Edna."

"And you are? Is that it? You want to settle down and have babies and grow a beer belly suddenly?"

"Yes. Not the beer belly part, maybe, but yes." He huffs out a breath and she savors the remnants of mint. "I want those things with you." She feels the smile in his voice rather than hears it, because she's closed her eyes, unable to bear the look in his.

"No, you don't," she whispers. God, why does she feel so *right* when she's around him? She wants to believe him. "Since when is being a family man something on your radar?"

"Since I met a girl that made me start fantasizing about all those things. *You*, Edna Edie. I want to be with you. I'm going fucking crazy without you, you know that? I can't stop thinking about you. I found myself writing 'Edna Mackenzie' all over a piece of paper the other day, like a fucking schoolgirl."

Edie opens her eyes to laugh, but when she sees the heartache clear in his, she halts. "And here my mom warned me you had stalker potential," she says. The words are meant to be a joke, but they come out soft and tender.

"Marry me, Edna." He pushes his body against hers, pinning her to the wall behind her, and he moves his hand down her face to hold her chin.

She closes her eyes again and shakes her head. "No. I barely even know you, Trenton. I just met you three months ago, I can't marry you." The last words come out in a strained whisper that betray any conviction.

When she opens her eyes, she finds his darting back and forth between hers, searching for understanding. "So that's why? Because it's too soon?"

"Huh?" she asks, eyebrows raised. "Yes, three months is too soon."

"But not 'no' because you're in love with someone else. Because of Zeke the—I mean Zeke."

With a resigned sigh, Edie shakes her head and drops her gaze down. "No, not because of Zeke." She looks back up at him. "And you're an asshole. He's not a geek."

"That's a shame. I love geeks, I aspire to be one someday. And marry one in particular." She opens her mouth to interrupt him, but he stops her with his mouth, pressing her in a soft kiss that removes all words, all coherent thoughts from her mind. Kissing Trenton feels like coming home, and her heart melts with a rush of wondering why she ever left at all. She returns the kiss with all the greediness she wants, unable to help herself. His mouth on hers is the very thing she has been dreaming about the past few weeks without him. His easy laugh and mischievous grins have been haunting her, causing tears in how badly she hurts in missing him. The feel of him against her now is a force she's helpless to stop, because it's everything she needs.

When Trenton finally breaks away, panting, she brings her fingers to her lips as if to savor the contact.

He sighs, hanging his head down. "Please. Let me put a ring on you, Edna. Please, baby." He looks into her eyes. "I love you and I need you. You're it, you are the one."

"I am?" she asks, her voice weak.

She drops her eyes to his mouth, both watching and hearing his next words. "Yes. The one," he says, his voice low, the words escaping his lips with reverence. "I want to make you my wife. Raise a family with you one day. Hear you drive me fucking crazy with all your ideals that knock my pompous self on my ass, in a good way. I miss your enthusiasm for all the things you love in life."

Edie smiles, lifting an eyebrow. "You just miss the sex."

She expects him to deny it, but instead a sly grin slips across his face. "Yes."

"That's all we ever were, remember? Just fucking." Her tone is teasing.

"Edna," he says, pressing his hips into hers and threading his fingers through her hair. "That wasn't fucking," he says, leaning down to softly brush his lips over hers. He pulls to the side and drags his lips along her jawline, sending shivers down her spine and heat between her legs.

When his lips reach her ear, he whispers. "That was making love."

thirty-seven

. . .

lori

MY HEAD IS throbbing as I open my eyes the next morning, and I realize I'm about to experience a hangover for the first time in years. Sweet little Edie sure does have moms that know how to party.

I groan as I lift myself off their couch. I see the glass of juice and plate in front of me, with some crackers and a bottle of Ibuprofen ready and waiting. I smile at the gesture and greedily down the goods, willing the ache in my head to dissipate.

I rise and use the bathroom, steal a glance in the mirror and pinch a little life back in my cheeks. I drag my fingers through my hair and rummage through my purse for some ChapStick. Satisfied and feeling a little less cloudy, I head back out to the living room, listening for any signs of life. It's dead quiet, though, minus the hums of appliances and someone using what sounds like a hedge trimmer outside. Unsure what to do with myself, I plop back down on the couch and reach for a magazine on the table beside me. I smile when I see the framed photo of little Edie, wide, bright blue eyes and matching sunny grin. She looks about nine or ten, in those last stages of girlhood before the awkwardness of a temporarily too-large nose kicks in and blemishes dot one's face. She's standing on a beach in front of a sloppy sandcastle, hands in fists on her hips and looking proud. I can't help but feel a sadness in not knowing her in those years.

But I get it. Now that I know the truth, I get it. I would have done the same damn thing.

ERICA HAD BRAVELY UNRAVELED HER story with me over lemonade and shots of tequila. I watched her toss that first one back with determination, as if sharing was going to take courage. I followed suit and took my shot, though with far less determination, and plopped down my glass, noting the squeeze of Jessica's hand comforting her wife.

She told me about first meeting Richard. How—like me—she had been swept away by him. She loved the way he filled out his suit, the confidence he exuded, the way he looked at you like you were the only person he saw. I remember those same looks all too well.

Erica was hesitant at first, given their age gap, twenty-plus years between them, but eventually she caved and allowed herself to fall into his arms. That first night with him, on the terrace of his hotel room, the crash of waves providing their ambiance, she knew she was done for. She admitted to having the sneaking suspicion he was married—he had the tell-tale sign of a strip of pale skin on his ring finger. The ghost of a marking indicating his attachment. But she ignored it, choosing to believe his story of being recently separated, on the verge of divorce.

It was at that point that I reached for the bottle in front of me and took my next shot. It's one thing to know about these things in general terms, but another entirely to hear the details of Richard's calculated deception, his disregard for me. I had squeezed my eyes shut as if that could magically shield me from the wave of hurt, and Erica offered to stop.

But I told her no. I needed to hear each and every piece that I pretended didn't exist for so many years. It was time.

When Richard's sparks of jealousy appeared, Erica started to worry that she was making a real mistake. He had shown up unannounced at a bar where she was having happy hour with some co-workers. She had been talking to another man—a younger one—and Richard had snatched her arm with a sharp squeeze, taking her outside and shouting, accusing her of leading him on when she really felt he was too old for her. She burst into tears, wanting to reassure him she felt no such thing, that she cared for Richard. He took her back to his hotel, where they made wild love, and Erica was torn between feeling an immense pull toward him and feeling scared of his mercurial moods.

That's when I took another shot, a tremor in my hand as I raised the glass to my lips, felt the burn down my throat followed by the sour zing from the lime I quickly shoved in my mouth. It was nearly too much, sitting there listening to this, but I had to. I knew moving through this could offer some semblance of my own healing.

I began to chime in similar memories I had held, memories I hadn't told a single soul about in detail. Jessica and Erica stretched their hands out to me, then, and the next thing you know all three of us were wiping tears as we rehashed the wrath of Richard.

Erica ended things with him soon after that happy hour incident. It wasn't that she had found out about me and then decided to break it off, it was that she could see signs of a darker side of Richard. He refused to accept it at first, and there were several more instances of him suddenly and unexpectedly appearing. He'd show up on her doorstep, pleading his apologies, then storming off in rage when she turned him away. She was torn, because she cared for him, but was trying to remain levelheaded and follow her instincts, knowing their relationship was toxic.

Then came the day Erica got some news. She had been struggling with her cycles and had undergone a battery of tests, eventually learning she had a hormone imbalance with a warning that fertility might be a struggle. Erica knew what that meant—get pregnant sooner rather than later if she wanted a chance to have a child.

"So you chose Richard," I said. "You took advantage of his continued pursuit and threw caution to the wind for the bigger thing you wanted."

"Yes," she whispered.

"How many tries did it take?" I asked. I knew the odds would not have been in her favor. I knew it wouldn't be so simple as the one time.

I was right.

"It took a year."

"A year?" I gasped. An entire year of his continued infidelity with one woman. Something about that felt like a slap across the face. In my mind, I believed his infidelity was him getting caught up in the moment with someone. Momentary lapses in judgment, surely fueled by alcohol and nothing more. Surely not prodded by actual affection for someone that wasn't me. I thought back to that time, how Richard had been in good spirits with me. I thought we were in this beautiful space together, in a wonderful rhythm.

All the while he was living an entirely separate life during his trips to the Sunshine State.

Erica went on to explain that she hadn't planned on actually staying with him. She figured she'd play along, give it a couple tries, hopefully get pregnant and then never see Richard again. She was going to change her phone number, move into a bigger place with the baby, finally open the daycare she had always planned to. Vanish.

But as time went on and she still wasn't pregnant, she felt herself falling for him, drawn in to his magnetic pull. She stopped caring about her plan. As long as she had Richard, she would be okay. I sat there listening and nodding. I understood that feeling all too well. Richard was dangerous like that. The longer you were with him, the more you needed of him, like a drug.

And also like a drug, the more you started to feel like shit.

Erica's rock-bottom day came when he forgot to take off his damn wedding ring. "I was devastated. I felt so stupid for ignoring all the red flags, and I thought about who this woman was. The wife of Richard."

I lifted my hand from my armrest. "And here I am."

She nodded. "Here you are."

"So what did you imagine about me? Back then, I mean?" Call me crazy, but I was dying to hear what the unassuming mistress thought about the wife she accidentally learned about.

"It's hard to say. I think I blocked it out as much as I could. He was crying to me and telling me he was in love with two women, that he couldn't help it."

I scoffed. "I don't doubt he truly believed that. How did you react?"

"Internally? I wanted to erase him out of my life and get the hell out of his hotel room. I was heartbroken and angry, but also scared. I knew rushing out the door wasn't an option, he would only follow me. I couldn't do that, especially because I had just found out I was pregnant."

"Did he know you had been trying?"

Erica shook her head, explaining that Richard had already made it clear he felt he was too old to be a father. Turns out it was probably just that he was too married.

"But I was scared of how he'd react if I told him we were done. So I kept my news of my pregnancy to myself, and told him I still loved him. I just had to make it through the next twenty-four hours." Her eyes welled once again, and fat tears rolled down her cheeks as she looked down at the trembling hands in her lap. I can imagine how torturous those twenty-four hours were. To have to lay in bed with a man that you knew could be dangerous, had completely deceived you, because walking out on a man like that isn't an option. Not a safe one, anyhow.

I understood. She did what she needed to do. She played along.

It's then that I realized some of the best actresses aren't the ones on screens or accepting golden statues, but they're the ones trapped in spaces with shattered and dangerous men, and their roles are a performance of a lifetime. Of a life to preserve.

When Richard left town the next day, Erica did her final act of her performance. She made herself disappear.

I WANDER TOWARD THE MUFFLED sounds of the motor rumbling outside, followed by the sounds of branches being cut. The scratchy Florida grass beneath my feet makes me smile. It's different yet familiar. Same lush green as home, same carpet to offer a playground for little people taking their first steps or chasing each other in games of tag, yet this grass is more hardy, in a way. I like that about it.

I find Erica chopping away at the bush in front of her—a victim to her hedge trimmer. She's dripping in sweat, and I'm thankful to see that she, too, is not immune to this heat. Her long hair is swept back in a messy bun at the base of her neck, sporting a white baseball cap to shade her face. She sees me and grins before turning off the trimmer.

"Don't stop on my account," I say.

She drops the trimmer down and grabs a pair of pruning scissors that lie stretched out in the grass, waiting to be of service. "I might kill this thing if I continue. Here," she says, nodding over to a pair of gloves tossed on the driveway. "Grab those, wanna help me weed?"

I glance down at my delicate hands that haven't had to do a single bit of outdoor manual labor in years. Sure, I do the occasional weeding and whatnot. But as I stand here watching Erica in her obvious comfort zone, wearing dirty overall shorts and a sports bra, commanding her garden, I feel a little silly to recognize how out of the elements I've been.

I bend down and roll up my linen pants to my knees, then slip on the gloves, making my way over to a patch I hadn't noticed yesterday when I was first standing at the Mackenzie front door and admiring what I thought to be a pristine garden.

I suppose we all have our own weeds of imperfection if we look hard enough. There's something comforting and lovely about that.

"Sweating cures the hangover," Erica says, as if that explains everything. Which it kind of does. "Jess is at work, but I'm on my summer schedule." She wipes some sweat from her face with her shoulder. "And that means four weeks off. I open back up mid-July," she says, referring to her daycare business.

I nod and pull away in gentle tugs, loving the feeling of being here in a garden, working to maintain its beauty. So strange to think that less than twenty-four hours ago, I had no idea who this woman even was, really. Still don't entirely, though I feel like I'm a whole lot closer. And now here we are, commiserating in the joint regret of our tequila decisions and redeeming ourselves through good old-fashioned yard work.

We work in comfortable silence for some time, and I'm lost in my thoughts as I yank away the unwelcome cancers of the garden, and pat at the dirt to level out the holes left behind. I think about all that was shared and revealed last night. Not just in Erica's pursuit of Richard to help her conceive, despite her internal warning system, but the other part too—did I mention that?

Right. I'll explain. It's the part where Richard had been in town again some years later, and one of Erica's former co-workers had revealed she had a daycare business now. Low and behold, Richard goes there and waits for her to walk out and lock up for the day, only to find Erica with four-year-old Edie on her hip.

"You have quite the frown on your face, Lori," Erica gently nudges me from above with her knee. "Come on, what's on your mind?"

I look up at her and laugh. She crouches down next to me and gathers all the weeds I had pulled, jumbling them in a bunch. She rises and walks into the garage, tossing the weeds in a large brown bag. "Bloody Mary?" she calls after me.

"God, no," I groan. I rise to follow after her, peeling away my gloves. We wander into the house, a blast of cool air-conditioned air hitting me like a blessing.

She laughs and we walk into the kitchen. She washes her hands, then pulls out two glasses and fills them with water, handing me one. "So, how you doing today?"

I grab my glass and drain it like it's a serum that will give me the gift of eternal life. When I finish and place it down on the counter, I sigh. "I keep thinking about the day that Richard found out about Edie."

Erica nods knowingly, placing her own glass down and opening the fridge. She starts pulling out eggs, bacon, an assortment of cheeses. I wash my hands too, my stomach grumbling as I'm quickly aware of the breakfast we're about to indulge in. "It was one hell of a day," she says. "What's making you think about it?"

I fold my arms over my chest. I think about all she had said last night. After a few blissful years of Erica quietly raising her baby girl, Richard had come to town and had seen little Edie. Imagine his shock at seeing a little girl who was his spitting image. Erica and Richard had shared a silent exchange out front of her daycare, neither one of them saying anything, but Erica ever so slightly nodded at him. Yes—yes, this little girl in my arms is your daughter. She said it was the only thing she could think to do. Denying it seemed impossible, when the look of hurt and anguish in Richard's face was so clear.

Too bad he turned on his heels back to his car, then raced to the nearest bar to get roaring drunk.

I sail over to the eggs and bowl Erica had pulled out, and I start cracking. The plop of each yolk settling itself into the bowl soothes me. "You must have been so scared, not just for yourself, but for Edie."

I glance over to Erica as she nods. "I was. He'd shown aggression before, but nothing like that night."

You see, once Richard found them, it wasn't hard for him to track down her new home address, thanks to her business. He showed up later that evening after seeing them at the daycare. Jessica and Erica had been living together at that point, and when Jessica answered the door with Erica behind her, he pushed his way through, saying nothing but grabbing Erica's throat in his hands, demanding to know if that was his daughter. He pushed her onto the floor with Jessica rushing to call the police, and it wasn't until Edie toddled her way into the foyer—seeing this man on top of her mother and bursting into tears, cowering away in a corner—that Richard released Erica.

"Do you think it was seeing Edie that made him stop?" I'm asking because of a slew of my own realizations. The way that Richard never showed aggression to Reggie, only kindness, which influenced me to stay. The way I knew there was a tormented-but-loving soul underneath all those terrifying layers of Richard.

"Yes," Erica whispers. She checks the heat of the skillet on the stove and takes the bowl from me, now filled with a whipped concoction. She pours it into the skillet with a hiss. "It was like I could see the darkness lift from his eyes at the sight of her. It woke something up in him. His rage obliterated, and he just let go of me, rose back up and walked right out the door, out of our lives. Not another word."

I nod. "It always amazed me the way he could turn it off like that. He was never once violent in front of Reggie."

"You think he saw abuse of his own mom as a kid?" she asks.

I sigh. "I'll never know for sure, but I suspect as much, yeah."

There's so much sadness I feel for my Richard in thinking about this. What if he had gotten help, would that have worked? Could he have possibly healed? A part of me thinks so. He always hated himself after the bad moments. So much regret, he'd feel, unlike other stories I'd heard from similar abusive relationships with a narrative of "You made me do it." It wasn't quite like that with Richard.

I feel a regret at never pressing for therapy. It was a time when therapy wasn't as prevalent as it is now, but I do believe he would have been open to it if it had been. He wanted to be better, I believe. At the very least, if I had pushed for it and he didn't follow through, I would have known where his true intentions lay. If we never ask the question to portray our need, then we'll never know if the potential we believe in could ever truly exist. But it's scary to ask, that's damn hard to admit. Easier, we tell ourselves, to power through with what we know.

Still, I wish I had tried. For both of us.

"The thing that always gets me," I start to say with a big breath, "is I hate to feel like our love wasn't real."

"I felt love for him too, Lori. I get it."

It's hard to explain this to Erica, but it feels like something I want to process with her. "No, I mean...I know that it was an abusive relationship. Yet I still hate that terminology. Makes it feel like the love we had was some hoax. He had a whole other woman and yet I *still* feel like I want to convince myself we had real love." I look up at Erica as if she can magically get me to let go of that delusion. "Why is that?"

She dishes out the eggs onto plates, then opens the air fryer for the bacon. "Maybe it was real. Just on the wrong scale of things."

I twirl a strand of my hair between my fingers, curious what she means. "How so?"

Armed with tongs, she places multiple strips of bacon on each of our plates. "Men like Richard need to feel powerful in their love," she answers casually, like she's thought about this countless times before. "It's because they love from a place of deprivation. For them, it's a constant need of reassurances, so they can feel on top."

I nod. "Sounds like Richard."

She hands me my plate and we make our way to the table in the breakfast nook. "Don't beat yourself up over it. There was love there. Just not the kind you deserve."

We take our seats, and I think about that last big fight we had, shortly before he died. When I thought I might die by his hands and the suffocation of a goddamn nightgown. He had been back from a work trip—Florida. He was so sad that night, and he tried to walk away from me. I know now he had just learned about a daughter he never knew. His ultimate mistrust he so vehemently felt, now officially confirmed in his mind. Even still, he had tried to walk away from me that night. It doesn't excuse his actions, I know that. Nothing can excuse rage and violence like that.

No—but sitting here with Erica helps me do something else. It helps me forgive myself for the times I believed in Richard. I wasn't a fool to do so, only a fool in not holding him and myself to a higher standard.

And it helps me forgive myself for my own wrongdoings.

Last night, Erica had asked me if I had thought she was a horrible person for keeping Edie from Richard, and from the rest of his family. Or for tricking Richard in the first place to getting her pregnant.

I had told her no, because I had done a similar thing, but I didn't share what. Last night seemed like her story to tell.

Today feels like mine.

EMPTY PLATES AND STOMACHS FULL, I begin to share with Erica my own small confession that I've not revealed before.

"So, Erica?"

She smiles. "Why do I get the feeling I'm going to need a three-day silent meditation retreat after what you're about to say? Lots of bombs being dropped here all around."

I laugh. "Maybe not quite as big as others, but I guess this right here feels like it already is my retreat."

"Though not silent," she says, pointing to me.

"No, not silent," I smile, shaking my head.

"Go on, I'm listening."

I begin to explain about my first husband, my girlhood love and father of my twin babies. I explain that I had been able to guess that Erica had taken advantage of Richard in hopes to get pregnant, because I had done a similar thing. She tilts her head to the side with a smile, saying she wondered if she'd get the rest of that thought I alluded to last night.

I sigh. "James and I were crazy in love from day one. And until the very end."

"Fairy tale stuff," she says with warmth, like she sees it and knows.

I nod. "The real deal, yes."

"So? What happened, what went wrong?"

I shake my head and shrug. "Absolutely nothing."

She wipes her mouth with her napkin and frowns. "Okay?"

I push my plate aside and rest my forearms on the table. "Just a little panic that I had. When we were in our sophomore year of college, James had this internship opportunity down in Georgia, and we had taken a road trip there for his interviews."

She leans forward in her seat and stretches to grab my hands. "It all starts on a road trip, doesn't it?"

I huff out a laugh, keeping to myself the irony of her statement.

I continue. "We got to our hotel, he got ready the next morning, and he looked so handsome in his suit. It looked *right* on him, and I kissed him goodbye and wished him good luck, with this wave of fear washing over me. I paced around in the hotel room waiting for him, so excited for him and what he might have in store, but simultaneously terrified that he would be spending the summer down here without me if he got the internship."

"You wouldn't have been able to join him?" she asks. I see the furrow of her brow and can feel the genuine empathy in thinking about the wild torment of young love.

"No," I say, shaking my head. "I couldn't join him because he'd be in housing with other college students, and my mind rolled to all the people he might meet, other young women with similar brains and talents to his—far smarter than me," I say with an eyebrow raise and laugh. I appreciate how Erica doesn't attempt to offer platitudes to counter that thought.

"So when he came back to the hotel afterwards, buzzing with excitement over how well it went, I seduced him. I was never great about taking my birth control, and he knew that, so as often as possible he'd back up with a condom. I knew he hated them, though, so while I waited for him to come back from his interview, I hid the condoms deep in our luggage. I knew that when the time came for him to wrap up, and none could be easily found, I'd be able to convince him to go on without one. We'd be hot for each other and swept up in the moment."

"And it worked," she finishes for me with a small smile.

I smile too, thinking of that magical moment of telling James he would be a father, scared that I had made a simple yet horrible mistake. And then him scooping me up and talking to my belly, warning our creation of the reckless parents he or she had. Total ownership of his own role, and zero remorse over that mishap. Only joy.

"No regrets, though, right?" Erica offers. I see the depths of the meaning of that statement in her eyes.

Because of course there's not. Regret of those choices we made all those years ago, even the pains endured in the aftermath of those choices, to live in regret would mean regret of our children.

I think about Lace, about Anna and the choices she made with falling for someone in the worst of circumstances. Then realizing she was pregnant. Raising the child alone, only for her child to become ill. The torment she must have felt in losing her child.

And I somehow know that, like Erica and myself, there's not an ounce in her motherly bones that would have taken any of it back.

I laugh, shaking my head. "No, love."

"No," she agrees.

"Not a single damn one."

***

ON THE PLANE RIDE HOME, I lean back in my seat and think about the strangeness of the past two days. I went down to the Sunshine State on a hunt for answers, but instead I received so much more. It feels like those two women ended up unlocking a tiny blockage to my healing. I stretched out my heart and allowed a most unexpected connection with them, and in doing so, I settled into acceptance and forgiveness.

I've held so much shame in my past choices, I realize. But shame holds no value, does it? Shame only steals from our sense of self-worth, little by little. We can have guilt, sure. We can feel remorse for mistakes made, even the ones that we would still make again and again if given the chance for a redo. There's always more to understand if we are to fully grasp the reasoning behind our actions. We can hold guilt and self-compassion in the same hand.

But shame only smothers us and slaps an unjust identity on our existence. A fundamental character flaw if we believe in shame's luring message. I'm relinquishing that shame, once and for all.

I'm smiling like a fool as my fellow passengers and I land and shuttle ourselves like cattle off of the plane. I make my way through the terminal and look down at my phone to check on Reggie's location, hoping she's not had to wait too long as I see that she's in the cell phone parking lot. I open my text messages to let her know I'm making my way through the airport, and I see that she's sent me a link. I click on it and see the article load. I scan it in disbelief, my eyes repeatedly running over the headline as if it'll change if I read it one more time. I'm surprised by the smile and emotion I feel in reading this simple little line.

MUSIC SWEETHEART RUBY FRANCESCA FIRES LONG-TIME PUBLICIST JULES ARNOLD, SHOCKING INDUSTRY INSIDERS

thirty-eight

. . .

dom

THE HISTORIC MEDITERRANEAN-STYLE mini resort tucked away in a corner of Palm Springs provides the perfect secluded oasis for the wedding everyone has been looking forward to, Dom must admit. With a main house surrounded by citrus and olive trees and dotted with multiple smaller villas, the entire guest list has their very own home away from home to lay their head in between the parade of festivities. A backdrop of mountains and palms provide the landscape to perfectly frame the sprawl of fountains, gardens, stone pathways and overall rustic flair. Every corner of the place seems to offer an enchanting appeal. If you didn't know better, you'd think you were on a retreat in Portugal or Spain, not a mere two hours from the bustle of golf carts careening through film studio lots and doctors' offices awaiting injections of faux youth.

Despite all this beauty surrounding him, and the anticipation of walking his daughter down the aisle in mere minutes to pass off to her awaiting love, Dom is feeling regret.

After an entire summer of hearing nothing from Lori, but with assurances from Reggie that she was doing well, just working on herself, he had hoped for a more exciting reunion. He had seen Lori at the welcome dinner last night. In fact, had been seated at her table along with Reggie and Xavier, Joey's parents, and one other couple. But unlike past times when Dom and Lori would be thrown together, Lori did not slide up next to Dom and make subtle arm touches or twirl her hair in mindless flirtation.

No. Instead, she had said, "Good to see you, Dom. Congratulations." That was it. The rest of their interactions were within the confines of side conversations with the other table guests, whenever they would be overlap. He found himself watching her with longing, as seeing her in person was proving to be far more difficult than simply not having the physical reminder of her.

And the pit he has had in his chest ever since yesterday has taken up shop and settled itself in. But he's attempting to shake away the feeling. Right now is about the ceremony, followed by endless hours of music and waves of fine cuisine, dancing and cigars and a night he knows will go until dawn.

Ruby beams up at him. "Alright, handsome. Don't forget to have just the right amount of smile as you walk me down. Lots of big money we'll be getting for these photos." Ever the performer, even on her wedding day—well, pretend wedding day as Joey and Ruby had quietly tied the knot officially in their home a few days ago. Had he shed a tear during their union? Hopefully none anyone could see. But it was all in pure joy for his daughter and new son-in-law.

"Please, they don't care about me. They care about you two," Dom replies.

"The pass-off is a big moment. Make it count," she says with a playful shove as she links her arm in his.

Her dress, designed by Lucy and Lila's mom, the talented L. Delphi-Ray, is cream and dotted with an intricate splay of red, pale pink, and cream flowers that seem to be growing right off the fabric like a walking garden. Her dark curls are tucked at the nape of her neck, and even in high heels that Dom could never in a million years imagine walking in, her petite frame appears about eight yards shorter than his. But his daughter's force is mighty, there is no doubt about that.

"How are you feeling with your new PR firm?" he asks her. He had been shocked as hell when Ruby told him her plans to fire Jules, and while he had pride in her willingness to do right by him, he didn't know that it was worth jeopardizing his daughter's career.

Ruby keeps her gaze straight ahead, waiting on her cue. "Good. We'll find our rhythm in time." She squeezes her father's arm in reassurance.

"I appreciate what you did, but I still worry it was a rash decision. What if there's repercussions?" He hates to press the issue, but as they are standing there getting ready to execute yet another public image game plan, it's on the forefront of his mind.

Ruby waves away the thought. "Please, Dad. Like what? Slightly less aggressive tactics that will lead to fewer sales or fans?"

"Precisely."

She shakes her head. "No, not a concern."

"Should it be? You've worked so hard to be here." There are no words to express the pride he has in his daughter and her success. He hates the thought of there being any hindrances to it because of him.

"I have worked hard to be here, yes," Ruby nods. "And I've accepted the fact that this job, this platform comes with a certain amount of responsibility and expectations. Like this," she says, gesturing her hand to the waiting guests and photographers mere steps away ahead of them. "I can and do have a lot of fun with that.

"But inevitably my popularity will decline at some point. And the day that I'm doing this in chase of more and more numbers— that's the day of my moral death. The real gift of this job isn't in achieving some goal of sold-out stadiums, it's the ability to make an impact in sharing my art, and creating something that speaks to people, plain and simple. That's the real meaning, right?"

"True," he replies tentatively.

"Dad, listen," she says, turning and taking a good hard look in her father's eyes. "You kept reaching out to Lori even after she shut you out. Why is that?"

He shrugs. "Because I love her."

"Exactly. You love her and you wanted her to know that, and you were showing courage in the vulnerability in that. Even if she's not giving you much back right now, for whatever the reason may be, she's receiving something in your honesty—it's letting her know that she has your heart. And that's huge, especially coming from someone like you, because you're not really an emotions kind of guy. But the meaning is there, and she'll receive that. No matter how it all works out, that's what's important." She turns back to face forward again. "I keep that in mind in my career as well. Even if the outcomes aren't always what I want, I'm doing this for bigger reasons."

With Ruby's arm in his, they begin to take their first steps. "Such integrity and wisdom, my daughter has," he smiles as the swell of the instrumental version of one of Ruby's hit songs rises. The mellow sound of strings reverberates around them, and he gives her arm a squeeze.

With the cameras flashing and guests beginning to rise, Ruby grins up to her dad. "Glad you think so," she says through her smile, aware that all eyes are now on them. "Now get your game face on."

Dom follows suit with a winning grin of his own. "I'll do my job to utter perfection, I assure you."

thirty-nine

. . .

edie

"YOU'RE RIGHT. I really am a bad guy. I'm only with you because I knew I'd get the chance to go to Ruby Francesca's wedding," Trenton says with a grin as he cradles Edie in a sway to the famous couple's wedding song. As soon as any other couples were invited to join the newlyweds on the dance floor, Trenton had been one of the first to jump up, pulling a laughing Edie behind him.

They spin around to Buddy Guy's "Feels Like Rain," and Edie smirks. "Incredible, since I only just found out I had this most unlikely invite." She had about died when she received a personal phone call from Ruby herself, thanking her for her work in tracking down the other half of the letters, saying that she understands Edie is the long-lost family member of Reggie and Lori. Ruby said she has found that the family bonds we form no matter how or what stage of life we are in are priceless, and Edie's role in the family tree now meant she was in Ruby's inner circle as well.

Edie just gaped into the phone. Trenton had to take it from her and respond, introducing himself as Edie's hopeful fiancé, and then

Joey Conti chimed in the background saying Xavier had said good things about him, and Joey hoped Trenton could make it as well.

That's when Trenton froze, and suddenly both of them were staring at one another in stunned silence.

Of course they dropped everything, scrambled to sign their NDA's and assurances that they understood the no cell phone rule that would be enforced the minute they entered the resort.

And here they are now. Swaying in a dance to the wedding song of Ruby Francesca and Joey Conti. Actor/model Lila Ray is in attendance with her fiancé—some famous photographer. Musician Grayson Atkinson is there as the Man of Honor to—not Joey—but Ruby, though word on the street is there's some beef between the photographer and Grayson.

It's all a little wild, and Edie's head is spinning.

"What's with the shrine over there of the old lady?" Trenton nods in the direction of a massive photo display of what is apparently Joey's late grandmother, a woman by the name of Mama Z. You'd think the celebration was for her.

She frowns. "Yeah, I asked Lori about that. Apparently, she was quite the force, and the mega-ness of the shrine is a little bit of teasing exaggeration? A kind of joke that Mama Z would love because they think she's watching from heaven or something?" It was an odd display in that it dominated the area dedicated to a handful of other loved ones lost.

Trenton nods. "Huh. Okay. You know what else is strange? This wedding song, don't you think?"

She smiles at the man in her arms, looking incredible in a tux when here Edie thought he'd never look as sexy as when he's in his usual suits. "How so?" she asks.

"It's talking about rain and hurricanes. What kind of love song is that?"

She lifts a shoulder. "I think that's the idea, Wroe. The beauty and passion, and the inevitable storms we endure through it all."

She tilts her head up, inviting a quick kiss, then pulls her head back, explaining, "We can have both."

He tucks her into his chest to lead them through a spin before leaning her back in a mini-dip. "You know," he says, staring down at Edie's giggling face, "I read the book. *The Awakening*, and I read all about Edna." He lifts her back up and resumes their swaying rhythm.

"You did?" she asks, looking over his shoulder in disbelief as she mindlessly allows him to lead their dance.

"Mmm-hmm," he murmurs.

"But you don't read."

He pauses their movements to meet her gaze. "For you, baby, I did," he smiles before gently pushing her back, holding her hand and raising it above her head to prompt her in a spin.

She twirls herself beneath his arm and back into his chest. "And? What did you think?" It's amazing to Edie how much this makes her happy to hear. It shouldn't really matter all that much, it's not *her* favorite book, just her moms'.

Trenton licks his lips, as if contemplating how to respond. "I mean, it wasn't my favorite, if you know what I mean."

Edie throws her head back in a laugh. "I do. I really do."

He grins. "Is that a preview to a phrase I might one day hear you say?"

Edie's heart rate quickens in her chest. This man right here, nothing like who she imagined herself one day ending up with. Especially at only twenty-two years old. She hears her moms' voices in her head warning her to take her time, to date more and not settle down. They had come around to accepting Trenton as a thing in her life for right now, but they still urged her to experience all she can, because she has her whole life ahead of her for love.

Edie's thinking to hell with that. Sometimes you just need to follow your heart, because there's no guarantee what tomorrow will bring.

"Yeah," she finally whispers, gazing into his warm brown eyes. "It is. I'll marry you, Trenton Wroe."

He freezes, his body suddenly rigid, and Edie briefly worries she made a mistake, that she's calling his bluff just like the countless bits they've done before. He never really meant it because she's always so good at sidestepping his bait.

But then he takes her hand, pulling her away from the dance area and around a corner, his head turning side to side as if looking for something. He eventually settles them into a small and secluded garden pathway, the smell of citrus and the flicker of torches enveloping them. They stop and face one another again, and she scans his face, seeing the flicker of nerves in his eyes.

And when he drops down to one knee, Edie gasps. He reaches in his jacket pocket and pulls out a box. He opens it.

Inside is a ring. She gingerly pulls the simple gold band and oval stone from its velvet cushion, lifting it as the etching of an inscription catches her eye. She scans the words—*How everything you are.*

forty

. . .

lori

I BLINK AWAY the fog of too little sleep, stretching and smiling in the massive bed of my very own bungalow on the resort. I look up at the wood beams above, loving the cozy feel of the Moroccan decor of this small 1920s villa. I'm still on East Coast time and realize that it's early, still dark out, and I only fell into bed a mere four hours prior. The wedding festivities were still pulsing, but my feet could no longer stand the ache of my heels. I'm always far too proud to take them off, though, so I had quietly escaped and nestled in my room with a good romance book and a stolen glass of wine.

But it's time to wake up and execute my plan.

I reach over for my phone before realizing with disappointment that I have none. Confiscated in the need for security and privacy. Which is fine, really. Some things are better done in person.

I rise and drop my feet to the cool floor, the ripples of the stone offering a kind of massage to counter their ache. I make my way through the villa and get myself ready, throwing on leggings, a tank, and a cardigan, unsure of how early fall weather feels at this hour in Palm Springs.

Once dressed I step outside and inhale the desert air, so different from the dampness the East Coast would offer. I pad out to the bungalow I'm looking for and walk up to the quaint arch of the doorway. With a heavy breath, I knock.

In the agonizing moments of awaiting a response, I scan around the area, taking in the inky purple black of the sky and the mountains beyond. I can hear some muffled music and quiet chattering off in the distance, die-hard party guests still lingering in their merriment, but there's no one within my line of vision.

I knock again, louder this time, and am rewarded when I hear his low voice grumble, "Hang on."

When Dom finally opens the door, I can't help but laugh. His black hair is a disheveled mess, he has on his tuxedo pants, which I'm guessing were the first thing he could find to put on before answering, and his white shirt is unbuttoned and exposing his smooth and tanned torso, the peak of his tattoos revealing themselves beneath the fabric.

"Lori?" he says in confusion, as if I'm an apparition.

"In the flesh," I grin. I nod my head behind me. "Walk with me?"

A FEW MINUTES LATER, DOM now dressed more appropriately in jeans and a gray long-sleeved t-shirt, we make our way up the small dirt path lined with rocks and cacti. My eyes slowly adjust to meet the demands of navigating in the dark. I'm looking at his hand, wanting to grab it, but unsure if I should. That hand is calling to me, though. I feel ready to take hold.

I decide to go for it, and the look of surprise followed by relief I'm met with settles my nerves a bit.

"So you don't hate me after all?" he says with a cock of his eyebrow before returning his gaze to the path ahead of us. "Watch your step," he says, motioning to a mini boulder jutting out on my side of the pathway. He pulls me in closer to him to save me from the potential stumble, and I breathe in his scent of remnants of cologne combined with laundry detergent.

"Oh, God, no."

"Okay," he says, his tone sounding unsure.

"I could never hate you. I know what happened wasn't your fault."

He sighs in what I'm guessing is relief, squeezing my hand. "You heard Ruby fired Jules, right?"

"I heard, yes. I'm sure that was a tough decision to make." I don't share my next thought—how glad I was to see that. I know how important Ruby's career is, and making a call like that wasn't smooth sailing, I imagine. But it felt like someone was finally in my corner.

Ruby had reached out to me, expressed how disgusted she was by the way someone that is supposed to have her best interests in mind had so recklessly done something with zero regard for her or her family. Jules had claimed it was all in the name of stirring up more anticipation for the wedding. Ruby knew that was a stretch, especially given how fiercely her father tried to stay out of the limelight as much as possible. She expressed her apologies for the hurt or doubt it potentially caused me, and wanted to know if there was anything she could do to make it right between her dad and me. I told her no, because I had already felt his love for me, and that when the time was right, when I was ready, I'd give us another chance, certain our story was just getting started. She expressed how happy she was to hear that.

But I did request one small favor, if she was willing.

"Anything," Ruby had said.

"Invite Edie, my stepdaughter and the finder of the Dog Tags letters, to the wedding?"

She had laughed and said if that's all I wanted, it was an easy request to make happen. That if I considered Edie to be family, then she did as well.

I look over to Dom and think about the beautiful daughter he has, and my heart swells at knowing the future we're about to have together with our joined families. I hope he knows the excitement I feel in that.

"I still care about you, Dom," I say softly. "I want you to know that never went away." He's quiet, I'm guessing he's not sure what to say. I sense he's afraid to, but based on his texts, on his courage in facing my mother and expressing to her his feelings, I know he's not given up hope.

I try to make myself as clear as possible. "I'm ready now, is what I'm saying."

He stops walking and releases my hand, wrapping his arms around me and pulling me into him.

"Thank God," he whispers, and I laugh, feeling so good to be in his embrace once again. But it's a different good this time around. A steady feeling that has lost the previous desperation I could sometimes feel.

Something we should all remember is that love born out of deprivation can be dangerous. That was my love for Richard, and I imagine it was the love of Dog Tags and his Lace. In many ways it may have even been my love for James, but there's something different about the kind of love story that begins in youth, isn't there? When fragile identities have yet to be formed, the bond of young love has the task of growing and fulfilling those identities together. I do believe that James and I had that power, and that if he and our son were still here today, we'd be just as fiercely thirsty for one another as we ever were.

But love in our later years of grown-up living needs another kind of nurturing, and to be able to bond with someone, we must first be complete within ourselves. This past summer I've been working on that. It's required speaking hard truths and taking ownership of my mistakes, even if I'd still do them time and again.

It's required finally facing therapy and resurrecting the pieces of my heart that I felt too scared to face, but in doing so, I was able to sit with my grief and hold its hand with tenderness, instead of pushing it aside. In that, I have finally found my ability to be complete.

"I care about you too. More than care," Dom says, and I love feeling of the rumble in his chest against my cheek. He's told me he loved me various times throughout this summer, but he doesn't say it now. I'm guessing he's not sure how, and I'm okay with that. I did just barge in on him in the wee hours without a warning.

We release one another and resume our walk, slower now as we stumble our way up the path with him holding me against him, his arm snaked around my waist. It feels like heaven, even if what is supposed to be a ten-minute hike might be more like an hour if we keep up this pace. I laugh and share the thought, but he just kisses my head and keeps holding me.

"How come you have barely talked to me since we arrived?" he eventually asks.

I shake my head. "Too much going on, it wasn't the right time. Not in the middle of everything."

"Man, I wish I had realized that twenty-four hours ago," he grumbles, and I give him a gentle squeeze.

"You want to know where we're headed?" I ask.

"I trust you have something good in mind."

"Indeed I do. A good spot for a sunrise view, apparently. It was a little blurb in the welcome brochure."

"You actually read the brochure?"

"No cell phones. Lots of down time," I explain with a laugh.

"Sounds like you made good use of your time."

We continue on in comfortable silence, sidestepping rocks and me trying to ignore my fears of other nocturnal creatures. After several more minutes of our warm and heavenly, if not slightly impractical, walking hug, he releases me, reaching down to hold my hand instead as we continue our steps. At one point he raises my hand for a kiss before dropping it back down again, and I look ahead on our path and see the start of more light up beyond the mountains.

I glance up at his profile, waiting for him to say something, as I have a feeling he's got something on his mind.

Gaze still held ahead of him, he finally speaks. "I know I may not be the love of your life, Lori." My heart pinches as my mind flashes briefly to my James. I internally smile at that love, and return my attention back to Dom. Despite the temptation to do so, I don't correct him or try and counter the thought.

He pauses his steps and turns to look back down to me, body framed by the now-purple sky. I can just barely make out the flicker in his eyes. "But I want you to know..."

"Yes?" I encourage him.

"I *need* you to know that I believe you're the love of mine."

epilogue

· · ·

AS DOM AND Lori make their way up the bend, to the promised spot sure to "dazzle and delight in a quiet abyss as one watches the sunrise spill up over the mountains," they soon realize they're not alone.

Perched on a boulder are the silhouette of a couple, her head on his shoulder, and as they step closer, they realize it's Reggie and Xavier.

Lori laughs as she plants a kiss on her daughter's cheek. "Found the secret spot, I see," she says. "Mind if we rain on your parade?"

Reggie lifts her shoulder and takes in the sight of Lori and Dom. Her eyes glance over to Xavier, and they share a silent exchange, both of them sporting slow smiles, like a secret confirmed. "We'd love your rain," Reggie finally says as she looks back up at them.

They hear another round of footsteps and look behind them to find the tall blonde frame of actor and model Lila Ray, and her photographer fiancé Simon.

"Steal your sister's baby?" Reggie asks, nodding toward Simon who is sporting a baby carrier holding Noah, Lucy's son.

"We offered to keep him for the night," Lila explains. "But

apparently little Noah here doesn't like missing out on anything." She leans into Simon and pokes her nephew's cheek before allowing his tiny fist to wrap around her finger.

Soon more footsteps can be heard, and they turn to see Grayson making his way up the path, open champagne bottle in hand and grin stretched ear to ear.

"Well, what do we have here?" He looks down at the bottle in his hand. "Wish I'd brought more champagne," he says, handing the bottle to Reggie.

She tips the bottle to take a sip, wiping her mouth in a laugh as she pulls it away. "Anyone else?"

"I'd love some," Lila chimes in. "Think this is unsanitary?" she laughs before taking her own pull from the bottle. She offers it to Simon, who shakes his head, then she passes it back to Grayson.

The gang watches with some apprehension as Grayson takes another sip, eyeing up fellow Brit, photographer Simon Sharp, and the baby attached to him. They have history together, apparently history that didn't end well. But after a moment, Grayson scans the group and slips into a small smile. "Nothing sacred anymore, huh?" he says, waving the bottle to reference the sunrise perch in front of him that they'd all found. "And here I thought I'd enjoy some quiet time alone." He lifts his eyebrow, and quiet chuckles roll through. He cocks his head over to Simon. "Good to see you," he says with a small nod, and Simon nods too. Grayson darts his eyes down to the baby on Simon's torso. "Looks good on you."

Lila smiles, murmuring, "Yes, it absolutely does."

Joey and Ruby make their way up last, and the small crew cheers and hollers in laughter at their arrival, both of them still in their wedding gear, though Joey has lost his bowtie, and Ruby has hiked up her gown, the skirt bunched together and held with a scrunchy, a makeshift bustle fit for teenage girls looking to make a baggy t-shirt more sexy.

"Mom would die if she saw that," Lila laughs, referring to the designer brain behind Ruby's creation.

"Good thing she's not here, then. Right?" Ruby smiles. Lila and Ruby were not always friends, exactly. More reluctant participants in one another's lives thanks to mutual loved ones. It's good to see them in this lighthearted exchange.

"Secret's safe with me," Lila promises.

Once everyone finds their spaces, scooting over to allow the newlyweds the best perch on the middle boulder, they pass the bottle around and sit in comfortable silence. The quiet rustles of nature surround them, and the sky pops a kaleidoscope of colors on the brink of its transition from night to day. The expanse of sleepy mountains and terrain stretch out as far as the eye can see, dotted with sharp edges of aloe and various cacti, and each one of them realizes in their own way, the beauty of our world, of this life, of each moment that we are allowed the nurture of breaths to be had. No matter the hikes and hurdles we've endured or the moments we'd rather forget. No matter the crisis or the wars, internal or otherwise. To exist right here and now is the greatest gift.

Lori thinks about the difference between the East Coast sunrise over glittering ocean water, and the West Coast spills of light over the various elevations of the landscape. How beautiful both are in their own ways.

Lila thinks about the unlikely turns her life has taken, and the confidence she has managed to find to navigate it all. She looks at her fiancé and admires how sexy Simon looks holding their nephew. She decides to hell with waiting for marriage or the right time in her rapidly rising career, she wants to start a family the minute they get back to their villa.

Ruby thinks about how much she's looking forward to falling into bed, finally allowing a deep sleep with the man she can now call her husband. She knows she'll dream countless lyrics and melodies, all inspired from the perfection of the past few days.

And Reggie thinks about the peace she feels with seeing her mother to her left, body cradled in Dom's embrace. Everyone knew it was only a matter of time before they got together. Reggie looks up at Xavier and he kisses her temple, and her mind wanders to their children, Ronnie and James. As much as she's enjoyed their little getaway here, she can't wait to get home and squeeze their babies.

As the sun slowly makes its entrance, the glow offers its own gift of light that—like a watercolor brush bleeding colors on its canvas—creates new waves of hues that shift and transform. Promises of another day to be seen.

Assurances that they are all here. All living, because once again, for today at least, they were lucky.

They awoke.

acknowledgments & thoughts

As soon as I wrote the last words to this book, the final in my beloved Dog Tags & Lace series, I burst into tears. And then I emailed my editor, crying, "No one told me how hard it would be to say goodbye!"

Saying goodbye is a part of life, however. When I taught Group Counseling at a local community college, and we'd get to the lesson on the final phase of a group, I would explain to my students that facilitating the closing is an important part of the process, as learning healthy endings is a crucial life lesson.

That doesn't make it easy, though.

Our "negative" emotions offer healing messages ("negative" in quotes because there are no good/bad emotions. All emotions are necessary and should be embraced). Anger sends the message of an internal value system we feel has been compromised. Fear lets us know we need to prepare for something. And sadness teaches us what we need to let go of.

To tackle grief in my writing in the way I did here was by far my biggest challenge as a writer yet. In fact, it took me a hefty amount of rewrites of those first couple of chapters before I could figure out what I was doing. I was subconsciously keeping Lori at arm's length, not allowing myself to get in there and feel her pain. I would re-read what I'd written and think, "I don't feel her. She's just a shell," and I realized it was my own fear holding me back.

So I allowed my fear to help me prepare, and I dug into my own cedar-lined trunk of memories. I pulled out my old journals, digging for ones where I had been feeling raw grief in all shapes and sizes. I resurrected crushes breaking my heart, and the loss of what could have been. I peeled back the curtain on the grief of moving away from friends, or from the job I didn't get that I thought I was *for sure*, perfect for. I found entries from the time of my miscarriage, something many, many of us have experienced. There were countless varieties of grief captured in those pages of my journals over the years. Grief is our emotional reaction to loss, and revisiting moments of mine was wonderfully therapeutic. If you don't already—journal, my friends.

Lori's pain of losing both her child and her love—it was heart wrenching once I finally allowed myself to feel her. I felt her anger, her fears, her denial, her sense of being betrayed. I cried with her and journaled on why the world can throw us these things, and how we're supposed to make sense of it.

In my therapy office I have sat with clients that have lost children, and I'm always amazed at the ways we can laugh together while also carefully navigating something so painful. People's strength in the face of hurt is powerful, and this is the message I hope to send to both my clients, and to my readers through these stories. That we can hold multiple emotions at once, that we can feel both wonder and hurt; they don't need to be separate entities but instead, a delicate and beautiful juxtaposition in our hearts, the result of lived experiences. This juxtaposition was my entire inspiration for the Dog Tags & Lace series, though I'm not sure I'll ever lean away from this most valuable lesson in my writing. It will remain an undercurrent pushing along my characters and their stories, and my wish is for you readers to learn and process through them while escaping in a good book where you can fall in love and get a happily ever after.

Thank you, thank you, dear readers for doing so with me. I write for you.

Thank you also to Jacqui Muller who patiently trudged her way through those first chapters while I tried to get a grasp on this story. Our discussions surrounding the birthing of my tales always lead to the best conversations of life and philosophies of the messiness of being human. I'd be lost (or writing far more chaotically) without you.

Thank you to Jen Denver and Sarah Crimian for being absolute reader guinea pigs in those early days of this book as well. You cheer me on when I need it most.

Meg Sponseller and Carly Pinato, I know you will forever hold Daddy X and Joey, respectively, in high regards as your first VZ loves, but I'm so happy Trenton comes in as a close second!

Many thanks and applause for Lauren Rowe, who has so patiently cheered for and guided me through all things Booksta-gram. You're so much cooler than me, but I'm learning :)

To my childhood friends Christine Hall and Catherine Skeans, whose love and support inspire me to write great female characters that form gorgeous bonds. Catherine—you spoke the most beau-tiful eulogy at your father's funeral when we were just seventeen, a speech (with song) I will never forget. That memory often came up for me as I wrote this book.

To my favorite pen pal, Lynda Hambright. Also known as my editor that I was absolutely MEANT to have. Not only are you the description queen to my brain that forgets not everyone *sees* all that I see so vividly, but you're an incredible master of words in your own right. Your insights and wisdoms feel like precious gems I get to hold, and I could not have picked a better person to help bring my tales to the next level.

As always, to my husband Matthew for inspiring every great book boyfriend that I write. You show me what it means to be loved as one deserves. Our love story will always be my favorite :)

And to our babies, who were at the forefront of my mind as I wrote a book focused on mothers and children. Thanks for choosing me as your mom. When you're fifty, you can read this. No peeking.

A note on Lace—her story was inspired by a group of German teenagers opposed to the Nazi regime, called the Edelweiss Pirates. Reading and learning about these courageous kids was awe-inspiring, and in another life, I would love to create more tales inspired by their tenacity and morality. As the daughter of parents who were born in Germany near the end of WWII, I was always fascinated to hear the stories of my grandparents and their own opposition. There's more I'd love to say on this, but I'll stay in my lane and steer you towards the experts on this subject. A resource I used for my research in writing is the book *The Edelweiss Pirates: Teenage Rebels in Nazi Germany*, by Dirk Reinhardt. May we all remember to hold beautiful rebellion in our spirits when called upon.

about the author

A believer that life is all about the great stories we live to share, Vanessa Zian loves helping people find the heart and ah-ha moments in their own tales. Her two loves are romance novels and tapping into underlying emotions.

When she's not writing or reading romance, Vanessa works as a therapist, helping clients heal through the powers of introspection. She writes with the same goals in mind—to find value in the conflict and strength of character in beautiful stories, and to celebrate our happy endings.

Vanessa lives in Delaware with her childhood crush-turned-husband, their four kids, and their rescue pup Mikka.

And lots of high heels.

Readers—please consider leaving a rating or review! As someone brand new out here, it's not only so appreciated, but vital to helping me keep writing.

Join my newsletter where I will randomly ask for character name ideas, offer therapeutic tidbits, share sneak peeks, etc! Visit
vanessazian.com
Email: Vanessa@vanessazian.com

facebook.com/VanessaZianWrites

instagram.com/vanessa_zian

tiktok.com/@vanessazian

www.ingramcontent.com/pod-product-compliance
Lightning Source LLC
Chambersburg PA
CBHW030110310726
48970CB00004B/1224